ALSO BY

LUCIA FRANGIONE

Cariboo Magi

Espresso

In a Blue Moon

Leave of Absence

Paradise Garden

All published by Talonbooks

GRAZIE

A NOVEL

LUCIA FRANGIONE

TALONBOOKS

Talonbooks
9259 Shaughnessy Street, Vancouver, British Columbia, Canada V6P 6R4
talonbooks.com

Talonbooks is located on xʷməθkʷəy̓əm, Sḵwx̱wú7mesh, and səl̓ilwətaʔɬ Lands.

First printing: 2023

Typeset in Sabon
Printed and bound in Canada on 100% post-consumer recycled paper

Cover and interior design by Typesmith
Cover image by Typesmith

Talonbooks acknowledges the financial support of the Canada Council for the Arts, the Government of Canada through the Canada Book Fund, and the Province of British Columbia through the British Columbia Arts Council and the Book Publishing Tax Credit.

Library and Archives Canada Cataloguing in Publication

Title: Grazie : novel / Lucia Frangione.
Names: Frangione, Lucia, author.
Identifiers: Canadiana 2022047723X | ISBN 9781772015089 (softcover)
Classification: LCC PS8561.R27755 G73 2023 | DDC C813/.54—dc23

I dedicate this novel to the late Paolo Frangione and my extended family in Palazzo San Gervasio who so warmly embraced me. And to my distant cousin and faithful translator, Antonietta Saponara, who made my visit possible. Though this novel is a work of fiction, their generosity and love inspired it.

PART I

CHAPTER ONE

THE CYCLE WARD

— Graziana —

The walrus heard the key at the front door. It gasped. It stiffened. Who was there at this ungodly time of the morning? Herman's moderate voice called out from down the hall.

"You up?"

The walrus exhaled with deep disdain. Obviously, it wasn't up. Why would it be up at 6:30 a.m.? Is this the freaking army now? Does Herman not understand the concept of privacy? The walrus rolled over to the side of the bed, flatulence being part of the ritual. It swung its legs over the side of the mattress and rocked several times to gain the momentum to stand.

It slept in stretch pants and an XX-large grey T-shirt and felt it didn't need to change. It brushed its teeth and washed its face. It rubbed the whiskers under its chin, long and unfettered. It lifted each pendulous breast and ran a cold cloth underneath. With great effort, it hoisted the bottom of its belly that folded over its groin and wiped the cloth along the forty-ninth parallel of its body and then let the belly flop down again. It brushed its long greasy hair and twisted it up into a bun, showcasing the balloon of blubber around its neck.

Today it seemed harder to breathe. It blew its nose, then looked in the mirror to make sure all was clear on the home front. Normally it tried to avoid catching its own reflection. Its eyes were the only part of its body it still recognized: two brilliant-blue life preservers swallowed up in a sea of neglect.

Herman called out again, "Don't wake up Hazel just yet."

Why would the walrus wake up the nut? Let her sleep, for

god's sake. It waddled by the nut's door and peered in. She was still snoring. The sheets and blankets were twisted into a violent heap. Shaggy, dirt-coloured hair was plastered against her cheek, thin enough for her large ears to poke out. She was almost cute, in a baby-hyena sort of way. Why did she insist on wearing those damn flannel pyjamas? They're too hot. The nut's legs were getting long and lean; the pyjama bottoms were far too short now, her calves jutted out. Her mouth, slightly open, revealed a glint of canine teeth. Seven years old already. She didn't look so disordered when she was asleep.

The walrus preferred it when Herman was still working as a superintendent paramedic. "Super-" was appropriate for Herman. The walrus could easily imagine the cape. First responders can retire, but they never stop responding. Herman had married the walrus's mother when the walrus was very little, but both the walrus and Herman insisted he should never be called "Dad." Herman kept a respectful arm's length when it came to parenting, leaving it to his wife. But when Mom died, he had taken it upon himself to assume the mantle. And since retiring from his paramedic work, he made it his new occupation, his mission, in fact, to "save" the walrus and the nut. He moved down the street, and the walrus already regretted giving him a key.

Yup, there he was, sitting at the kitchen table. He'd made himself a cup of coffee, no sugar, double cream. He seemed very pleased with himself, formal even. The blue plaid of his pressed shirt was full of right angles. He was wearing relaxed-fit, high-waisted evangelical jeans.

"Herman ... for god's sake! I was still asleep. Don't just barge into my house like you own the place, okay? It's creepy."

Herman shot his eyebrows up, the only sign of the blow. He folded his hands on the table, which the walrus noted was washed and set for three.

"Technically, I do own the place."

Already exhausted by the imperious truth of him, the walrus laid a hand towel on the chair and sat down. At some point today, it expected to bleed.

"That's how you're going to start the morning? Throw that in my face?"

Herman eyed the walrus for a long time, saying nothing. He took a sip of coffee. The table was an eight-seater lady with thick ankles, the only hand-me-down from Mom that the walrus could take. Grocery bags were still on the counter; lettuce waved at them, calorie-free.

"You want a coffee, Graziana?"

The walrus sneered and slumped back into the chair like a teen. "Oh please, help yourself."

"You still seeing that Dr. Norma about your depression?"

"Is that your diagnosis?"

"Well, can you still call it grief? I just want to make sure you have the support you need."

"Fat lot of good it's doing me."

"Don't blame Dr. Norma for that."

The walrus looked down at its bulbous knees.

Herman poured the walrus a cup of coffee and resumed his place at the head of the table. "I came in early before Hazel woke up because I have something important to tell you." He cupped his mug in a gesture of prayerful thanksgiving. His thumbs were as wide as griddle pans, and his fingernails were clean. He smiled the smile of the righteous.

"I got a call early this morning from Mark Hildebrandt, you remember him? He used to work with me in Red Deer, but then he moved to Rocky Mountain House when his wife became head of the thrombosis unit there. Anyway –"

"Of course I know Mark. I went to high school with him!"

"Okay, well not everybody remembers everybody from high school."

"He was a very good friend. He came over with Sheila all the time. You know that!"

"If you don't want to hear this, Grazie, then I can just go home. Never mind it's the best news you've had in twenty-one years."

The walrus stopped all motion. Twenty-one years? What did he mean by that?

"So, Mark was on shift last night, and they got a call about an MVA, right? Guy in a Mercedes-Benz convertible went right off a cliff, fell, and rolled about two hundred feet, likely dead on impact. Took a while to get to him, the fire department had started rigging up a rescue. Anyway, once they got to the bottom to pull the guy out, they noticed the idiot had his pants undone, his dink still hanging out –"

The walrus laughed in surprise: Herman said "dink."

"– and when they found his phone, a dirty video was still playing on it."

"Ew!"

"Yeah. Happens more often than you think. So, in case the guy was married or such, the fellows started to do the family a favour, tuck his pants in, erase the viewing history on his phone ... but when Mark saw the ID in the wallet ... he realized ... well, he recognized the name and then looked at the face and – sure enough! – told them to let the pecker be found as is. And he ... he called me and ... thought you'd want to know."

"Me? Why."

"Bad business and all."

"Who was it, for god's sake?"

Herman looked at the walrus: "Ivan."

"What?"

"Ivan Vidal."

The walrus swallowed – walnut – stuck – throat.

"Licence plates were from California. Cops came on the scene, and apparently Ivan had stolen the car from an elderly lady in San Francisco. Maybe a relative."

Bitter-sharp.

"There was cocaine in the glove compartment."

Can't – swallow.

"Ivan has a beard now, and he's going grey, but he's still recognizable as the so-called personal trainer he once pretended to be."

The walrus did not believe it. "It can't – It's not."

"It is. I mean, I only met the guy once or twice, but Mark knew him. And though it was all a long time ago, that guy had a distinct sort of look. And Mark, well, don't tell anybody this, but Mark sent me a picture and, sure enough, it's him."

The walrus wanted to see.

"No, it's not appropriate for civilians. And besides, I erased it."

"You can retrieve deleted photos in your trash. I have a right to see."

Herman gave the walrus a measured look again. "Will it, do you feel ... Be honest with me now. Do you feel it will help?"

"Yes."

Herman dug into his pristine pocket and retrieved his phone. He clicked a few times and then cautiously handed it over. "You can't tell anyone, *anyone*, that you saw this photo. Ever. Mark is risking his career sending us this. It's just his upper body, but you can clearly see his features, and that he's stone-cold dead. Even from the photo you can tell there's no life in him. You know, when we're on the job ... we try not to look at the ... it's just a vic if you don't look at the face. You sure?"

The walrus took the phone as one would take communion. The walrus turned the photo sideways and enlarged it. The shape of the head in the picture was immediately recognizable, that shaggy squareness. The walrus zoomed in. Prosaic, round, harmless nose. Handsome chin. Thin, dirt-brown hair parted in the middle, oddly, his ear poking through. Vacant brown eyes. Surreal. Shouldn't it feel ...? Ivan. Ivan. Young Ivan flooded the walrus. The smell of new running shoes and car-interior leather. The taste of orange Gatorade. He exuded unearthly confidence for such a short man: early twenties, movie-star handsome, biceps so tight they looked plastic. Brown flashy eyes, small hands and feet. Neat. God, he was a salesman, promised all sorts of end results and brought in more memberships to the gym than the owner had ever seen. He hustled in the elderly afraid of falling, he enticed bored housewives, he bolstered white collars who were softening and widening. He made red-ribbon promises to track-and-field kids. Everyone followed Ivan into the gym to become their best selves. He had trained with Charlie Glass. He had the latest athletic techniques. His car had California plates. He dared to wear purple T-shirts with the sleeves cut off.

The walrus at the time had already won all the local ribbons and medals: 1,500 metres, 800 metres, long jump, relay – a regular Marion Lois Jones. Pictures of Olympians were plastered on every closet and locker door and binder cover. Grade ten: won provincials. Grade eleven: went to nationals. Grade twelve: shooting for world. The walrus had known her potential, had felt it. She was tall, lean, fierce, and farm-kid strong.

Ivan Vidal rattled off the names of muscle groups and talked of torque and leverage and the psychology of sport. He was all about elongation of the stride, smoothies with greens, white-meat protein, and the evils of wheat. The walrus's high-school coach introduced Ivan to the top track performers, and they trained as a team and then one on one. Ivan drove the walrus home in his second-hand Corvette, and they talked like adults. Always respectful. Other girls would gossip. They made fun of his small hands and what he might be overcompensating for with his hot rod. They were jealous of the time he spent with his star athlete.

Training with Ivan worked. The walrus won provincials, easy. Won second place in nationals. Training for worlds, he made his protégée promise to keep him on as coach for the Olympics and not hire some European douchebag.

Press weights, jump rope, sprint until the lungs bleed. The greatest obstacle is fear of success.

"I want you to jump from this box to that box. We need to work on your trust, Grazie. Jump!"

Jump.

Ivan moved the box another foot away.

"Jump, Grazie!"

"I'm afraid –"

"You're afraid of your own greatness. Of your own power. Trust me. You can do this."

Jump.

Another foot away.

"The average person can jump ten feet. This is only five. Don't think, just do. Jump, Grazie!"

Jump.

Another foot away.

"It's not the distance, it's … it's going to overturn, Ivan."

"No, it won't. I'm holding it. It's made for impact and so are you. Jump!"

"I don't feel safe."

"Good! Nothing remarkable is safe. Haven't I been right about you all along? Now jump! Jump! Jump!"

Jump.

Topple! Rip! Thud. The walrus can still hear the inside of the body tear apart. The left knee's anterior cruciate ligament snapped. The medial collateral ligament shredded beyond repair. The tibia cracked. Blood flooded the injury hot, hot, hot. The walrus was rushed to the hospital; the surgeons tried to repair what they could, but really, it was over.

Ivan's credentials were demanded, exposed as fraudulent, fired. His Corvette roared up to the walrus one rainy day, spraying dirty water all over her crutches. He shouted from the car:

"They weren't in the gym! The phys-ed teacher or the doctor. You and I both know the truth. It's you! It's your self-sabotage that ruined both our lives!"

At high-school graduation, a note was tucked into the walrus's locker. Ivan's scrawl lay vulnerable and small across the page, the penmanship so curled into itself, it looked fetal.

"Happy Graduation. You look beautiful in green. I didn't have the courage to talk to you in person. I'm glad to see you're off crutches. You were a champion, Grazie. You could have gone all the way. I'll never forgive myself. I wish you all the best in life. Ivan."

Thirteen years later, a good thirteen years, under a ten-speed, tick, tick, tick, downtown Calgary, ding! In through the door a late customer called. Him. Ivan. He'd come across the profile on Facebook. Still his handsome fit self but less polished, more scruff. Kinda good. Came with flowers, all white, the expensive ones. Good shirt, a brown leather jacket. The kind that complements those with hair that can't decide if it's brown or blond. Amazing! The walrus had opened a bike shop and found a sport for a compromised knee. Incredible! The walrus cycled from Vancouver to Halifax. Ivan was full of flattery. Fantastic! Tell me more!

How they ended up in bed … Was it a teenaged fantasy realized? Or did it just feel good to finally have power over him? The thing about his hands – true. He kept slipping out. And talking! God, he talked about himself non-stop. Bullshit stuff. Cut the walrus off. Armpit hair bristly. Something sick started to snake out and hiss in the tiny stuffy bedroom. That after-sex sudden feel of creepy. Creepy. Was he high, maybe? Why did the walrus let him in? He knew the address now. He knew the fire escape was here by the bedroom window. He had her phone number. He talked on and on, wouldn't get out of bed even after the walrus had showered and changed. He lay there, flattening all the pillows, and yacked on and on about personal growth. CrossFit. The stock market. That bitch Jean Ruth who ripped him off. Dabbling with Buddhist meditation.

"Those phone calls when someone hangs up?" he asked sheepishly. "That was me."

Long day, time to go, the walrus needed to get to work early. He interjected with jibes and jokes. Finally, coat on and at the door, the universal message of "Get the hell out," the hurt, the genuine surprise, the rejection. The slow putting on of socks.

"See you Tuesday?"

"Think I'm busy. I'll call."

Don't we all know that means not at all?

Letters, letters, phone calls. Stopped by the bike shop three awkward times. Every swing of the door at work a ding – jump! Ding, jump! Had to make it brutally clear.

"Ivan, I don't want to see you, ever again. Please. Stop coming by."

"Grazie, I love you. Don't be afraid of love."

"No."

"We are entwined, you and me."

"Do I have to file a restraining order? Do I have to call the police?"

Left quietly, but why why why why why not call a friend? Why did the walrus think that waiting half an hour made it safe, confirmed that he was gone? Stupid stupid stupid fat stupid ugly stupid idiot lock up dark parking lot SLAM SLAM cement-littlerocksintheface digging in small hands (huff huff) gloves grab came prepared clawing clawing the walrus tried to gagging gagging jaw smash and rip the shoulder off the shirt.

Beforeyouknowitsdone.

Zipandgone.

Crum ... ple.

Crum ...

ple.

So.
Fucking.
Tired.
Get.
Home ...
Fell ... asleep.
Here? In the parking
Lot.
Weird.

Broken. Tooth.

Right ...

Oh.

Right ...

Sleepy.
Get.
Home.
Just.
Get.
Home.
Key key key in the lock so hard to put the –
Like it will hurt putting it in the –
Insert insert insert insert worst fucking word ever
Shaking so hard –

Wash wash wash.
So
Sleepy.

Wash wash wash in the shower with the water on hot hot hot.
Bed. Pee. Bed. Pee. Bed. Pee. Bed.
Garbage starting to stink. Taste of metal in the mouth. Idiot you have to drink water or you can die.
Why didn't the walrus ...? Stop? Think? No. Wash wash wash. Washed it down the sink. Stupid. Evidence gone. Stupid! No use to call police. To say what? He had small hands?
And Mom is sick, stage four, and doesn't need this –

Can't work. Can't enter that shop with the ding, with the –
Bills coming through the slot. Doesn't it hurt to have a letter
shoved …?
Piling up.
Piling up.
Too tired to open any of it.
Back to bed.
Throwing up.
Wait.
Wait.
How long has it –?

No blood.

Slip.

Under the water.

Walrus.

Became so huge.

Can't see
genitals.

— Herman —

Ivan Vidal was found dead on impact, MVA, Rocky Mountain House: distracted driving. No other vehicle was involved. Graziana requested evidence of his death. She then slipped into a stuporous state. I would not say she was catatonic, but she seemed to be experiencing mutism. Having no known history of psychosis, this was alarming, and my first conclusion was heart attack or stroke, given her morbid obesity. I called an ambulance and they rushed her to the hospital for tests. Dr. Norma Kulpas was alerted.

Unfortunately, Hazel witnessed her mother in this state. Naturally she was upset. She overheard the EMT say Graziana would be assessed and then monitored for several days in the Peter Lougheed psych ward in Calgary. Hazel thought he said "cycle ward," where she imagined her mother might be doing some bicycle riding to feel better. I felt it was best not to correct her at this time and removed Graziana's old bicycle from the shed and took it to Pump & Pedal on Fourth Avenue for a tune-up and tire replacements.

I watered my plants and alerted my neighbours that I would be staying down the street at Graziana's house as Hazel's guardian until Graziana recovers. Graziana is not receiving visitors. She has been medicated and is being closely monitored. Her motor and communication skills have normalized.

I hired a cleaner, Amanda Copping, who will come tomorrow to tidy the house. In the meantime, I have taken out the recycling, which was significant, and organized Graziana's papers, which were strewn all over the house in unkempt piles. I cut and fertilized the lawn, and I've done six loads of laundry and made dinner for Hazel and me. Hazel tells me she only eats white food. Luckily I made chicken on rice, which she ate a slight amount of. She did not eat her broccoli, but she did eat some raw cucumber rounds that I set out. I decided it was best not to press the matter tonight. She had chocolate ice cream for dessert, and I noticed an immediate burst of hyperactivity and irritability.

Hazel had a lengthy temper tantrum when I refused to allow her to watch television beyond the limit of one hour. Her emotions ran wild, and she was physically violent when I removed her to her room for a "time out." She screamed and cried and kicked at the door from 7:30 to 11:30 p.m., whereupon she fell asleep from exhaustion, having collapsed on the floor in a full sweat.

Unsure of her sense of privacy at this age, I left her fully clothed and carried her sleeping body to bed. At 4 a.m. she woke up crying, having urinated in her sleep. She seemed very embarrassed for me to find out, but I assured her that in my field as a paramedic, I had seen plenty of grown women and men who had voided their bladders in times of distress, and she mustn't blame herself.

I ran her a bath, and she seemed confident that she could clean herself adequately and wash her own hair. Her mattress was soaked, so I set it out on the back porch and threw the bedding into the laundry. I suggested she sleep in her mother's bed while I took the sofa. At 6 a.m. she woke again because she urinated in her mother's bed. It wasn't as bad and didn't soak the mattress, so I was able to simply deal with the sheets and address the external shell of the mattress with some vinegar and water. She took a shower. Next thing I knew, it was seven. I made breakfast and got her off to school. Though she was very tired, I thought keeping her on schedule would give her a sense of normalcy and distract her from her mother's absence.

At eleven o'clock I received a phone call on the home line from the principal who said that Hazel had had an incident with another child at recess, and I was to collect her immediately. In person, the principal informed me that Hazel was arguing with this student before biting them in the arm so hard they had to go to the hospital for three stitches. I explained briefly to the principal, Ms. Faulk, that Hazel's mother had been hospitalized for reasons still to be determined, likely the catalyst for Hazel's behaviour. I also informed the school that I was the guardian to be contacted for now and would deal with the situation appropriately. (Thank goodness I was on Hazel's approved list of contacts.) Ms. Faulk seemed relieved that I was in charge and admitted that Graziana had always been resistant and disengaged from any conversation regarding Hazel's developmental issues.

Ms. Faulk explained that though this was Hazel's first significant physical assault, she had a complicated and difficult social and educational history at the school, and every teacher had brought her to the principal's attention at some point as their primary concern. She said Hazel was in the special-needs class and worked with a teacher's aide, Julie (Ms. Julie Perloff), who spent significant time with Hazel one on one. It had been suggested to Graziana that Hazel see a psychologist and get thorough testing done, get a real diagnosis for what may be a disorder. Staff at the school were not qualified to say whether Hazel suffered from ADHD or audio-processing disabilities, but they suspected one of these may be the case. When I asked for more details, Julie was brought in to speak with me.

Hazel sat in the other room while she explained that Hazel seemed to have troubles processing the information that she hears; she may actually not hear it. It is difficult for her to sit still for any length of time, and she often engages and disturbs the other children who are trying to learn. She seems to lack emotional maturity, has several outbursts daily, and experiences social isolation. She is physically agile and adept, though. She also shows great creativity, has a wonderful imagination, and shows musical ability with her sense of rhythm and pitch. She has a love for animals, can be very entertaining as a verbal storyteller, and excels at visual art. Julie suggested testing as well and confirmed that Hazel would have to be suspended from school for her sake and the sake of others while we all "formed a new strategy." (This over three stitches. You'd think

Hazel had brought a switchblade to school and stabbed the kid in the stomach.)

When I asked what other parents did in these scenarios, the teacher's aide reiterated testing and suggested a psychologist for ongoing therapeutic sessions for anxiety management. She brought up diet, too (avoid sugars and highly processed foods), and talked about the importance of regular exercise, ten to twelve hours of sleep at night, and the calming effect of a consistent schedule. Julie seemed relieved that I was receptive to these ideas and that I was there to support both Graziana and Hazel at this time. Then she informed me of the various alternate approaches to education one might take: homeschooling, private schools, and gradual reintegration into the public-school system. Seems to me this is all fancy talk for: "We don't want to deal with a problem child. We want to sing songs in a circle and draw giraffes and get paid for three months of holiday a year, thank you very much, Mr. Taxpayer."

When I tried to discuss the incident with Hazel, she couldn't concentrate or sit down with me or even put a sentence together. She barely even made eye contact. She didn't understand why she couldn't see her mom. Admittedly, I led her to believe her mother was still in the "cycle ward," biking a great distance in an effort to get healthy. Hazel wasn't sure why she was left behind. I told her the doctors were the ones who said her mother had to cycle on her own and that it wasn't her choice. That much, at least, was accurate.

I bought a new mattress for Hazel's room and waterproof mattress covers for both beds, and Hazel went to sleep rather early, without any protest about the TV. I made an effort to limit her liquid intake. Despite that, she urinated in her bed around 4 a.m. The damage was mitigated. She had a quick shower and did not urinate in her sleep again.

I have decided to keep her at home while I set up appointments with a child psychologist. I will not move forward with testing, especially not without Graziana's approval, but the suggestion of having a third party for Hazel to talk to and learn anxiety-management skills from sounded reasonably non-invasive. I will focus on creating a stable and healthy physical environment and assess for myself where I feel she is at with her learning in terms of the basics of reading, writing, and arithmetic.

Grumpy threw out all my best "just for snack" cereal, even though I told him it was just for snacks and not for real breakfast. And all the chocolate! Gone! All the tangerine Pellegrinos, my favourite favourite favouritist pop of all time. He opened them all up and poured them down the sink, and there were lots. Mom is going to be so so so mad because she pays a lot for them at Costco. Mommy Mom Mom Mommy Mad Mom Mad Mom Mad Mommy – yeah, that sounds best, like a band name, oh yeah, I play lead guitar for the Mad Mommies! No, wait, it should be Mad *Mummies*! Like the guys with the bandages covering their eyes and their whole bodies and they're stumbling around, but then they would not see their strings on their guitars and they would fall off the stage and that could be hilarious! Only the drummer mummy could keep banging things like: BAH BAH BAH BAH –

"Hazel, don't thump on the chair while I'm driving please. We're going to stop in here to do the recycling. Come and help me lift this bag. We'll do pop cans first."

It stinks in the recycling depot like if a garbage monster took a big pee and never flushed. Everything is sticky, and the man with the blue gloves keeps yelling, "You can't recycle that, it's soft plastic!" or "Put that in this place, not this big container!" Who cares, sticky man. You like yelling. Grumpy got even more grumpy. Where does the soft plastic go then? There is so much soft plastic it could make its own planet. Who even needs soft plastic? It's not even beautiful. I hate it when people make sh–, I mean stuff that is not beautiful. I want to carry around my apples in a velvet bag – that would be magic! Dark-blue velvet like the bits on Belle's dress. Not this shit shit shit – HA HA HA! Nobody can hear me say "shit shit shit." Hey, this wine bottle has stuff in it still! I could drink the rest of this wine and nobody would even know I was drunk –

"Hazel! Do NOT put your lips on that bottle, you don't know where it's been! Are you nuts?"

"Mom calls me the nut because I'm NUTS. Warghawargh-hawargha!"

"Don't swing the – sorry, sir – she's – this is her first time here. Don't swing the bag around, Hazel, you could break the glass inside and cut yourself, and you're bugging people. Stop. This is where the tin cans go, this is where the plastic containers go, see?"

"Bug bug bug bug!"

"Are you trying to bug me?"

"Bug bug bug bug."

"And what would bugging me accomplish? What's your endgame, Hazel?"

"End what?"

"What I mean is, when you bug me on purpose, how do you think that's going to turn out for you?"

"You bug me, so I bug you. I get you back."

"Well, I certainly don't mean to bug you, Hazel. What do I do that bugs you?"

"Boss me around."

"Well, to be fair, that's my job right now. See that bin over there? That's where you put the milk and the juice cartons. It's not plastic, it's –"

"Who gave you that job to boss me? Not me, not my mom, not my teachers!"

"Circumstances, Hazel. I would be a bad grandpa if I didn't step up and take care of you."

"I don't need you to take care of me. I don't care about circumferences."

"Circumstances. Oh no? Then what would you eat?"

"I don't know, you threw all the good stuff out!"

"That's a beer can. That goes in the huge bin over here."

"How am I supposed to know what's beer and what's juice?"

"Look at this. It has a *B-U-D*. That spells *Bud* –"

"Beer is called *Bud*?"

"And it's blue. Anything *B* goes here."

"Blue buddy?! Beer is a blue buddy?"

"Oh, lots of people think beer is their blue buddy, but actually all they get is lazy and fat from drinking it."

"Don't you drink beer? Doesn't that make you lazy and fat?"

"Sure, I'll have a cold beer on a hot day. But not this crap. I'll drink one beer. A real beer."

"What's a real beer?"

"Blue Buck pale ale."

"*Blue Buck* has two *B*s too!"

"Very good, Hazel. And you know what it's called when you use the same letter several times in a sentence? Alliteration."

"A little what?"

"Maybe that's too advanced."

"A little what? Do you think I'm stupid? I'm not stupid. I'm just crazy!"

"You're not stupid, and you're not – Hazel, don't smash those, careful! God, give me patience."

"A little what?! Tell me!"

"Okay, okay. Put the bag down!"

"I'm recycling!"

"No, you're throwing things around, dang it. PUT. IT. DOWN!"

"Don't YELLLLLLLLLLLLLL at me. Don't GRAB! OWIE!!!!"

"That did not hurt. Sorry, sir, I'm just going to take her outside. We'll be right back."

"You're grabbing my arm!"

"I'm allowed to grab your arm when you are being violent. What I'm not allowed to do is hurt you. But if you hurt yourself by flailing around like a wild animal, then it's your own dang fault. Okay now. Take a breath."

Whoooo-haaaaaaaaa.

"Take another breath."

"You take a breath!"

"Let's both take a breath."

Whoooo-haaaaaa.

Lots of bees around this recycling place. They like it. And somebody is stacking up all the egg cartons. Like for a hundred million eggs. Are there that many chickens to make all those eggs for people to eat? That's a lot of eggs. I don't like eggs, except the white part is okay with ketchup. Grumpy likes to look straight into my eyes. It's hard to look away. One, because it's hard. And two, because he has really light blue eyes like a watered-down blueberry Freezie.

"Okay, Hazel. Alliteration is when you repeat a letter lots of times in a sentence: 'Blue Bud is a bad beer because it's … bland.'"

"You're making a beer poem."

"Ha ha, yes, yes, I am! That is precisely why I am a paramedic and not a poet. And that poetic device –"

"Device?"

"Sort of like a tool you use to make poems – the repeating *B*s – is alliteration. Can you say that word? Alliter–"

"Alliteration. Duh. Doris is dorky but not dumb."

"Okay. Maybe it's not too advanced. Well done, Hazel. Let's finish up now and get out of here, okay?"

When I was little I called him Grumpy because I couldn't say Grandpa and it was so funny, but now it is not funny because it is true. He's a Grumpy Grumpy GRUMP.

"Okay, last bag. I'll do it or it will take forever. You can wait in the car."

I want to say a bad word now, but I won't because I don't say bad words, except sometimes a very quiet *shit*. But if I did say a bad word about Grumpy, it would start with a word that is like a donkey, and it would end with a big HOLE.

"Don't kick the back of my chair, please."

Grumpy's car smells like him. Like laundry. And and and a shoebox maybe in a closet. With a stone in it. A magic stone would be nice. I'd keep it under my bed and maybe it would turn into a gecko. I always wanted a gecko, but Mom said I would like it for three days and then get bored and forget to feed it and she'd have to do all the work and it would live until I was in university and I still wouldn't take it because my roommates wouldn't want a reptile in their room and worms in their fridge because you have to feed them worms or crickets. Gross and cool.

"Look, there's Maxine!"

I wave at Maxine from Grumpy's car, but she doesn't see me. I think it's cool to have a name with an X in it. I have a Z which is almost even better, except Hazel is the name of a witch and that's what Stephen calls me at school: Witch Hazel Witch Hazel. He is so mean. He is mean to Geoffrey too but especially mean to me.

"Is Maxine a friend from school?"

"Yeah."

"Do you want to say hi to her? I could pull over."

"No."

"Okay."

Maxine is wearing her cool Keds that have kittens on them. Her dad works in the oil fields and he's never home, but he makes a lot of money. They have a big house with one two three levels with stairs, you know? And a boat in the driveway. A boat! With wood on the inside. I want to curl up in there, it's so cozy, like a tent.

I went to her house once and I spilled hot chocolate on the white sofa and her mom was pretending not to be mad but she was really mad and she asked me if I did it on purpose because I thought it was funny but I didn't know why I was laughing. Only because it looked like runny poo. And Maxine had a birthday in November and she invited Cheryl, Kiki, Olivia, Priyanka, Sunny, Phoebe, and Elizabeth, but not me. They all got loot bags that had purple rings and pretty pencils with little panda bears on them – that was alliteration – those panda pencils were so cool and they all brought them to school and I didn't have one. So Mom went to Salvation Army and bought me a REAL RING and we knew it must have been from a princess who dropped it when she was riding horses and a farmer found it and put it in the store and it has magical powers to give me an invisible tiger who is very soft and gentle and can eat pandas if he wants to. I wanted to wear my ring to school but then I dropped it down the sink and Mom says that's why she doesn't buy me nice things.

"Where are we going?"

"You'll see."

I wonder what would happen if Grumpy drove his car through that fence and off the side of the road and over the cliff. I wonder if instead of fall fall falling and crash crash crashing to the bottom, we would discover we could fly and then we'd be famous because we'd have a flying car like Shitty Shitty Boom Bang – what's that old-fashioned car's name? I hate old movies because everyone is sooooooo happy. Smiling like dorks. That's not real. Nobody smiles that much, especially not adults.

"Why are we going here, Grumpy?"

"I thought maybe it would be fun to see how fast you could run."

"I love running! How fast do you think I can go, Grumpy? Faster than you?"

"Oh, yes, probably faster than me. I could time you –"

"There's a stopwatch on your phone. I could show you –"

"Oh I know, and this –"

"But I'm wearing snow boots!"

"This is a running –"

"I won't be as fast in snow boots –"

"Try not to interrupt me when I'm –"

"Because they're all heavy and floppy. I need to go home and get my runners –"

"Do not interrupt –"

"Run run run run, open the car, Grumpy! Open open open!"

"Hey. Look at me."

"Open open open!"

"Stop kicking my chair and stop interr–"

"Open open open! Ha ha ha ha ha!"

"Hazel. Look at me. Hazel. Hazel, look at me. Breathe, honey. Big breath. One –"

"Why do I always have to breathe?"

"We all have to breathe or we'd die."

Sigh. Whoooo-haaaaaaaaa. One.

"Two."

Whooo-haaaaaa. Two.

"Three."

Whooo-haaaaa. Three!

"I brought your runners. They're in the trunk. This is called a running track, and it's made to absorb the –"

"You brought my runners? Whoopie!"

"Absorb the impact so it's better for your joints. Okay, get out of the car, kid. Before you drive me crazy."

I love the park I love the smell of grass I love little yellow butterflies. Mom says they are moths but my favourite colour is yellow so I say they are the only real butterflies because they look like butter! I also like the snow time and icicles and frost. I am going to run with my magic tiger. His name is William. The ring went down the sink but he didn't go down the sink. He stayed with me full time. But sometimes he goes out at night to hunt, I think. He's nice to me but sometimes he scares me like I think he's going to tear my throat open with his teeth when I'm sleeping.

"Okay, you have to warm up first, Hazel. Let's rotate the ankles to the right."

I love my runners. They're dirty now but they're still cool. They're black, and black is cool.

"To the left. Luckily we've had some warm days and the track is clear."

Grumpy's hair is nice and wavy like a wave. Like a silver wave with dark underneath, sort of like maybe if the ocean was brown and the waves were on top. Like a swirled-up dirty ocean but still nice.

"Grumpy, after this can we get an ice cream?"

"Ice cream in the winter? And now stretch out the back of the legs like this. It's called a lunge."

Lunge sponge grunge tunge. *Tunge* is not a word unless you didn't know how to say *tongue* or went to the dentist and got your mouth frozen and then said, "Dottor, you fwoze my tunge! Bahahaha!"

"Pardon? Okay, now stretch out the arms. Cross over like this."

"Grumpy, that's so silly! We're not going to run with our arms! Or are you going to time me doing a crab walk or a backward crab walk? Yeah, we can do them all! I can show you! And maybe cartwheels too!"

"Oh, I'd like to see cartwheels. Now the neck, but do it gently like this. You never want to make a full circle. Hazel, gentle with yourself! I just said you never want to make a full –"

"I'm like a dolly, see? I can turn my head all the way around!"

"Bloody exorcist child."

"What's an exorcist?"

"Exercise. Child. Exercise! Okay, now start at the white line and when I say 'go,' run as fast as you can to … See that first white line right at the end?"

"Yeah! Go!"

"No, no, WAIT, Hazel! Come back. When *I* say 'go.' How can I time you if I'm not ready?"

"Right right, okay. I'm ready, Grumpy! I love running, I love it!"

"Your mom used to love running too. She was the fastest in her whole school. Did she ever tell you that?"

"How can she run if she's SO FAT?"

"That's not very nice."

"Why isn't it very nice if it's true? She's faaaaaaaaaat. She can't even WALK! And now she thinks she can ride a BIKE? All by herself? That's stupid! Probably her fat fat fat stomach is going to get caught in the bike gears! She's going to crash and fall off a cliff and DIE! And it will be her own fault! And I won't care! I won't even give a SHIT."

"Well."

I don't know why, but sometimes I feel like I want to cry and there's no good reason.

"Well, Hazel, I think you would give a shit."

Like right now. My eyes got all stingy with water and so I just looked up and pretended the sun is burning my pupils. And by the way, Grumpy said *shit*.

"As I was saying, when your mother was in school, she was very fit and she was very fast. And I would drive her out to this track, and I would time her."

It's winter but there's no snow except in the shadow places under the trees. Little humps of white snow like sleeping arctic foxes. Some people say that climate change is what makes our snow so weird in February, but Grumpy doesn't believe in climate change. He said it's all a bunch of baloney and the weather has always been up and down like a see-saw.

"I think you have your mom's legs. You're built like her."

"What, fat?"

"She only got fat after she had you."

"So I made her fat?"

"No, just ... sometimes women get heavy after they have babies."

"But not super fat like my mom is super fat."

"Please speak about her with more respect, Hazel."

"Who cares? Mom is only your stepdaughter, not your REAL daughter."

"Anyway ... underneath ... before, when your mom was young, she was a great athlete. So, maybe running is in the bones?"

I never had baloney before and I asked Mom and she said it was disgusting, like a flat hot dog. But I like hot dogs, so she bought me a pack of baloney and I ate the whole thing in two days for lunch.

"Your mom had a lot of energy when she was young, like you. And she was the fastest in her whole school and the whole city. Do you know the name of our city, Hazel?"

"Alberta?"

"No, that's the name of our province. But your mom was the fastest girl in the whole province too."

"Who cares?"

"What's the name of our city though?"

"Canada."

"No, that's the name of our country. I mean the city, the one we're in right now. Smaller than a country or province."

"I don't know. I can't see how big it is! San Francisco?"

"San Francisco? Land's sake, where on earth did you get that?"

"Earth?"

"That's our planet. No, our city –"

"Can we run now?"

"Our city is Red Deer."

"I want to run!"

"What's our city?"

"Earth!"

"What's our city, Hazel? Did you hear me?"

"I want to run!"

"What's our city?"

"Grumpy!"

"What's our city, Hazel?"

"CALIFORNIA!"

"No."

"Canada!"

"No. Maybe you didn't hear me."

"401 MacKenzie Crescent!"

"That's your address. Can you look at me for a minute? Good. I want to know that you can hear me. Our city is Red Deer."

"Why did they call it that? I don't see any deer. Only in the country when we drive to your old place where Gramma used to live, and the deer were brown, not red. Brown with white bums."

"So, Hazel, what is our city?"

"Red Deer."

"Good. Now, you're running to the –"

"First white line, got it!"

"And ... GO!"

RUN RUN RUN RUN RUN RUN RUN RUN RUN RUN RUN RUN RUN!

Only when I run does my brain fuzz out all the tigers and blues and oranges and MOMMY and and GRUMPY and STUPID MAXINE and cars beeping and smelly garbage on my shoes and the snotty in my nose and I become long long long like a pencil and my head is the pointy part. SHARP! I could prick you! SHARP SHARP SHARP! Hazel with a Z. Zzzzzzzzz. When I run, everything gets quiet in my sharp pointy head and I feel the most like me.

"And ... TIME! Holy cow, Hazel, twenty-eight seconds!"

I didn't know Grumpy could be fun. Usually he just watches hockey or mows the lawn.

— *Beloved* —

Our beloved has returned to Us unfettered by flesh yet feeling foiled. Not realizing his state, not comprehending the new dimension. His energy hurtles back into Our presence: aghast, still shivering with the memory of bleeding out, his face sticking to the ice.

"Not the Mercedes, oh my god, no! Granny's gonna kill me. She loves that car. I was gonna give it back. I was gonna ... Shit! I'm not insured, I'm sure I'm not insured under her coverage. I gotta, I gotta, I gotta run! I gotta wipe the steering wheel of my prints, I gotta get up and ... Maybe they'll think it's stolen. What the ..."

Beloved notices that he's looking down at his own inert body. He observes his still chest. He looks into his own unblinking eyes. His belt buckle is frosting up, his pants are open. His penis is poking out from the slit in his underwear, like a tiny pink fetal elephant.

"No no no no no. Please, please, no! I'm sorry, okay? I'm sorry! Wake me up, wake me up! People are coming! I should have never been driving while high and ... oh my GOD. My pants are down. Pull my – you gotta pull my – Not Mark Hildebrandt! That fucker hates me! That six-foot Mennonite do-gooder, not him, not him. Fuckin' paramedic loser. Too stupid for med school. Shit shit shit! He sees me. They're taking pictures of my – Wake me up! You can't leave me to die like this! This isn't FAIR! YOU CAN'T DO THIS TO ME! You put the ice on the road. You set me up! You should be ASHAMED! You're mocking me! Why are you mocking me?!"

Mockery is personal. Are We a person? Our beloved forgets his very nature is constant choice and he can choose again. He's been carried out of carnage into the coolness of Our consciousness to do so.

Stay. Settle. Be consoled.

"Don't leave me out there in the snow with my dick hanging

out and my head cracked open! They're laughing at me. I'm dead or I'm gonna die. Why am I not dead? Why can I see all of this shit? NO MERCY! Of all the people, Mark Hildebrandt. You know he called me Speedy, Speedy Gonzales, every time he saw me at the gym. But You reward him. That redneck racist asshole. He gets to live! Flip YOU! Why can't I say *FROG*?!"

We decided to replace your flagrant Fs with funny ones. Love does not welcome abuse.

"Listen, You flapjacks, I want back in! Send me back! Now! Why am I flooding talking to the air? You don't exist, and if You do I sure as Frito-Lay wouldn't want to know You. Because what kind of joke was my life? You toy with humans like a cat with a mouse? Is that it? I didn't have a faceless chance in hell. Born to an alcoholic mom and no dad, because she was a frankincense whore and didn't even know which of the six hundred johns she fricasseed that I flinching came from. And Granny Camila was just as bad but won't admit it. Fend for myself, and then that Freudian gymnastics teacher, Mrs. MacDonald, started getting me drunk at the age of twelve and asking me to go down on her in the locker room when everyone else was gone. What kind of forked-up ship is that? And then I frosting hate that guy Voight who failed me in math and lowered my GPA so bad that I didn't have a chance at getting into a decent finking university. FLOSS THAT. Not my fault I got mono! I finally get out in the workforce, and it's the worst economic crash since the Dirty Thirties, thanks for that. Fracking bartender and waiting tables. Oh, and love the dyslexia. Could have been a fibromyalgic electrician or some damn thing if I could forklifting read straight. Bad enough You only let me grow to a ferreting five foot six. Are You kidding me? With a dick the size of a fizzling cocktail wiener? Women always, ALWAYS laughed. It's not FAIR!"

You were born into peace and liberty at a time of great invention and freethinking. You were born as part of a privileged race and gender, and your citizenship was that of a country possessing great wealth, opportunity, and charity. You never

31

knew hunger, war, or disease. You were gifted, you were loved, you were admired, you were comely.

"Who the hell says *comely*? Who the frogurt are You anyway? God's femmie frigate secretary? I want to talk to the Big Man."

We are All.

"I mean the guy with the white beard and the – the Father – the Dude. See? He doesn't exist! So I don't follicle know who the hell You are, some Goddess wannabe or – cuz a Holy Mother? Ho ho ho, yeah, that's not gonna work for me. Are there three of You?! I can't tell. Stop being everywhere, will ya?! Wrapped in a peach-coloured frolicking sunset! Flan You!"

We are All. We are genderful.

"Oh, You're All, are You?! Then explain to me the starving kids in Africa? What kind of omniscient being invents the kind of bug that eats out the eyes of children? What kind of omnipresent Lord creates a psychopath who mass-murders innocent people? And isn't it amazing that the Muslims were all born knowing the 'one true God' and the Christians were born knowing the 'one true God' and the Jews were born knowing the 'one true God' and they're called to kill millions of people, all for the sake of Your holy name?"

We believe you've bastardized the arguments of exorbitantly wealthy celebrities. They divert their own discomfort away from being worshipped and extraordinarily blessed, knowing they could be doing so much more for the underprivileged. And you, in turn, are using them to divert from your own discomfort. Do you really want a discussion?

"No. I don't want to hear from You at all. Just send me back!"

By design, We do not interfere with your choice to return, but We urge you to seek transformation in this place first. You've regressed. Please stay in Our presence and heal. Rest.

"No way, get me out of here. Send me back."

What do you choose to bring into the world?

"I choose to have a great big prick!"

And what do you offer others, besides a great big prick?

"Others? What did others ever do for me? I'll stick it to the assholes!"

Are you sure?

"Do it!"

We have a placement.

"Beam me up, Scotty!"

Begin.

And there he goes, into a puddle of emerald green, deep in the Amazon forest, filled with crystal-like, slender stalks of mosquito eggs.

CHAPTER TWO

STICKING POINT

— Graziana —

The walrus knew it had to stop referring to itself as the walrus. Dr. Norma Kulpas had been saying that for years. But when it looked in the mirror, that's what it saw. When it poked at its heart, that's what it felt: waterous. That should be a word: *waterous*. The walrus was logged full of dark brackish sea, blubbery and heavy and thick-skinned.

The walrus at least allowed itself to look more like a "she." It would be a long road before it would even want to reclaim its sexuality, but it did have the strength now, the courage, to admit it might have a gender. The walrus had made small steps forward with self-care. It bathed now. It cut and brushed its hair. It plucked the hairs off its chin. One of the nurses cut its toenails and painted them blue. Other patients here at the psych ward in the Peter Lougheed Centre worked hard for their right to wear street clothes or gain access to their cellphone again. The walrus was content to stay off the grid and in pyjamas. There was no need for good behaviour.

That said, the walrus started reading again. It only had the energy for light lit, so it dabbled with Dan Brown, a chapter here and a chapter there. Crafts were soothing, though lame of course. It felt silly doing them, like it was either at the beginning or the end of its life and only capable of using crayons and yarn. The walrus wasn't half bad at watercolour. There was a dignity to it; it was unforgiving and required the nicer paper.

Medication was taken faithfully. The brain felt foggier and

clearer at the same time. As a voluntary inpatient, the walrus was kept from excesses. It was eating a balanced, moderately healthy diet and going for walks around the courtyard on its gimpy knee. Sometimes it got on the recumbent machine while watching TV, mostly to avoid thinking. It had lost fifteen pounds in five weeks. The walrus had never been fond of stepping on the scale but was astonished to learn when it was first admitted, that it had ballooned up to three hundred pounds, more than double its usual weight. It struck the walrus that ever since the incident with Ivan, it had wrapped itself entirely in a blubbery second body.

"Obesity is common among those who have been sexually assaulted."

The walrus already knew this from sessions with Norma.

"Rape is about power, not desire."

"Yes, I know. Can't you just ask to read my therapist's notes so we don't have to repeat ourselves?"

Dr. Norma Kulpas was in Mexico this month. Besides, the team at Peter Lougheed wanted their information first hand.

The walrus liked Norma. Her GP referred her several years back. It was a long wait but worth it. Norma's a psychiatrist, so she's covered under medical. The walrus started sessions with Norma two years ago, when the nut entered school full time. Norma never pushed meds but tried to make headway with cognitive behavioural therapy. They both agreed: the walrus progressed to a certain point and then seemed stalled. Parenting the nut was exhausting. The fatigue and numbness made it hard to care about anything. The walrus had a good mother growing up. It understood how it was failing in comparison. The walrus and Norma talked all about childhood, Mom's cancer, the nut, Herman, Ivan. It was like chipping words into ice. Theories were laid down and understood, but everything was frozen solid around it. Nothing ever moved. Until now. Now the walrus was liquifying into puddles of grief and rivulets of shame. It could barely breathe: waterous, waterous.

Peter Lougheed leaned in, wearing purple and smelling of

ranch dressing. "Perhaps you haven't allowed yourself to feel, to hope, to heal … because even though you have had no contact with Ivan since the assault, he's always been out there."

"Watching."

"You think he was watching you?"

"He was always watching."

"With his death … how do you feel?"

"A little sad. In an abstract way. I mean, he was a human being. But mainly I feel relief. Tremendous relief. So why did I have a mental breakdown?"

"You're starting to feel again. Perhaps like ice on a river, breaking in springtime. You know that loud crack? Graziana, perhaps this is you beginning to thaw."

"Maybe I don't want to thaw."

"Why not?"

"Maybe I can't live with myself."

Peter Lougheed kept the walrus in for further observation. Words like *disassociation*, *trauma*, *PTSD*, and *depression* were whispered in hushed tones. The staff didn't seem to object to the walrus asking for no visitors – not even family.

"Maybe it isn't depression. Maybe I just don't care? Maybe I'm a bad parent. I haven't seen my kid in weeks and I know she's better off."

"What makes you think she's better off without you?"

The walrus shrugs.

"Why do you think you're a bad mother?"

The walrus flinched at the *M*-word.

"I … I haven't been mean or anything, I just haven't been … much. It's my fault the nut is a problem child. On top of contending with … where she comes from, I let things slide, you know, like printing and reading. I let my kid stay up and watch movies and eat junk food just to keep her quiet. There's something … I'm afraid of her. And I don't know why. She's only seven years old. And she's a playful, imaginative, funny little girl. I mean, she makes me laugh. We sometimes laugh."

The walrus isn't sure why the thought of laughter brings her to tears.

"But my kid doesn't get on well with others, and I have this feeling she'll always be troubled. I know that's horrible. Even when she was born, I couldn't ... I couldn't stand to breastfeed. I mean, what kind of monster doesn't want to breastfeed? I did it at first for the colostrum. And everyone was watching me at the hospital. But I hated every second of it. This creature feeding on me. As soon as I got home, I pumped and gave her the bottle within a week. She was never a huggy baby, thank god. Always wriggling out of my arms, and I'd just as soon put her down."

"Do you think you suffered from postpartum depression?"

"Oh god, I don't know. Is it supposed to last eight years? I didn't even know I was pregnant for the longest time. I just thought I was losing my periods because of the stress. And then when the thought crossed my mind, I couldn't bear it. I didn't want to know. I pretended it wasn't happening. And then it just felt ... too late to abort. And I didn't have the capacity to think about giving it up. I was sick with it, so sick. That's when I really started to put on the weight. The muscles in my leg atrophied, and I've got a bad knee, so I couldn't work ... God, listen to me."

"I want to hear it. Tell me more about Hazel."

"She's ... I can't ... To be honest I have a hard time looking at her. She always has her mouth open. She's a mouth-breather. She's ... it's hard to explain, but I think she's disordered. She's going to grow up to be a drug addict or in jail."

"Does she exhibit violent tendencies?"

"She hasn't killed and dissected the neighbour's cat or anything if that's what you mean. But she has a wild temper and will lose control, yeah, and flail around and break things. She used to have a real problem with biting when she was younger, when I had her in daycare. One place kicked her out. She had a Métis friend for a while, Walter, and she was real gentle with him. But he was a foster kid who ended up getting adopted by his aunt or something and moving up north."

"Does she have friends now?"

"She's never brought anyone home from school, and I never arranged anything. The only playdate she's had was with Maxine. I think her mother felt sorry for her. Anyways, something went wrong there, of course, and the nut was never invited back. She's been to Geoffrey's place. Geoffrey is a kid with autism, pretty high functioning, but he does a lot of bouncing on a big ball and is non-verbal. She met him through one of her special-ed classes. I don't think the nut has very high self-esteem. I don't think … she's happy."

"You call her 'the nut,' right?"

"Um … yes."

"Do you call her the nut out loud? Does she know it's your nickname for her?"

"Um … yes. Is that bad? It can't be that bad. It's kind of cute. Like Hazelnut."

"Does she remind you of him? Physically?"

"I've been over this with Norma. God, I'm tired."

"Graziana, does Hazel resemble Ivan?"

"I think I'm done here for the day."

"Does she have his hair colour, his shape of nose?"

"Yes, yes, she does! And I know that's an issue. Norma and I have talked about transference and it comes and goes. Seriously, I can't keep my eyes open."

"Yes, that is a stress response. Does your daughter self-harm?"

"Not on purpose. No. But she's always hurting herself because she never pays attention. Falls down the stairs, walks into poles, so clumsy. She'll stare at the TV for hours like a zombie and I have to admit, I don't give a shit. At least she's quiet for the evening, gives me a break. I told you, I'll be the first to admit, I'm a shit parent. I don't think … I don't think she even knows how to brush her teeth properly. When and how did she learn to wipe her bum, I don't know. I just hope it's being done.

I don't comb her hair and she gets these terrible knots and once I just told her to cut it all off if she hated it and she did, and she looked like a complete disaster, and I left it. One of her teachers cleaned it up with sewing scissors. Whatever. They keep calling me in to the school, but I have no answers for them, so I just don't go anymore. What can you do about a kid who doesn't care about anything or anyone?"

"You mean your daughter."

"Of course!"

"Does she … Is she capable of empathy?"

"I don't know. She's pretty self-absorbed. She'd have to pay attention to feel any sympathy for anybody else. She's just take take take take, loud loud loud loud. I'm afraid to turn my back on her. She's so … wild."

"What would she do if you turned your back on her?"

"Oh, I don't know, nothing I suppose, but she might, like, jump on me, jump on my back, smash my head against the wall … small … hands …"

"Graziana?"

Crum … ple.

"Graziana?"

Crum …

ple.

"Stay with me, stay with me, tap your legs like this, stay in your body, Graziana."

Sleepy.
Sleepy.

Must get

To bed.

Must

Sleep.

— *Herman* —

Education: I hesitated putting Hazel into any homeschooling program, having had no contact with Graziana, not knowing her wishes. This past month, Hazel has not attended school. She has been under my continuous care, and I feel I am providing her with a stable and balanced environment. She is beginning to show improved results in her ability to concentrate and socially engage.

As formerly indicated, I wanted to assess for myself Hazel's basic educational level. I'm not an expert, of course, but she may struggle with dyslexia because she often inverts her *B*s and *D*s. Though she loves telling stories verbally and she loves drawing, she is very averse to learning how to read or write. Her stories are often quite violent: people falling down holes or leaping off cliffs and dying. She doesn't show the patience to sound out words. She tells me her teacher lets her write out words phonetically instead of learning the actual spelling. This may be true, but I don't see the sense in it. We had quite an argument about that.

She flat out declares she can't read because she's "stupid," and she can't write because she's "dumb." I asked her to tell me who told her that, and she said, "kids at school." It seems helpful to keep our lessons together very short and very focused with a chance to earn a sticker on her progress board. I have decided to follow the alphabet. I include physical activity and healthy snacks as a break between our work on writing, reading, and the basics of arithmetic. I have also included some geography.

It has taken me a good week to figure out how to get her to sit down and learn anything at all. And although the progress is slow, there has been progress. She can add and subtract digits up to ten. She can write out a few very basic words, though she still hasn't any command of spelling, capital letters, or punctuation. She is willing to sound out words for a brief time, but at this point it's safe to say she cannot read. I have started to read to her every night as a replacement for TV, something she really seems to enjoy. Right now, we are reading *The Hobbit*. She interrupts me a great deal with questions or tangents, and I often lose my patience, but we have managed to get to chapter three.

Physical health: I took Hazel in for a full physical exam, which she hasn't had since birth. She is generally healthy. She is low in iron and underweight but very tall for her age – four feet and five inches. The doctor said she needed more exercise based on her muscular development. She confirmed my suspicions that white sugar, caffeine, pop, and highly processed food can aggravate hyperactivity. Judging from the contents in Graziana's cupboards, those seemed to make up most of Hazel's diet until now. She was also behind on her vaccinations. Luckily, all she was missing was her Tdap-IPV. I approved the inoculation.

Having done some reading about attention span and the relationship to diet, I also took her in to see a naturopath, who tested her for allergies. I'm not usually into all that witch doctor stuff, but it confirmed my suspicions that Hazel has an intolerance for wheat and milk products, so there must be something to it. Since removing these from her diet, I have noticed that her nasal passages are clearer, and she no longer snores. She has also alerted me to the fact that her vagina is often itchy, so I hope these changes to her diet also improves that. She seems to not become as irritable after meals. The naturopath did say that wheat can cause a rage response in some people. We found out that Hazel is allergic to soy. It causes her to itch and lends itself to her feeling both irritation and rage. As I've come to realize, soy and its derivatives are in nearly every packaged food. Therefore, we have been eating fresh vegetables and meats, and I've had to learn how to cook completely from scratch. This has been a struggle. She insists on only eating white food, like potatoes, apples, chicken, and cucumber. I have been able to introduce white fish, pork, navy beans, snap peas, rice crackers, devilled eggs, thin carrot sticks, celery with a non-dairy dip, cashews, and sweet potatoes. Amazingly, she will eat a spinach-artichoke quinoa cake. Generally, she rejects anything that is dark green.

I also took Hazel to the dentist. She had never been in her life. Her teeth were in bad shape. I am unsure how often she brushes them. Six of them had cavities: two in her newly erupted back molars and the rest in her baby teeth. Her other permanent teeth are fine. That said, she has a significant overbite and crooked incisors and will definitely need braces. We moved forward with cavity repair and scheduled an appointment for Invisalign. Hazel was rather brave about it all despite the poking and prodding.

I also managed to get her in to see an optometrist and her eyes are just fine.

I am teaching her how to throw a baseball and a frisbee. We have been going to the pool, where I have registered her for Canadian Red Cross swimming lessons. She was eager to get out of level one with all the little kids, so they tested her and moved her to level two. It's hard to watch the lessons because she interrupts the teacher and disrupts the others terribly. I have stopped observing. Running is still a favourite activity, and I bought her a skipping rope. She has decided to put on a "dance show" for me as a daily after-dinner special. She raids her mother's closet, finds music on her tablet, and puts on a rather flamboyant number. She tells me she'd like to take dance lessons. I can't imagine her being able to focus enough to accomplish any group choreography at this point, but we will see. Note: Investigate a dance form that is not ballet and find out when classes start.

Social skills: I strongly believe Hazel will have a better chance at making friends if she stops snorting mucus. Now that her nasal passages are clearing, she doesn't sniffle as often or wipe her nose on her sleeve. That said, I've had to try and teach her the basics of covering her mouth when she coughs or sneezes and saying "excuse me" when she passes wind or burps. The largest obstacle is teaching her how to eat with her mouth closed and to not talk when her mouth is full. I am teaching her how to say "thank you" and "please" but progress is slow. In fact, at this point, I don't see any progress at all. There are many other social issues to tackle with Hazel, but already I feel I am introducing more rules than she can handle, and our days seem to be one long confrontation.

Hazel has seen the child psychologist twice. I don't know what goes on in there except crafts. Hazel made a stress ball and something she calls slime. In my opinion, someone is getting paid two hundred and twenty dollars an hour for doing nothing in particular.

Having never raised a child before, I have new respect for my late wife, Nunzia, who did the lion's share of parenting with Graziana. I also have new respect for teachers. I protested their latest strike, and now I feel they most certainly do not get paid enough. I wish I was still working, so I could receive the dental benefits. Caring for both Hazel and the house has been a full-time job with no pay, and there is nobody to do it except for me. So much for bloody retirement.

Hazel does not ask about her mother.

— *Hazel* —

Who is Lan? Grumpy says, "Lan sakes child, lan sakes." ALL THE TIME! Well, I can't help it if I'm STUPID! And then he tells me nobody in our family is stupid.

"How do you know? Maybe I have dumb DNA!"

"Your mom is smart. She got good grades in school, and she used to run her own business, a bike repair shop –"

"Nobody knows my dad. Maybe he had dumb DNA."

"Oh, I don't think so."

"What do you know? You're not my real grandpa! You can't boss me!"

"Of course I'm your real grandpa."

"No, my real grandpa was a motorcycle rider from Italy who died in a car crash before my mom was even born!"

"Listen, a dumb person wouldn't even think of DNA, especially at the age of seven. That's smart. You're smart. But you're not being very nice right now."

"DNA isn't smart. It's just science. Duh!"

"Who told you about that anyway? About the motorcycle?"

"In school we did a family tree and I said I was German like you, but Mom said I'm not. I'm half Italian and half question mark."

"Well, I'm your real grandpa according to the law. Because I married your grandmother and adopted your mom, and I wish Nunzia was here right now because she'd do a much better job of wrangling you."

"Wrangling me? What's *wrangle*? Sounds like a cowboy. Sounds like you want to lasso me, Grumpy, and drag me behind a horse like they do in the Stampede, so you're the one who is NOT VERY NICE to KIDS or COWS!"

"Lan sakes, child, I can't win."

Lots of kids in my school like pop music but my favourite is old-fashioned. James Brown. "I feel good! Badabadaboopaba! Like a nugget of wood, yay. Doobie do do do. I feeeeeeel good, chinga chinga chinga choo, like a nugget of wood ...! Badabad-abadaba! So good, bam bam, so good, bam bam, soooooooooo good! Zoo doot do do do do DO!"

I got a needle last week. It was HUGE. But I was brave. So brave that Grumpy got me an ice cream, even though he says it gives me SNOT.

I'm glad I'm not in school. School is sooooooo boring! I hate it! And the kids are MEAN! Now I get to skip. Oh, yeah! Grumpy got me a skipping rope! I can go fast. See? (Skip skip skip skip.)

"Do you feel like you've worn off some of your jitterbugs? Heaven knows you could light the whole city with your energy."

"I don't have bugs."

"Jitterbugs. It means when someone moves around a lot. It was even a dance."

Grumpy is very funny when he dances the jitterbug. He moves his bum around and shakes his hair out into his eyes and scoots his feet around like this (scoot shake scoot) and it only lasts for two seconds. I have this feeling in my head that he will never dance it again. It was just for me. Like a secret.

"Hey, kiddo, you were asking about your grandmother, Nunzia, and your mom's birth father, so I thought I'd show you a picture."

"What's this book?"

"It's called a photo album. We took pictures and put them in books before we ever had computers."

"Coooooooooool. Who is this pretty lady?"

"That's your grandmother, Nunzia. Though because she's Italian, you would call her *Nonna*."

"I never met her."

"No. She died a few months before you were born. It's really too bad. She would have loved you."

"She would have wrangled me like a cow you said."

Grandma Nonna Nunzia had TONS of black hair all done in what Grumpy says was a ... f– ... faucet? Flip. And she had on high-waisted jeans and a fur coat.

"She had good fashion!"

"The seventies are back, I guess. This was before I met her when she was probably ... oh, maybe eighteen. Just before she left Italy."

"I like her eyebrows."

"And this guy –"

"On the motorcycle? That's my grandpa?"

"That's ... your mother's birth father, yes. They made a baby before they got married."

I know all about making babies. That means he put his penis in her vagina. Gross. How did he get into her underpants if she was wearing high-waisted jeans? So weird. I guess he must have surprised her when she wasn't looking. I would have been mad and so embarrassed. I would have just kicked him right in the face and not let him. I would have SCREAMED!

AHHHHHHHHHHH!

"What on earth are you screaming about?"

"Just pretending I was making babies."

"Well ... if you're screaming like that you're doing it wrong."

I wonder if Grumpy ever had sex. Nah. Gross. He's not gross. He probably has a penis because he has a zipper on his pants but it's only for peeing. Gross. Why am I thinking of PENISES?! They are so disgusting! But also kind of funny. I saw one in a painting on an angel, like an angel in the sky with a ... a ... a cupid! That's what I saw. Cupid. And he had a little boy penis between his chubby legs and it looked like a baby's finger poking out from a round white pierogi.

"His name was Baggio. I don't know his last name. He was an engineer who worked at the FIAT factory near Nunzia's hometown. They were going to get married but he –"

"Got run over on his motorcycle."

"Right. So then your grandmother, Nunzia, when she realized she was going to have a baby, her family in Italy was not very happy with her. So she moved to Canada to live with her zia Cinzella and zio Antonio –"

"Za za za what?!"

"*Zia* means 'aunt' and *zio* means 'uncle' in Italian. So, her aunt Cinzella and her uncle Antonio. Cinzella looked after the baby while Nunzia went to school and learned English. This was in Toronto."

"Is that my mom with the lunch kit and the shorts?"

"Yup. Isn't she cute?"

"She's so small. She's smaller than me."

"We all start off small. Even me, but that's a different photo album. And this was their house."

"Nice flowers."

"And then Nunzia took driving lessons and got a job with Telus and eventually moved to Calgary because she got transferred. She was a very strong woman. Very smart. So brave to have raised a child on her own and to learn a new language."

"Is that my mom? Why does she have that thing around her head? Did she hurt herself?"

"No, that's a headband. They were real popular in the eighties."

"Is that my mom running?"

"Yes, I told you, she was very fast. Ver–"

"Who's that?"

"Wow. I can't believe this picture is in here. This was ... well, it was her coach for a while. He was a bad coach, and she got hurt with her knee because the jerk didn't know what he was doing."

William, my invisible tiger, doesn't like to get wet. The good thing about that is, if you are a good swimmer and take lessons, even with babies, and want to get away from him, you just have to jump into the swimming pool or the ocean or a lake and he won't go after you! And the other good thing, if he's your friend, you can also use him as a towel because his fur is sooooo soft.

Four plus four equals eight. But four minus four equals zero. I always draw fours wrong because sometimes the arms are closed and sometimes the arms are open and I wish people would make up their minds about fours!

Today was *L* day. So I learned the letter *L*, the big one and the small one, I like *L*. *LLLLLLLLLLLLLLLL*. I'm glad I have an *L* in my name, it's almost as cool as the *Z*. Hazellllllll.

I spelled all *L*s today: *last, let, live, lock, lump, lyric. Lyric* is the hardest because *y* is hard to write, but it is also my favouritest. Grumpy says *favouritest* is not a word but it is so. It is in the Hazel dictionary. And then we had llllllemonade and lettuce for a snack!

I go to Shannon's office now. Shannon is a lady who knows how to make slime and stress balls and she talks a lot about breathing. She's nice. But sometimes she's really nosy. Like none of her beeswax. I told her that.

If you go into Mom's closet, it smells like her.

The pupa cracks open and the silvery beloved slides out, stretching its long legs, extending its wings, preening its long prick. It shimmers, light enough to walk on water. It skates to the shore, to the shade of a bromeliad, to let its wings dry and its exoskeleton harden. It is ready to fly. Hungry, hungry, it buzzes for nectar.

It is immediately crushed by the foot of a capybara and swallowed up by mud.

A new pupa cracks open and the silvery beloved slides out, stretching its long legs, extending its wings. It does not stop to preen its long prick. It skids along the water, quickly finding shelter on the top of a sunny rock; it will dry its wings faster. It wills its exoskeleton to harden quickly. It flies low and cautiously towards a heliconia.

Mid-air, it is snatched by the whiplike tongue of a harlequin frog.

Another pupa cracks open and the silvery beloved slides out, stretching its long legs, extending its wings, and brandishing its long prick, defiantly. It glides silently on the water, on the guard for predators. It finds shelter on the backside of a strangler fig snaking up a tree. It lets its wings dry and its exoskeleton harden while it plots out a plan. It buzzes its way back to the very same heliconia, buzzes high, too high for frogs. It sucks nectar fervently. It moves on. It dodges another frog tongue to find another heliconia. It sucks nectar fervently through its glorious prick. It moves on. It feeds and flies, gaining size and strength and confidence over the course of the morning. It emits its prowess through an enticing buzzing sound.

The buzzing is matched and then drowned in a deafening whir. A swarm of others come up fast from behind, engulfing it. It lands on the bark of a podocarpus. Suddenly, a male jumps on top of it, pins its legs down and penetrates its body without permission. It is shocked to realize that it must then be female.

Its assailant buzzes off to die.

The beloved is left filled with his assailant's sperm coursing through its body, and a new great hunger arises.

Blood. Blood! BLOOD!

It smells blood first on a howler monkey and pricks him by the ear. It sucks up hot red revenge. It sucks up the blood of his mate. It sucks up the blood from their baby. Who cares? It doesn't feel a thing!

Blood. Blood! BLOOD!

It continues this bloodsucking throughout the day, preening its magnificent prick after each successful extraction. Then it sluggishly lays its thick belly down on water and voids its eggs.

It and its kin are swallowed by a grebe.

The Beloved continues to pursue its desire to prick, bleed, suck the life out of things. We were hoping it would tire of this, but the Beloved never once asks for another placement. The constant recycling of its energy moves it from pupa to pupa, buzz to buzz, swat to swat, from Ecuador to Brazil, whereupon it comes across humans. This is particularly satisfying for it, to suck blood from men and women and their children.

"Hey!"

Yes?

"Listen, I don't know what kind of suckhole humans you have me hooked up with down here, but their blood tastes weird; they're sick. Some of them are lying around without any energy. Some of them are really hot with a fever. I don't know if a bug can catch a bug, but I have enough to worry about with frogs and birds, you know what I'm saying? Put me somewhere healthy!"

You're carrying the plasmodium parasite. It causes malaria.

"I have malaria?!"

Yes. You are infecting the population. Some of them have acquired immunity, and some of them have been vaccinated, but not all of them. They are quite isolated in this village.

"Oh."

Are you ready to make another choice?

The beloved falls silent for a while, thinking. Then all of a sudden: "You kidding? Mosquitoes! Yaw! Number one killer in the world, bitch! I totally forgot about that. I determine their fate. You don't get more powerful than that."

It makes you glad ... to be spreading a disease?

"You saying I don't have what it takes? Think I can't handle the responsibility?"

The respons–

"Think I'll be a pussy and wimp out? Send me back! Now!"

Another pupa cracks open and the silvery beloved slides out, stretching its long legs and extending its wings, and glides expertly across the water to a sheltering leaf. It lets its wings dry and its exoskeleton harden. It sucks nectar from passion flowers. It copulates on the side of a latrine. The thirst for blood comes. It sucks nectar from orchids. It is delaying a blood meal. This gives Us hope. But the thirst for blood grows. It tries to draw a blood meal from a goat but gets swatted by the tail.

Pilar gently approaches the left of the goat with a pail to milk; Baby Benigno toddles by her side. Easy prey for the beloved. It buzzes right up to Benigno's chubby face. It smells the innocence. The beloved buzzes away and approaches Pilar's ear, noting the slender curve of her neck, the fullness of her lip.

"You think you can laugh at me? You think I'm small? I can kill you and everyone dear to you."

The thirst for blood grows. Blood. Blood! BLOOD!

The beloved drives its prick right into Pilar's neck. Then the beloved sticks it to Benigno behind his tender knee. And just to make the picture complete, the beloved takes the time to circle around the back and bite the elder son, Mal, on the forehead.

Smack! The beloved's guts spread across Mal's hand, full of bloody banquet and eggs. Too late, Mal, too late.

The beloved returns to Us.

"Did I kill them?"

We have no reason to give you that information.

The beloved is silent a long time. Then it admits, "It didn't feel the way I thought it would."

Would you care for a rest?

"I want to know if I killed them!"

Why? It won't make your decision to infect them any better or worse.

"I know, I know! It … it isn't about me! I want to know about them!"

Why?

The beloved is silent again for a long time. "I want to be high. I want to get drunk. That's all I want."

Why would you want to do that?

"Does there always have to be a reason?"

Yes. By nature there is always a reason. But please, come and heal; come and rest. Be with Us.

"Fuck no. I want to get the highest and the drunkest I've ever been in my life!"

We have a placement.

"Do it!"

Begin.

And in he goes to the centre of a light-blue spotted waxwing egg. He's nestled in with his five siblings in a wee cupped nest. He's four metres up, next to the trunk of a pine tree, just north of Svappavaara, Sweden.

CHAPTER THREE

TIME TO FLY

— Graziana —

The walr–
She.
She must stop calling herself bad names. She is not a walrus.
She is a woman. And she is sure that Herman was not happy to
learn that she is no longer at the psychiatric hospital. She did
not allow the ward to disclose her new location, and he did not
press. She did finally give him a call. It was brief.

Apparently, the nut … No. She had to stop saying that.
The … daughter … the –
Hazel.
Hazel is an innocent child.
Hazel is an innocent child.
Hazel is an innocent child.
Hazel was doing well. This gave her great relief. She never
doubted for a moment that Herman would take good care
of her. My God, he put her in swimming lessons and was getting her Invisalign. He asked permission to homeschool! This
made her laugh. But maybe juvenile military training would be
good for the … *Hazel*. He wanted to meet in person. She agreed
and gave him her location. He was shocked to hear she was four
hours away, near the Saskatchewan border. She asked him to
give her a couple more weeks before meeting.

She had been thinking of all the ways her daughter was her
daughter. She could pore over a photo now, almost comfortably.
The transference had settled down. Hazel had Ivan's mousy hair

colour and square head and brown eyes, but she had the swoopy half-moon Italian chin. She had her side of the family's strong limbs and wide back. She had her feet, good feet. She could probably run! She could probably be an athlete. The wide curvy mouth, who knows? Some recessive gene. But it was charming.

And Hazel grew a sunflower from seed when she was five. Right! She brought it home from kindergarten in a Styrofoam cup and placed it on the kitchen windowsill. She watered it faithfully. She sang to it. The damn thing grew. She planted it in the front yard. It thickened and fuzzed and towered to six feet. It flowered. It bowed its head. It turned into seed for the birds to eat.

Parenting had been mostly inert, distracted, barely functional days. To think of her own absence in her child's life was excruciating now that she was feeling every slicing dicing thing. But the wal– ... *she* was also starting to remember and cherish the brief good moments she managed over the years. They made play dough, paper snowflakes, they played "go fish." They ice-skated at Bower Ponds and had hot chocolate with marshmallows between frosty mitts. In the summer they'd go to Sylvan Lake, and she'd watch Hazel splash in the murky water and build leaky condos with sand pails. This didn't make up for everything, of course, but she hoped that Hazel had a few tender memories.

The wal– ... *She* met Vera at the ward. Vera was a woman in her seventies who still had black hair, hardly a strand of grey. She wore nun shoes and patterned, thick skirts. She had a brother who struggled with schizophrenia and ended up at Peter Lougheed now and then. She came to visit him for a week and donated several beautiful handmade quilts to the ward. She helped make snacks and conversation. Vera ran a bed and breakfast near Medicine Hat on a heritage-site ranch. She had a bunch of rooms and several guests, and the busy season was coming. Her son used to help her out, but now he'd become a filmmaker and the other boy has decided to live in a yurt and raise horses. In short, Vera could use an extra hand doing laundry and cleaning and gardening, and she offered the walrus a job. The wal– ... dammit ... *She* wasn't convinced she'd be very good at helping with such chores, but Vera insisted she could teach her. Room and board in exchange for labour. A safe place for her to land.

Her new room at Vera's was in the basement along with the quilting supplies and the canned goods. It was dark and quiet, and she could sleep twelve hours at night, which was important, apparently, for her mind to heal.

Vera was very particular about how to clean a bathroom and make a bed. The wal– ... *She* had a hard time with the details, with caring. But Vera was persistent and made her do things over and over again. Sometimes Vera could harp on, which annoyed her, but she really had nowhere else to go, and she knew Vera was doing her a favour. She had learned how to clean a house well enough from her mother, but Vera had her own method, which she insisted on. She printed out a very extensive laminated checklist that she had to cross off with a dry marker and hand in every day for every suite.

Bathroom:
- Do a spiderweb check with the fluffy duster that is taped onto the end of the hockey stick. Also check for dust on the light fixture.
- Use a green scrubby with the rosemary cleaner on the sink first, the bathtub second, the toilet last. Do not use that scrubby again: it is now dirty.
- Use the toothbrush in the glass in the bucket and a tiny bit of bleach if you notice any grout discolouration.
- Use an old washcloth now in the same order to wipe down all the surfaces with hot water and the spray bottle of natural cleaner marked "Bathroom/Kitchen." Be sure to check the inside of the medicine cabinet and include wiping down the walls near the toilet for "man spray." Do not use that cloth again: it is now dirty.
- Use an old dish towel to polish the mirrors with the

spray bottle marked "Vinegar" to clean the mirrors; then use it to polish the taps on the sink and then the tub. Finally, use it to wipe down the drops on the tiles, double-check for any hairs in the tub (sometimes they are stuck onto the shower curtain), and then wipe the toilet seat dry.

- Fold the toilet paper into a point.
- Check to see that the liquid soap is topped up and that the pump is not gummy.
- Vacuum the bathroom floor with no attachment, doing all the baseboards.
- Take a new cloth and wet it in the kitchen sink and wipe down the bathroom floor on your hands and knees, spraying with the bottle marked "Rosemary."
- In the medicine cabinet, you will see peppermint oil. Dab some around the ring of the tub plug to discourage insects.
- Once the floor is dried, put the bathmat on the side of the tub, make sure it is straight, and double-check again for any hairs or fuzz that may fall into the tub. Adjust the shower curtain so that it hides the taps and is out far enough to dry, around one-third of the way across the tub, making sure the fabric is on the outside of the tub and the plastic liner is on the inside.
- Fold a hand towel into thirds and place it on the towel ring.

It took her a long time to clean, but she had from 11 a.m. to 3 p.m. to do it, and after a few weeks, Vera stopped double-checking her work. The repetitiveness and completeness of it was soothing, admittedly.

"Gives a person a sense of purpose and accomplishment," Vera would say while spanking the pillows into a fluff. "Can't fix the world, but we can make the bed."

Vera cooked healthy simple meals and harvested things from her large garden. The woman never seemed to stop creating beauty, night and day. Her husband, Lloyd, was a retired minister, and he was often in his workshop. He made backgammon and crib boards and beautiful salad bowls that he'd piece together intricately out of different wood. He had done the whole interior of the house, all the wood floors, gorgeous. He never said much but once in a while Vera would make him laugh. And when he did, he didn't make a sound. He just scrunched up his eyes and nodded with a silent, open mouth.

After cleaning, Graziana would go for long walks way out into the farmer's fields before dinner, down the hardscrabble roads. Her knee would swell up, but she'd ice it when she returned home, and it would be fine the next day. She'd help prepare dinner and clean up afterwards, and she'd learn little tricks of the trade:

- Put the pastry bowl and measuring cups in the fridge for half an hour.
- Never throw out the potato water.
- Add a piece of beet to your steamed carrots to help them keep their colour.

Norma was back from Mexico, and she was having phone sessions with her once a week. Norma agreed it seemed time to contend with family. So Herman drove to the ranch. Red Deer to east of Medicine Hat. He did not have the nu– … the girl … the daughter, *Hazel*, with him. That would have been too much. He drove up in his blue truck, wearing his blue plaid shirt, his wavy hair perfect. How can his pants not even crease when he's been driving for four hours? He met Vera, very cordial. He shook hands with Lloyd who came out of the shop to say hi. Vera made them tea and scones and then absconded to the sewing room.

His tone was even, but she could tell this was an effort.

"I'm sorry you seem angry, Herman. But I'm not mentally well."

"I'm not angry. Never mind me. I'm fine. What I don't

understand is why you can't even speak to your own child. She's only seven years old."

"I –"

"I don't care what kind of nervous breakdown you've had. Folks these days have a name for everything. I'll tell you what it is: selfish and irresponsible and downright cruel to a child – a CHILD! What kind of lasting damage do you think that kind of neglect does to a little girl?"

"I –"

"And now I find out you're not even at the Peter Lougheed but out here on holiday at a lovely B & B?"

Crum ... ple.

Crum ...

ple.

Stay awake, stay awake.

She tapped her hands on her thighs in a rhythm, tap tap tap tap.

Herman snapped. "What in tarnation are you doing? I'm talking to you!"

"I –"

"You what? You're just ... you're just being dramatic to make yourself look crazy."

Tap tap tap tap.

He looked away, annoyed, shook his head, crossed his arms.

Tap tap tap tap.

"I tap. I tap. I tap to stay in my body. It helps me ... not black out ..."

"Okay, okay."

"It's a technique."

Tap tap tap tap.

He watched her out of the corner of his eye, resigned. "Listen, we don't have to talk about all that just yet. I'm not here to have you flipping out on me again." Herman looked around nervously. "Where's the lady who owns the place?"

Tap tap tap tap.

He watched her tap. He looked away. "Nice house they have here."

Tap tap tap tap.

"Yes."

"And people drive all the way out here to sleep?"

"Yes. She's ... the rooms are very nice. She's a very good cook, Vera. Makes good jam."

Tap tap.

"Ah. Well, she's got a big garden. And chickens, I see. Fresh eggs. Me, I prefer hotels. I don't like sleeping in other people's houses and having to make conversation in the morning. These muffins are good though I have to admit. What's this stuff called? It isn't whip cream."

"Devonshire. Devonshire cream."

"Fancy."

Tap.

Herman spread cream onto his scone liberally and then topped it with a blob of strawberry jam.

Tap.

"She make this too?"

"Yes. I made this batch with her, actually."

"So, you're learning things. Good."

"Yes. I ... I started a quilt for Hazel."

Herman munched his scone and then sipped some tea. She'd never seen him drink tea before, especially not out of a teacup. He lifted his pinky. She found this amusing. Herman looked up and sighed.

"Graziana, I don't want to set you off or anything but ... maybe you can just tell me ... whatever you can."

She took a deep breath.

"Ivan Vidal is the ... is ... Hazel's dad."

Herman set all his crockery down. After a moment he said quietly, "Well, the way you reacted to the picture, it got me wondering. Now that I look at her, Hazel does resemble the guy. But I never put it together before because, well, how on earth did you end up with the creep all those years later? Why? What possessed you?"

She straightened out her spoon and fork into a perfect line by her plate.

Herman sat back. "You don't have to tell me."

She smoothed out her napkin. She put her hands back on her thighs. "Well, Herman, he showed up. At the bike store. It's a long story, but ... the short of it is ... he ... Hazel is the product of rape."

Herman's eyes got wider than they had probably ever been since birth. He pushed back from his chair and stood up. He went down the stairs and headed out the door and down the hardscrabble road heading to the farmer's fields that she had walked down for the past few weeks. She sat in the silence of their aborted tea and tapped gently, briefly. It felt good to tell him the truth. She did not expect that. It felt good, like a well-made bed.

Scone crumbs had managed to fall down her shirt, and they lodged themselves in her tight line of cleavage and prickled her skin. Making sure she was not in view of anyone, she dug between her massive breasts and wiped the sweat and crumbs out between them with her napkin and tossed it into the wash basket. She then stood up from the kitchen table and wandered over to the window to watch Herman. He had made it all the way to the end of the lane where you either turn left to the highway or right to the Crabsons'. He hung his head and stood there for a while. She watched him. He stared out at the horizon. He looked at the ground. He was talking out loud. Then he stopped. He stared out to the horizon again. He put his hands on his hips, like a winded runner. Then he stood very, very still for about ten minutes. The moment he turned around she vacated the window and set to boiling more water and cleaning the dishes. Up the stairs he came and sat down in his chair. He looked as though he was about to say something very official or maybe cough, but he remained mute, his eyes reddened.

At the loss of knowing what to do, she simply said, "Sorry."

He shook his head and stretched out his hands towards her across the table in a gesture of group prayer. She cautiously extended her hands and he enveloped them in his large paws, his griddle-pan thumbs crossed protectively over the top. It seemed so strange to be this close with someone she had lived with nearly all her life. She wept while he stayed stoic, and they kept holding hands, quietly, beyond the point of being embarrassed, a teacup shoved slightly to the left at an angle that might suggest it would topple but never did.

"Maybe don't come home yet?" offered Herman. "You've landed a good job here. You seem to be getting better."

"I am."

"And I just got Hazel onto a schedule. I mean, it's not my place to tell you what to do with your child ..."

"No, makes sense. I want to come back capable."

"I can understand that."

So they agreed. She continued to live with Vera and Lloyd from May until September. She was able to decrease her lorazepam down to zero and stayed on the Lexapro at twenty milligrams per day. She had lost fifteen pounds in the psych ward and with Vera, another thirty, simply because she was moving. She was down now to two hundred and fifty-five pounds. It was easier to get up from a chair.

One Saturday morning, after a particularly strong cup of tea and a nourishing session with Norma, she decided to call home for the first time since she was taken away, six months earlier. To her surprise, Hazelnut answered, bright and cheerful.

"Hello? Hazel, it's ... Mom."

The little voice sighed. Paused. Then Hazel rattled off impatiently, "Wrong number, dumb dumb." She hung up.

She had started a quilt. Yellow. The nut ... *Hazel* liked yellow last she knew. Vera raised her brows. Not often is there a request for yellow. How delightful. The contrast colour would be purple, but she chose orange and light green with cream. Vera suggested a pattern called Girl's Favourite and hooted, remembering a scrap of fabric she had in storage that featured squirrels foraging for nuts.

She tried calling home again, a week later. This time Herman answered. He put Hazel on after some muffled warning she couldn't hear. The girl's voice was small and tight.

"Hello."

"Hi Hazel. It's –"

"I know."

Long silence.

"I'm sorry I've been –"

"You're not sorry! You're riding your bike!"

"I'm what?"

Long pause.

"You've been gone half my life! When are you coming home?"

"I'm sure it feels that way, honey. We've never been apart this long, have we? I've had a very big shock ... to my head. I found out the man who hurt my knee and who was not very nice to me, like, really not nice ... well, he died. And ... how do I explain this? Um. That was the shock to my head. But also, you know, Nonna died before you were born ... I've been a ... I've been a tired mom. I'm sorry."

She didn't want to weep on the phone. She had no idea what was happening on the other end of the line. Hazel was uncharacteristically silent. Vera peered around the corner, concerned. She waved her off, reassuringly. She sniffed.

"Are you still there?"

"Yeah."

"Anyway, I've been trying to deal with that. And I did get a little bit better when you first went to school, and I started doing therapy."

"When you did breathing on the yoga mat like HAW HAW HAW."

"Yeah."

"And then you stopped."

"Yeah. Anyway, this big shock to my brain means I had to go to a place where people could take care of me and I could get better."

"And ride your bike. When are you coming home?"

"I ... It won't be for a while yet. But I have gotten a lot better by resting and talking to the doctor and –"

"What does 'a while' mean?"

"I don't know."

"Then don't bother! We hate you!"

Hazel slammed down the phone.

Uhhhhhhhhhhhhhhhhhhhhhhhhhhhhhhhhhhhhhhhhhhhhhhhhhhhhhhhhhhhhhhhhhhhhh ...

The dial tone honked in her ear, one long vowel of "F– you."

She eventually hoisted herself out of the chair, placed the phone back in its cradle, and shuffled downstairs to the quilt room. Half a Girl's Favourite was strung out with pins and needles. She decided to press out a border slowly and carefully. It was a belligerently positive bright yellow. It would define the shape.

My stepdaughter finally made contact a few months back, and I'm relieved to know she's safe and relatively sound. She's been diagnosed with PTSD due to an assault I was not formerly aware of and is currently being treated for depression. Her obesity, lethargy, and disconnection from her daughter are tied into her trauma. This also explains why she seemed unable to grieve the death of her mother in a way that I considered healthy. She rarely talks about Nunzia; she does not have family photos in her house; she wanted none of her mother's belongings, except for some of the jewellery and the kitchen table.

For the past eight months, Graziana has become far more stable, thanks to her medication, exercise, diet, cognitive behavioural therapy, EMDR (tapping), and neutral environment. She's living across the province and video-chats with Hazel once a week. The death of Ivan Vidal triggered an anxiety response. I don't understand much of it in psychological terms, but I now understand a bit better as to why she's had a hard time raising Hazel.

Note: Research transference.

Graziana could make more effort communicating with Hazel, though, and she hasn't once hopped on a bus to come see her. Mind you, Hazel is giving her a run for her money, but I can't help but feel that Graziana should try harder. It seems cowardly and mean-spirited. When Graziana first asked what Hazel knew, I admitted that I told Hazel she was cycling. I explained the misunderstanding of *psych ward / cycle ward*. I confessed I removed her bike to a repair shop and then stored it at my apartment to confirm the ruse.

Graziana laughed at this. "*Cycle ward*, not a bad idea. I always feel good on my bike."

We agreed it was best to let Hazel think she was on a long

bike trip. It seemed less hurtful and confusing than her mom choosing to live in a different house.

Hazel is sleeping on a regular schedule, and her mood seems to be more even. She's doing well with her Invisalign and consistently brushes her teeth. She will now eat asparagus and broccoli if they are covered in "cheese," a sauce made from brewer's yeast.

Against my better judgment, I decided to homeschool. She's about halfway through the grade-two level now, though most kids her age are halfway through grade three. I can't believe I've been teaching since spring and I haven't completely lost my marbles. Part of why she's caught up a leg is because I kept her studies going throughout July and August, much to her chagrin. During those two months, she liked peeking at our homeschooling portfolio. I think she was proud of her accomplishments laid out in a way that she could clearly see. When we weren't studying, we were at the lake. We also spent most of our weekends at Ed and Connie's. Hazel loves the farm animals and is getting to know her cousins. They learned quickly that she does not have the attention span for board games but could play tag in the hay bales for hours.

I am pleased that Hazel makes the effort to sound out hard words and is beginning to read simple books. She was doing well with addition and subtraction, but she is very averse to multiplication and division. I don't know why. God, give me patience. She can name all the provinces now and their capitals and our country, and she's starting to learn the continents. I have to constantly review these though, or she quickly forgets. It has helped to link images to places – Alberta has oil and the Oilers hockey team, and Edmonton is close to where Uncle Eddie lives, my older brother. I bought her a globe that also functions as a night light.

She has been having playdates once a week with Geoffrey, a boy on the spectrum. His mother had called with the suggestion. He's non-verbal, but he plays piano and Hazel dances to the music and talks his ear off, so it seems oddly symbiotic.

Geoffrey's parents seem grateful, anyway, and it gives me a few hours of alone time, which I greatly need.

I also have her going to some homeschooling events, and when it's a play or a movie or anything with a story, it seems to hold her attention. I know she will be relatively well behaved during the performance itself, and I don't necessarily have to volunteer to go along. She did very well watching *La Bohème*, and I'm glad I did not have to sit through that. The field trip to the Alberta Legislature buildings in Edmonton, however, was a complete disaster. We had to leave halfway through; she was bored out of her skull and very disruptive.

Hazel has been excelling at swimming; her instructor says she's "physically intelligent." Hazel liked the sound of that. She's now at Red Cross Level 3. She is still not great at paying attention to instruction, but she can certainly focus when it's time to do laps and she's timed or it's a race. This is what frustrates me: she pays attention when she wants to.

There has been little to no progress with Hazel's manners. I have resorted to bribery. I set out three dollars at the beginning of the meal and every time she chews with her mouth open or talks with her mouth full, I subtract a dollar. She usually loses all her dollars within the first five minutes. So then I broke down the dollars into quarters. She loses all her quarters too. I don't remember Nunzia having to do this with Graziana. My main concern is that I have extremely limited parenting skills with little time to research. I am halfway through a recommended book called *Smart But Scattered* by Peg Dawson. It is useful.

Hazel has started wetting the bed again. I am not sure if it is on purpose or not because she seems to find great comfort in ending up in her mother's bed. My back isn't doing very well sleeping on the sofa. Because I have sublet my apartment, I am here full time. Hazel did not like that I moved my clothes into her mother's closet. She threw quite a tantrum.

Note: Ask Dr. Shannon if I should move into Hazel's room instead.

Hazel's nightmares about plummeting continue. She's often

falling away from her mother, or her mother is falling into an abyss or off a cliff and carried down into deep water. It doesn't take a genius to know what this is about. Hazel has gone from being angry and silent about her mom to crying at night and wondering why her mom won't just come home. I don't have a satisfactory answer for her.

Note: Ask Dr. Shannon if therapy is doing Hazel any good or if she is just making cheap crafts and charging a lot of money for it.

Hazel has become more affectionate. She will crawl onto my lap while I read to her, and she often reaches up to hold my hand when we are walking to the park. I find this quite touching, as Graziana was not an affectionate child towards me. I have never experienced this sort of fatherly interaction. We fight a great deal, perhaps more than ever, but I've grown very fond of the dear little pup.

Grumpy isn't very nice. I would say he is a jer with a *k*. He's always telling me what to do. Nothing I ever do is good enough. I am always doing things wrong. He made me do school all summer long when every other kid on the planet of Canada was playing in the park and going camping!

I have to sit still, I have to stop talking so much, I have to wash my hands when I just washed them. And I don't know why we have to learn division when we can just use a calculator. It's so dumb! Sometimes division is with the little house that goes over the number and sometimes it is with the teeter-totter – make up your mind! At least with multiplication it's just with an X. Grumpy says I am lucky he is not teaching me the "new" way to do multiplication because it is even more confusing. And why do I have to write *science* instead of *siens*? You know what I mean? And I used to think swimming was fun but now Grumpy is like, "Come on, do Level 4! Swim faster! Keep your head down!" What I REALLY want to do is hip-hop dancing, but Grumpy says it's expensive and besides I wouldn't pay attention. He also says that hip-hop just teaches kids how to be a smart aleck. So then I asked if I could do jazz dancing and he thinks it isn't right to teach young kids to act like grown-up ladies (because they wiggle their bum a lot in jazz and push out their vagina like THIS. I know what that's called, that's called SEXY, but Grumpy doesn't even KNOW that word I bet!).

I miss TV. I know I'm too old for Treehouse, it's for babies, but I like it, it makes me laugh. *Toopy and Binoo*. Toopy's a crazy mouse! And I just wanted Annie's macaroni and cheese once, just once, and Grumpy yelled his head off, "Eat what I put in front of you! Annie's is crap!" NO IT ISN'T! MY MOM MADE IT AND MY MOM DOES NOT MAKE CRAP! GOD! I just wanted it once as a snack. I don't care if I'm allergic!

Grumpy says I shouldn't say *God*. I should say *gosh* because it hurts God's feelings. Whatever. I said, "You believe in God?"

And he said, "No. But some people do. So it hurts their feelings."

"Mom and me are spiritual, not religious!"

"Where did you hear that load of crap? You either follow the Lord or you go to hell. Sorry to break it to you, kid. There's nothing in between according to Christians but wishful thinking."

As if Grumpy knows God. And what is hell anyway except feeling bad, and I already have hell.

I think I should run away to Brazil. *B* is for *Brazil*, which is a country in the condiment-al ... um ... South America. Grumpy made me learn that. *C* is for *China* and they have my favouritest animal, the tiger. Back to Brazil. Brazil, if you don't know, is a country. It is very big and green with a flag that has a blue ball. They play soccer there and eat BBQ and they have the Amazon, which has monkeys and parrots and jaguars, animals I all love. It doesn't look that far away on the map. I bet if I just started walking straight down, it would take me three days. I wonder if Mom rode her bike to Brazil. She's been gone so long. She's probably in China.

When the beloved is first nudged out of the nest, he can't believe his luck when he spreads his wings, pure reflex. He flutters madly in the wind as he plummets and then ... begins ... to fly up! We never cease to love watching this moment for birds.

Not remembering himself fully, flooded with instinct, he does have a sense that he used to dream of flying, and now the dream is true. He also has a sense that he didn't expect such a blessing. We were hoping that he would remember what it is like to feel gratitude. But instead, he flies with the underlying foreboding feeling that something is chasing after him. Something he deserves.

What is it with our beloved and this idea of deserving?

All he really remembers, or thinks he might remember from before the egg, is wanting to be high. And high he goes! Oh, he is gorgeous! A dapper beige with hints of black and grey and white and red tips on his wings. He is small but agile and voracious. Rowanberries are his favourite: plump and red and juicy. He can't get enough of them.

When the forests start to freeze over in Scandinavia and berries are few, he flies with a flock of feathered friends to the north of England. There, the berries are still on the trees, but they have fermented. They taste different but still divine. And what ... what is this feeling? No pain at all! No fear of cat or hawk or judgy females finding fault with the way he's built a nest or the lack of red on his wings, being a juvenile ... no. He no longer cares about those trivial things. He just wants to eat another deeeeeelicious berry!

He realizes he is, quite frankly, pissed. "I'm completely loaded! How hilarious!"

Our beloved feeds until berry juice drips sloppily off his stubby little beak.

"Whoooooootwhoooooo!"

He steps off the rowan branch and spreads his wings and fliiiiiiiiiiiiiieeeeeeeesssss.

SMACK!

Right into a bedroom window, breaking his neck.

Now he's back with Us, his head at an uncomfortable angle.

"Ooh my head ..."

We let him know, gently, that he can straighten it, that there is no pain here.

"This is all some joke to you, isn't it?"

The things you choose are sometimes ridiculous. Would you like to rest?

"No. I think my whole problem ... my whole problem is I never got laid enough. Even as a bird, I died so young I didn't mate once. Give me that. Give me sex sex sex sex. I just want to fuck. Day and night. Just that. Can you at least do that for me?"

Day and night?

"Are you deaf?"

That is very extreme.

"DAY AND NIGHT!"

We sigh. *There is a placement.*

Our beloved gives us a strange sort of wobbly salute, and he says with a wink, "I'm up for it."

And in he goes: a mammalian, a marsupial of the Great Divide, Australia. A brown male antechinus to be exact, no larger than a mouse. He is birthed, and he suckles greedily on the teat of his mother in a forest just outside of Kioloa.

CHAPTER FOUR

PILGRIMAGE

— Graziana —

Graziana always liked her name. She was named after her mother's mother. That's how Italians do it. Mom took Grazie to Italy when she was three, too young to remember anything. Mom went back to the old country a couple of times on her own because Grazie was in school and Herman hated to fly. Nonna died when Grazie was thirteen from a different kind of cancer. She was a stern Catholic and a great cook. She had the swoopy chin and the strong legs.

Aside from a few family recipes and her distinctive name, Graziana was disconnected from her Italian heritage. She was never taught the language; she was not raised Catholic. Her biological father died before she was born. All of Italy slow-cooked down to her mother. It didn't matter if it was Roma tomatoes, Pinarello bikes, dried hot peppers strung in a window, or Giuseppe Verdi. Anything Italian made her ache with grief.

Lloyd had been asking Grazie to cook some real "Eye-talian" food since she arrived. Vera, preferring things plain in deference to her heartburn, didn't champion the idea. But they did have a bumper crop of tomatoes that fall and Grazie simmered up a simple marinara over penne.

"Do you ever think of going back to the motherland?" Lloyd asked, after savouring a mouthful.

"Not really. Why?"

Vera perked up. "Ooh, what a wonderful idea. Grazie, you could visit your mother's village, learn a few words of Italian.

What a beautiful way to mark her passing. And your ... new beginning."

Lloyd nodded in agreement. "A pilgrimage. It's a practice in all the major religions. The Muslims head east to Mecca. The Jewish folk flock to Jerusalem. Hindus bathe in the River Ganges in Varanasi. The Buddhists, Bodh Gaya (if you've heard of the Bodhi Tree). Christians will go to Bethlehem, but we have other pilgrimages too, like Santiago in Spain is a popular one. I think there's one to Rome as well. I mean, there's gotta be."

"Pastor's in the house!" winked Vera.

"I'm not religious," said Grazie.

Lloyd took another bite. "I don't think you have to be. Me being a pastor, I do believe you'd get the most out of it if you do it prayerfully in communion with your Maker. But I think pilgrimage is a part of instinctual human activity. When we want to make sense of ourselves and clearly see our path ahead, we often travel back to our beginning. Give or take. Or you can just head to Red Deer." Lloyd sopped up his last bite of noodle.

Grazie thought about the last few times she video-chatted with Hazel and saw her sweet, sad, petulant face. She wouldn't stay still enough for a decent conversation. The moment things got the least bit serious, Hazel would jump up with some new dance move or barrage the screen with raspberry farts. Sometimes she'd just leave the room. Once, only once, she pressed her scraggly little head against the camera and just breathed.

"Do you want me to come home, Hazel?"

"Not really."

Vera passed around the spinach salad and offered seconds.

"It's a victory for me to go to the grocery store," said Grazie. "I can't even think of going back to Red Deer yet. With Herman having completely rearranged my house by now and Hazel raging at me."

Vera dotted her lip with her napkin. "Not even for Christmas?"

"Herman is taking Hazel to Ed and Connie's."

Lloyd and Vera shared a look.

"I'm so …"

Vera nodded.

Lloyd reached over. "It's okay."

"I'm so afraid of relapsing."

"We have B & B guests through to January second, and we have the holiday craft fairs coming up, so it pleases me to have your help. The boys will be around for Christmas dinner, and we'll go to church, but you have the whole downstairs and can come and go as you need."

Her time with Vera and Lloyd was coming to an end, they all knew it. Vera was able to keep her employed during the Christmas season, but there just wasn't enough work to keep her on in the new year. Could she find another job?

Grazie tapped her legs under the table. They were still there, she still had legs. She could walk down the aisles of a grocery store now. She could scratch items off a list. She swirled her tongue around her teeth. She could think clearly enough to do her banking and fill Lloyd's tank with gas and talk with Hazel and Herman once a week. The scallions from the vinaigrette stung the sides of her tongue pleasantly. She was getting stronger. She could talk about her mother and make a family recipe and sleep soundly all the way through the night without waking. The pleasant clatter of crockery and cutlery allowed her to take a breath. A bright blue sky opened up in her mind, a sparkling sea, a winding road through cypress trees. She was starting to believe she could someday open her bike shop again. She might be able to parent Hazel and accept Herman's help. She would actually love to go to Italy. Ivan was getting smaller and smaller, and Grazie was growing straighter and taller, like a tree that'd had a strangling vine hacked off. This was the first time in nearly nine years she could even think about the future. The first time in nearly nine years she dared to dream.

Graziana did not come home for Christmas like I expected her to. Being a man and all that, I can't possibly relate to what she's going through with the ... with what Ivan did. But I also think she should get her head out of her arse, pull up her bootstraps, admit she has wallowed in her own self-pity for far too long, and get on with life. Heavens to Betsy, why am I raising her child, for land's sake? *Frustrated* would not be too strong a word.

I have to say I'm also relieved. I've worked hard to get this house in order and give Hazel some semblance of a healthy environment. I don't want Graziana waltzing back in here with her slop slop slop and bags of chips. So on that point, I agree with her. Come back ready to act like a gull-darned grown-up or don't come back at all.

I'm not really sure if we should still be lying to Hazel. She still thinks her mom is riding her bike in the "cycle ward." At first she thought this meant her mom was on a stationary bike watching TV in a kind of hospital room. But now she thinks her mom has cycled clear to China! And as unbelievable as this sounds, what's more unbelievable is a mother living four hours away from her child and not coming to visit. How do I explain that to a seven-year-old? No. It's less complicated and less hurtful for her to think her mother is on some epic faraway trip. When she presses her mother for details on FaceTime, Graziana is vague. "Oh, I saw some horses today" or "I don't really know where I am, I didn't pay attention to the signs" or "I don't like to talk about it, Hazel, it's just something I have to do. Someday you'll understand."

Graziana thinks she'll be ready to come home by the spring. Hmph. I'll believe it when I see it. She got a temporary receptionist job at Impact Health Physiotherapy in Medicine Hat for the new year. The lady went on maternity leave. So at least she's getting out some. Lloyd and Vera are awful nice still taking her in. I doubt they're charging her much for room and board. Graziana brought up this cockamamie idea about ending her "hiatus" with a pilgrimage through Italy. She said that her therapist, Norma (what's with all these doctors going by their first names?), thinks it would be great "closure." *Closure* is a word that can justify anything. There's a path called the Via Francigena she wants to cycle instead of walk (easier on her knee). She'd love to go from Milan to Rome, then head to Nunzia's village in Potenza to meet extended family. But it's all pie in the sky because she can't afford it, and even thinking of organizing such a trip is too stressful for her.

Now, as much as I think this girl does not deserve a European holiday for neglecting her responsibilities, this was the first time Graziana expressed any sort of grief related to her mother. I knew Nunzia would have loved the idea. So, call me a sentimental sucker, but out of respect for my late wife, I decided to pay for the whole damn thing.

I did some research and sure enough, the Via Francigena is an ancient pilgrimage, even older than the camino in Spain from Oviedo to Santiago. The first documented journey was by the Archbishop of Canterbury. He started in England, travelled through France and Switzerland, and then went down to Italy all the way to Rome in the thirteenth century. Merchants and pilgrims have used it ever since. The interest in the Via Francigena has been newly revived, and a trail for bicycles has been marked out. I found a Via Francigena app with itineraries through the viefrancigene.org website.

I guessed Graziana could cycle seventy-five kilometres or so a day, tops. And she wouldn't be in a rush. She could push the bike uphill. I mean, the kid cycled across Canada in her twenties. Sure, she has put on a lot of weight, but she's also been getting healthier this year. I think she could do this trip, especially with three months to train. I decided to book it for her for the month of March.

On the back roads and trails mapped out by the app, Milan

to Rome is about 1,100 kilometres, give or take. That's about eighteen days. I figured she could use a couple of days' rest, including two for travel. Then I added another day and a rental car for her to see her mother's hometown in Potenza. Twenty-three days in total, about the extent of what my pension could afford.

I set up her bike rental (which seemed cheaper and better than trying to fly her own bike over), I booked her flights, her rooms, and recommended places to eat. I downloaded each leg of the journey onto a GPS. I surprised her with this travel package by sending it all off in the mail for Christmas. Well, you think she'd be grateful? Nope. Didn't hear a word. Finally I called to make sure it didn't get lost or something. She was nervous on the phone, thanked me with some trepidation. I guess I overstepped. She probably wanted to plan it out herself. Then don't complain to me that you find planning too stressful! What's a guy to think? And she wanted to pay me back, but I told her to save her money. Then she blubbered on the phone wondering why I was being so nice to her (I was starting to wonder myself). I said the reason was plain and simple: "We're family."

Darryl and Brian don't agree. We meet for doughnuts and coffee on Saturdays. They always rib me for being a chump and letting Graziana take advantage of me. They don't know her. They don't know what Ivan did. They don't understand how needing help has been hard on her pride. Normally you can't even mow her lawn without her taking it personally.

After a few days, she called me back and thanked me properly. She said I did a great job of choosing things, and she felt she would be well enough to go in three months. She said something about it feeling like making a bed. Whatever that meant. I think it was positive. With this big bike ride, at least something of what we have told Hazel will be true. The details of the "cycle ward" can be unravelled later when Hazel is older and may better understand.

Though Graziana did not come home for Christmas, she did make Hazel a quilt. She did a very nice job. Vera says she's the best quilter she's ever taught. Grazie wrote a short note to go with the gift and mailed it. I rewrapped it and put it under Ed and Connie's tree. It was hard to explain to Hazel. She wouldn't open it at first, so we left it under the tree all day. The little pup must have snuck out in the middle of the night to open it, because when I knocked on her door the next morning to wake her up, she was wrapped up in her mother's gift, tight as a piggy in a blanket.

Hazel and I put up our own tree as well. We decorated it with Nunzia's ornaments I had in storage and the trinkets Hazel had with her mom. Since Nunzia's passing, I either didn't feel like putting up a tree just for myself (it seemed silly), or I was in my apartment where there wasn't much room. This was the first time in about nine years I saw some of these things. I have to say it threw me into quite a sadness that I had to kick to the curb for Hazel's sake. She was feeling it too, explaining to me about the time she and Graziana made a popcorn chain together, and showing me the popsicle-stick skis they'd painted and the stocking her mom had sewed with her name on it.

Ed and Connie's farm was a welcome distraction. I believe Hazel tires of me, and I have to admit I tire of her. She met her Grand Prairie cousins, who were two and three years younger. This combination seemed to work very well. The younger kids thought she was hilarious fun. I noticed when Connie told Hazel to close her mouth when she ate, Hazel kept her mouth politely closed for the rest of the meal.

I was glad to have the quilt under the tree for Hazel. She has not let go of it ever since. She drags it with her everywhere she goes, a long cape worthy of an empress.

— Hazel —

I got a quilt from my mom for Christmas. It was all wrapped up and under the tree at Uncle Eddie's and Auntie Connie's. I asked how did Mom get it there and where was she? Grumpy said she mailed it and he took off the brown paper and then rewrapped it in Christmas paper so it would be pretty. I wanted to see where the package was from, like if there was a stamp, you know, or an address, but Grumpy said he threw the paper in the fireplace already. He couldn't remember where she sent it from exactly, but it was from far away. How could he not remember where she was? Why won't she tell me when I call her? I asked Grumpy if we could fly to her as my Christmas present from him and he said no it was too expensive, even though APPARENTLY he doesn't know where she is! I asked if we could fly if it was my Christmas present and my birthday present (February 9) combined and he said it was still too expensive and he hated to fly. So then I asked him if I could make her a picture and if we could mail it and he said yes. So he *does* have her address! I think he's making it all up and she's living around the corner and just doesn't want to see me.

But for sure the quilt, which is an old-fashioned kind of blanket, is from my mom because she knows more than anyone that my favourite colour is yellow and my second favourite is orange and my third favourite colour is green. She wrote me a very small letter which I can read because her printing is very very neat:

> Dear Hazel,
> I made you a quilt to keep you warm this winter.
> This pattern is called "Girl's Favourite." I am getting
> better and better with all this cycling. I am excited to
> be a way stronger, happier, and far more fun parent.
> I hope you have a good Christmas with Grumpy
> Herman. And be nice to him and listen to what he

says, okay? Remember he's almost seventy, and it
isn't easy keeping up with kids.

xo
Mom

It isn't easy keeping up with moms, Mom. Wherever the hell you are. I hope you're cold on your bike. I hope you shiver.

There is comfort to be found living so close to the ground. The beloved also enjoys being quiet and inconspicuous for a change and being a night prowler. He is well into the forest and away from pavement, windows, and human beings as a young marsupial mouse. He munches on insects contentedly. He likes centipedes in particular, with their popcorn-crunchy shells. He avoids the airborne vectors. He catches and eats a frog. He is quite pleased with himself. He has never liked amphibians.

He is a handsome little fellow. He looks at his fur and feels the colour is familiar. He has a comfy spherical nest in a tree hollow hidden in a respectable neck of the woods. But something is missing ... what is it? He feels as though he was sent on a mission and then forgot the briefcase with the top-secret information. What is he here to do again? His intuition tells him it is important. When winter hits, suddenly so do his hormones, and the hormones of all the brown antechinus population. His body begins to vibrate:

Must mate must mate must mate must mate must mate
must mate must mate must mate must mate must mate
must mate must mate must mate must mate must mate
must mate must mate must mate must mate must mate
must mate must mate must mate must mate must mate
must mate must mate must mate must mate must mate
must mate must mate must mate must mate must mate
must mate must mate must mate must mate must mate
must mate must mate must mate must mate must mate
must mate must mate must mate must mate must mate
must mate must mate must mate must mate must mate
must mate must mate must mate must mate must mate
must mate must mate must mate must mate must mate
must mate must mate must mate must mate must mate

> must mate must mate must mate must mate must mate
> must mate must mate must mate must mate must mate ...

For two straight weeks, he copulates day and night, day and night:

> must mate must mate must mate must mate

In a violent sexual frenzy:

> must mate must mate must mate must mate

Biting the backs of necks:

> must mate must mate

Leaping from one female to another:

> must mate must mate

Even when he starts to ache, he does not stop.

> must mate must mate

Even when chunks of his fur start to fall off.

> must mate

Even when internal bleeding turns him gangrenous.

> must

He does not stop.

> must

He copulates himself to death, dropping cold, still, and senseless with exhaustion.

The beloved returns to Us, beaten.

"You are sick, twisted monsters to think up an animal like that."

You are part of the creative process. Your choice is part of why such lives are born. And you are not the first one to demand such an existence.

"Well, it's your fault for giving me the option."

Option is part of the design.

"You suck as a parent! You know that? I mean, if you really are the Almighty, Father or Mother of the Universe or whatever. Haven't you ever heard of a child needing healthy boundaries? You don't just keep giving the kid everything it wants! Kids don't know what's best for them! How about some goddamn guidance here? Like, 'Don't touch the stove, it's hot.' Like, 'Don't have sex day and night for weeks on end or your skin will fall off!'"

Ah. You forget the guidance We have offered and continue to offer. Are you asking for guidance now?

"When I request something that is going to hurt me, just say no."

Wouldn't obstructing your free will hurt you more?

"Yeah, you must be female. You always answer a question with a question. I don't know why I bother. You don't give a shit about me. You probably think this is funny. If you even clock me at all. Bitch."

You are our beloved. We see all. We grieve. Are you finally ready to rest?

"Yes, but not with You."

The beloved turns away from Us and thinks for a good, long time. A great heaviness starts to seep into his eyes, and he bends low with fatigue. He finally speaks. "I want to be completely alone. I do not want to be touched. I don't want to talk to you or anyone. I want very few options. Put me in the middle of a mountain. No, wait. Put me on Pluto. No, wait. I don't want to see stars. Put me at the bottom of the ocean."

The bottom of the ocean is very deep.

"Exactly! That's what I want."

And lonely.

"Perfect!"

And dark.

"Good!"

Are you … punishing yourself?

"Leave me alone! I know what I'm doing. I know what I want. Like You said, don't obstruct my free will! Put me at the very bottom of the ocean. Nothing can eat me there. Nothing can have sex with me there, and nothing can bash my head in. I'll just float."

We have a placement.

The beloved barely nods. Then down, down, down, down he goes into the Mariana Trench. A solemn, pale sea cucumber sifting through the sediment.

PART II

PART II

CHAPTER FIVE

SWALLOWED BY A WALRUS

— Graziana —

Hello?

I don't know …

This is me, Graziana.

I have never been a religious person, but I've always considered myself spiritual. I'm not entirely sure what that actually means, if I'm being honest, except that I believe there is something connecting us to the earth and to each other. And I have to believe, in fact, I do believe, there is Great Good in the world, alongside great evil. I used to wonder about predestination and karma and "You reap what you sow" and all that. But now I believe random, violent, senseless destruction happens, and random, outrageous beauty and life happen, and we don't deserve any of it. Perhaps the more connected we are to the Great Good in ourselves, the earth, and each other the better chance we have of … hmmm … navigating this life.

Norma suggested that I journal every day while I'm on the Via Francigena. I resist the idea. It seems wanky. Vera and Lloyd assumed I would pray, and they are praying for me, probably, as I speak. They call me a child of God and say I am the beloved. I understand this to mean I have Great Good inside of me. This is my way of "praying" and staying connected to it. Norma has a thing with the Catholics. She doesn't like them. And she glommed onto the fact that my mom was Catholic, even though I was never raised in the church. Norma says it doesn't matter. Culturally, I was raised with the concept of "original sin," and

I should throw off the shackles of that. She wants me to believe I am enough.

But let's face it, I'm not enough.

The walrus has led a small, rather useless, fearful, watered-down life. It ... she ... no, *me*. Me. I've done harm to myself and most certainly to my daughter, not because I did anything, but because I didn't do anything much. I find it depressing as hell to think that I am enough, that I must generate everything myself and that this is it. I need to believe there is some Great Good that I can connect to, something that is beyond me and yet also inside of me, growing like a seed. Hopefully I can grow Good quickly, like Vera's scarlet runner beans.

Hazel is an innocent child and she has Great Good in her. I have to believe she is not a random act of evil but rather a random act of beauty. She isn't a curse; she isn't Ivan's way of making sure he continues to overshadow me. How could he have even known I would get pregnant? He isn't a devil. He doesn't have the power to fertilize me with an evil spawn. It is hard to believe he is dead. Next to Mom and Herman, he has been the greatest influence on the wal– ... on me, on who I am, and who I have become. He was wrapped into my greatest achievements and my worst nightmares. How many nights did I writhe in guilt for not having the mental wherewithal to call the police? The strength to face him in court. Morally weighing the damage he could do to other women against letting my daughter and everyone else know she was a product of rape. Now he's dead as a doornail, and I'm relieved. But also ... strangely, I am mourning him.

Now that I think about it, he had to have known about Hazel. She's probably the very reason he stayed away. He wouldn't have to pay child support, or, who knows. He must have been stalking me from afar. He had to have known about her. Right?

That would make Hazel a kind of talisman.

January to March flew by quickly. I worked, I biked at the gym, I did chores for Vera, I ate, I journaled, I slept. I called Hazel for her birthday, but she refused to speak to me and has refused ever since. I should have hopped on a bus to see her. I was probably well enough. I should have made more of an effort. But I also didn't want to force myself on her. She didn't want to see me, she didn't want to talk to me, she doesn't want me home. Maybe she and I both know she is better off without me. Well, one more month, Hazel, then I'm coming home. And we'll sort out what's what.

CALGARY TO LONDON

I arrived at the Calgary airport four hours early. I wanted the extra time because I had never flown outside of Canada before. Even walking left instead of right towards the international gates instead of the domestic ones was exciting for me. The food court was more expansive and had a wine bar. The shop windows tempted my need for comfort with their cozy wool throws and warm leather satchels. "We know you have baggage; why not be stylish about it?" The clientele were better dressed in London, and the sea of white faces was now speckled with other shades of humanity. I had to be careful not to stare. Living in Red Deer is like living on the lily-white ass of the Anglosphere: you can't get any paler. Today was the first day I had ever seen women wearing niqabs. And yes, I had to look that up.

There was a direct flight headed to Tokyo. I towered over the crowd of passengers as I passed. The world was expanding before my eyes. This earth isn't just on TV. There actually is an Africa, an Asia, a Middle East. I seemed to have let my privileged life collapse me. I stopped moving and closed my eyes. Breathe, breathe. Until a kid pulling a princess suitcase clocked my heel.

"Sorry," I said, apologizing for existing.

When I got to the British Airways counter with my luggage, the sleek brunette at the scale took one look at me, examined her computer screen, and diplomatically smiled: "Oh, you're in seat 32E; that's sandwiched right in the middle of the plane. Let's see if we can find you something more comfortable. Luckily, the flight isn't full, so I can reassign you. In the future, consider purchasing a premium seat. They're more roomy."

As she tapped her fingers over her keyboard, I was suddenly aware of the long lineup behind me, the whirling noise of the conveyor belt, the annoying beep of the travel-assistance carts, the announcements, the noise, the gummy sweetness left in my mouth from bottled water, the stale smell of recycled air.

The British Airways brunette winked and handed the walrus a new boarding pass. The walrus accepted it gratefully and quietly as its head swam and its heart pounded and its wide flappy cheeks burned with shame. It found the first empty seat it could. What was it thinking? A walrus is too heavy to fly. It flounders and flops on the rocky shore, scraping its blubbery belly. It submerges into the murk. It sinks. It does not go to Italy.

It knows ... *She* ... She knows she needs to tap.

She pulled out the tablet and pretended to type. The tablet was on her knees, so she felt the tapping. She. Me. Grazie. Coming back up for air, inhaling, exhaling, typing *A* to *M* without even thinking:

Mamamamamamamamamamamamamamamamamamamama mamamamamamamamamamamamamama ...

One step at a time. Calgary to London. All I had to do was sit. I could do that. I was good at that. Sit and watch movies. I entered the plane and passengers looked up at me nervously. Indeed, I was too large to fit comfortably in one seat, never mind a centre seat, so the British Airways brunette had been wise to give me an aisle and an empty seat beside me. My gut spilled over the armrest, so I put it up and let my arm and thigh swallow half of the adjacent seat. I was at the very back of the plane, near the washroom; the smell of urine and cheap soap was in my nostrils for ten hours, but I was too nervous to care.

I did get to do some biking at Vera and Lloyd's in September and October, but it got too snowy after that. I lost another thirty-five pounds though, September through March, which brings me down to two hundred pounds, a total loss of a hundred pounds. My skin hangs around my belly and my arms like white bags of lumpy oatmeal, and it really flops when I exercise. I actually feel skin pain. But I have much more energy, and I'm starting to recognize my face again. I've been seeing a doctor at the drop-in clinic, and she's very pleased with my weight loss. She says my blood pressure is greatly improved; I am no longer considered borderline diabetic. I no longer get sores on my back or rashes between my fat rolls, my acid reflux hasn't been acting up as much and I'm losing weight at a healthy rate.

The other thing I did to prepare for my trip was try to learn a bit of Italian. I used Duolingo. I had remembered a few things from my mother, but she never did make a concentrated effort to teach me. Mostly I learned from her: *occhi, orecchie, bocca* ... *uno, due, tre* ... *vieni qui, basta, aspetta* ... and, inadvertently, *stronzo, Madonna*, and *vaffanculo*. It was comforting and also painful to learn more of the mother tongue without the mother and to taste new old words in my own mouth.

On the plane I watched *The Upside* and *The Favourite*, two films for better or for worse about the relationship between the afflicted and the helper. I couldn't help but think of my odd relationship with Herman. As Mom would say when I misbehaved, "Herman, he is not your father, remember, Grazie. You need to be careful and thanks be to God he is so good to you. Not every man would be so understanding about a bastard."

She didn't have an expansive English vocabulary, but the words she had she never minced.

LONDON TO MILAN

I had a four-hour layover in Heathrow. I went to the first restaurant out of the gate and ordered fish and chips and mushy peas. I shuffled along the halls for a while, not daring to go into any of the shops unless they were bookstores. Fat girls are allowed to read. I purchased a duty-free water and chocolate bar and my first postcard to Hazel. I thought good and hard about what to say to her in the small space afforded to correspondence, and when I finally did pull out my pen to write, it exploded in my hand. Pressure from the flight, I suppose. I washed the inky flood off in the washroom, purchased another postcard, a stamp, and a pen, and wrote.

Dear Hazel,

> I am at the airport in London, on my way to
> Milan, Italy, to cycle a famous path called the Via
> Francigena. The doctor recommended I do this as
> part of my cycle ward. I am working hard to be
> healthy so that I can be a good mom. I won't be away
> for much longer, four weeks. I hope you can forgive
> me. I love you.

Mom

I mailed the postcard before I had time to doubt it.

I sat under a flight schedule board and waited. It had been a while since I really looked at the people around me. I watched a young man holding a broken banana with both hands. His expression was so alarmingly dejected one would think someone took a bite out of a vital part of him. He was caught in some thought that had rendered him completely motionless this afternoon while he waited for his flight. His stillness, his guileless sadness, his half-eaten arrested fruit – was it his metaphor for love? Suddenly, my sad banana man shifted and popped the rest of it in his mouth and folded up the skin like a carefully guarded secret. It was important for me to see a man, peeled, to that degree.

An elderly lady with modest pearls was sitting pertly by Harrods, all dressed up for the other side. Across from me, an Asian girl was cuddled up to a leggy German Amazon with "fly off your face" eyebrows and a wild faux-fur jacket. Their Australian third-wheel friend in silver sparkle pants was clearly low status and kept trying to make jokes in order to belong. They were headed to Barcelona. The Australian was probably going to get ditched by the time they hit the tarmac, but she'd be okay. She had the face of a nurse. Everyone had their story lived out between their arrival and departure. Nothing like an airport to dissolve any feeling of being on a unique hero's quest.

Last night, while having nine o'clock tea with Lloyd, I said, "What if some gelato truck hits me into a ditch somewhere between Milano and Pavia? I feel as though I am going to die."

Lloyd, a man of few words, looked up calmly while testing another oatmeal cookie and said, "Oh, that's normal."

"Is it?"

"Sure. You're about to significantly change your life. It is a kind of death."

Lloyd had a way of saying the most profound things in the simplest of ways. It's probably what made him a good pastor.

My flight to Milan finally appeared on the departures board. I waddled down towards my gate with a stroke-victim smile: one half of my mouth was upturned in an excited grin and the other half was agape with anxiety. The flight was full, and I was jammed in beside a tiny, well-dressed man in an impeccable grey suit that matched his perfectly combed hair. He never looked up from his paper. Luckily, I had the aisle, so I sat on one butt cheek for two hours, trying to keep my arm and thigh from pressing up against his.

Herman had told me that upon landing at the Milan airport and going through customs, I was to spend the money on a cab, because I would be too tired to navigate public transport. He also knew I did not have the energy to enter a big unknown city, which is kind of a shame: to fly into Milan and not see Milan. But, as Norma says, maybe this is only my first trip to Italy.

I stood on the platform for the taxis and immediately was shuffled into a big yellow car. I stuttered out the name of the small town I was headed to: "Boff-Boff-Boffalora? Sopra Ticino?"

The cab driver waved his hand impatiently, not understanding me. "In English. I speak English."

"Okay, well, I'm going to a town called Boff-Boffa –"

"Boffalora sopra Ticino? You go there? You sure? Why?"

"Um, my B & B … Il Giardino Fiorito."

"Best you speak English. Gimme Google Map, the address."

I handed him my phone. He examined it, grunted with a nod, and we were off. The taxi drove half an hour or so into rolling hills and farmland; I was quite surprised. I never imagined Italy with fields like back home. But instead of barbed wire, there were crumbling rock walls; instead of a herd of two hundred cattle, I saw two cows. Instead of horses, I saw a donkey with long fuzzy ears.

Down we went into a valley, and there was this little town full of very old yellow stone buildings the colour of dusty lozenges and a few modern condos and homes around the outskirts. Herman had estimated the cab ride would be thirty-five euros, but the cab driver asked for ninety! Apparently it was the standard rate for any cab leaving the Milano airport. I saw the sticker on his window too late. I hadn't even begun, and I'd already blown Herman's budget. My mind raced. The credit card he gave me had a limited budget. This would eat into my miscellaneous fund. I was trying to work this all out in my head while sitting in the back of the cab, my heart thumping, my head getting sleepy, the driver gently inquiring, "Okay? Okay? You okay?"

He reached over and tapped my shoulder. He tapped me. Awake. He dropped it to seventy.

I hoisted myself out of the cab and stood with my two bike panniers in front of my B & B. Its cheery yellow walls were browning like a ripe pear in the shadows as the sun was going down. I didn't realize the cab was still behind me until I heard the driver say, "Hey, you, americana."

I turned around. He had been staring at my bum. "I'm Canadian."

"You are a big beautiful woman. You will love Italy, and Italy will love you." He smiled and nodded approvingly at my wide bottom and drove off while lighting a cigarette.

I was so surprised, I just laughed.

My B & B had a quaint geranium-potted garden. My hostess – I barely remember her – was a tiny woman in her sixties with shiny, black, short hair and a darting head. She reminded me of a raven. My room had light-blue closets and a bookshelf full of Italian cookbooks and some travel guides, and two very small, white, starchy twin nunnery beds and one of those big old-fashioned wizard-worthy keys for the room door. As soon as my hostess pecked at the towels and left, I sat down on one of the tiny beds and giggled. "I can't believe I'm here."

I pushed the twins together. I was too tired to eat or do anything else but have a shower, drink a glass of water, and go to bed. I figured I would sleep with my girth on the twin to the left, and the twin on the right would give me room to flop an arm or a leg. But in the middle of the night, I slipped between the beds and landed on the floor with a tremendous thud. It was so loud that I woke the raven up. She squawked an alarmed inquiry in Italian; I didn't answer. Did I shake the plaster loose around the chandelier under me? I laughed and crawled back under the sheets of the nunnery.

I couldn't sleep after that. "Wrong number, dumb dumb, wrong number, dumb dumb, wrong number, dumb dumb, we hate you."

She sat up in bed, covered in a sweat of shame.

The walrus didn't deserve to be here. The walrus had no business being in Italy. Nunzia would be deeply embarrassed by her daughter, stupid enough to allow a predator in her bed, idiotic enough to carry the pregnancy, only to utterly fail as a parent and deeply damage an innocent little human being while burdening a man who should be enjoying his retirement.

The walrus knew what to –

Tap tap tap.

The wal– ... She stared out the unfamiliar window into the

dimly lit street. Tap tap tap. She touched the starchy thickness of the white sheets, the slight bumps on the oranges left in a ceramic bowl. She ... I sighed heavily. Each sigh lifted the sun, finally, into the sky. "Wrong number, dumb dumb" settled into the crevices of the cobbled streets.

I was served breakfast in the garden on a patio table with a starched white cloth and matching embroidered napkin featuring little blue flowers on the corners. Breakfast in Italy means a cappuccino and a pastry. No eggs. No bacon. Certainly no kale smoothie. I was starving because I hadn't had supper the night before. My hostess must have seen the look on my face, and she gave me an additional piece of smooth fresh cheese called *asiago pressato*, a chunk of tough bread, and a beautiful, fresh orange.

Already exhausted from jet lag and lack of sleep, I packed my panniers, bleary-eyed, tied the laces on my new sports shoes, and took a deep breath. I walked down the narrow street to the next stop on Herman's itinerary: "In 450 metres you'll come to Doctorbike." How was that possible? Was I in the right place? Why would there be a bike rental store here? Everything was terracotta houses, budding wisteria, and skinny cats. But sure enough, I crossed a bridge, and there, on the other side, was an unexpected hub of spandex super-sporty cycling activity! Helmeted bikers buzzed like hornets to and from their nest: a CUBE bike shop hanging off the edge of a leafy canal. I walked in, and Giulia and Massimo, two athletic, beautiful people in their late thirties, greeted me. They had been anticipating my arrival and shouted out my name and strode over to give me hearty hugs and kisses on both cheeks. I hadn't had that much physical affection in a long time.

They had set out a bright-orange CUBE hybrid bike for me, and we fitted me for a helmet. Next, they gave me a bike lock and attached a water bottle and my panniers. They kept yelling out to the bikers coming and going from their shop that I was biking from Milano to Roma. The look of surprise on everyone's face! I suppose I would be surprised too if I saw a timid, obese woman setting out on an epic journey. Massimo handed me a tire repair kit, nervously, unsure how he would explain it to me given our mutual lack of language skills. My hand gestures helped let him know I knew my way around a bike. He kissed and hugged me again with familiarity and relief. I bought a bottled water from their pop machine, which I discovered far too late was *frizzante* and not *naturale*, and guided my bike towards the busy trail that ran alongside the canal. Massimo confirmed what Herman's itinerary said but in flippant broken English as he waved generally to the west: "Canale" (hand gesture: turn right), "Abbiategrasso – dopo – normale." I wondered what "normal" was according to Massimo. He put his arm around Giulia, and they waved at me as I planted my wide ass on the tiny bike seat and set out on my wobbly odyssey.

The canal was gorgeous, and I biked along it for a good fifteen kilometres. It was a beautiful day; the cycling was super easy, no hills. The trail was filled with families pushing strollers and young lovers holding hands and waving at butterflies. It felt safe, rural, and friendly. The only downside was the down under: the bike seat. It was not built for a woman's pelvic width. Ooh the undue pressure put on my sitz bones! I ended up standing and leaning forward for a lot of the ride, which caused my thighs to burn hot, hot, hot. I stopped just past Abbiategrasso at a pretty little B & B that Herman had chosen for me. It had purple petunias in the window boxes. It professed to be a Top Residence and an Agriturismo Spa, in the hamlet of Arioli. It was an old farmhouse and inside were sleek-looking beds with striped coverlets and a large dining room with a beautiful old wooden roof, empty except for me.

Their specialty was gorgonzola, and I had some of it and their homemade salsiccia with some crusty bread and pear and olives. Perhaps it was because I was hungry, but I had never tasted anything so delicious in my life. I walked briefly out into the fields, if nothing else, to get some circulation back into my posterior. A German shepherd on the back porch watched me warily. I stared out at the peach-coloured sky and watched the sun set over the rows of tilled reddish-brown earth.

I felt nauseous, maybe from the travel and the happy stress of being there. When I breathed a little deeper, shame flooded into my lungs.

I don't deserve to be here.

It isn't about deserving. It is about healing.

Yes, but I could be healing in Strathmore.

Often Goodness comes in an extravagant abundance. Much like suffering. Both can colour the entire sky, like this sunset.

Sometimes the Great Good talks to me. Part of my unravelling. At this point, why not? I allow it. I picture Hazel wrapped in the stars of her Girl's Favourite quilt. Perhaps I am being romantic. The quilt could be rejected and tightly bound in a plastic bag, stuffed into the top of the linen closet beside the Christmas placemats I never use.

I headed back and had a shower, rinsed out my socks (I only have two pairs), briefly checked in with Norma to tell her I had made it, and went to bed.

PAVIA

It was easy to get turned around in the small farming villages along the way to Pavia. Streets spiralled out from the churches and snarled into dead ends. Panic-inducing traffic circles were everywhere, and they starburst into narrow one-way lanes. Buildings slammed up beside each other with no green space. In Italy, streets aren't labelled on posts at intersections; the names are placed on the sides of buildings – sometimes. I am so used to the grid-like precision of Canadian city planning, I found it quite perplexing. But otherwise it was a sunny flat ride through grain fields and groves of chestnut trees. Once in a while, a male biker would fly by me in brightly coloured, full-body spandex, riding a super high-class Bianchi, Cincelli, or Pinarello. "Buongiorno!" And then they were already out of earshot. Otherwise, I had the Via Francigena to myself.

By the time I rattled into Pavia, kachunk-kachunk-kachunking over cobblestones, it was about 4:30 p.m. I steered my handlebars towards huge stone cathedrals, my elbows vibrating. The tiny winding streets were absolutely packed with locals and tourists strolling in the sun, heading for a glass of wine at a restaurant patio in the piazza. Along one of the cement walls, a poet had plastered their words onto fragile white paper that fluttered as I cycled by. Beside a recycling bin sat a green-glass wine bottle, a "damigiana." What a satisfying shape. It reminded me of my bottom. Why can't I find that a satisfying shape?

I locked my trusty steed against a sign that likely said No Parking and waddled tentatively over to an outdoor patio with the romantic idea of sipping a glass of Chianti in the square while writing my next postcard to Hazel. I pretended not to feel everyone staring at my straining bike shorts, trying to wedge myself between the metal chairs, "Scusi, scusi ..." I finally managed to squeeze behind an empty table and sit. Oh, glorious sitting! What a marvellous invention! My legs were dotted red, and my chest was blotchy with sweat. I took off my biking helmet and felt the breeze blow through my mottled, sweaty hair.

Dear Hazel,

I am in Pavia today. It is in northern Italy, in the province of Lombardia. I am riding a bike called a CUBE. Some of the buildings here date back to medieval times, like thirteen hundred years ago! My favourite thing so far is a long bridge across the Ticino River, the Ponte Vecchio. It has a tiny church in the middle of it! One of the things to eat here are frogs, but Mom is going to eat polenta instead, which is sort of like Cream of Wheat. Thinking of you!

Love,
Mom

My waitress looked like a show pony, with strong, horsey legs and a high ponytail. She sported some sort of rockabilly tattoo with skulls and roses, and she had severe straight black bangs. When she brought my Chianti, she also tossed me a plate of free appetizers with it, like a zookeeper might throw food at a gorilla. I may have devoured it much the same. Near the end of my glass, I remembered I wasn't supposed to have alcohol with my medication. I wandered woozily around the duomo. In front of the church was a statue of some muscled hunky god of the sun, riding a horse blessed with very shiny gold testicles. I must have been tipsy, because I stood underneath those bountiful balls and laughed for quite a while. I mailed my postcard, then out of respect for Herman, who had carefully researched my itinerary, I tracked down the Chiesa di San Pietro on my phone, as he suggested. It supposedly housed the remains of the partying philosopher Saint Augustine of Hippo, the patron saint of brewers. However, the only remains I found were the remains of a mass. I knew enough from my mother how to make the sign of the cross and genuflect towards the altar, but then I scooted out respectfully, not understanding a word.

I headed to my B & B early, starting to feel myself crash. Attenti al Lupo was its name. It was a sprawling old house with a big green garden and a whimsical sage-coloured shed that had a chandelier in it. My host, Marianna, stored my bike in there among spidery rakes and broken pottery.

The great thing about travelling slightly off-season is that I got the place to myself. The airy and feminine B & B had flowy white curtains and high ceilings. Marianna was a welcoming beauty in linen, her silver hair complemented by excellent silver earrings. I had a shower, washed my shirt and bike shorts, hung them in the poetic bathroom window, did my Italian lesson, and munched an apple I had picked up at a market on my way in. I believe I heard the Great Good SHOUT (It had to shout because I was not listening):

Graziana.

"Um … am I delusional from exhaustion? Because I did just cycle thirty kilometres."

Graziana.

I automatically got down on my knees. Why? Maybe Norma was right about Catholicism. Or maybe I saw too many churches today. Is this my head talking to me? Is this illness? Why a posture of servitude and humility? It's not really my jam. Well. There was a handy little carpet there at the foot of the bed, a perfect size for making oneself prostrate before the … whatever this Voice was.

You haven't really listened to your heart or your body since you fell off that exercise box that Ivan made you jump towards.

"Oh, we're going to go there, are we?"

You miss your baby.

"What?"

Sssswwwooooshhhh … The dam burst. Sorrow poured out of my mouth, out of my eyes, out of my ears, as though I were one of those marble-fountain sea monsters spurting water out of curious places in an endless stream from an unseen well.

I miss my baby.

I miss my baby.

I miss my baby.

Hazel Hazel Hazel. I did not name you after my mother, Nunzia. I only gave you the *z*.

It is hard to explain how I was comforted. It was a vision, like complex vein work, of decisions, of timing, of season, of impulse, of life, of the ebb and flow of things beyond my understanding. I saw my baby heading towards a collision between a punctured egg and a violent sperm, and her little light was placed inside and closed the hole and made it whole. And out from her burst an avenue with its own joyful trajectory. She was a gift.

She is still a gift.

I then felt a sense of urgency. I had wasted so much time being angry. I had been spiritually idle. I had –

You are beloved. As you are. We hope you embrace that Truth.

I slept soundly.

— *Herman* —

Since her birthday on February 9, Hazel has slipped into a despondent state that I've never seen her in before. She kept expecting her mother to show up on the day, even though I persisted, sternly, that she would not because she wasn't well and she had said as much. Graziana has been gone for well over a year now. I had begged her to visit Hazel before she left for Italy because Hazel wouldn't take her calls anymore. Graziana was concerned that it would set her back right before her big trip. She did, however, sew Hazel an apron and sent it in the mail.

When I gave Hazel the apron on her birthday, I lied and said her mother had mailed it directly to the post office with no return address and I didn't know anything more about it. Hazel knows I'm lying, which has created a distrust between us. She opened the package and read the note solemnly. She did not try on the apron.

The party was a failure. Hazel did not want friends over; she just wanted to stay at home without any distractions in case her mother came by. Despite her wishes, I invited Geoffrey and his family and three siblings she'd met through the homeschooling association: Mikayla, Sienna, and Eli. Hazel was listless and distracted. She was belligerent and bossy during the games, insisting I didn't have the rules right, and she didn't eat her cake, only the icing. She was downright rude to her friends, not saying thank you for the gifts and actually criticizing what they bought for her. It was embarrassing, frankly.

I really started to wonder why I had arranged for Graziana to do a cycling trip to Italy. How did I end up indulging her big self-pity party, and why did I allow myself to get suckered into paying for it? Maybe this was all very, very wrong. Who did I think I was, trying to parent Hazel? I thought I could do a better job. Well, obviously I am lousy at this and wrong. Nobody can replace a mother or a father.

Hazel pushes around her food and barely eats, to the point of concern. She refuses to swim; she just dog-paddles absent-mindedly towards the middle of the pool. I told her if she didn't pay attention to her lessons, I'd end them. I was forced to follow through due to her insolence. I offered to sign her up for piano or hip-hop or baseball, but she was not interested in any of it. She keeps saying she wants to watch TV and eat Annie's, so I have given in. She gets to do this on Sundays. I figure this must be a memory she has of her mom. She sits in front of the TV, wrapped up in her quilt, and barely eats the macaroni.

I stopped her sessions with Dr. Shannon because they seemed to be absolutely useless. Shrinks have done zip for either of the girls, as far as I can see. Hazel's homeschooling has been nothing but a big fight for months. She will engage with her instructors online and work eventually, and she will attend the group events, but it's been next to impossible to get her to accept any instruction from me.

If she wasn't such a handful, I'd ask Connie and Ed to take her in. But I can't do that to them. Their health isn't what it used to be, and they're very busy with grandchildren. I've never felt so dang useless in all my life. I don't know if there's a much worse feeling for a man.

— Hazel —

Eight is a big number. I remember when I was a little girl and I was happier because I didn't know any better. But now I understand things and it's hard to pretend you don't know and pretend to be happy when you're older and not as stupid and can see what's real. What's real is people don't like me.

Some kids came to my birthday but it's only because their parents made them. And you could tell they didn't know me very well and that they didn't pick out the gifts, their parents did, because if you knew me even the slightest bit you'd know that I do NOT like doing origami because I have problems with what is left and what is right and see things backwards sometimes because I am dyslexic. And I do not like pink, so why get me a craft where I have to make a stupid pink purse with diamonds on it? Do you ever see me wear pink or diamonds? No. Do you ever see me wear a purse? No. I hate things I have to always hold.

I like popsicles. I like decals you can put on your jeans. I like blue nail polish. I like paper I can draw or paint on. I like iTunes cards and fancy drinks at Starbucks that Grumpy never ever goes to. I like stuffies. I like phones and cameras (but I know those are expensive) and I would like a scooter or a bike and maybe a dog.

Grumpy says his present is a class. I can take a class like a sport or something. I think that's a dumb present and I don't want it. He also got me a subscription to a magazine about animals. Mostly it's writing and not many pictures. To be honest, it's boring.

Mom sent me an apron she made somewhere … who knows? And with it she included a recipe for Vera's chocolate chip cookies. Whoever Vera is. Never heard of her. Maybe that's her new daughter: Vera. Mom wrote that when she gets home we will make them together. But guess what, Mom? If you were actually around for my life you'd know that I am allergic to wheat and milk and there is soy in chocolate and sugar makes me hyper. If you're so "sick," Mom, why don't you come home? If you're so sick, Mom, why do you have the energy to do sewing with Vera? If you're so sick, Mom, why aren't you in a hospital? If you're on a bicycle to get healthy, then how can you sew? How dumb do you think I am?

And Grumpy is a liar. I know he's lying. I just don't know why. But deep down, I do know. Deep down I know that Mom doesn't want to be my mom anymore. I always knew Mom didn't like me, but I thought maybe because she was my mom that she would have to love me. But obviously that is not true. And Grumpy is only taking care of me because of "circumstances," he says, and besides, nobody else will.

Not a single teacher or student from the school calls me ever. It's been over a year. Not once did they say, "Hey, Hazel, are you learning anything at home? We missed you at recess. We'd like to know if you can spell now." Not Miss Catherine, not Mr. Shaw, not Mr. Sandu, not Julie, none of the students. Nobody even asked me why I bit Peter. Did they even know he told me I was retarded so I should kill myself? Doesn't that matter at ALL? Did he even get in trouble for saying "retarded"?

Maybe he's right. Maybe I should kill myself. The only person I thought maybe liked me was Dr. Shannon, but I don't get to see her anymore because Grumpy says she is not doing anything useful for the two hundred and twenty dollars an hour he was paying. Two hundred and twenty dollars! No wonder she was nice to me. And now that she's not getting her money, she doesn't give a shit. She hasn't called the house once. She hasn't knocked on my door or even my window or sent me a letter after all the private stuff we talked about. I'll probably never see her again. I hate Dr. Shannon now. I HATE HER.

When I think about all of this, I take my fingernail and I rub it on the inside of my leg where nobody sees until it bleeds. I scratch it, not because I'm itchy but … I don't know why. I just do it.

I saw Janine at the park and I told her I was being homeschooled and she laughed and said, "Well that makes sense!" And that's not very nice because the homeschooled kids at our school who sometimes come in for special events, they get picked on for being weird. So I know what she meant: that I'm a weirdo.

And now that I'm eight, I know it's true. I am a weirdo. I'm skinny and as tall as a twelve-year-old. I have a strange square head and my hair isn't blond and it isn't brown, it's just sort of like a mouse. It's "mousy," says Grumpy. And I'm a year behind school which Grumpy says is because I don't try hard enough. But what does he know? I TRY! But sometimes my eyes get tired and my head can't think. It's full of ... like ... if you stuffed it in a really grey cloud.

I feel inside of me that I am going to die. I'm not saying I want to die but I'm saying I might as well. When you realize nobody really likes you, it's really hard to want to do anything at all because, why? What's the point?

And where is my dad? Whenever I asked when I was young, Mom said, "You don't have a dad." On my family tree it's half question marks. I had to put my tree up on the wall at school with all the other trees and it was half question marks. Even when I told Mom I knew about sperm, she said, "That's my business, you don't have a dad, end of story."

End of story.

I am eight years old and already I have an end of story.

— *Beloved* —

Sea cucumbers, drifting in the dark with their rudimentary organization of cells, can't really grasp a sense of time. Sometimes the simpler creatures have a greater understanding of the profound. A sea cucumber does not experience time by length, but by depth. And this sea cucumber's time is thousands of years down, deep-diving into the endless darkness. It drifts along, cold, alone. If it had a mind, it lost it long ago. If it had a will, it had broken. If it had pride, it had oozed out and dissolved.

It is Us. We intervene. We think upon what the beloved has asked for. Indeed, sometimes a parent must say no. He is absent-mindedly drifting over the diatomaceous sludge, bumping into the odd, little grey brains on the bottom of the sea, the mono-thalamea. Without trespassing his will, We send a current to gently drift him up without him being aware even as he is lifted two thousand metres off the Mariana's floor, high enough to encounter a sea lily. Though the beloved did not have eyes to see the lily's bright-red beauty, he yearns to perceive colour. He feels the faintest desire to commune with it, to touch its undulating fronds. But instead, he tucks himself into himself and asks in a frightened whisper, "Is that ... you?"

Yes.

"I didn't know you could be here."

We are everywhere.

"Why ... would you want to be here?"

You are Our beloved.

"How can I be?"

He shakes his head and curls up tightly. We understand he is done talking.

Mind if We sit with you?

He nods, barely. So We sit. We sit for a long time. A transparent telescope octopus tiptoes by on all eights. Later, a trio of terrifying hatchetfish dart into view, making the Beloved gasp at their bulging eyes and gaping, skeletal maws.

They aren't here for you.

"They feel like ghosts, like lost souls!"

They are. For now.

The Beloved senses them flicker away, leaving him to float in the black emptiness. He floats for a long time. "Lost souls. How does one become ... found?"

By asking to be.

"There must be more to it than that. Isn't there ... what do they call it, a reckoning?"

Yes. One must be found out to be found.

"You know all about me. You know how hideous I've been."

Yes. But do you know?

"Of course I know! Doesn't it make you angry? The things I've done? The cruelty? The words I've said, the havoc I've inflicted, the selfish greedy mean ... mean! The taking. The grabbing. The ripping apart of things. The infecting!"

Yes. It makes Us angry.

"I ... have a child. I've done nothing for her. She doesn't even know me."

She doesn't.

"And good thing. She might have a chance if she doesn't know she comes from a bad seed. It's just not enough to feel sorry. I don't know how anyone can forgive me and maybe I don't even want them to. What happened to me? Anger. Anger crawled into the centre of me, made me rotten. And I invited it. The last time I felt clean ... I don't remember. Maybe rescuing worms from sidewalks on the way to school after a rain. I had to, they were so weak, laid out plain. I was a small child and dark. Just enough Mexican in me to get kicked around by the white kids and not enough Mexican for me to belong.

"Grazie, when I was her coach. The way she would look at me, so trusting. She was sixteen, seventeen, I wasn't much older. We were the same, you know. Single mom, didn't know our dads. Athletic, driven. Believed in the here and now, not some god. We liked Tom Waits and Cheezies. The Canadian kind: Hawkins. I did lie about my credentials at the gym, but I knew what I was doing from experience. Why I pushed Grazie to jump. Her trust in me felt so good. Like an addict with a drug. I ... I had to know if she would hurt herself for me. It wasn't logical, the impulse overtook me. I didn't dream it would damage her so badly.

"And despite that, despite all that, she gave me another chance when we met up years later and I blew it. I don't know how I blew it, I don't know what I did wrong. She sensed this thing inside of me, crawled up and creepy. One minute she was inviting me into her room, making love with me, the love of my life, and I was the happiest I had ever been lying next to her on the pillows, thinking: we'll finally belong now, we'll finally make a home. Maybe we'll open a gym together, have a couple of kids. Her mom, Nunzia, will call me son. Herman will approve. She'll make that big bowl of mussels and the spaghetti with the little clams, and we'll all sit around the table and tell stories and laugh. I'm dreaming this on her pillows, and she gets quiet and leaves the bed. She puts on an ugly sweater and thick pants. She looks at me with a kind of disgust, like I was a little worm laid out plain. To be stepped on. To dry up and die, stranded in a desert of cement."

The beloved sighed deeply.

"I planned it. I actually planned out when and how to take her. She was right to be wary of me. What kind of man rapes a woman?"

"She carried our child. She can't get rid of me! My almost-life dangling in front of me ... sweet little baby. Poor little fucker looks just like me. How can Grazie stand it? And yet some of me hopes she sees that little child and remembers there was also good in me. I couldn't watch anymore. I went back to live with Granny."

The beloved calls out into the watery deep. "I'm sorry, Grazie. I'm sorry."

The beloved looks Us straight in the eye for the first time. The beloved weeps. And people wonder where all the salt water of the sea comes from. He weeps and weeps and weeps until there is only room to laugh. Then, he finally lets go of everything. He floats up, up, up ...

And he is swallowed by a walrus. Whereupon he returns to Our Vastness.

Are you ready to rest?

"Yes."

Finally.

We fold the beloved into gentle petals in the centre of Our flower. The softest of all landings. The safest of all havens. The most wholesome of wholes.

Sleep. Deep.

The brightest of all angels once asked Us how we could love such a hideous child. But We do.

When the beloved wakens, We feed Our dear one with milk and honey. We wash the beloved with dew. We restore the marrow in the beloved's soul bones. We sing, gently, and cradle the beloved. We bless him with silence, and let the child stretch his spirit out, spread-eagle, on a bed of grace. Then We let the beloved run with no obstacles, across the sky at twilight, skipping through pink clouds and diving into the deep-blue mist of mountains and touching fingertips to star points weightless in the milk of Our universe. The beloved becomes aware of the space within the pattern that makes up its existence. The formula, the frond, the familiar collection of feels. The sound of circles, the circle of the sun, the moon, the earth, the North Star. The persistence of pulse. The dawn. The dawning. The beloved is never alone. The beloved has never been alone. Alone does not exist.

CHAPTER SIX

LIFE FLASHING BEFORE ME

— *Graziana* —

BELGIOIOSO, LOMBARDIA

Dear Great Good,

I woke up in the breezy whiteness of my room in Pavia, and I could barely move. Overnight, my thighs had hardened and tightened, and they throbbed with big, deep aches when I first tried to bend my legs. The bottom of my bum swelled up like I had two tennis balls stuffed in my underpants. It was alarming and hilarious when I noticed my oddly shaped new booty. I was up several times last night to drink water, stretch, massage my legs, and basically writhe in pain. This morning I didn't know what else to do but shove my gloves down my pants for more padding and head out to buy some ibuprofen.

I scoured the streets to find the big blue cross of a pharmacy and found one that opened after espresso and pastry time: the bakeries and coffee shops open first here in Italy. Who am I to insult the culture? I had a croissant and a cappuccino alongside a couple of men in construction pants and a cleaning woman with a kerchief and an extremely pale Swedish couple with enormous backpacks. I guessed they were Via Francigena pilgrims as well, going by foot. I nodded to them.

I've been trying to follow the navigation on the app. After a while, I gave up and stuck generally down and to the left, happy when I reconnected with the blue-and-white VF Cammino stickers stuck onto stop signs and the sides of medians and barriers. It didn't take long to cycle out of Pavia through residential streets and back roads. Then it was all pastoral. Green crops dotted with small stone villages, and once in a while, through the trees, I got a peek at the Po River. The sky was a cheerful blue with puffs of sheeplike clouds.

On a particularly deserted stretch of farmland, I stopped for water from my bottle and decided to roll my jacket into a neat package and shove it onto the B-clip pannier rack over my back tire. As I continued to cycle, the hood popped out and got caught in my gears, grinding it all to one shredded Lululemon stop. The jacket was firmly jammed in the spiky cogs, running all the way through to the back gear shifter. I turned the bike sideways to release the back wheel, but my jacket was jammed too snug to remove with my bare hands. I had a tire replacement kit but no tools. How foolish of me. I stood in the middle of a field on a dirt road with no buildings in sight, wondering what on earth I was going to do.

After about ten minutes, over the hills roared a small, dusty, green truck. It screeched to a halt when it saw me and my fallen bike. A young farmer leaped out of the driver's seat. He had brambled, curly blond hair and wild eyes: a Raphael cherub on speed. He also had a huge bandage on the back of his head, like, stuck there, on top of his thick hair. There was no shaved area to indicate a head surgery, just a big ole band-aid.

"Hai bisogno di aiuto? Cosa è successo alla tua bici?"

I stammered, "Sono spiacente, parlo italiano un po, io stupido! La mia giacca ..."

But my cherubic, head-injured farmer had no time for my apology. He was too busy spewing a fast stream of Italian: incredulous, stumped, calculating what to do.

I offered, "Tagli? Giacca? No problemo." What I was trying to say was: "If you had a knife you could cut my jacket, I don't mind." (Did I want to ask him if he had a knife?)

He headed back into his truck, muttering about getting something from home. He started talking out loud in his vacant vehicle. Was he on the phone, or was he talking to one of his personalities? Was he plotting to kidnap me? He could easily overpower me. What if he did have a knife or a gun? This was why women should never travel alone. He could throw her in the back of the truck, gag her, tie her up, put a burlap tarp over her body, and nobody would see or hear the walrus – not that anyone was around. He could drive the walrus to his farm and throw it into a shed with the pigs and cut off a flipper while –

Tap tap tap. Walrus. Predators smell fear.

Tap tap tap. She must not let her mind run away with itself. This was a kind young man who had offered to help. A kind young man with a brain injury. Tap tap tap. I pulled at the jacket gently while rotating the gears. The farmer returned and by this time, I had loosened the fabric enough to remove the back wheel without damaging the bike. The hood, however, was still jammed in the cogs. He pulled out a screwdriver and was able to stab through the jacket enough times to jimmy it free and save the day.

"Grazie, grazie! Tu ... um ... Dai tempo e intelligenza ... per ... mio ... molto gentile, grazie."

I hoped my smattering of words said to him that I was grateful; he'd been very kind.

He gave me two thumbs up and said, with an Italian British accent, "Bond. James Bond."

I watched his truck disappear over the hills. There are good men, safe men, kind men. I tapped my chest until I could breathe properly again. I righted my bike, mounted it, and pushed the pedals into motion.

Along the dusty road, past burgeoning crops, I waited for spiritual engagement.

Just be. How about that? Accept the gift of being.

Admittedly, I've been in a resentful panic today trying to keep up with Herman's rigid itinerary. I wanted to do it justice because he obviously paid so much money and had gone to such great effort to arrange it for me. I cycled back a loop because I missed the turnoff for the Belgioioso castle. "Must see the castle," says Herman. Why? Is that rich family's history more important than the history of the people who tilled the earth in these fields by the Po River? Is this architecture more important than the barn I passed with the gorgeous and oddly ornate loft windows? Is it possible Herman wouldn't be bothered if I saw the castle or not? Is it possible he's just trying to help and not trying to boss me around? Because, to be honest, I'm far more interested in observing the little bird at my feet pecking at crumbs than some dead guy's monument to his own vanity.

When I got to Belgioioso, I sat at a caffè right beside the big brick wall of the castle and belligerently ordered an espresso. I sipped it for an hour, until I saw a security guard close up the castle gates to the tourists. This was the main attraction in the city, and I missed it with glee.

"Take that, Herman Bossypants. Ha! I don't have to see anything I don't want to."

I sipped a second espresso very, very slowly. Nobody in Italy thinks this kind of pace is weird. What's weird is ordering a coffee to go. People in Italy sit for a cappuccino or latte or stand by the counter for an espresso, and they enjoy the beverage they paid so much for, a beverage carefully prepared for them. Really, when I think about it, coffee culture in North America is so stupid. We mash plastic lids over a barista's beautiful pattern created over a crema with microfoam. We ask for our coffee hot and then carry it around until it's lukewarm. And how can one enjoy a coffee fully while driving in the car or talking on the phone? It's like having sex while watching the hockey game. Nobody's really paying attention to who scored. One should treat a good cup of coffee like a good friend: look it in the eye, pay attention, take time with it. I vowed never to take coffee to go again.

And then I harrumphed. This, coming from me? I can't say I have any real friends anymore. Not that I see regularly. I keep up some Instagram correspondence with former chums, but nobody lives in Red Deer, nobody comes to visit, nobody's been invited, nobody has seen me as the walrus, and I certainly don't post selfies. The problem with slowing down is I start to catch up with myself. I start to think of the only person who might truly miss me, my daughter, and how I've done her such ... violence. Really. Neglect is violent.

Just be.

A handsome couple walked by me, openly and loudly arguing. This is also normal in Italy. So is the dog barking in a Juliet balcony flanked with wisteria, so are the old men in sweater vests sitting beside each other on the park bench. They've probably been doing this for sixty years, and amazingly, they still have something to laugh about. Just "being" is part of what I am beginning to love about Italy. It is perhaps why the Italians, like their slow cooking, live a long life with more *gusto*, which means "flavour." I have cooked my life on high and have simply avoided scraping too close to the bottom where the burnt parts are.

The young couple returned from around the corner. She pulled at her cheetah-print bomber. He ran a ruddy hand through his dark hair. She laughed, they kissed. They started arguing again. She pushed his chest with her hand – push, push, push – until he was back across the sidewalk, then she kissed him again and flounced off. He lit a smoke, then called out to her. She didn't answer; she just wiggled her bum. He shook his head, took a drag from his smoke, and slid a lighter back into his fine leather satchel that he was man enough to wear.

I cycled past the front of the castle on my way to find my B & B. It was dilapidated and surrounded by a high fortress. Doves were roosting in the corners of its former glory. I stopped in Monteleone for groceries, water, and a tube of toothpaste for my *spazzolino*. Isn't that a fantastic word for "toothbrush"? This meant cycling with a shopping bag off one handlebar because my panniers were full, but I wasn't that far away from my destination, according to the map: a picturesque amble through the famous wine region of San Colombano al Lambro.

A shrine to the Madonna del Latte loomed at the edge of the vineyard. There is so much about Catholicism I don't understand. Shouldn't that Madonna be gracing a dairy farm? No matter; I continued on. The vines were row upon row of brown, shrivelled bodies with their two bare, gnarled arms hung on trellises. They reminded me of hundreds of crucifixes. Some of them were just beginning to bud, like Jesus with green pompoms. Oh my, this vineyard split off into a hundred little paths that all became mountainous and very, very pebbly. The paths were so rough I had to get off and push my bike. The vineyard was impossible to navigate, having not been plotted by satellite, and I turned around several times while going up, up, up. Perhaps the name Monteleone should have cued me. Wait, did that mean they had mountain lions? Grazie, don't be silly, you're not in Canada anymore.

Ahead was a small, round elderly man with a bike as old as him resting on the side of the path. His pants were a light faded blue, and the waistline bowed around his belly, held up with straining suspenders. He was in the ditch picking some kind of plant beside baby wild asparagus.

I asked, "Trovi i funghi?"

He smiled and shook his head, showing me a long green herb I couldn't place. He said something about "verdura ottima." I nodded. He was very happy to have a chat with me and asked me where I was from. When I explained that I was biking from Milano to Roma, he made a joke about the pope blessing my bicycle. My bike was damn heavy, and it looked as though I would have to push it up the rest of the mountain with only fifteen minutes left before check-in. I bid the forager farewell.

"Piacere!"

"È stato un piacere!"

Up and up and up I went, my grocery bag banging against my handlebars, pedals catching against my calves. Grapevine after grapevine, where the hell was I? I finally reached the summit and a paved road and eventually my B & B. Peeking through the jamb of the huge metal locked gate, I could see it was a large, sprawling, well-kept brick acreage with a cheerful, chilly pool and potted pink geraniums. Was there a note? No. There was a bell; I rang it. No answer. I texted the number I had. Monica, the hostess, said her son, Alessandro, should be there, but alas, he was not. He forgot. He was on the road. It would take ten minutes.

Monica was wrong. Alessandro kept me waiting nearly forty minutes. Monica kept asking if I was still okay and still waiting. I wrote: "Aspetto. Con la bicicletta." I stretched my wobbly legs, all red and blotchy. I drank water until I had to pee. That was dumb. If I were a man, I would have urinated my signature on the fancy metal fence. But being a sitter, I'd just end up mooning the innocent neighbours and leaving an undignified puddle. I muttered to myself, "Oh Alessandro, you are going to get a piece of my mind when you decide to show up for la turista."

A mustard-coloured Fiat pulled in, full of gorgeous young people, and I gave them my best frown. I did not wave, I simply righted my cycle and headed in first through the gate. Out from the driver's seat glided a young, handsome, well-spoken, well-groomed Alessandro, smelling like sunshine and looking like a cologne ad. Damn him. I knew he'd look like this. He spoke excellent English.

"I apologize for keeping you waiting. My mother asked me this morning to let you in and I simply forgot."

I stammered and blushed. Suddenly I was a fourteen-year-old girl? "Oh, no worries."

He was already far ahead of me, efficient with the mundane task of showing me around, in order to return to the languid gorgeousness of his life.

The suite was decked out like an expensive room in an art hotel. Everything was swoopy: the kitchen cupboards were curved like a white wave, the fridge hidden within, the leather sofa shaped like a leaf, real art over the bed, superbly crisp high-thread-count sheets under a classy duvet, and in the bagno, a rainfall shower head. I had to admit, this was worth the wait. I cooked my cibo, washed my body and clothes in the shower and went to bed.

I woke up two hours later to a dog barking. I would be cycling through Orio Litta tomorrow. Herman told me nothing about it. When I looked it up on the internet, the most famous thing about the town was the rabid wolf that attacked sixteen people before it was killed. Fourteen of those people died. Was the dog outside barking at a wolf? I'd seen a badger sort of animal as roadkill, lots of geckos, and a road sign warning for deer, but wolves? Do they roam the vineyards looking for lost tourists? My last B & B had "Lupo" in its name. Is this a thing?

I turned on the side-table light, pulled out my phone, and googled "wolves in Italy." I should not have done that. Italy has wolves indeed, and the population is on the rise. The wolves live in the mountains, and where am I cycling?! In the mountains! Didn't Herman know this? Didn't he think of predators? I'm a succulent, easy target, all meaty and sweaty, huffing it up every vertical on foot. Wolfie teeth digging into me. Jumping on my back.

Crum ... ple.

Crum–

Tap.

Tap tap tap tap tap tap.

Glass of water, turn all the lights on, breathe. Breeeeeeathe.

Trust me.

Not this again!

Look at the facts. Read.

Okay.

With fear and trembling, I googled "Orio Litta" again. Yes indeed, the wolf attack was the first thing mentioned. It happened in '65. Well before I was born. Was there a more recent attack? I double-checked ...

1765. The wolf attack was in 1765.

I chuckled. Okay. Perhaps the rabid wolves had been dealt with in the last two hundred and fifty years. Here I was, at midnight now, unable to sleep. Even the neighbour's dog had gone back to bed. The Great Good was otherwise quiet tonight. Was it because I was obsessing about wolves instead of doing what I was supposed to, which was to just be? Does Good get pissed off? Is it even ... Good?

Here is how you're going to die: you are going to die an old woman, of bodily dysfunction.

Bodily dysfunction? That's weird to know – to know that. And yet I did know, deeply, in that moment, it was true. Probably a heart attack or stroke like my grandparents. Both options sounded much better than being torn apart by a wild animal. I guess that meant I would also not die by a desperate intruder, psychopath, knife attack, gun, strangulation, drowning, being pushed off a cliff and falling on my head and breaking my neck, internal bleeding caused by violent rape, suffocation, bludgeoning ... A woman thinks of these things.

Remember the Pilgrim's Prayer?

Right. I had seen an Italian Psalm 121 on the side of a church in San Leonardo, and apparently it was the Pilgrim's Prayer. I looked it up.

Psalm 121 (King James Version)

1   I will lift up mine eyes unto the hills,
      from whence cometh my help.
2   My help *cometh* from the LORD,
      which made heaven and earth.
3   He will not suffer thy foot to be moved:
      he that keepeth thee will not slumber.
4   Behold, he that keepeth Israel
      shall neither slumber nor sleep.
5   The LORD *is* thy keeper:
      the LORD *is* thy shade upon thy right hand.
6   The sun shall not smite thee by day,
      nor the moon by night.
7   The LORD shall preserve thee from all evil:
      he shall preserve thy soul.
8   The LORD shall preserve thy going out and thy
      coming in from this time forth, and even for
      evermore.

I loved "thy shade upon thy right hand." I read it again and looked down at my palm. I was under the side-table light at the time, and no matter where I turned my hand, there was some shade afforded in the shadow that is always there. It was found between my fingers, between my knuckles. I could turn a number of ways, but there was always shade somewhere on the landscape of my body, on the landscape of my soul.

Did I believe in that psalm? It promises that God will preserve my soul no matter what my comings and goings are, no matter the happenings of the moon and the sun. I put a lot of energy into unreasonable fears. I put a lot of planning into avoiding death, and yet I do not fear death. I fear violence.

You are holding on to the memory of those whom you've been intimate with, including Ivan. A piece of each of them is being carried inside of you, held captive.

I hold onto the good memories because they remind me that my sex life wasn't all bad. But why do I hold onto the bad memories and replay them in my mind? I hold on because if I forget, if I forgive, or if I let go ... he gets away with it. Someone has to keep vigil. Someone has to remember the wrongs he did.

I remember. I keep vigil. Leave justice to Me. I am more interested in your health than in his transgression. It is time to let all the stories go now and to heal.

I was asked to go through the list of every single person I'd been intimate with and to decide to let them go. To exhale them from my body.

Start at the beginning.

What is the beginning of when I first felt sexually hurt? I guess when I was seven. I ran naked down the hall from my bedroom to get my swimsuit hanging on the curtain rod to dry, and Herman caught me and raised his voice: "Get your clothes on, you're not a baby anymore. That is not what a proper young lady does." When we were playing capture the flag, I was on the shirtless team. My mom yelled at me to never take my shirt off outside. I was even younger then, maybe five. Yeah, they didn't handle that very well.

"Cover up, you look like a slut," was a common mantra from my mom. "Herman is not your dad, remember?" She told me I wasn't to wear things that could tempt him. This was despite the fact he was never home, and when he was, he was glued to Mom. He barely acknowledged my existence. It wasn't Herman who gave me the creeps, it was my mom. I wasn't allowed to wear low-rise jeans or crop tops or short shorts or miniskirts or close-fitting T-shirts or anything with a spaghetti strap. "If you give a boy at school the hard on, then he can't help it. Especially the teenagers, they go wild, Graziana. All the blood rush out of the head and into the other head, you know what I mean? If you get them hard, then it's your fault whatever comes next."

So I inhaled ... and exhaled ... my mother. That's not the piece of her I wanted to hold.

I inhaled and exhaled Herman. Because though I never once felt anything creepy from him, my relationship with him was constantly sexualized by my insecure mother.

Then, the leering, obsessive cousin and the innuendo-spewing high-school teacher, my first boyfriend in college, the one-night stand in Winnipeg, the tattoo artist with the dragons on his belly (do I have to let go of him?), my first great love, John, who loved me but not enough to marry me.

I inhaled and exhaled them all. I decided not to replay the stories over and over in my head anymore.

Then ... Ivan.

"I need help to do this; I can't on my own. I want to let him go but he's woven into the fabric of my –"

We are also woven into your fabric. You can pull out the Ivan thread and you will hold together.

And there he was. Not bad Ivan, but shiny-biceps, purple-shirted Ivan, my friend, welcoming me into the gym, sneaking Hawkins Cheezies.

I inhaled. I exhaled.

Then a flash. The teeth – the rip – the –

No need to keep replaying the story. You've done the healing work for years. Now, breathe in.

I inhaled.

And pull the thread out; release him.

I ...

I ...

I ...

Exhaled.

Once I decided to let him go, I felt something in me snake out. Then my feet, wide and sturdy, suddenly grew roots. My hard shell, the top of me, felt so light and ready to burst wide with green. Like an acorn. The Great Good invited me to sprout in a valley nourished by a river.

You are safe. You are new. You are free to love and be loved.

I lay there in my Italian movie-star bed, full of frond, full of spring, full of bloom.

Hazel is missing. She disappeared on April second, sometime between 9 p.m. and 8:30 a.m. I put her down to sleep, and when I knocked on her door to wake her up, she was gone. I searched the house and yard and the nearby parks by foot, and then I drove around the neighbourhood in my car. I went to the school and Dr. Shannon's and walked through Bower Place and the Parkland Mall (Hazel is fascinated by malls) and called all the friends I had numbers for.

She was nowhere to be found.

I searched until noon, when I contacted the authorities. The police were here immediately, and soon after, a social worker named Janice interviewed me. Janice looked around the house wanting to see which room was Hazel's and which room was mine. She asked to see Hazel's drawings or a diary. There was no diary (thank the Lord), but there were pictures. Lots of tigers and birds and big round-eyed girls. A tiger on a bicycle flying off a cliff. Pages and pages of angry scribbles. One of them said, "I hate you, Mom!" And another said, "F F F, HERMAN!" And then there was a long story about a piece of popcorn and a mouse that wanted to learn how to explode that made absolutely no sense and ended mid-sentence. Janice asked for photos of Hazel. She examined the bathroom and the kitchen, including the contents of our fridge. She then sat me down for an interview which she recorded. I asked for a copy of the transcript:

> JANICE: Herman, may I call you Herman?
> HERMAN: Yes.
> JANICE: So, let me make sure I have this right. Hazel's mom had been raising Hazel on her own as a single parent until she had a mental breakdown and ended up in the Peter Lougheed hospital's psychiatric unit. The breakdown occurred after she learned that Hazel's

biological father had been killed in a car accident? Hazel has never met her biological father?

HERMAN: No.

JANICE: Hazel did not hear that her biological father was dead?

HERMAN: Not to my knowledge. As far as I know, only Graziana and I know that Ivan Vidal was Hazel's biological father. Hazel has no information about her father at all.

JANICE: And did Ivan know he had a child?

HERMAN: I ... don't know. As far as I know, she never saw him again after ... after she conceived. I really don't think Hazel ran away because of her dad.

JANICE: So after Graziana – What a lovely name. Is that Spanish?

HERMAN: Italian.

JANICE: Does it mean "grace" or "thank you"?

HERMAN: I don't know.

JANICE: After Graziana went into the psych unit, you took over as guardian.

HERMAN: Yes.

JANICE: And you are Hazel's maternal grandfather.

HERMAN: Yes, I'm Graziana's stepfather.

JANICE: Stepfather. And your wife is ...?

HERMAN: Deceased.

JANICE: I'm sorry. How long ago was this?

HERMAN: Eight and a half years ago.

JANICE: So just before Hazel was born.

HERMAN: Yes. Nunzia, my wife, she didn't know Grazie was pregnant.

JANICE: She didn't? Graziana didn't tell her?

HERMAN: No.

JANICE: Why?

HERMAN: Well, I don't think she was happy about the pregnancy. It wasn't planned ... and her mother would have just been upset.

JANICE: Upset?

HERMAN: Worried. But Grazie hid it well because, well, she started putting on a lot of weight really quickly, so we just figured she was letting herself go. She was about five months along when Nunzia died.

JANICE: How did she die?

HERMAN: Ovarian cancer.

JANICE: I am so sorry. That must have been very hard for you.

HERMAN: She was the love of my life.

(pause)

HERMAN: And Hazel. Hazel is an exasperating child, but if anything ever happened to the little pup, I'd ... anyway. She's very dear to me. Would you like a glass of water?

JANICE: I'm good. Please take a moment if you like.

HERMAN: I'm okay.

JANICE: So your wife passed away, and about four months later, Hazel was born.

HERMAN: That is correct. Graziana closed her bike shop. She qwned a bike repair shop, but with the baby ... anyway, she couldn't afford to live in Calgary anymore, and she was out of work and at home with a newborn. Nunzia and I had a rental property here in Red Deer, and I suggested that Graziana move in.

JANICE: That was very generous of you.

HERMAN: Well. What are you going to do?

JANICE: And you lived where?

HERMAN: Rocky Mountain House. I was a paramedic superintendent until I retired five years ago. Then I decided to downsize. I sold the house and moved to a condo down the street. I wanted to be closer to the girls.

JANICE: Would you say you have a good relationship with Graziana?

HERMAN: (sigh)

JANICE: Stepfather, stepdaughter – it can be complicated. I understand.

HERMAN: It's distant. If I could do it again, I would have been more involved in Grazie's upbringing. I met her when she was still very little, and she never did know her biological father.

JANICE: Why?

HERMAN: Oh, he died in Italy, an early boyfriend. Nunzia wasn't even eighteen. Motorcycle accident. She left Italy for Canada because having a child out of wedlock didn't go over very well with those Italians; she's from a small town in the south. And when Nunzia met me, I was ten years older. She always made it clear that I wasn't the father, that she would do the parenting herself, that I wasn't to "bother myself" with the "burden" of raising Graziana. Really, I think she just didn't want me meddling. And I worked very long hours. But I think we missed out, you know? We could have been closer, Grazie and me. Now, that said, we've always been cordial. I've always let her know I was there for her.

JANICE: You've certainly proven that. I think you've been incredibly supportive.

HERMAN: Well. Clearly, Grazie was struggling. But there's only so much I can do, right? The two of them cooped up here all day ... she was getting more and more housebound. She worked briefly at Safeway, but for the most part she's been unemployed, on welfare, down on herself. Anything I tried to do to help she just grumped at me, got really defensive and belligerent. I'd come over and shovel the walk and instead of a thank-you she'd say, "I was going to get to it! Stop pressuring me!" She wasn't going to get to it.

JANICE: Any other relatives?

HERMAN: Some on Nunzia's side, all in Italy, as I said. Except for a cousin in Vancouver. Hazel's never met any of them. And my brother Ed is up near Edmonton on a farm. We see them about once a month. Ed and Connie.

And then Hazel plays with their grandkids. It's a really good time up there. They're wonderful people.

JANICE: Thank you for filling in some of the history for me. Do you mind if we revisit what happened after Grazie went to the psych unit? You took guardianship of Hazel, and the next day she had an incident at school?

HERMAN: Yes. She bit another student hard enough he had to get stitches.

JANICE: Why did she bite him?

HERMAN: I ... I don't know.

JANICE: You never asked?

HERMAN: I just assumed she was upset about her mother.

JANICE: Was she bullied in school?

HERMAN: Not as far as I know. If anything, she had a history of being aggressive, even violent with kids. They didn't want her there; she was disruptive. They kept throwing around possible learning disabilities.

JANICE: Like what?

HERMAN: ADHD and audio something-or-other, but I figured that was a pile of bull and they weren't qualified to say. Hazel just never grew up with any discipline.

JANICE: And what does discipline look like to you?
(pause)

HERMAN: Setting boundaries. Time outs. Saying no. Finishing what you start.

JANICE: Wonderful, yes, a child needs structure. You are so right. Did you have Hazel tested for disabilities?

HERMAN: No, I was waiting for her mother to return. But like I said, I think it's a pile of bull. I don't think there's anything wrong with Hazel intellectually. In fact, I think she may be brighter than the average kid. She speaks in a kind of stream of consciousness, which some people may call a disorder or see as a bad thing. It can surely be hard to follow. It's completely different from me. I'm very ... I guess what you'd call ... linear. Some might say anal. Isn't that an ugly word? How did that get into our

129

vernacular? That we call detailed people anal? Anyway, I think Hazel's just plain honest. And I think she sees the world … in poetry. If that makes sense.

JANICE: I love that. I love the way you put that. "She sees the world in poetry."

HERMAN: And people expect a lot from her because she's tall. They think she's ten or twelve, but she's only eight.

JANICE: Well, I sure do want to meet this remarkable little big Hazel. And you decided to homeschool. Why?

HERMAN: I wanted to see for myself where she was at.

JANICE: I see. And what are your conclusions?

HERMAN: Is this really necessary? I'd rather get out there and keep looking for her. She's very upset.

JANICE: Upset? You think she ran away?

HERMAN: Yes. And I'm afraid she's liable to hurt herself. I didn't check down by the river. There are bike trails there. She always liked it there.

JANICE: "Liked"?

HERMAN: Likes. She still likes it.

JANICE: You think she's liable to hurt herself.

HERMAN: When she's out of control. When she's distracted, she doesn't think. She'll walk right into traffic.

JANICE: Has she tried to hurt herself on purpose?

HERMAN: What a question!

JANICE: Has she?

HERMAN: The girl is eight years old! She's not going to slit her wrists!

JANICE: You'd be surprised. Eight-year-olds can self-harm when in distress.

HERMAN: No. She doesn't hurt herself on purpose. Good Lord.

JANICE: Does she self-harm in any way? Like cut herself or hit herself or stop eating?

HERMAN: No.

JANICE: How has homeschooling been going?

HERMAN: My conclusions are that Hazel is an imaginative,

high-energy child who is very emotionally sensitive and willful, and she needs a firm hand. Whether she realizes or appreciates it or not, and despite our many, many arguments about her homework, she's doing much better now that she's homeschooled. She's caught up to other children her age, and she thrives with a healthy diet and a predictable schedule.

JANICE: I certainly commend you for keeping a clean and orderly home. You could come to my house if you're ever bored! And I see you have plenty of fresh food; do you enjoy cooking?

HERMAN: I wouldn't say I enjoy it. I see the benefits of having a balanced clean diet. I also try to get Hazel exercising.

JANICE: Good. Now you said Hazel is "willful, and she needs a firm hand." What does a firm hand look like to you?

HERMAN: Oh, this again. If you're implying that I hit her or abused her in any way, that is not the case. I've never laid a hand on the child, except to hold her down from hurting herself.

JANICE: Herman, I don't mean to imply anything. I just want to understand. How do you hold her down?

HERMAN: Oh for Pete's sake. Are you serious?

JANICE: If I'm Hazel, how would you hold me down?

HERMAN: She used to have temper tantrums, not so much anymore, and she'd flail around, completely out of control, throwing herself at the door or whatever, so I'd hold her arms.

JANICE: So if I'm Hazel ...

(Janice starts flailing her arms.)

HERMAN: I'm not going to –

JANICE: How would you hold my arms?

HERMAN: I'm not going to hold your arms. Please, please, don't.

JANICE: Okay, do you hold her from the back or from the front?

HERMAN: Well, I don't know!

JANICE: Do you hold her with your full body?

HERMAN: Any way I could grab her. I don't mean *grab* her, I mean, I would try to hold her.

JANICE: And when you held her, did it hurt her? Did her skin bruise?

HERMAN: No!

JANICE: Did you raise your voice?

HERMAN: Probably! To be heard over her bellowing like a wild animal.

JANICE: How would you hold her? On your lap?

HERMAN: Are you implying something sexual?!

JANICE: Was there a sexual relationship between you and Hazel?

HERMAN: No! What kind of sick question is that? You are SICK for even asking that.

JANICE: I have to ask that, Herman. It's my job to make sure children are safe in their homes.

HERMAN: She *is* safe!

JANICE: Well, something made her feel "unsafe." She was running away from something. She wrote "F F F, Herman!" for some reason.

HERMAN: I know the reason! It's because she found the bike!

JANICE: What bike?

HERMAN: Her mother's bike. It's a long story.

JANICE: I have time.

HERMAN: When her mother was taken to the hospital, Hazel overheard the paramedics say she'd be at the psych ward, but she thought they said "cycle ward." So when Graziana left home and didn't even communicate with us for the longest time, I hid her bike in my storage unit and, well, I told Hazel that her Mom was cycling, that the doctors told her it would be good for her to go for a long cycle. The cycle ward. And that's why she didn't come home. As far as Hazel knew, her mom took her bike and has been cycling for a year around the world or some damn thing.

JANICE: You said Graziana didn't want to see Hazel?

HERMAN: I didn't say that. She had a mental breakdown and needed time away to heal. She did make phone calls and sent letters and gifts. Hazel knows her mom is coming back for good in four weeks.

JANICE: Where did Graziana go to heal?

HERMAN: She lived with a couple on a farm near Medicine Hat for nearly a year, helping out with their B & B as a maid.

JANICE: How did that make you feel, Graziana abandoning her child?

HERMAN: Angry, of course. Poor Hazel. What a horrible and selfish thing to do to your little girl. But I have come to understand now, because I went out to see Grazie, that Ivan, Hazel's biological father, was a terrible man. He'd been in her life on and off for thirteen years, and I think he may have forced himself on her.

JANICE: You think Hazel was the product of rape?

HERMAN: That's what Grazie said, yes.

JANICE: Oh. Well. That makes sense of why she stopped working. A rape on top of her mother's death and an unexpected pregnancy. She never pressed charges?

HERMAN: You'd have to ask her about that.

JANICE: She didn't choose an abortion.

HERMAN: Pardon?

JANICE: Nothing. I was –

HERMAN: We don't believe in abortion. That would be murder.

JANICE: Are you religious, Herman?

HERMAN: No. I just have a respect for life is all.

(Pause. Janice gets up from the table.)

JANICE: I think I will have that glass of water.

HERMAN: Help yourself. You think abortion is all right, I suppose.

JANICE: We're not here to talk about what I think.

HERMAN: Well, help me understand then. Would Grazie be better off without Hazel?

JANICE: Well, Herman ... it depends what you believe. Some may believe that a woman has a right to choose. Some might believe that Hazel could have been born later, at a time when Grazie was more prepared, had a partner, was mentally well.

HERMAN: Then it wouldn't have been Hazel.

JANICE: The point is, Graziana chose to keep the baby. We have to make room for the idea that it wasn't an easy choice.

HERMAN: Hazel is the best part of Grazie's life, and she doesn't see it. She doesn't treat her that way. I think Hazel could give her a sense of purpose if she let her. Hazel is a gift out of all of that mess. She's ... a joy. She can be very joyful.

(Herman begins to choke up.)

JANICE: Can I get you a tissue?

HERMAN: Oh for heaven's sake. No. Let's get this over with.

JANICE: I don't mean to upset you. I'm trying to understand the family dynamic that Hazel has been brought up with. I hear what you're saying, but I want to also acknowledge that Graziana was likely deeply traumatized, not just ambivalent or lazy.

HERMAN: Yes, yes, they have a name for everything. ADHD, PTSD, whatever.

JANICE: And being deeply traumatized would have made it hard to mother. She wouldn't want to be triggered. She must feel that Hazel triggers her.

HERMAN: It doesn't help that Hazel looks the spitting image of him. Ivan. Same little square head. Same colour of hair. Same kinda teeth.

JANICE: Can you understand how that might be hard for Graziana?

HERMAN: Yes. But it's no excuse for abandoning her daughter.

(pause)

JANICE: Hazel thought her mother was cycling all this time but came across her mom's bicycle. How did that happen?

HERMAN: I completely forgot. I went into my condo storage unit, where I kept it hidden, to get my rototiller, and Hazel tagged along and there it was. Hazel flipped out.

JANICE: I'm confused. I thought Graziana was actually on a cycling trip?

HERMAN: She is now. But she only left a few days ago. And she's rented a bike. Turned out to be cheaper. Anyway, the problem is, Hazel knows I lied. So now she doesn't believe a word I say. And she's known I've been lying for a while now because her mom gave her an apron and a quilt she made in Medicine Hat, and I had a hard time explaining how those items magically appeared. For sure I wasn't going to tell her that her mom was a few hours away and simply didn't want to see her. For a year!

JANICE: You were trying to do the right thing.

HERMAN: Yes.

JANICE: So you said Hazel flipped out. What does that look like?

HERMAN: She screamed, "Liar, liar, liar," and so forth, and she started kicking me in the shins and punching me.

JANICE: And what did you do?

HERMAN: She ran into the corner of the storage room and sunk down and started weeping and screaming, so I kind of stood by the door, having her corralled, and waited for her to calm down. It took about half an hour for me to even get a word in. I'd started to say, "Hazel, your mom is on a bike trip, she just rented a bike." But she wouldn't let me finish a sentence. She'd yell "Liar!" or

"Shut up!" over what I had to say. Then she got really quiet and just looked at me with a hard glare. And that's when I said, "Hazel, your mom HAS been cycling ... in Canada. But when she decided to go to Italy, she rented a bike and I stored her bike in here." Hazel didn't ask any questions; she just looked at me with a kind of hate and then started to cry softly. That lasted for another, I don't know ... an hour maybe? Then I asked her if she was hungry and maybe we could go for burgers. She got into the car silently. She ate her burger silently. She went to bed silently. And that was the last I saw of her.

JANICE: I see.

(end of transcript)

And that's basically it. The rest was just a wrap-up. That's how it went. It was one of the worst experiences of my life. Cop cars here, the neighbours all looking, wondering. Meanwhile, Hazel is out there somewhere completely helpless, angry, and lost. I'm sick, I'm just sick about it. I drive around for hours and hours. I come home to check if she's returned and then I hit the road again. I can't sleep, I can't eat. Being a paramedic, you see terrible things. And all those things are coming back to me, but with Hazel's face: the child drowned face down in the river; the child hit by a car, the middle of her stomach crushed like a pancake. The child raped and strangled and left in the trunk of a car. The child beaten so badly she dies of internal bleeding to the head. Don't talk to me about PTSD – the things I've seen. The things I've had to carry around with me every goddamn day of my life. No, I'm not a religious person. Anyone who sees that much carnage, they know that life is precious because when it's over, it's damn well over.

I am a very good liar and I didn't think that was such a good thing but today it will be very very useful. You's fullllllllllllllllllll! Ha ha ha ha ha! You's fullllllllllll of lies, you liar liar pants on fire. Hazel the super liar super super fire pants!

It will also be a good thing to be a good stealer. Steaaaaaaaaalllllller!

There is no joke there. But I like that word: *steaaaaaaaaaalllllller*. And I hope I'm good at it. Because I can't buy a ticket, or they'll know I don't have my mom with me. I can't remember ever stealing before, though Mom told me when I was little, I used to grab chocolate bars at the grocery store lineup and try to stuff them into my mouth before she could take them away.

I know that the big buses with the grey dog on them go to Calgary in the morning time because Mom and I took them quite a lot for shopping when she needed clothes because she says the malls in Red Deer SUCK. But they don't suck, they just didn't have clothes for MOMS WHO LIE! Guess where I got the good lying from? Eh, Mom? EH?

GreyHOUND! That's it. That's the bus with the dog. Greyhounds are racing dogs. In the olden days they raced dogs and horses and sometimes chickens and sometimes turtles and sometimes snails (that would be boring, but I have heard about it, I'm not lying about that), and now they just race cars. It's too bad because I'd way rather watch a dog race.

Oh my God my heart is racing so fast – I feel like *I'm* in a race! Except I wouldn't be a greyhound, I'd be a wolf! A grey wolf! And nobody would ride me because they would be afraid of me! But I wouldn't care because I would be way faster than a Greyhound and I could get to Calgary way faster. See you, suckers!

Probably Herman is still sleeping because I got up before him. I am not calling him my name for him anymore, G.r.u.m.p.y., because he doesn't deserve it and I'm not little anymore and so Herman can F off. Talk about a liar! But he's not a smart liar like me because otherwise he wouldn't have shown me the – I wanna – I'm gonna – F this stupid stupid bush with the prickles! I'm gonna stomp on you F'ing prickles!

STOMP STOMP STOMP STOMP! LET GO OF ME! Stupid thorns. Ripped my F'ing T-shirt! Ow!

He shouldn't have shown me the bike. That was stupid. That was a stupid move if you were gonna lie about something and then DUH, it's right there in front of me.

People are starting to fill up the Greyhound building now. I'm super proud that I found it because it was a very long walk out of Morrisroe and past my school and down the hill and over the bridge and past Rotary Park while it was still dark. I was scared but mostly I didn't give an F and I have my invisible tiger with me. Except I always worry that when I'm in the dark, the tiger, William, will forget I am his friend and he will bite me in the back of the neck and sever my artery. That's what cougars do. They attack kids and kill them so fast by severing their artery (which is a big vein) that they don't even know they're dead! Uncle Eddie told me that because he goes hiking in the Rocky Mountains and knows all about wildlife. He had no solution for why kids get killed except that nature is cruel. He always says that: "Nature is cruel."

I knew Greyhound was downtown and near City Hall. I know City Hall because it has a park in the front. It took me some time walking around but I found it. It was easy because it was getting light out and not many cars were around. I hid when cars came so they wouldn't find me and tell Herman.

I had lied awake all night – *lied* – isn't that funny? I sure did lie! And I thought about how I was going to run away. I thought and I thought and I made up a good plan. At first I had a long list of things I was going to take and then I kept saying to myself, "Hazel, do you really need your bathing suit? You don't know if you'll end up swimming. No. Hazel, do you really need your toothbrush? No. Hazel, do you really need a pencil? No." All I needed were the clothes I had on, a sweater, and all my saved-up birthday and Christmas money, which was thirty-eight dollars and twenty-five cents. And it's really heavy, the money, like it's making the pocket of my sweater hang so low it almost bangs against my knees, but I like the sound it makes, KACHUNK KACHUNK KACHUNK.

One time at the Greyhound, Mom had to go to the bathroom for a loooooooong time and I was out on the bench by myself and a guy who worked there asked where my parents were because it wasn't safe for me to be alone. So I'm gonna wait until there are lots of people so nobody can tell I'm alone. I hope there aren't spiders in these bushes. I don't want them crawling up my legs and living in my pants all the way to Calgary. One could crawl in my hair and then have babies and then my head would be full of baby spiders. I am one hundred percent positive that must have happened to someone in the world before. Hopefully not me.

Oh, oh, oh! There's my bus! It says ... Ca– ... lgary! Oh my God, okay. I hope hope hope somebody is going on the bus with another kid and then I have to steal it because kids' tickets are different from adults' tickets I think. Oh there's a lady. She is on her phone and she has a stroller, maybe that baby is too small for a ticket but she also has a boy who looks maybe five. I remember when I was five. I remember when I was young and had no problems. You are lucky, boy. Lucky to just wake up in the morning and think, "I don't have to worry about anything because my mom is right there making breakfast." Yeah. Well. Suck an egg, little boy. I'm going to steal your ticket. Deal with it. Where is her purse? I think ... it's hanging outside the diaper bag. If only the little boy would stop looking at me. Maybe cuz I'm looking at him. I'll go away and come back.

Oh my God, I got it! I got it! I got it! I'm not supposed to say *God* because it hurts God's feelings. GOOD! I hope I hurt your feelings, GOD GOD GOD GOD! I want to laugh but I also want to cry really hard, like my throat hurts like after you throw up, like little rocks are in there. Okay, okay, I need to breathe.

The little boy started playing on his iPad, and the mom was still on her phone and the baby saw me but who cares? The baby can't talk, SUCKER! I even pulled out the right ticket the first time. It says "Child." If I believed in angels, I would say they were helping me get on this bus. But that's dumb of course. Angels are for kids who sleep in big houses with fluffy white pillows and have boats in their driveway. Angels are for kids who still believe in the tooth fairy. Lame. I had to tell Grump– Herman when I lost my front tooth to pretend he's the tooth fairy and slip in at least a toonie under my pillow when I'm for-truly sleeping. He said he figured it was only a quarter because a toonie was too heavy for a fairy to carry. I told him fairies nowadays understand a kid can't buy a single thing with a quarter. Like, not even one Chiclet or one Tic Tac because nobody sells small stuff like that. It isn't the olden days!

We are starting to line up now and I'm trying not to watch the lady with the kids, but I can't help it because now she's looking for her ticket that I stoled. She's asking the boy if he took it and she's raising her voice. I feel bad, he didn't do anything. Parents always blame their kids. It's your own darn fault, lady, for not paying attention. Don't you know there are people who are stealers?

She has on a nice purple leather coat and a really fancy stroller, the lady I stoled from. She can totally afford to buy another ticket. I don't feel bad. She says "shit" really loud. She's heading back to the ticket booth, yanking on her boy's arm and the baby is crying. DON'T FEEL BAD, HAZEL, you need this ticket more than she does! Now I need to get on the bus without the driver asking me where my mom is because once Mom went on without me to teach me a lesson because I was fooling around and they would not let me on the bus without her and I started crying and then she finally came off the bus to get me and the bus driver told Mom to not hold up the bus schedule just to teach me a lesson. Yeah, Mom. That was so embarrassing but now I know I have to find a … I think I need an old lady. Old ladies always take the bus. And old ladies always talk about how they walked to school by themselves or rode horses by themselves and back in the olden days you don't need to always have an adult around so they wouldn't think it's weird that I was alone. Either an old lady or someone Japanese. Because when I watch Japanese cartoons, the kids are always walking around by themselves.

Mushroom hat. Is she coming to stand in line for Calgary? I hope so I hope so I hope. Oh, she is! Walk slowly, Hazel ... be cool. Old ladies like me. I have no idea if Japanese people like me, though, because I have never met a Japanese person. I have met a Chinese person (Meghan in my class) and an Indian person (at our grocery store – Mom says he wears a turban on his head because he is from India and his name is Nadeem and he's super nice and super handsome and if I was my mom, I would have a crush on him) and a Vietnamese person (Poppy, she is the cutest girl ever and she has nice glasses and always really cool clothes. And even though she's older than me, she's tinier than me, and so we never played together, and besides she's super popular, but if I was less weird and could pick my friends, I'd pick her because she does wisecracks. That's a kind of joke that is said when your lips are straight). But old ladies like me unless they are the grumpy old lady kind of person instead of the talk-a-lot old lady kind of person. I hope I have found the right old lady! She has a nice fuzzy green coat, I like it. Looks like a mossy rock.

"I like your coat and hat!"

"Oh, why, thank you, dear. The hat's called a tam. A tam-o'-shanter. We Scots like our tams."

"Looks like a mushroom. What's a Scots?"

"Oh, I was born in Scotland is all. But I've been here most me life. I am rather fond of your yellow pants, dear. You remind me of a daffodil."

"Thank you. Yellow is my first favourite colour."

"Well then, we are kindred spirits. I have always had yellow curtains in me kitchens, no matter what house I've lived in. Yellow curtains."

"Can I sit with you on the bus? My name is Hazel."

"Good to meet you, Hazel. I'm Doris Noble. Where's your mom or dad? Surely, you're not travelling alone, wee one? How old are you? Ten, twelve?"

"I have a ticket."

"I see. I'm surprised you're allowed to travel by yourself. Aren't you afraid?"

"No. My ... dad is waiting for me on the other side. It's totally safe."

"My, my, kids are so independent these days! When I was growing up, I always had to have a chaperone."

"What's that?"

"That's a big brother, usually, who makes sure no other boys come near you."

The lady with the purple leather coat and kids is trying to pay for her ticket fast enough to join us. Her fingers are like frightened little birdies. I feel pretty bad but not bad enough to tell her I stoled it. The little boy turns his head and looks straight at me.

It's time for Doris and me to get on the bus and Doris goes first and I hold her hand. I know that will mean the bus driver thinks she's my grandma, aaaaaaaaaaaand he takes my ticket no PROBLEM! The lady with the purple jacket gets a ticket in time and rushes on the bus, breathing hard like she's ran a marathon. I'm glad. I'm glad we both got on.

Me and Doris sit together the whole way to Calgary. I am a genius stealer and liar. How's that for "retarded," Peter? Peter is so dumb and mean he doesn't even know it's wrong to say "retarded." Like, nobody says that word anymore, grow up, son of a redneck stupid-head. Peter is a fart. Peter is a stinky fart that you can't even touch because all he is is bad air. I can blow him away. Stupid Peter.

I like the blue chairs on the Greyhound much more than the red chairs on the city buses. They are more cozy and way bigger and there's a place to put my feet but both Doris and I are too small and our feet dangle down and then it is very easy to want to kick the chair in front and I have to remember not to.

Doris is now a pretty good friend, I'd say. She has blue veins popping out on the back of her hands, big as earthworms. They are very cool. I want to poke one so badly to see if it moves but I don't. She has a tiny purse with lots of jewels on it and she opens it up and gives me a green round peppermint. It is the best peppermint I've ever had in my life. She won't let me try on her hat though, her shamble tam, not because she's mean, but because she says her hair is really thin, like bald, like a bald man. I really want to see a bald lady, but I don't ask because Doris is my friend and I know she is embarrassed. She is going to go see her son who is in the hospital with a heart attack. Doris said it was very strange to have a son who is a senior citizen and who isn't doing as well as her in the health department. She blames her son's wife, Shantel, for giving him the heart attack. She said the wife is a "harpy." I think that's an old-fashioned word for *bitch*.

I am starting to worry that Doris will want to meet my dad now that we're getting to Calgary. But I think I know what to do. I just need to look for a man who isn't too old, isn't too young and isn't too scary. We get to Calgary and it's super crowded, thank God, and I give Doris a big hug and a kiss on her powdery white cheek.

"There's my dad, Doris, thank you for being my friend. I hope your hair grows back and your son gets better!"

"I'd feel better if I saw –"

I don't hear the end of what she is saying because I am running into the crowd looking for the perfect dad ... there's one! There's one in a stripedy sweater and cool jeans! He's ... oh – he's got a baby in a stroller and I think a wife, too bad! He's got to be my dad, or Doris will worry, I can feel she's watching. I should hug him, I should, but it's so weird to hug a total stranger.

I say, "I love your sweater, you look like a tiger!"

I hug him and he's super surprised, like I knock his glasses off a little. The baby is staring at me with a goober coming out of its mouth – gross, babies can be gross – and the wife opens her mouth. I have to say something, so I say, "I have a pet tiger, but he's invisible. Sorry to be a weirdo but I just like to hug people sometimes who look like they could be a good dad."

The wife asks me, "Where are your parents?"

"Here."

"Where?"

"My dad is … buying me a chocolate bar in the café."

I look over and I see Doris is still looking and she is waving at me. I wave back. The wife says, "What's your name?"

"Hazel."

"Well, Hazel, I'm Leslie and it's not very safe to go up and hug people, especially men you don't know. Is that your nonna?"

"No, just a nice lady I met on the bus."

I have to stall until Doris goes away. "What's your baby's name?"

"Jordan."

"Is that a boy or a girl?"

"We don't believe in infant gender assignment. Until we are sure of how Jordan wishes to identify, we just call the baby Jordan."

I don't know what the F she is talking about. I ask, "Does Jordan have a vagina?"

The wife looks surprised and I'm glad I made her blush. I don't really like her. She's like all bristly, like when a dog doesn't want you to pet her and she's maybe going to bite you. You know those bristles on the back? That's the wife. She has the perfect name: Leslie. It sounds prickly, like *restless*. That dog is Leslie, better not pet it.

"I don't feel comfortable discussing my child's genitalia with a stranger."

The dad finally talks. "Jordan has a penis."

This makes his wife mad. I see that Doris is looking away now, heading towards the taxi so I say, "Bye, Tiger Dad! My dad is in the cafeteria!" And I run run run into the crowd.

The cafeteria has lots of people. I go way back to the back and hang out by the place where people put their milk in their coffee. I steal a sugar because I'm hungry. I stuff the packet in my pocket with all my heavy coins. Sometimes babies are handy. There is a baby here, an older one with pigtails and cute chubby legs and a pink toque. Her mom has given her a muffin with blueberries, but she pushes it away and so the mom puts the muffin back on the tray and picks up her baby and walks away like the whole thing is garbage! It only has one bite out of it! So it's not gross. I make sure nobody is looking and I take the muffin and put it in my pocket too. I know lots of times it's okay to ask for a glass of water. I do that with my mom because she says pop is too expensive. I go to the front of the line and ask for water and the guy behind the counter gives me a glass. I am so thirsty.

I peek back out into the bus station and the tiger dad and his Leslie wife and penis baby Jordan are gone now. Whew.

The Greyhound in Calgary is right downtown, right near the big Calgary Tower! I don't know where I am going or what I am doing but I know I want to see the tower and I can see it from the bus station, so I walk until I find it. I cross some very big streets and I am careful to look both ways. I am super proud of myself. I get to the tower and it's like the bottom of the hugest tree in the universe! Inside the tower (I am surprised I can walk right in), are lots of shops and stuff and a theatre that looks like a movie theatre but maybe it has real people. It starts with a *V*. Ver-something.

But more than mysteries I like lunch. I have five loonies from my piggy bank and there is a place that sells ... Vietnamese buns? I don't know what that means but it smells good. I ask the lady for a sandwich and I tell her I only have five dollars and she squints at me and says I should ask for two more dollars from my parents. I tell her my parents are at the theatre and asked me to buy my own sandwich. She gives it to me anyway. Then I ask if I could get a Coca-Cola for no money and she says no but she gives me a glass of water. That's okay. But after I drink it, I sure have to go pee.

I see a bunch of people going into the theatre and giving the person standing there a ticket. I think it would be fun to see a show. But how? How do I get in? Oh ... Oh my God I am so good at this – I say, "Excuse me ticket lady, my grandma Doris has my ticket, sorry, I went out to get a sandwich, can I go in and find her?" And they let me in! I use the bathroom and then peek into the big theatre. It's really pretty. Wow! And dark. There is a clump of empty seats right at the front and almost everyone is sitting now so I take my chances and sit in one right at the front and lucky for me, nobody comes and boots me out!

The show is called *Might as Well Be Dead*. So, I like it already because I have felt that very same thing. There is a man who is grey all over, his hair, his suit, he's called Wolfe or something. But he doesn't look like a wolf. He looks more like a tired Santa Claus. And then there is another guy with a suitcase and a cool hat. I guess it's for adults because everyone is laughing and I don't get it. But the skinny guy likes milk instead of wine so I kind of like that because that's like being a kid. They just talk talk talk and then a pretty lady comes in and then talk talk talk. The walls slide on and off. I fell asleep but I like theatre a lot. My favouritest was a show called *Zorro: Family Code* at a place called ... I don't know, it started with an *A*, in Calgary, a theatre. Because they had a lady with a sword and they were Spanish and they wore masks and lot of black and I wanted to be just like her because she was so cool.

Even though I fell asleep, this is the best day ever, in my whole life.

Holy man, does it ever get dark fast outside. The show is over and when I come out of the Calgary Tower, the sun is setting already. I am starting to feel scared. Cars go extra fast at night zoom zoom across my face. I wait for the red light, but I am afraid that even a car won't obey it and run right into me. Smash me underneath it. There's a big iron horse on the sidewalk and it's kind of cool but mostly it freaks me out. I wish I had Doris, I wish I had that striped-shirt dad, I wish I had –

I just need to find a shopping mall because they're really big and the lights are on all the time and I'm small and I can find a place to hide in the plants or under a bench or in some clothes.

Or maybe I can stand really really still and they will think I am one of those ... what do you call them? Those pretend people, big dollies in the window? I'm a good hider. All I see are restaurants and banks and this street is closed off, no cars. Just guys with dirty pants and beards playing guitar. And GOD people are nosy! Lots of people are staring at me. "Where's your mother?" "Are you alone?" "Where you going, little girl?" "Are you lost?" I wish my money wasn't so loud in my sweater, KACHUNK KACHUNK KACHUNK. I see another lady staring at me in her high heels: "Mind your own beeswax!"

I walk and walk and it gets darker and darker and I'm afraid there is only going to be bars and weird shops for cameras and phones but then ... BINGO! I see it! Something called the Core! A beautiful mall with big white sort of dinosaur-tail sculptures on the outside, and on the inside ... the roof is all shiny and glass. Like, it's the superest, specialest mall I've ever been to. Way better than Bower Place and Parkland Mall put together. People in here have very nice clothes on, nicer than mine. They are rich, I think. There is no store for XX-large liar moms in here I bet. Just pretty things for really healthy girls and really healthy boys. I am supposed to say "healthy," not "skinny" says Herman. Because sometimes skinny people are not healthy and sometimes what you could maybe call a fat person could be super healthy. But make no mistake, my mom is fat and not healthy and a liar in a bad way because she never did have to lie to me ever. She just did lie to me because she doesn't want to be my mom, she wants to leave me by myself because she doesn't love me.

Crum ... ple.

Crum ...

ple.

I ...

I ...

I can't get sad. If I get sad, people will see and then they will ask me where my mom is and I'll have to say, "I have NO IDEA, SHE JUST LEFT ME!"

I need to find a bathroom because ... my nose is running ... Stupid tears, stupid. DON'T CRY HAZEL YOU ARE TOUGH AND YOU HAVE YOUR TIGER!

Tiger tiger tiger beside me, eat that old man sleeping on the bench, just kidding. Bite that boy's leg, just kidding again. Though it would be pretty cool to see an invisible tiger bite somebody. There's the bathroom sign of the lady wearing the dress but I look more like the man because I am wearing pants and I have no boobs because I am only eight. I wonder which place Jordan the baby with the penis would choose. I don't feel like I belong in either bathroom, but I guess I'll go to the one my mom goes to. GOD it stinks in here. I am going to blow my nose and then get the hell out. Teenaged girls doing something in the corner, trading ... oh, I think tampons? I know what tampons are because I found some under the sink and Mom told me about it. You stick them in your vagina. GROSS! Why is everything scary today? Uncle Eddie is right. Nature is cruel!

Okay. Let's go find a Chapters. I like books. Well, I like pretty books with pictures. I don't like to read very much because the letters and words flip around on me. Grump– I mean HERMAN says that's dyslexic. But what does he know about it? He doesn't have my eyes.

Furniture, ladies' clothes, jewellery, who cares, baby stuff, Shoppers Drug Mart. That will do okay. I'll look at the maga-zines. Maybe if there's a cartoon or a comic I can buy one with my money. It's really bright in here. Like, so bright the light is almost blue. Like, maybe being inside Shoppers Drug Mart is what it's like being inside an igloo when the sun comes out? Ooh, better get out before it meeeeeeeeeelts on you, tiger! Lip gloss. I like lip gloss. I can try this one because it's a "sample." My moth – I've tried samples before. This one tastes like cherry.

Crossword puzzles and little kids' colouring books and then food and fashion and cars and gardens and who cares? Nothing cool. I'm tired. I'm feeling very tired.

"Thank you for shopping at the Core. The mall is now closed. Please make your way to the exit."

Oh no! They are closing up the stores, pulling those little gates across. I need somewhere to sleep. Why didn't I figure that out earlier? Hazel, you are so stupid stupid stupid! You never think! You stupid bragger! You can lie and you can steal but you can't make a decent plan for your own future! Where are you going now, huh? Huh? And don't cry! And don't talk to the tiger because you know deep down William is not real and he is not going to save you. STUPID! Wait, there's H&M, they haven't closed the gate yet. Scoot!

I sneak in beside the dresses and hide deep behind them. Nobody sees me. I don't think so. I peek out. I see the lady at the counter with some keys, she's talking to the cute boy she's working with. I think they're flirting. She's wearing a sweater that is also a crop top and it's fuzzy and pink like a baby flamingo might be, no wait, they have feathers, like a baby duck might be except it's pink. Why are baby ducks fuzzy? Ducks have feathers. Maybe baby flamingos are fuzzy too.

Whoa! She almost saw me. I'll hide in here with the long dresses, they almost cover my feet. I just hope she doesn't look down and I hope the money in my sweater doesn't clink together. I hope my breath isn't too loud. It seems loud to me. But maybe my ears are extra super hearing right now because I can also hear my heartbeat and normally I can't. BaDum baDum baDum baDum in my ears. Jingle jingle, she's pulling the gate, I can hear the cute boy.

"Goodnight, Visco."

"I am so not Visco! Bro."

"I am so not Bro. And just kidding. I know you're not Visco. I just know you hate it."

"Thanks for that. You got a ride?"

"I walk."

"You going which way?"

"Sixth."

"Wait up."

I think she grabs her bag and then she locks up, locks me in the store! I hope the lights don't go out. I wait and wait and wait.

So quiet. Weird to have the mall so big and so quiet and so bright. I'm so tired. I don't think anybody is around, but I am afraid of someone catching me in case.

I tiptoe underneath the dresses, stepping over the metal bars and knocking things down. Shoot! And I see jeans and shirts and skirts and winter jackets! Perfect! I crawl quickly on my knees to the middle of the winter jackets hanging in a circle. They are the big puff-puff kind with the fur on the big hoods, they are just like pillows! I pull three down underneath the circle and make a nice bed with one and a nice pillow with the other and a nice blanket with jacket number three.

Okay. This is a pretty good idea. It's very cozy. I smile. But then ... there's nobody to hear me, and I cry and I cry and I cry. I don't even know why. I feel so little, like a tiny mouse with all my fur rubbed off of me and no cheese. I find a T-shirt and use it for a Kleenex. Sorry, H&M, I made snot on your shirt. All my coins fall to one side of my hoodie pocket and I wish I could disappear. I lift up my sleeve and scratch where I usually scratch on my arm. I scratch and scratch and scratch to hurt myself until I bleed. I don't know why, but bleeding makes me feel better. Or like ... it hurts on the outside like it hurts on the inside. I don't know. I just do it. Owie, owie! I don't care – bleed, bleed, you stupid – !

Stupid ...

Stu ...

The beloved has been pondering his presence among Us. He's been ruminating about his placements on Earth. He's been exploring his matter. He expands and spreads so he can skate on sound waves and speed with light. He sprinkles himself across the Milky Way, he rolls his eyes, "at one with the cosmos." And although he can join it all, try as he might, he can't escape himself. He contracts into the size of a sesame seed – no, smaller: a grain of sand. Magnitudes smaller: an atom! Wait. The smallest thing he's ever heard of: a quark! But he cannot disappear. In fact, he triples himself. He furrows his brow over the mystery of being a being. And he shakes his head over the confounding truth that We are everything and everywhere and yet intimate enough to speak. How can that be? He cannot escape Us, and this is both a comfort and a discomfort. Finally, he strides forward, his exasperation thrown up in the air.

"What am I to do with me?"

Sit by Us. We will discuss.

We sit together and watch the sun fattened and flattened into a persimmon as it folds into the horizon, like the freshest of cracked farm eggs.

What would you like to do with you?

"I have … appreciated the rest. I feel like I needed that. And I feel … safe with you. And that's new. Let me tell you. I sure do love not having to look over my shoulder every five minutes to see if there's a frog or a hawk or a cop car. My ankle doesn't get sprained here, I have no stomach growls. My eyes don't get sticky and heavy. I'm not wondering what grub to scratch up for dinner. And now that my heart isn't always beating beating beating, … it's so quiet within myself. All that mad drumming of blood pumping pumping through my veins, all of me has stopped racing. To not be alive on the earth is a huge relief. Thank you. You know, when I was a kid, especially around the age of thirteen, I was willing to die for this kind of peace. I thought about how I'd do it. Tried it once."

We remember. And your mother was struck with sudden menstrual cramps so intense she left work early, just in time to find you on the bathroom floor.

"So that *was* you."

It was all of Us.

"Well, I didn't do much with that second chance, did I?"

You obtained your driver's licence and started picking your mother up from the bar at night so she didn't keep driving home drunk. That saved lives. You were a good friend to Armand.

"He was a bully."

You understood he was a bully because his father beat him. You allowed him room to feel anger. You let him talk. You let him be silent.

"I helped him beat up Ken, and we were horrible to Carrie."

There is also that. You worked in the home for the aged, and you invented ways to make your clients laugh.

"Yeah, I've always liked old people. They're not so judgy, they're generally very appreciative."

You took extra time with Elsa at the end of every shift, played marbles with her, because you knew she never had visitors.

"She was so old, everyone in her family had died on her, even her kids. She could be mean. Mean old bitty. Easy for me, though. Just made me laugh. And she could roll more fours after sixes than I ever did see. 'Okay, Chuckles,' I'd say. 'If you don't want your pudding, use it for fingerpainting on the window, see if I care.' But, you know what I mean. When she died, I stole her gold earrings. Pulled them right off her ears. Overall, I did very little good in the world and I would say, overall, I did a lot of harm. So, I'm wondering ... what's the deal? You haven't blown me to smithereens, so I figure you must be keeping me around for something. Is this the fattening up of the lamb before the slaughter? Are you waiting for some reason to send me to hell? Is there a hell?"

Yes.

"But then I think, why would you go through the trouble of teaching me, of finding me placements, if you were only going to throw me into the fire and burn me up? Or send me to a place of eternal torture, or whatever hell is."

Hell is something beyond your comprehension. At present.

"Well, I guess it doesn't matter because I don't think you're sending me there. I think you've been preparing me, or hoping I'll improve and learn and be better in order to be something useful. Am I not built to be useful to you or anyone? What do I need to do to contribute? To honour your creation?"

You need to participate in your reckoning.

The beloved gasps and cowers with fear. "I thought the bottom of the ocean for thousands of years of dark isolation might be enough of a punishment."

We didn't say "punishment." We said "reckoning."

"I thought it would purify me: all that salt and silence. But I don't feel clean. If you test me on my goodness, I am quite sure I'm going to fail."

It isn't a test. A reckoning is an understanding of the patterns you've created with your soul. Think of it as a weaving. The dark threads that you introduced and then continued to needle in and out of your life, the pattern that you allowed to repeat started to take over. You became more and more entrenched. We need to untangle and pull the coarse black thread out.

"Truth before reconciliation. As they say."

Yes. Wise words from the Originals.

"I don't know if I have the strength."

Are you asking for strength from Us?

"Yes."

We give you strength.

The beloved stands and waits to feel the difference. He cocks his head. We pull the thread. The beloved sees: he is Ivan in the parking lot with Grazie, glove over her mouth, shoving her against the cinderblocks, pulling down her jeans, bashing her hip bone against the cement.

The beloved gasps and shuts his eyes. "Out out out! I want

that out of me! Please! I am so ashamed … I've never forced myself on a woman before. I said sorry and I meant it. Is this when you punish me? Do anything, just don't make me look at that."

We pull the thread. The beloved sees: Louise, wiping her nose through tears, packing up her clothes into a box labelled "Miscellaneous." Toe poking through her sock, ringlets in a knot. Accepting Ivan's embrace. Seeing his tears, meeting his goodbye kiss, then backing away, while he grabs for more.

"That was breakup sex."

She asked you to stop, and you didn't.

"It was right before I … it was only a couple of seconds."

You held down her legs for the longest thirty-two seconds of her life. She cried.

"So did I. I knew it. I know … I'm sorry Louise."

We pull the thread. Wren, splayed out on a frat-house downstairs sofa with a dying kitchen party thumping around upstairs.

"That was completely consensual."

How could it be consensual when she was delirious with drink, incoherent and unresponsive?

"What was her name?"

Wren.

"I was also drunk, but no excuse. Wren, I'm sorry."

We pull the thread. Lucy. Sitting at the table, touching at the eggplant-coloured bruise swollen on her chin, the smell of schnitzel frying.

"No, no, you have it wrong. Lucy was raped by somebody else. Some stranger jumped her in her car."

Yes, and six days later she came to your house for a business meeting, or what she thought was a business meeting.

"Well, okay, that was the carrot I dangled; she was very career-driven. But I invited her to my house, to make her dinner. Everyone knows that's code for sex."

Lucy's look of utter surprise when Ivan, flipper in hand, apron around his middle, hands her a glass of wine.

She told you she had been assaulted. She showed you her

bruises. She told you she hadn't been tested for STDs, and that she was in no position –

"It's not my fault she changed her mind. And if she didn't want it, why'd she come over?"

She needed the work. It was a free meal, a kindness, from a trusted colleague.

Ivan flips the schnitzel and sneers, "Did the guy know he was raping you?"

"Yes," Lucy answers, shocked, her head starting to swim; she has to sit down.

"But then she started warming up. She walked into the living room, she liked my art. Talk about mixed messages. She didn't say no."

She didn't say yes.

"She changed her mind!"

No, she didn't.

Lucy walks into the living room, heading for her jacket flopped across the chair. She says she isn't feeling well, and she's ready to go home. She'll walk. Ivan kisses her on the mouth, despite the fact there is absolutely no invitation. Lucy pops up to the top of the ceiling.

"Where did she go? She was right there, kissing me back."

No, she wasn't. She was floating on the top of your picture frames, wondering if they were dusty. She was crawling along your windowpanes like a trapped fly. She was thinking your light fixtures were the cheap ones from Ikea she had in her last apartment, and how she'd like to smash the bulbs. She had no idea what her body was doing.

"She what? Well, I'm not a mind reader!"

Ivan on top of Lucy, her eyes a blank, her arms limp, going along with his motions in a complete daze.

"I ... I thought ... they say the good-looking girls just lie there, like showing up is enough."

Lucy – later – explaining to Ivan in the hallway between the dressing rooms, while the janitor is wiping down the elliptical machines. She had disassociated, she didn't remember, she felt she had made it clear. Ivan should have never. So selfish, so stupid, to have taken. Ivan says they have mutual friends, they move in the same circle; he calls her a liar and a crazy slut.

"Well I'm dead now. I hope that makes her happy."

It does. She calls it karma.

"How do I say I'm sorry, then? How do they forgive me?"

That is not their obligation.

We pull the thread: Tara. Catholic girl still in her school uniform, the plaid skirt just above her knee, tidy ponytail, purple eyeshadow. A poster of the Cure. Writing in her diary.

"No, for sure you have that wrong. She stayed a virgin."

Tara writing, "I think I will kiss Ivan but that's it, I've told him." Tara and Ivan necking on the sofa. She pushes away his hand from her breast.

"She was always saying no, but she was really meaning yes. It was this thing between us. She wanted me to make the moves so that she didn't have the Catholic guilt."

Tara wakes in the middle of the night to see Ivan in her bedroom, naked. The house is empty, parents away for the weekend. He pins her down and pulls up her nightie and puts his mouth between her legs. She screams and cries and tries to get away.

"If she didn't want it, then why did she cum? Why did she stay with me for six months?"

She stayed with you to try and make it work. You told her it was her fault, that she had tempted you by wearing tight T-shirts. You told her that God would punish her if she slept with anyone else. She had a nervous breakdown at the age of eighteen. She couldn't go to college.

"Over that little thing?"

That little thing was her faith. That little thing was her agency.

"I didn't realize ... Actually, that's not true. Something inside of me knew."

We pull the thread. Mrs. Carol MacDonald in the locker room, well after gymnastics practice, her Toyota the only car left in the school parking lot. She lays a clean towel across the bench and removes her underwear; Ivan enters, twelve and pimpled and carrying a social studies book about World War I.

"We don't have to ... yeah, I don't count that. I ... exploded all over my ... I don't want to look at this."

Mrs. MacDonald pulls up her skirt for viewing and places her hands in strategic places; the boy's face crumples into red sweat.

"I DON'T WANT TO BE THERE!"

We pull the thread. Ivan's mother in a loosening housecoat, blue-and-red flowers, polyester black lace, laughing, blowing a cigarette circlet. Yet another "uncle" smelling of beer and corporate sweat, grabbing at her while she straddles his waist and plays with his hair. Little Ivan opening his bedroom door a crack to hear the animal sounds coming from down the hall, eyeing the bathroom, afraid to cross from door to door in case he sees what he is trying not to hear. Half-eaten TV dinner, gluelike white mashed potatoes left cold in the corner of the plastic plate mould. All the Jell-O gone. Books lined up on the shelf. Little Hot Wheels parked in perfect chromatic order. Bed with the brown checks, made. Hot urine running down his legs, spreading darkness along his powder-blue penguin pyjamas. If only he was out there on an ice floe, cool and white and clean and quiet, with his favourite kind of bird.

The beloved becomes as little and chubby-cheeked as he was, as he feels. "I should have known not to hurt people like that. Of all the boys ... I should have known."

We both sit and stare at this long thread with despair.

"Where is she? Mom is dead. But where is she?"

We touch into the Earthly, just outside of Florence, South Carolina, to the flower We know she is resting on.

The beloved closes his eyes tightly and covers his ears. "I never said I wanted to see her! Take me back! Take me away!"

She won't speak. She will sense a familiarity, but she won't know who you are.

The beloved opens his eyes, tentatively. He gasps, surprised. "This is it? She's a butterfly?! Who asks to be a butterfly?!"

One who yearns to understand the beauty and importance of fragility.

The beloved stares hard at the impassive, fluttering monarch hovering over a frilly pink milkweed. "Why does she get flowers? She doesn't deserve wings!"

The anger of a tantruming toddler fills him, and he yanks out the dark thread of his life. Instead of letting it go, he swings it over his head like a lasso, gathering the pressure of a late-spring thunderstorm, pushing warm air up and cool air down. Delicate wings flutter.

We tell the monarch to fly.

There's no reasoning with a storming child, cycloning in that much raging sorrow. The beloved throws the dark thread straight up over his head with the currenting winds, connecting earth to sky, pulling condensation down, down, down to the fields through the centre of him, like clutching at the ankles of angels and dragging them to their knees as they scuttle to get away, kicking up dust, pulling down red sunset maples from the root. The cyclical pipe of wind rolls and ravages along the dirt, hurricaning hurt just off of I-95. The Beloved roars beside the Pee Dee River, rattling the roof of a Southern Baptist church, scattering boys playing softball in a field of sawgrass and rabbiteye. The tin of a roadside peanut hut shakes and shimmies like a steel drum. The woman inside, Charlotta, stops pulling at the density of her kitchen, sets her head wrap aright, wipes her apron over the boiling pot, and rushes out to her stoop.

She stares agape at the beloved snaking up the sky. "Act of God my ass," she mutters and then shouts, "Be gone, devil!"

Then Charlotta senses what she does not yet understand. She breathes in the revelation, calls it a gift, this reckoning, and We agree. She listens to her soul, despite the fact her skirt is flapping against her legs in the wind like two frantic crows, despite the fact she could be smote any second. She knows a tantrum when she sees one, having raised six kids. She yells out to the immense hurricane tearing up the world in front of her, "Hush down! Hush! That's enough. I see you. I hear you."

The beloved is stopped short of blowing her to smithereens, or at the very least, blowing Charlotta to Charlotte. Who is this woman who dares to stare into the eye of his storm? Who is this warm mother?

Charlotta whispers, "You're safe now, child. Let the Earth go."

CHAPTER SEVEN

THE IMPORTANCE OF BUTTERFLIES

— Graziana —

ORIO LITTA, LOMBARDY

I sailed down the mountain from my glamorous B & B in San Colombano al Lambro and rode along a freeway until I saw the scruffy old path of the Cammino and the familiar little sign of the pilgrim beside it. I dodged butterflies and smiled as the sun flickered through new forests with their beautiful symmetry. I watched swallows and robins scout for worms. The Po River rolled beside me; old dusty green tractors rumbled in the earthy fields that met the horizon. Once in a while, another cyclist passed me. I felt refreshed and well and light in my soul. I hadn't felt this happy in ... well, maybe ever.

My odd presence has people coming up to me on the street (usually men around my age) and asking me incredulously where I'm from. They guess Canada or Germany. Is that where they think hearty pale women who aren't afraid of inclement weather and long distances come from? There is admiration. Yet something tells me if their wives decided to do the Cammino solo they would not be so impressed.

In the afternoon, a couple of easygoing, long-limbed local chums cycled along the path with me, half-heartedly, laughing, cracking the tops off a couple of beers they had in their backpacks, drinking and cycling one-handed. It was effortless for them to catch up and pass me. Then I passed them when they stopped for gelato. And then they passed me while I paused to admire a church and munch a carrot. They called out, teasingly, suggesting I was slow or some such, so I retorted, "È la Via Francigena! Un cammino, non corsa!" – a walk, not a run. To which they laughed and waved me off.

Generally speaking, there's a way of talking in Italy that is punchier than what I hear in Canada. People raise their voices and it has nothing necessarily to do with anger. This was my mother. I hear her cadence, her tone, everywhere. I remember her saying she lost her first job in Canada over it. She was an excellent dental assistant and though she never quarreled with the dentist or the patients or the receptionist, her emphatic way of speaking alarmed them; they always felt scolded by her. They sat her down in a nervous circle and said her volume was "inappropriate in a professional setting." She laughed at first, then realized they were serious enough to let her go. From that point on, she adopted what she called her "Canadian voice," a soft false purr with a plastered-on smile, which, if you ask me, was far more terrifying. But I can see in Italy she would have been able to breathe. She would not have to worry about scaring people with her unapologetic opinion, her bombastic frankness and open joy.

Just as I was pondering my mother, I had my first sighting of a female biker on the Cammino. She wore full-body blue-and-white spandex. She had a shiny helmet with goggles, and she was lean as an insect. She flew past me and yelled something in German akin to "Move over, slowpoke!" I'm not entirely sure she was embracing the spiritual concept of a Cammino, but she was glorious all the same.

It was a seventy-kilometre cycle today, and I finally arrived at my "hotel." The picture of it on the Expedia link looked like a lush holiday family resort. In reality it was a thirsty, dust-covered truck stop plunked in the middle of a highway cloverleaf. It made me nervous to weave my dirty little bike past large solemn trucks still hot from the highway. I wasn't sure where to lock up, so I dragged my CUBE up the stairs and in through the front door. A man behind a well-stocked bar kindly rushed to my aid. With few words, he hoisted my filthy steed over one shoulder and carried it across the breakfast hall to a back storage room with swinging wood-slatted doors.

"Is more safe here," he said, carefully placing it beside humongous cans of peeled Roma tomatoes and clean boxes of bottled water.

Then he gave me my key and pointed to a staircase behind the bar to my room. When I stepped up the creaky stairs and found my door, I gasped at the room's austerity. It was clean and large with tall, shuttered windows, but it looked like the corner of a dark funeral home. The room had four chaste and hard single beds in it, everything draped in a sombre maroon, and the cold marble floor had just been disinfected.

I patted myself with a facecloth, changed my shirt, and tiptoed nervously back down the stairs. I searched for a postcard at the bar. There was one of the opulent Villa Litta Carini, a sight I did not see. Would sending this be disingenuous of me? Oh well. Then I followed handwritten signs that led to the attached ristorante. To my surprise, the hallway opened up into a huge banquet hall filled with about eighty men sitting at tables with starched white tablecloths: truckers. A female server approached me from the side and smiled, reassuringly: "Non ci sono problemi, tranquilla. Come. They good guys."

The truckers sat in fours, each on their phone, probably to wives and children. Not a single greasy baseball cap or dagger tattoo in sight. They were clean-cut family men, many in button-down shirts, sipping from their five-ounce glasses of red wine. I was glad to have my own preoccupation with family. I ordered a delicious spaghetti vongole, and this pellegrina had a Pellegrino. I tried not to get tomato spots on the white tablecloth or my postcard when I slurped up the noodles.

I wrote:

Dear Hazel,

*I am near a place called Fiorenzuola d'Arda. I was
thinking today about my mother and how she used
to laugh with her whole body, like you. She had a
big operatic voice that she tried to keep quiet around
all the scaredy-cat Canadians, but then she let it rip
when she got home. She would yell when she got
angry, but it was never really scary, just loud. And
Herman would grin and say to her, "Are you going
to break some dishes now, Nunzia?" And she would
say, "Herman, those are the Greek, not the Italian.
I never smash a dish in my life!" I think I grew up
being extra quiet, trying to give my mother the hint
that she should tone it down. And now I am thinking
I should have been more like her. I am at a truck stop
right now, surrounded by men I'd call the salt of the
earth. Like Grumpy. I always felt safe and protected
around him, and I know you do too. And for that,
I am thankful. Love,*

Mom

Was that the sort of thing a person writes to an eight-year-old
child? I didn't know. Once back in my funeral home of a room,
it struck me that what I was doing, this chatting with the Great
Good, was prayer. If it was indeed so, then perhaps I could ask
the Great Good to intercede. This opened up a whole can of
worms as I sat contemplating predestination, divine interven-
tion, and the futility of wishful thinking.

"I know you're not my spiritual credit card, that I can't just
go shopping with your Divine power, but if you could give Hazel
some comfort and peace tonight, I'd appreciate it."

I have heard your intercession.

Intercession. I didn't know I had these ancient words in me.

163

— *Herman* —

Hazel was found this morning at 7:45 a.m. in the H&M store at the Core Shopping Centre in downtown Calgary. A night watchman heard her whimpering while doing his rounds. She had hidden in a clothing rack and fallen asleep there overnight. She gave him my phone number and he said he'd wait for me to come pick her up. He had contacted the authorities and they were conducting interviews and said I could start driving out.

When I arrived at the mall, I expected to find a very sheepish and scared little girl. Instead, Hazel was wearing new sparkly clothes, all in yellow, and she was sipping on an A&W milkshake, kicking her legs under the table, munching on French fries, happy as a lark. She had made a good friend out of Munish, the aforementioned night watchman. Apparently he was a father of three, and when he wasn't on mall security, he played saxophone in a jazz band. He took it upon himself to buy Hazel a completely new outfit, except for shoes, because she had urinated all over herself during the night in her sleep.

She had also urinated on two ladies' winter jackets at H&M, both size-small. One was the colour of a raw chicken, and the other was the colour of horse shit. I had to buy those damaged goods, of course – that set me back nearly four hundred dollars. I don't know a single person who would even wear such ugly jackets. And thanks to Munish, I had to pay for Hazel's new garish "ensemble" – another fifty bucks.

He shrugged and said, "Yellow is her favourite colour."

He kindly covered her breakfast. He didn't have to do that. He was a very nice man, and he didn't look at me like I was a criminal, which I appreciated. He just said, "I'm a father too. Kids will be kids." Sure. But I doubt his children had ever run away 150 kilometres and wet their pants all over hideously ugly ladies' wear.

Hazel didn't apologize, she didn't explain, she just kept

cracking jokes with Munish. Oh, they were laughing it up like two old friends. Meanwhile, I sat there in the mall's food court with three garbage bags full of clothes that smelled like piss. Of course the police and another social worker had to get in on the whole thing and interview Hazel before I could gain custody again. Whatever Hazel said convinced them that I wasn't an axe murderer, and she was allowed to come home. That was a long, silent ride, let me tell you. Once she lost her audience in Munish, Hazel was quiet as a mouse. I asked her if she was going to apologize. She said nothing. I didn't press the point, because I was so angry I was afraid of what I might say if I did start talking; so I just turned up the radio. She didn't even complain about my choice of station, and I know how much she hates country.

We had another interview with Janice at the house. She suggested I keep the therapy sessions with Dr. Shannon going. She also encouraged me to let Hazel know how much she means to me. Right now, let me tell you, all I want to do is throw my golf clubs in the back of the car and take off to BC and find myself a lakeside cottage and a cold beer.

That evening though, at supper, about halfway through, I noticed Hazel was chewing with her mouth closed. This was partly due to the fact that she wasn't talking to me, but still, I think effort was made. She also, halfway through dinner, remembered to put her napkin on her lap. Then, and let me tell you, I nearly fell over, she cleared her plate and mine without having to be asked and set them in the dishwasher. She didn't scrape them properly, but it wasn't the evening to criticize. I was still very angry, but this softened me up to see what was perhaps a bit of remorse.

I asked her to sit down at the table, and she did. She looked frightened. I realized I'd never seen her frightened before, not of me anyway. This softened me again, so I tried out what Janice had recommended.

"Hazel, you look scared."

"Because you're super angry at me."

"Yes, I am. Why, do you think?"

"Because I peed on jackets and you had to pay for them. I will get a job and I will pay you back, Herman."

"You're calling me Herman now?"

"Well, you're not my real grandpa."

"This feels pretty real to me."

"I shouldn't expect you to be my grandpa when you're just Herman and you shouldn't have to take care of me if you don't want to."

"Who says I don't want to?"

"I can tell."

"Well it isn't easy. You haven't made it easy on me, Hazel." At this point the little pup hung her head, and I felt bad for saying it. "But it doesn't mean I don't want to take care of you. Sometimes the hardest things are the best things for you. Like math class. Or eating your vegetables. Or reading a difficult book. Taking care of a child is not an easy thing, especially if you're an old fart like me in your late sixties and don't know what the hell you're doing half the time." I made her snort when I said *fart*. "And yes, I'm angry and frustrated, Hazel. But mostly I'm scared."

"Why are you scared?"

"Well ... honey, I'm scared I might be doing this wrong."

"Doing what wrong?"

"Taking care of you."

"Grumpy, you are the best taker-carer there is. It's me. I'm stupid and horrible. No wonder Mom left."

"Little pup, you are not stupid, and you are not horrible. You are clever. Nobody is like you. So many people wish they were unique, and you can't help yourself. You are so creative, Hazel. And I think you're pretty strong. On the inside and the outside. You will find your way. You will. Your mom left. She did. I won't pretend she didn't."

"I don't want to talk about it."

"That makes two of us. But it wasn't your fault. And yes, you did use your smarts to do a bad thing, but I know it's because you're upset that I lied to you about your mom. And I'm sorry. I just didn't know how to tell you the truth. If you want to call me Herman, well, I am not going to stop you. If you don't think I'm your grandpa, that's your decision. But I'll tell you this much, Hazel. You are my grandchild, and you always will be. And you are one of the best things that's ever happened to me."

I don't think I actually realized all this until I said it out loud. I rather surprised myself at how emotional this made me. I guess I was also tired, it had been a stressful day. But after I said those words, Hazel decided to forgive me. She came over to the back of my chair and wrapped her arms around my neck and stood there and cried, kind of hugging the chair and me at the same time. And then, as a joke I guess, to break the ice, I started singing an old Hank Williams we heard in the car, in a country twang that Hazel hates, but it made her laugh.

> Did you ever see a robin weep
> When leaves began to die?
> Like me, he's lost the will to live
> I'm so lonesome, I could cry
>
> The silence of a falling star
> Lights up a purple sky
> And as I wonder where you are
> I'm so lonesome, I could cry

Sometimes you have to decide who you want as your family and I have decided that I want Herman to be my grumpy. I don't know yet if I decide I want my mom to be my mom. Right now she can go suck an egg. I think that is such a funny expression – who sucks an egg? But Grumpy said it once and it made me laugh so now I say it.

I met this lady, Janice, and she was pretty nice, but she was even nosier than Dr. Shannon, who is another person I have decided is not my family. She can go suck an egg because she never called me once since not seeing me. Janice asked me about why I scratch myself on my leg and I said I didn't know and she was okay that I didn't know. She just said kids do that sometimes when they are in distress. I like that word, *distress*. When I think of being in distress, I think of being in a dress that is all raggedy and torn like Cinderella and it's kind of wrecked but kind of beautiful too because sometimes holes in dresses on the bottom and on the sleeve can make skin peek through and then it's kind of mysterious and shows you the person underneath. Kind of swoopy. I like that. Like the raggedy clothes are leaves and you are the tree. Then birds might sit on your shoulder. I think that's why birdies liked Cinderella.

Janice asked me a lot of questions about Grumpy, questions that made me uncomfortable, like questions about the bath. Like, of course I take a bath by myself, what am I, a baby?! It was kind of weird. But the more I told her how good he was, the more she wondered if I was saying those things just to be nice or because I was scared. But I talked and talked and proved that even though Grumpy can be stubborn and say "Lan sakes" and have a million rules and, well, how can I say this nice? Even though he is so old-fashioned, he is good. If I closed my eyes and tried to think of a picture that would be safe, it would be Grumpy. Grumpy sitting at the table with his blue shirt. Maybe with his cup of coffee. He is safest after he has had a cup of coffee. Then you can talk. If he has not had his coffee, it is better to be in a different part of the house. He is a good teacher and I am learning. I can read now, a little bit, and that isn't because of school, which will never be my family, but because of Grumpy. He knows I can do things. He says I'm clever. Nobody said that ever before. And sometimes he makes me laugh. Janice liked to hear about that. Like when Grumpy crosses his eyes and makes a silly face he calls his Mildred Machinbosch face. I don't know why.

And besides, Janice saw our house. She saw how clean he makes it and the broccoli in the fridge and she really liked the chores with the gold stars on the corkboard that Grumpy made. She liked it that we were all done *The Hobbit* and now were on book three of Harry Potter. She liked it that my mom made a quilt and an apron and that she was going to write me postcards when she was biking. I told her I was not holding my breath for that and Mom can suck an egg. Janice did not tell me to be a nicer daughter. She just nodded like it was okay that I was mad, so Janice is fine to me. She shook Grumpy's hand. But I am learning now. She doesn't care about me, she is just doing her job. But I would say that she did her job pretty good and then she left.

I am glad I ran away. Because now I know I can do it and I can do it again if I need to. I asked Grumpy to tell me about my mom, the whole truth, because I can take it. And anything he knew about my dad. Grumpy told me the hardest thing first. He told me my dad was dead. That didn't make me sad like crying but sad like tired. Really disappointed. What is the point? I can't ever see him now. When he told me that, I went to bed and didn't want to talk about it.

But the next day I did want to talk about it. Grumpy brought out the photo album and he found one little teensy tiny picture of Mom and Ivan in the middle of a bunch of kids that looked like a sports team and I knew it right away when I saw the face: that was my dad! His name was Ivan Vidal. Isn't that the coolest name? Having a *V* in your name is as good as having a Z or an X.

I look so much like him. He was really handsome and young and smiling. His arms had muscles. Mom was very young too, like a teenager. And she was so fit and strong. I didn't even know it was her except when I looked really close I could see it was her eyes. Grumpy is right, I have long legs like her. Her knees are like my knees. They are not pokey, they are like pug dog faces. That's what I think anyway. My knees look like pugs. So funny! If I wiggle them I can pretend that they're talking to each other. Grr … woof woof! Anyway, Mom was really beautiful in a way that she sort of looked like a boy and sort of like a girl. Do you know what I mean? She was not pretty. She was better than just pretty. She was interesting. And so serious. She was not smiling in the picture. She was thinking of running. She was thinking of winning. You could tell. Like if I could make a bet, I would bet she would win. And she did, says Grumpy. She was the best runner in all of Alberta out of the girls. Alberta is our province and it includes Calgary and Edmonton and they are way bigger cities than Red Deer!

Grumpy said Ivan was a mixed-up person and he doesn't know anything about him except that Ivan and Mom used to do sports. And then when they were older, they saw each other again and "got together," which is Grumpy's polite way of saying they put their penis and vagina together, and oops, they made a baby: me. Now, I'm not a little kid anymore. I know that babies can come sometimes when you are not married and you don't have to be married and you don't even have to be a boy and a girl, there can be two dads and two moms. But I do know that you only stay together if it doesn't hurt, and Ivan hurt my mom's feelings and maybe she hurt his and, anyway, Mom told Ivan to bugger off. Grumpy said "bugger off," and then he said sorry, and that I shouldn't repeat it because it's vulgar. We should instead say Mom told Ivan to go away and not come back. But I think *bugger off* is the perfect word to say to someone if they're bugging you and you want them off off off like a mosquito! "Get off! You bug!"

He said he didn't know if Ivan knew I was born. He also said that Mom felt Ivan would not be a good dad so she didn't tell him about me or me about him to protect me from having a dad who didn't care. This makes me mad because it didn't give my dad a chance to care because he didn't even know. Maybe if he saw me when I was a baby he would have cared because I was very cute. I had really chubby cheeks and hair that stuck straight up like a dandelion. Maybe if he knew he had a baby that cute he would have decided to be a nicer person and not be such a bugger. Maybe if he knew he made such a cute baby he would not have been so mixed up. But Grumpy thinks Mom did the right thing. Grumpy thinks that Ivan might have tried to steal me as a baby or hurt me.

This freaked me out big time. What kind of guy was Ivan? It started to make me think deep inside myself of when I am bad and just want to, you know, like, punch a boy at school or yell a swear word at a family when I see them together in the mall spending money on the best of all running shoes, or when I see a perfectly innocent little worm on the road and jump on it with all my might to squish its guts. I did that once and I can't stop thinking of that little worm. Poor little guy. Why did I do that? The worm was just trying to crawl to the grass. Why didn't I put him in the grass? He never did anything to me. I have cried for that worm lots. It's one of the things that makes me cry the most.

Maybe I am like my dad. Maybe I am the kind of person who would hurt babies. You see how this freaks me out? I am scared of my very self. I went to look into the mirror, right into my eyes and I asked my eyeballs very seriously, "What is the worst thing you would ever do to a baby?" And it freaked me out because ... because I right away could think of lots of terrible things to do to a baby. It would be so easy because it's just a baby. Like, I could stomp on it, like a ... Horrible horrible horrible! Why did I think that so easy? But just because I thought it, doesn't mean I'd do it, does it? But then I couldn't stop thinking it: stomping on the baby! The little fingers, the little tummy. Horrible horrible horrible! What if that is me?! The thinking in my head! I started to hit my head over and over and Grumpy caught me doing that and grabbed my arms to stop me and I kicked him by accident, and he said, "What child, what?"

I didn't tell him all of my thinking, but I said, "What if I'm scary, like my dad?"

And Grumpy said, "What did you learn about DNA? What can you get from your dad's DNA?"

"I don't know."

"Tell me what you remember. Tell me what you think you got from him."

"I think I got my hair colour. Maybe my teeth. The shape."

"That's right. And do you have any choice over that? Or were you born with those things?"

"I was born with them."

"And how to speak English, and how to walk, and how to learn a knock-knock joke – were you born with this in your DNA, or did you learn it?"

"I learned it."

"And the other day, when Janice was here, you told her you liked her pretty pink scarf. Did your DNA make you say that nice thing, or did you choose to say that nice thing?"

"I chose."

"That's right. DNA chooses your body; science will tell you that. But you choose your heart. Ivan had a perfectly healthy body and a sharp mind. He had very good DNA. That's the gift he gave you. You can feel good about your DNA."

"But Grumpy ..."

"Your heart has nothing to do with his heart. You are a brand-new person."

"But I can think horrible things."

"So can I."

"Oh, like what? What is the worst thing you can think of to do to a baby?"

"I could stick it in the garburator."

When Grumpy said that, he said it so quickly, I couldn't believe it! Then we both laughed and laughed and laughed!

And it made me feel better because Grumpy could have terrible thoughts in his head too but there's no way on this whole planet Grumpy would ever ever stick a baby in a garburator.

Grumpy said Mom could have aborted me. I didn't know what that meant. But then Grumpy explained Mom could have had me sucked out of her body with a vacuum cleaner and nobody would blame her for doing so. Between you and me I think Grumpy maybe has that wrong. I was wondering why he thought that would cheer me up. But the point is, according to Grumpy, Mom didn't have to keep me. She *decided* to keep me. She decided to grow me in her tummy. But she was scared to be a mom and didn't know how to do it. He said that her mom died, my nonna Nunzia, so she didn't even have a mom to show her how to be a mom and ask her questions. And she said that Ivan broke her heart, even though she never loved him, he broke her heart. I don't know how that works but it made me feel sorry for her. No excuses, but still. She did look pretty little in that picture with her pug knees.

I asked to have that picture of my mom and Ivan, and Grumpy made a copy of it on his computer and then gave it to me. I have the photo by my bed now. My weird mom and dad. I know I don't know him, but I feel like I know him. He has my square head. He has the same colour of hair. He has my teeth. I think if he had a chance to know me, he could choose to be better. I wish he wasn't dead.

Charlotta stares down the hurricane of the beloved. Being seen and being known, he releases his muscular grip on the dark thread that holds the underside of his humanity together.

Can you let go of the thread, Ivan?

He nods, asking for release, and so We rip it out of him, like filleting the spine from a fish. The hurricane collapses. The beloved hovers in scattered spirals over the field while Charlotta watches. Waits. Then she breathes. She knows she has been part of something holy, but she has no way of knowing what. She raises her plump warm hands to the sky and cries out:

"That's it, child, let it all go."

This flattens the beloved. He lies in a prickly cotton field beside the river; the smell of peanuts wafts through the air. He listens to the cars and trucks pull off from the highway. The banter of customers with Charlotta, the familiarity of the regulars. The crinkle of paper cups. The call of crows. The buzz of bees. The swoosh of pompous grass. Charlotta vocalizes her pain between customers, the arthritis in her knees. She sets herself down on a three-legged stool and huffs and puffs and sips sweet tea.

The Beloved lies there until nightfall, long after Charlotta has locked up her roadside stand and walked her tired feet home. Long after the dampness has settled on the white puffs of cotton all around him.

He stares up at the stars, longingly. "I'm never going to be a human again, am I?"

No.

"There are limits to grace."

There is no grace without limits.

"That's fair."

It's not about fair.

The beloved sighs. There are times We wish We did not have all the answers.

"So, this time I've spent with you. The animals, the stars, the sand, the hurricane, the bottom of the sea ... Is this a vision, or has it been real? Has this all been a reincarnation, Judgment Day thing, or has it just been my life-flashing-before-me as my psyche dies?"

Would it matter one way or the other?

"I suppose not."

Is there anything more real than the transformation of a soul?

"You answer me with questions; you know that's annoying."

If We gave you all the answers, you would also find this annoying.

"I like it that You're not a man. Or a woman. Both are complicated for me. I like it that You're ... You. Around You I feel ... clean. Like soap and sunshine. Clear water. The way a baby will stare at its own hand in wonder. A hot, blue sky."

Yes. And smooth stone. And song. A sprouted seed. The love between.

"You know what I really miss about being a human? That feeling of having just brushed my teeth. Or stepping onto a dock by the lake, the warm wood under my bare feet. A good sneeze. The satisfaction of shuffling a deck of cards. The complicated taste of black liquorice. Shifting a car into sixth gear. The crack of a ball against a baseball bat. Starting a campfire with a single match. My granny, Camila, the way her lipstick threads up through wrinkles, the way she laughs. The efficiency of a ten-minute nap. Singing, even though I am not a singer. Watching LeBron James do a two-handed dunk. Christmas lights. Times, dates, to-do lists. The smell of waffles. Holding a baby duck."

PART III

CHAPTER EIGHT

ELEVATION

— *Graziana* —

RUBBIANO DI SOLIGNANO, EMILIA-ROMAGNA

I started the day looping back to view the thirteenth-century abbey of Chiaravalle della Columba, near Alseno, and its exquisite line of rose-marble columns. (Thank you, Herman.) Near it, there was a courtyard full of modern marble statues, dated 2010, that seemed like they were perhaps a protest against war. There was one in particular that honoured world Indigenous populations. Or least, that's what I understood with my feeble amount of Italian. The statue was of a man wearing a cloak covered in many generations of his people. He carried them with pride. They protected him.

I didn't even know who my people were. This trip that Herman designed is supposed to end with me going to my mother's village, where apparently I still have relatives. I haven't decided whether I have the courage to show up or not.

I rolled away from the man standing proud with his blanket of peeping peeps and headed back onto the Cammino through farmers' fields. The frilly apple blossoms were out, like little girls lining up at the altar for their Sacrament of First Communion. Feral farm cats squinted at me from their crumbling perches.

I looked down at my legs. I was starting to recognize them again. They had some muscle now, definition in the calf. I felt far more steady on my feet. Before, I was an unsettling combination of heavy and breakable all at once: cinderblocks balanced on teacups. I knew if I ever fell, I'd smash myself to smithereens and there would be nobody capable of picking me up. I vowed to never return to that place of dangerous neglect.

The things I said to myself I would not say to my worst enemy, the body shaming I did to myself in front of Hazel all her life. Not only did I call myself a walrus, I saw one. I saw one in the mirror. There was no grace, there was no kindness, there was no care. What a horrible example to pass on to a daughter. I've taught Hazel nothing about the value of exercise, nothing about the need for a healthy, well-balanced diet, nothing about self-care. Yeah. I wasn't the mom to have a spa night with my kid. There was never any painting of toenails. I couldn't even reach my toenails.

My mother was a curvaceous, beautiful woman who always did herself up. Nunzia dressed modestly, no cleavage, skirts no higher than the knee, but her clothes did not, could not, mask her large breasts and plump bottom. She was unapologetic about wearing sleeveless blouses and pencil skirts and sporting a bright yellow or hot red or deep purple when she pleased. Her comfort with her own skin was the key to her sensuality. I knew, even as a young child, that men were excited by her, even though she gave them no particular invitation. Who wouldn't want to tuck into a warm, soft woman like that? She was equally confident with or without lipstick. She always tailored her shirts and always combed her hair until it was shiny. She put in her Jane Fonda workout VHS three times a week and wore her one pair of shorts, a green terry cloth ribbed with white I was sure she bought in the seventies. She knew how to make a garment last. I grew up knowing how to press a collar, how to fold a fitted sheet, and how to choose the freshest produce and the ripest melons. She taught me how to sear the juices into a chicken and how to simmer a succulent sugo. I've passed none of this on to Hazel.

I always thought my neglect was about Ivan, but now that I think about it, it's sure starting to sound like it's a lot about Mom. Was I mad because she left this world right at the time I needed her most? She was only fifty. Was I ashamed because

I emotionally checked out the last months of her life? Perhaps I stopped doing anything that reminded me of her because I did not have the capacity to grieve. But everything reminded me of her, so I became inert.

Blinded by tears, I had to get off my bike and stand in the middle of a field. I tapped my chest while my CUBE leaned against me with affection, like an old dog. I patted it all the same. Now that I was off my bike, I noticed heavy clouds from the north cycling in faster than me. By the time I got my feet back on the pedals, I felt the first drops of rain. Within no time, I was being pelted and realized the difference between buying a rain-resistant jacket and a rainproof one.

Pump, pump, up the hill! I am going to teach Hazel how to cook. Pump, pump! I am going to keep the house clean. Pump, pump! I am going to buy a bathing suit. I am going to sign up for mother–daughter activities at the community centre. I am going to get a freaking job! I am going to be a big, beautiful, healthy woman like my mom.

Another lean, mean, focused female cyclist passed me. Shortly after, I came blasting around the corner, out from under a drippy wood, and had to quickly swerve out of the way for two pilgrims on foot. They had huge backpacks on, and when I saw their faces underneath their rain hoods, I was surprised to see they were at least in their seventies. They resembled waddling ducks, splashing along in their oversized yellow slickers.

"Buon Cammino!" I wished them. They smiled and wished me goodness back with a wave of their walking sticks.

I made a quick stop in Medesano for a double espresso and then headed back out into the rain. After some huffing and puffing, I thought, "Who am I reporting my progress to? What am I here to achieve?" So I got off and pushed my bike. And it was then that I could listen. I heard the wild pheasant, the swish of grass between my sneakers, the satisfying crunch of gravel under my tires. I saw lilac and wild poppies and one flowering tree left at the top of a hill tilled for crops. The Great Good is in the walk, not the run.

I headed along the Taro River and stopped in the small town of Ramiola for a green apple. On my way over the bridge to Rubbiano, I entered an industrial area and smelled pasta. I thought I was losing my mind until I noticed a sign on the side of a factory: Stabilimento Sughi Barilla. Aha!

I soon came upon a quiet little village by the river and my gorgeous B & B. Herman had said this would be my fanciest stop due to the lack of choices along this leg of the journey. The laneway leading to the house was laid with two kinds of stone. The air smelled of lavender, and I could hear children laughing and the river rolling. The home was a freshly renovated stone building with a beautiful climbing rose rubbing its shoulders along the side. I felt intimidated ringing the doorbell while I was covered in mud, standing there like an abomination on the tidy front porch with its perfectly potted sage.

The hostess answered; her name was Tania. She had caramel-coloured hair swept up in an effortlessly gorgeous twist. Her eyes widened when she saw how wet I was and that I was on a bicycle, travelling alone. She led me into my separate suite. If I understood correctly, it was originally a stable that they converted into a guest home. Inside was all post and beam, with high ceilings and plaster walls, beautiful wrought ironwork around the large windows, billowy curtains, soft duvet, and fluffy towels.

I asked Tania if she could recommend a restaurant or grocery store that was close by. She spoke in excellent English, "Oh no, it's better if you eat with us. Too far in this rain. I will cook, but it will be simple."

How many people would offer to take in a stranger for dinner? Once I cleaned up and put on long pants and a sweater, I knocked on the immaculate front door again. I was invited up the stairs to their happy dining area, a fireplace to the left, a table surrounded by children to the right. Her husband, Pier, a thoughtful, handsome man, welcomed me in, warmly. The eldest boy, Marcello, a blond, well-mannered young fellow, poured me a glass of Lambrusco. Apparently, he swims. That much I understood. And then his sister, Marghe, whom I understood did gymnastics, offered me a plate of Parma ham with chunks of two-year-old locally made Parmesan. Oh, what a treat to be in the province of Parma!

Everything was so fresh and authentic, it exploded with flavour in my mouth. The other two children, Robby and Federico, two younger, dark-haired Bacchus cherubs, were plopping the bites of cheese into their mouths absent-mindedly, like it was popcorn. Didn't they realize they were munching some of the finest cheese on the planet? No. They had never had a block of North American rubbery bullshit mild-orange-dyed cheese product in their lives. Bless them and their gastronomic purity!

Then Tania served a perfect pasta, followed by tender eggs poached in cheesecloth, sautéed broccoli rabe, and salad. The dessert was fresh strawberries over gelato. Tania and Pier spoke English fluently, but the children only knew a word or two. I tried to say the few Italian words I knew, "Mmm ... fragole, grazie!" For their sake. I noted one of the cherubs had a Star Wars shirt, so I did my best Chewbacca. Somehow, we got onto the topic of pronouncing the Italian word for "cherry," *ciliegia*. Chee-lee-EY-ja! The kids coached me over and over and laughed every time my stiff Canadian tongue got the vowels muddled.

Tania runs a bar in Fornovo di Taro and runs this B & B – with four children. Pier sells mechanical parts, from what I understand, and travels with his work. How these two do all of this and still manage to sit around the table for a family meal is beyond me. It was interesting to learn that children start college in Italy at the age of fourteen, which means the parents often choose for the child what direction their career will take, what they will specialize in. I'm in my thirties and I still haven't figured that one out.

At some point in the conversation, I learned that Pier was a widower, and the two younger boys were from his first marriage and the two older children were from Tania's. Their little blended family seemed so cohesive that I could have sworn they had always been together. Pier spoke of his first wife with great sadness, telling me she died within a few days of giving birth to their youngest. She started bleeding and it couldn't be stopped. Within fifteen minutes she was gone.

He said, "It was h-rr-kin."

"Pardon?"

"It was h-rr-bk ..."

"Sorry?"

Then he said it loudly with grating clarity: "IT WAS HEART-BREAKING."

Oh my God.

How terrible I felt for asking him to repeat that.

Later, Tania, sighed and said softly, "It's a long story."

I'm sure it is.

But what a gift for me to see how these six people found each other after such a tragedy and came together to form a new family. It planted a tiny mustard seed of hope in me. But at the same time, it illuminated my emptiness. I couldn't get to sleep until four in the morning. I kept thinking of those boys popping Parmesan in contrast to Hazel eating cereal out of a box. I'd roll over in bed and felt Ivan's hands tugging at my breasts. No, it's just the sheets. Will every evening be warped by him?

The next day it thundered and rained so heavily that there was no safe way for me to cycle to Berceto, so I stayed another night and recalibrated Herman's itinerary. I had a quiet, healing day in my suite. I was able to keep the darkness at bay, mostly. Tania invited me up for dinner again. The antipasto this time was a white, soft substance I thought was a soft cheese. Nope. It was lardo. I took a modest portion of the deadly deliciousness, thinking about how hard I had worked to remove the lardo from my arteries. It was followed with a delicious and delicate risotto and salad. I not only had my best two nights in Italy with this family, but two of the best nights of my life. When I offered them money for the meals, they laughed me off and kissed me goodnight.

I headed back to my suite and lay in the comfortable bed with the best mattress since ... ever. Was it peace or was it Lambrusco combined with my medication? All I said to the Great Good was a simple thank-you before falling asleep. Oh, and I made two promises. The first: to start having proper dinner at the table with Hazel and invite people over. The second: to never ever again in my life buy shitty cheese.

— *Herman* —

We have replaced Dr. Shannon with a Dr. Cheryl Ching. We haven't met her in person yet, but I liked her no-nonsense approach on the phone. Dr. Ching has dogs on her website page, and I figure anyone who owns dogs has to be somewhat down to earth and connected to reality. One of the dogs is a Labrador puppy, which gave me the confidence that Dr. Ching could handle a Hazel. She's in great demand, but she'll be able to squeeze Hazel in for an appointment in two weeks. That said, lately I've been less worried about Hazel than I ever have been. We seem to be getting along well, and she has a renewed interest in school. It also helps a great heap that the weather is getting warmer and she can get outside and play at the park without it being a big slop pile of mud.

We should be getting one of Grazie's postcards soon, I suspect, though how long it takes for a postcard to get from Italy to Red Deer, goodness knows. To my great surprise, we got a different kind of letter this week. It was addressed to "Graziana Fidler or Whom It May Concern," and it was from a Ms. Camila Vidal. I don't usually open other people's mail ... but for Hazel's sake, I decided to see what connection Camila was to Ivan. I could tell from her legible handwritten letter that she was from my generation or older.

Apparently, Camila is Ivan's grandmother. He had been living with her in San Francisco. It was her car that he stole. He drove it all the way to Alberta, crashing it in Rocky Mountain House. She was devastated by his death. She said it took her a long time to work up the courage to go through his things and pack up his room. When she did, she found a file folder about Grazie. It had some newspaper clippings about her track-and-field wins, a blue ribbon, and her high-school graduation photo. It also had a business card of her bike shop, what Camila presumed was a lock of her hair, and another "personal item."

At the bottom of the pile was a photograph of a child in a playground. Camila felt this child looked a great deal like Ivan and wondered if indeed she had a great-grandchild. She did not wish to impose, as it seemed obvious Ivan was not involved in this child's life, but she wanted Graziana to know that Hazel was her only living relative left and she'd love to meet. Camila had a few family heirlooms she wished to pass on if that was of interest. She invited Grazie and Hazel to come visit her in San Francisco.

I decided "no more secrets" with Hazel, so I let her know she had a great-grandmother out there, and I read the letter with her, as cursive writing is still a challenge. Well, I don't think I've ever seen a child as excited as Hazel that day. You'd think I had told her she had a fairy godmother. I warned her that Camila could be cranky or crazy or goodness knows.

"Don't get fancy ideas in your head, child."

But there was no going back now. Hazel was bound and determined that we would take up Camila's offer, jump in the car, and go to San Francisco to meet her. Of course, that wasn't going to happen; I flat out shot down that dream. There was no getting Hazel over the border on such short notice.

That said, I have always enjoyed road trips. Many a time, when Grazie was little, we would drive out to Kelowna in a motorhome. My brother Dave lives there with his wife, Cathy. Good folk. We'd come back home with crates of peaches and tomatoes and cherries that Nunzia would start blanching and peeling, her big pressure canner hissing away on the stove. She had an old checkered red apron she wore on such occasions; it was the kind that tied around her neck. She called it her "Nonna apron."

Sometimes we'd leave young Grazie in Kelowna; she got on with Dave and Cathy's girl, Meghan. And we'd go as far as Vancouver to visit Nunzia's younger cousin, Marco. It was about twelve hours behind the wheel. Marco was a real flamboyant character who owned a hair salon. If you're thinking what I think you're thinking, you're right. Marco and Nunzia always got along. The "bad apples," Nunzia would say. They had both moved to Canada on account of their indiscretions, escaping the judgment of the old country. I liked Marco well enough, but it was the only time I'd see Nunzia smoke and get drunk. I didn't like it. I don't do it. I'd leave them to it, laughing over their bottle of wine and cigarette pack at the dinner table. Sometimes they'd go out dancing. Not that I was worried about her getting hit on or anything, considering the clubs they went to, if you get my drift.

I was touched that Marco flew out for her funeral. He came wearing an off-white linen suit that somehow magically never got wrinkled. I still, to this day, do not know how he managed that. Nunzia purchased me one pair of navy-blue linen pants in the eighties, and I never wore them because by midday it looked like I had slept in them. Anyway, Marco brought the biggest bouquet of flowers I'd ever seen in my life. Lots of those pokey orangey-red things: birds of paradise. He said he figured that's what she was now. He cried like a baby.

I remember thinking, "I wish I could do that." But I'd be ashamed of myself. I've never been one to show much emotion. And I just hate when people gather all around you and say, "I'm so sorry." What are you sorry for? You didn't give her cancer. Arguably, I did. I did not want children, and she was on the pill for twenty years. And besides, when you're the one arranging the funeral, there's too much to manage. Half the time I'm not sure what I feel, or I'll feel it three days later. Part of being a paramedic for so long, I figure. You cultivate a delayed reaction to trauma. And then you dissect the logic of it, the experience of it, like any other call. Except sometimes the call is your life. And you're the one in the back of the ambulance and the one behind the wheel and the one left like human jam on the side of the road, all at once. Is that what they mean by going to pieces? Nunzia's funeral – I was too chopped-up to cry. I barely even remember it. Mostly I remember wishing everyone would just get the hell out of there so I could go home.

Maybe it's time to reconnect with those folks in BC. Hazel's never even met any of them. That night, we called up this

Camila. Apparently, Vidal is pronounced "vee-DAL." Meaning "life." She seemed sort of defensive about the fact that her dad was Mexican. She mentioned three times that her mother was Dutch. What's wrong with being Mexican? Nunzia and I went to Mexico on our honeymoon and had a wonderful time. Real nice folk. We stayed with the locals too, not at a resort. Nunzia worked with an accomplished dentist, Yolanda, and they stayed close friends. We all went down to visit Yolanda's parents' place way down in Huatulco.

Note: Take Hazel to see the butterfly sanctuary if it is still there.

Yolanda's parents only spoke Spanish, which was okay for Nunzia because Italian is close enough to get the gist of what they were saying, but I was left largely out of the conversations. All I had to do really was nod and drink beer. Best vacation of my life.

Back to Camila. She didn't talk about being Mexican, she went on and on about being Dutch and long-time American. But she looks Mexican. You'd never guess Dutch. Ever notice how Americans love to tell you a couple of times just how American they are? And that up here with the polar bears in the "state" of Canada, we are living with a "socialist" government? Well excuse me, but I did not vote for Karl Marx, I vote for the Conservative Party. And no American I've ever met has heard of the War of 1812, when we burnt down the White House. Nope. I have a cousin from Milwaukee, Gary, and he always goes on about how boring Canada is. Well, if shooting up elementary schools and throwing people in jail just because they're Black is your idea of entertainment, you can damn well stay south of the border. I'll take my health care and hockey, thank you very much. Not that we're perfect here – ask anyone living on a reserve, drinking contaminated water, and being taken out for "starlight tours." Anyway, I digress. I see Hazel is wearing off on me. I go on tangents now. Ever notice that the tangents are often far more important than the original subject?

Back to the point: this Camila had a kindly voice, if not a tad uppity. She said she was seventeen when she had her daughter, Rose, and then Rose was seventeen when she had Ivan. Camila lived in San Francisco all her life. I could tell she was very moved to hear Hazel's voice on the phone, and to my relief, she simply laughed when Hazel went on and on instead of getting all annoyed with her wild tangents and fanciful stories. She called Hazel imaginative and vivacious. Hazel liked the sound of that.

Camila sweet-talked Hazel like mad. She said if we came to visit, she'd show her the Golden Gate Bridge, and we'd take a cable car to the pier to see the aquarium and have an ice cream and go to the theatre. Then she talked about Disneyland only being a couple of hours away. Hold your horses, lady. She's been planning this trip half her life from the sounds of it. She said Hazel could stay in Ivan's room and she had a guest suite for me. It all sounded rather exhausting and expensive. Also I explained to Camila that Hazel did not have a passport, and I'd need to get Graziana's permission to bring her over the border, even though I had applied for legal guardianship last year.

We agreed to meet up in Vancouver. Money didn't seem like much of an object for Camila, and she had been there before for Expo 86. Camila would fly in and Hazel and I would drive, and I suggested we could both stay at the Sylvia Hotel near Stanley Park. I chose it because it seemed fancy enough for Camila. It had an ocean view, was a reasonable price, and I could avoid driving downtown. If I take Highway 1 over the Lions Gate Bridge, I just have to take Denman up to Pacific. I hate driving in the city, but this seemed palatable.

Graziana was scheduled to arrive home from Italy in about two weeks' time, so we really had to get this done as soon as possible. Camila was game. Dave and Cathy are still in Kelowna, and they're glad to have us stop in. I even managed to track down Marco, and he got all blubbery on the phone that I even thought to call him. He's excited to meet Hazel. It's hard for me to believe, but it looks like we're taking our own kind of pilgrimage.

I would say that my whole life was pretty much craptacular until yesterday, when my great-grandmother wrote a letter and then called. And now we're going to go on a road trip to Vancouver to see the ocean! I have never ever in my whole life seen the ocean! I want to swim like a mermaid but Grumpy says the water is super-duper cold and I'd get hyper-thermos. But guess what? Halfway, we are going to stop in a place called Kelowna, which is by some real big lakes in the mountains and it's really pretty and I have an auntie and uncle there. Grumpy says it gets hot in Kelowna and I could maybe go in the water there, so I should pack a bathing suit.

Yeah, just in one day, suddenly, I have all these family people! I was going to say "not my real auntie and uncle" because it's Grumpy's family, but I've decided that Grumpy's family is my family, and they don't seem to mind, so I now have an uncle and an aunt and they have a big yard with cherry trees and apple trees and peach trees and pear trees and raspberries. And a golden retriever. Holy moly, can you imagine having a whole grocery store in your front yard? I'd be like plop plop plop, yum yum yum, m-rg-mouth-is-full-erv cherriezzz! Hrrr yummm! I like dogs. I wanna dog. I already know that this dog, whose name is Oola, is going to love playing with me. I already know that I am going to have a blanket and Oola is going to be my pillow.

And then, get this, we will go to Vancouver and guess what? My mom has a cousin there. Well, it was her mom's cousin and I don't know what that means for me except that I guess he's my old old cousin. His name is Marco. Grumpy says Marco is not going to like me calling him my old old cousin and to just call him *zio* Marco. It's kind of weird to call a total stranger "zio" (which is "uncle" in Italian) Marco. Maybe I'll just call him "Hey." But I think it is cool that I'm going to meet a real Italian because that is part of my DNA. And besides, Grumpy says zio Marco is a really good cook and very handsome and charming.

I said, as a joke, "Grumpy, does that mean zio Marco is like a prince?"

And he said right away, "Zio Marco is princely."

I've never seen anyone princely before. I wonder if that means he wears a lot of gold or he has horses or he waves like THIS when he gets out of his car?

And we have to go on our Vancouver trip right away because Grumpy says my mom is going to be back from Italy in two and a half weeks! And we need to be home when she gets back. When I think of this, of Mom coming home, of seeing her ... it's like my brain is a banana. It goes all mushy and yellow and squirts out sideways – blah. It's like when I think of my mom, I blink a lot with my eyes. Blink blink blinkedy blink. I've been wondering if I'm going to hug her and there's no way I'm going to. Not that I'm mean but she has to learn that you can't just hug a kid if you're going to leave your own girl for a year. Phone calls and presents don't really count. Like I said, Mom can suck an egg.

Grumpy says that he will move out of her room so that she can have her room back and he will go back to his condo down the street. But I think too bad, it's Grumpy's room now. Who is going to make me breakfast and do math? (We always do math first while our mind is fresh, says Grumpy.) Mom can go live somewhere else. Mom can live in the stupid condo of Grumpy's where she kept her stupid bike. Or she can just keep cycling all the way to Australia! Good luck crossing the ocean, dumb Mom! You can't just leave a house and then think it's yours when you come back.

Oh, oh, oh! I have to tell you about my great-grandmother, and by the way, she's a real great-grandmother because she was my dad's grandmother and that makes her great. And you know what? She *sounds* great! She sounds super-duper nice and she must be rich because she lives near Disneyland. And I think everybody who lives in California is a movie star or famous or at least really rich. And I know Americans have guns. I asked my great-grandmother if she was going to bring a gun and she said no. She would leave it at home. (Which means my great-grandmother HAS A GUN!) This may sound cool to boys at my school, or something like that, but if you think about it, it's really freaking weird and also scary that such an old lady has a gun because, for one, old ladies don't see very well.

She is going to take an airplane to Vancouver, and we are going to drive and meet her there. I've never in my whole life had someone that wanted to meet me before. Mostly people meet me and then they wish they didn't. Because I am a "handful," Grumpy says. And I always think that's weird because a handful isn't much. It can curl up, like a tiny pet, like a hedgehog, and you can have it in your hand or carry it in your pocket. To me, a handful sounds super easy and very cute, but I know that's not what he means. When I go see Uncle Eddie and Auntie Connie and all the cousins there, they are used to being around handfuls so they think I fit right in.

I hope my great-grandmother doesn't think I'm a handful in a bad way but in a good way. Especially because she's coming on an airplane. I hope she's not disappointed. I'm glad I have my new yellow pants to wear that I got with Munish. They are impressive and they don't have holes yet. I get holes on my knees because I am always pretending and lots of times that involves being an animal. I will also have to not be a handful for Uncle David and Auntie Cathy and Zio Marco. They've never met me. The good thing about this is: as far as they know, I'm a perfectly normal girl.

We the collective Beloved never force Our Grace onto the mortal beloved. The beloved must accept it. That is the very thread that has been reckoned with. But how is it, why is it, that the beloved refuses to take the next step with Us and embrace the New? We are enough, We are Everything. We are the Great Good. We are Kin, We are the Creator! Right now We create holy exasperation, because the beloved recoils. Why?

The things you love and miss about earth and your place-ment as Ivan are all connected to Creation. You are a creator. Creation continues. There is exhilarating industry to be had. There is wonder, there is pattern and sensuality, there is learn-ing and listening, there is Creation and caretaking. If you take Our hand –

"No."

Why?

"Just – no. Not yet."

The beloved sits. We do not believe they even contemplate.

Human hesitation. What a frustrating by-product of free will. The angels and the animals, they plan, they wait, but they are never idle with hum-hodgery. There is no end to Us, but if there was, it would be caused by this unholy stall. The sneakiest of all the devil's tricks.

CHAPTER NINE

TREMBLE

— Graziana —

PONTREMOLI, TOSCANA

In order to not throw off Herman's itinerary by more than one day, I combined two biking itineraries in order to catch up. It meant I wouldn't stay over in Berceto but carry on all the way to Pontremoli. It would be seventy kilometres. I felt strong and rested: piece of cake.

It wasn't until the morning I left that I looked at the actual route. The satellite map showed a long uphill stretch of desolate road. Vast swaths of dark, green, mountainous forest stretched on either side. Few farms. Few villages. The Via Francigena threaded through the mountains in a very different direction from the highway. If the thunder came again, if I popped a tire, if I broke a leg, I'd be on my own. And, oh my … Why didn't I take note of the elevation before I made this ingenious plan? I'd be cycling a thousand metres up!

I tried to calm myself. I filled two bottles of water and fixed them to the bike. I packed up my meagre bits of clothing and rolled them into tight little sausages. Surely they wouldn't advertise this route on the app if it was dangerous? My heart started beating in my ears. I had to tap. I stopped and listened for the Great Good.

You are afraid of so much of Us. Our mountains, Our lakes, Our oceans, Our forests. What if this is the best part of the pilgrimage? What a rare opportunity to be immersed in nature and quietude. What if you get to be safe, even though you are a woman? Let Us wrap you up in Our beauty. Fear is often the first step towards Awe.

How true. When I really examined what I was afraid of, it was the power of nature. In the face of it, I was small, finite, and insignificant.

You are significant. All are significant.

I thought of Emily Carr stomping through the western coastal rainforests under drippy red cedars, moss smudged on her bum, the middle of her cigarette damp and bendy. She never died from a cougar or bear. And those forest landscapes and seaside villages she painted weren't empty. They were populated with men, women, children, all living, hunting, farming, fishing, pilgrimaging in harmony with their surroundings. What did that say about me? That I was at such discord with the natural world around me? That I must map it and control it to feel safe? Have I allowed my life to be so colonized that it suddenly felt foolish to travel alone without a man to "protect" me? Why did I assume the mountains were empty, aside from a few wild animals just waiting to devour me? Why did I think nature even cared about my presence, let alone be actively malevolent towards me?

Maybe it hasn't been the concept or even an awareness of God that I have been kicking at all along. Maybe it's the institution boasting that it holds God within: tightly shrink-wrapped. Why would I want to be a part of a club that has ravaged so many? Why wouldn't I naturally resist the four walls and the very low ceiling of the patriarchy? Of course I resent the machine that says I am lost without it. Perhaps even I had too much self-respect to obey doctrines that kept me trembling in pallid fear, knees together, eyes averted, tongue bit.

Yeah. That's some of it.

That and the three shots of espresso I drank to bolster me.

One of my favourite things about my mother was her commitment to beautifying the work of living: "l'arte dell'essere donna." I'm not sure why she felt that was specifically female, but she certainly squeezed the juice out of life, whether it was ironing Herman's shirts to perfection or stopping to smell the rain in the air. Now I had to fearlessly squeeze the juice out of the next seventy kilometres climbing up the Apennines. It would be a long day. Why not enjoy it?

Berceto from Fornovo took five hours of biking, almost entirely uphill. I dragged my steed beside me on foot most of the way, cheeks puffing red and hot. But this gave me time to notice the wild primula and lupins, the colourful shutters on the sprinkling of homes, and how they accented the old stonework so beautifully aged, highlighting subtle colours under the sun: yellows, oranges, browns, greys. The sky was open and billowy, and the view of the gentle mountains, literally breathtaking. When does one experience such quietude anymore?

The chance to stop for water or relief was rare. I was grateful to come across a quaint old two-storey stone taverna about halfway to Berceto. Often places close in the afternoon for siesta. This door was open, and I heard voices inside: delightful! There was a bar with about five tables. I ordered a panino so stale I could barely choke it down. Two elderly ladies in dresses with socks eyed me with disapproval. What kind of respectable woman wears biking shorts? I greeted them with smiles – I would be "gentile." When I asked for the bagno, the elderly sweatered bartender pointed up the creaky stairs. To my immense dismay, the toilet was a standing one. My thighs were so sore from the mountain climb already that it was hard to squat aloft. I certainly didn't want to fall backwards against a wall that had been liberally sprayed with diarrhea chunks. Imagine the velocity it would have taken to accomplish these ... *objets d'art*. One of those three people down there did this. They knew it. I knew it. They didn't care.

When I returned, I sat and sipped my water and eyed the Italian cooking show that Scontrosa and Stanca (Bitchy and Tired) were watching on a TV above their heads. One of the panellists looked alarmingly like Justin Trudeau during his unfortunate goatee years. I didn't trust his judgment. The difference between Italian cooking shows and the North American ones is that the

Italians don't focus on their performance angst or competitive gripes. They laugh, they shout at each other. Then they roll the chestnut and fennel into the pasta while telling jokes. And then everyone eats.

I had a smattering of rainfall and some stretches of dark forest ahead, but I was never alone in the woods for very long without a car ambling by or an easygoing farm sprawling alongside a clearing, like a child lying in a field, cloud busting. It wasn't the deep, dark, thick mountain wood of Revelstoke to Golden that I had in my mind. I descended down, discovering Berceto, like one might come upon a nest of house wren eggs. Comforting, tomato-coloured terracotta roofs were huddled cozily together in familial fashion. Broad tracks of cultured green curved into the foothills. I would have loved to stop there, but I had many miles ahead.

I continued pedalling up, up, up through the stunning passo della Cisa; patches of crispy snow lay in the shade around the feet of some of the trees. At one point, I had to get off my bike again and just trudge ever so slowly along. I came across a caramel-coloured snail moving about the same speed. I could see dark, broody mountains and storm clouds in the distance, and I peered down into scrubby-brown and lush green valleys. Little villages would pop up unexpectedly with careful wrought-iron fences around stone buildings and bright-red shutters complimenting the pink in the blossoms of the cherry tree in the yard. Even garages and barns had beautiful stone and brickwork with window boxes full of marigolds. I cycled up to a church called the Santuario della Madonna della Guardia. But to get up to it, you had to climb – what? Seven steep flights of stairs?! Where was the kiosk selling the whips? Because this must be the church of self-flagellation. Not going in. Nope. The Great Good I know would not do that to me today.

I continued towards the upper Magra Valley, another three hours of cycling. The pilgrim posts started to resemble stone grave markers with a ceramic pilgrim stamped in the middle. The landscape was Mona Lisa mysterious and moody.

By the time I hit Pontremoli, I was shaking with exhaustion and cold. Pontremoli means "the trembling bridge." We trembled together. The Magra River runs white under several crescent-shaped bridges. The skyline is dominated by the light blue duomo of the Santa Maria Assunta basilica. The city is studded with stately buildings of past nobles: the Houses of Malaspina and Dosi. Overlooking the water are colourful pink and yellow palazzi with turquoise shutters and balconies. Foothills lie around the valley, far enough away to look fuzzy, like old guard dogs snoozing as the sun sets over them.

I hobbled over the bridge and into the city at around six in the evening. My legs barely worked. I greatly anticipated my B & B stay and a good meal. Pontremoli is famous for the Bianco Oro cocktail: a secret local recipe served in a wide, sparkling wineglass with a small lemon peel. Oh yes, something special. How I deserved it. Maybe wild boar with porcini? And for dessert, an amor: a double wafer stuffed with lemon cognac cream.

But first I had to wash off the mud. I wandered down the right street, found the cross street, and – nothing. My B & B didn't exist. When I asked the fellow in the store closest to the bogus address, he said he had never heard of it. I punched the actual name of the B & B into Google Maps, and it sent me five kilometres back up the mountain.

"Are you kidding me?"

The road I had to take to get there was steep, gravel, and rural. Often the rocks in the road were so large, I had to lift my bike because the wheels wouldn't budge. I did not just whimper the last two kilometres, I sobbed. I was delirious. Nobody was answering the phone, and I had no idea if the location I was headed to would actually materialize into this mythical B & B.

Farm, farm. Brush, brush. Vineyard, vineyard. Where was I? Heavy brush cleared, and after a few obscure little hand-painted signs, forks in the road, and potholes, I finally got to a gate: LunAntica, Agripodere Il Falco.

It was a tidy farm with large, refurbished stone buildings overlooking the valley. Windows winked in the setting sun, and this very handsome farmer strolled up with his overalls and movie-star silver hair. You'd think I was in an advertisement for artisan Italian cheese. Beside him, a white-and-black dog wagged its tail. His smile dropped when he saw my tear-stained face; he looked panicked. He didn't speak a word of English. I can't remember what I said – something like, "Buonasera signore, tu B & B bella – ma no vicina Pontremoli, ma up, up, up montagna! Stanco, so very stanco e freddo."

He looked immensely relieved when his long, lean daughter opened the barn door and marched towards us in her sweater and riding boots, her dark, curly hair caught in the breeze. I said to her, "Dove mangio stasera? No taxi!"

She said in clear, patient English, "Hello, I am Ilenia. We have a restaurant here. We feed you. Anytime you like. We make fresh. Agriturismo, sì? You okay?"

I took her hands in mine and pressed them to my bowed, mud-splattered helmet in deep thanks. "Grazie. Grazie. Sono spiacente."

She showed me to my austere but comfortable little room, whereupon I flopped on the bed in full gear for an instant nap. Inside their converted old stone barn was a cozy little dining room with a wood stove in the corner. A table for one was all set up for me. I met Ilenia's mother, Francesca, a slender ginger with diligent hands and sharp eyes. Apparently at LunAntica, they make their own olive oil, sambuca, and collect honey from acacia. That evening, she served me tender triangular-shaped testaroli, famous in the Lunigiana region. It's similar to a spongy crepe. Then she served cotoletta di pollo with lemon, a fresh salad from her garden, and potatoes with rosemary. Certainly, "l'arte dell'essere donna" was on full display.

The productivity of this small farm was amazing, and all the work was done in the last two years by the husband (Raffaele), wife, and daughter team. They decided to leave the city life and convert this old farm into what it is today. Lovely linen curtains and old stone walls, antique cabinets and heavy wooden doors. Yet everything that needed to be new was new: the plumbing, the windows. Sparkling clean. I had to admit, this paradise was worth the effort.

That night, I hit my pillow hard and fell asleep immediately. But my body woke up at two in the morning. HUFF HUFF HUFF. I wanted to keep cycling.

She kept seeing wolves nipping at her feet. And then the wolf was Ivan. And then the wolf was Hazel with those little spiky teeth. The wal–

She.

Tap tap tap.

I stared out the window. Being in the country, of course it was nothing but black. At first I found this impenetrable darkness frightening. But then I started to feel comforted. Blanketed. The night is a necessary part of the Good, of me, of everything. I breathed in. I breathed out. I could feel myself deeply shifting. Like I was recalibrating my very spine. My life was changing as rapidly as this old, dilapidated farm was transformed. Step by step. Thought by thought. Mile by mile.

— Herman —

Hazel and I packed up the Volkswagen, and we were on the road by 7 a.m. I thought it might be a chore getting Hazel up and at 'em that early, but she was ready before me. She was so excited about the trip. She was fully dressed in her bright-yellow outfit, suitcase beside her, coat on, standing straight as a soldier at the door by six. The little pup had also made us a snack for the road – peanut-butter-and-honey sandwiches, a couple of Fruit Roll-Ups, and two juice boxes. I must say, though, I am not a fan of any of those items, but I was impressed with her offering and swallowed it all down with great appreciation.

We started our drive with a light rain, but visibility was excellent by the time we hit Banff. It never dawned on me before that Hazel had never seen the mountains up close. I found it rather moving to see her little face pressed against the glass with awe, gazing up at the Rockies. She kept thanking me for taking her.

She christened the mountains with various names and was very excited when the mountain she named Castle Mountain was actually called Castle Mountain. She found animal shapes in the clouds in the sky and made stories up about them. Hazel was particularly amazed at the turquoise colour of the water caused by glacier silt in the Bow River and Gap Lake along the highway. She wanted to stop and go for a swim, but I told her it was mighty cold and we had a long road ahead of us.

I wasn't originally going to stop in Banff because of the cost of the Parks Canada pass and all the tourists, but the girl's sheer wonder at her surroundings changed my mind. This is what life with Hazel has brought me – unexpected detours. The former me would have found deviating from the plan very irritating. But the new me is starting to realize that often the best part of the day is the Hazel detour. For an older fellow like myself, change isn't easy. It's downright uncomfortable, if I'm honest, though I discover that the discomfort only lasts about five minutes, and then I get over myself and make a new plan. That's all. Just make a new plan. Hazel will disrupt it again, and then I will make a new plan again. So what? This is our whole deal. Mutt and Jeff. Abbott and Costello. Opposites can make for a well-balanced team.

Now that I think about it, the same could be said of my marriage to Nunzia. I'm not shy, per se; I'll go up and talk to any stranger I find interesting. But Nunzia was charming. She was the life of the party. She liked the attention. I'd rather hide under a rock. I hate having people looking at me in the sense of just looking at me, like opening gifts at my birthday party. Nothing worse. Everyone watching to see what my reaction is. Dreadful. My birthday is the only time of year I wish I'd never been born.

Anyway, today was going to be a Hazel detour. I called up David and Cathy and told them we'd be coming in later than expected; they didn't mind one jot. Hazel and I wandered down Banff Avenue and poked around the little shops. Hazel said it reminded her of gingerbread houses. We took a peek at the Bow Falls, and on our way there we came upon a herd of bighorn sheep. They were on either side of the car so close that Hazel could see the yellow of their eyes. That was a big hit. Then I thought, "Oh, what the heck," and we stopped in at the Banff Springs Hotel and went to the hot springs pool for a soak. After that adventure, we went to the Lookout Patio for the most expensive ham-and-cheese sandwich on earth. I really hate getting ripped off like that, but Hazel was hungry after her swim, and I didn't want to try and find parking back in town again. I guess a guy pays for the view. It was spectacular, I have to admit.

We had another five and a half hours to go before we got to Kelowna, so I let Hazel know we'd be driving pretty much straight through in order to get to Dave and Cathy's for supper. She fell asleep around Golden and didn't wake up until we got to Sicamous. Admittedly, I was glad for the quiet in the car, especially tackling the Rogers Pass.

I keep trying to picture Graziana in Italy. I know she's sticking to her itinerary based on the payments coming through on the credit card. I can't say I'm happy for her, out on this trip. As I believe I have mentioned before, I'm not all that clear what I'm "feeling" half the time anyway. And honestly, who cares? Feelings don't do much good for anyone. It's more a matter of what I'm thinking. What I'm thinking is, she'd better be good to Hazel when she returns, or I'm going to file for custody. Can I do that? Would I have a chance at it? Would Grazie even fight me?

I do miss having more of my own privacy. I think I would be a kinder grandfather if I was better rested and not running ragged with laundry and meals and homeschooling and Invisalign appointments. Though it breaks my heart to think of not living in the house with Hazel anymore and having that precious time. Like waking up the morning and seeing her sleepyhead hair all tangled, Spider-Man pyjamas. She insists on Spider-Man. She wants nothing to do with Disney princesses, strangely. Nothing whatsoever. Though she's aware of them. She'll make up princess stories in her head. She just doesn't want to wear the gowns or the crowns or anything like that. The princesses in her stories are always riding horses and taming tigers and building castles. She's really big on building castles with lots of families living inside. Lots of dances around the fireplace and big banquets with chicken legs and pies. It's always chicken legs and pies. Three-legged races too. These seem to always figure into her idea of what a royal family would do.

When Grazie was a child, she was quite a different little girl. She always had a mysterious side to her. I've never known what goes on in her head. Hazel, I know exactly what goes on in her head because she verbalizes everything. Grazie was much quieter, gentler, often glued to the side of Nunzia's leg. I remember being quite surprised when I first saw Grazie at a track meet. She'd always been quite bookish and never interested in sports. But I think it was group sports she wasn't interested in. Track and field, being mostly solo, ignited her ambition, I guess you'd say. She got gutsy and focused and quite competitive, you know, in a good way. And there was something we could finally talk about together. I'd drive her out to the track, I'd pick her up after practice, I'd take her to the gym … oh Lord. When I think of that creep and how I'd drop her off there with Ivan training her, not even questioning it …

When Grazie moved to Calgary to get her degree and opened up her bike shop, she still called Nunzia every single day. We'd drive down to the city often to pop in and see her. They were very close in a way that was just natural and mostly unspoken. Like a fawn following after her mother, watching how she forages, learning the nature of being a deer. When Nunzia was diagnosed with stage IV cancer, Grazie was around but not really present. She was mostly in a daze. Now I understand why, but at the time I didn't. I thought it was selfish and cold. But in typical Nunzia fashion, she didn't care about herself; all she was worried about was leaving her daughter without a mother. She'd say, "Poor Grazie, alone in the world, an orphan," like I'm some chopped liver. One day I said, "Nunzia, what about me?" She misunderstood and thought I meant in terms of being without a wife. She patted my chest, "You're a handsome man, Hermie, you won't be alone for long." She was wrong about that.

My thoughts were diverted as soon as we headed into the Okanagan Valley. Despite the fact that we were far too early for any fresh fruit, it was a great time of year to come. Not too many tourists, and everything was sunny and green. The cherry, peach, plum, and pear trees were all in bloom. The air was full of flowers and bees.

Today was the prettiest day of my whole life! First we got into the car very early in the morning and we drove past Calgary and all the way to Banff. If you don't know, Banff is a small really cute town that looks like maybe a fairy-tale kind of place. Grumpy says it's like the Swiss Chalets. I went to one of those restaurants once for Walter's birthday when he was my friend, and the restaurants didn't look like this. They just have weird chicken sauce but good ribs. Swiss Chalets, Grumpy says, look like places that fairies might live in, if fairies were really big. I think if I saw a really big fairy, it would totally freak me out. Like, you'd see one of those big pointy ears and wings and think, "You are going to poke my eyeball out if you nod your head, Miss Fairy Pants, so just keep your ears to yourself, thank you!" Mind you, if fairies were big, then you'd know for sure if they exist because part of why we don't think fairies or pixies are real is because they're small and they can hide easily. Now, you're probably thinking I'm eight and I still believe in fairies? Grow up! But I know what I know. What you can't prove, I am still allowed to believe in. And just because Grumpy was the lousiest tooth fairy ever (like so loud, that was terrible sneaking, he woke me up!), it doesn't mean that fairies, like, all fairies, don't exist. All you have to do is drive out to see the HUGE Rocky Mountains and know that this world is very very very big and magical mystery things can be hiding so easily everywhere! Especially in a mountain that looks like a castle.

The water here looks like turquoise. My mom had a turquoise bracelet. (I broke it – the beads went under the fridge and we didn't find them until Grumpy moved in because Grumpy actually cleans behind the fridge. I didn't know fridges moved but they do.) The water here is the same colour as Mom's broken turquoise bracelet. It's so beautiful I can't even believe it. Grumpy says it's blue because of crunched-up glaciers, and a glacier is like a huge ice cube so that means that the lake is super-duper cold. Like a slushy. I don't quite get that, but okay.

Then we went to Banff. Isn't that a strange name for a town? BANFF. It's so easy to say "BAMF" instead. "Banff" is like the sound slippers make on the ground when you're walking and the rubbery bottom kind of flips on the fluffy side with each step. Banff Banff Banff, I'm going to get some orange juice, Banff Banff Banff, I'm still in my pyjamas! Banff Banff Banff.

We went to see some huge waterfalls and they make a big racket, like, all the time! I think I would go deaf if I lived beside them, but I also loved them very much. It's interesting how you know something is dangerous but you kind of want to dive into it anyway. Waterfalls would be another very clever place to hide for magical creatures, because you never think to look behind the waterfall. There could be a secret passageway into the mountain where there's a huge cave and a whole hidden world that we don't even know is there. Like, not even scientists, because they think they know it's just water and rock and who goes swimming down a waterfall anyways? Nobody.

And on the road there were these sheeps with big circle horns on the sides of their head like Princess Leia! One was right beside me, right beside me in the car, I couldn't BELIEVE it! Walking on the road like, "La dee da dee da." They couldn't care less. No big deal. Cars. "You can wait for us, Mr. Herman! We're not in a hurry!" They have amazing yellow eyes. But not like zombie yellow but like golden yellow. One stared right at me. Like, into my SOUL. For a minute I thought the sheeps know there is magic and they know *I* know there is magic and we are making a promise right now not to tell anyone on the whole planet because then the magic would get wrecked. Like the Amazon forest. I read about that with Grumpy.

Grumpy was super surprising today and Grumpy is not a surpriser. He didn't tell me he was going to take me to any hot pools! But guess what? There is water underground that gets super hot (I'm not sure why) and smells like boiled eggs (I'm not sure why), but you can swim in it and it's warm as a bathtub and steam goes up into the air because it's all outside! I never heard about this in my whole life. I know that I know how to swim, but mostly because I'm light in the water and then I can feel little again, I went piggyback on Grumpy and he would slowly dip down into the foggy water and make this "du na … du na" shark sound and dunk me in. It was so fun! Grumpy looks completely different when his hair is wet. He has a round circle with no hair right in the middle of his head. I told him in case he didn't know. He knows.

Then we had a sandwich and we could see from our table all down the mountain, so pretty. But then I got super tired and fell asleep in the car. I was kinda upset with myself because I didn't want to miss anything, but Grumpy said we could see it on the way back home, which made me feel better.

The Okanagan has huge lakes, like I thought it was the ocean, and such pretty flowers on all the trees. We got to Uncle David and Auntie Cathy's and I had a double feeling. I had this feeling that I loved them right away, but I also had this feeling that I was to be careful not to break anything. That's because everything in their house is special. It's on purpose. Everything is art. It's not like they got it at the dollar store and thought, "Let's put pens in this plastic cup." Nope. Pens go into Auntie Cathy's pottery. Pottery is like cups and bowls made out of clay and it feels really good on your hands, like it gives your fingers a massage. She was happy when I said that. She said, "Texture is important. Not everybody gets that." But I do!

And Uncle David makes paintings of birds and lakes and trees and flowers and even a painting of his doggie, Oola. He has his own little house in the backyard that just has paintings in it and one chair and one big window. He calls it his studio. It's very squishy in there but he says it is his favourite place. My favourite place is the fireplace. It's super cozy and at night they put real logs into the real fireplace! I never saw that before! I thought that was just old-timey, but they actually heat their whole house that way. Amazing, these Okanaganers!

But let me tell you my favourite part. Besides dinner, which was very yummy salad with a kind of cheese macaroni from scratch, my favourite part was Oola. She has big brown eyes and long yellow fur and a swishy tail. She's a golden retriever. She let me pet her and pet her and pet her, and in the backyard she would go get the ball no matter where I threw it, and she'd bring it right back to me and drop it right at my feet. It was just like the movies but I didn't know that could be real. Sometimes I would just hug her. Auntie Cathy teased Grumpy that now he'd have to get me a dog. But I know in my heart that is not going to happen. Dogs are too messy for Grumpy. He told me so.

I wanted to sleep beside Oola on her dog bed, but Uncle David said no, that would be gross. I guess it doesn't smell too good, but I don't care. I slept upstairs on a mattress on the floor in a room with lots of sewing stuff. Auntie Cathy also does weaving. That's like making sweaters except they have no sleeves and they're really big and bumpy and you hang them on the wall. At first, I didn't understand why you would do that but then I remembered: "Texture!"

When I was up in my bed, because the house was so quiet, I could hear the adults talk even though they were trying for me not to hear them. They told stories for a bit about my nonna Nunzia I think. She would pick a lot of cherries, especially the sour ones, and make pie. Auntie Cathy got a kind of "about to cry" voice, then everyone got really quiet, missing my nonna. And then Uncle David told a joke and they all laughed really loud for a long time. I do that too. Sometimes I laugh to shake away all the sadness in my body.

Then they started talking about my mom. At first Uncle David was angry and so was Auntie Cathy, though Auntie Cathy was trying not to be. She was trying to be fair, she kept saying, "Let's be fair now." Uncle David said my mom was feeling sorry for herself and she was cruel to me. Then Grumpy said there were things they didn't know about my mom and that's all he was going to say about it. He had hopes my mom was going to "straighten" herself out. Uncle David said he was just feeling protective because I was "a dear little girl." Auntie Cathy said

I was bright and she thinks I am an artist. That made my heart beat fast in my chest hearing them say such nice things. I had no idea. How can they know me so well already?

I lay in bed thinking of my mom "straightening" out. She is crooked a lot, it's true, bent over on the couch watching TV and eating chips with me. What would she look like if she stood up straight? I don't know. She was always bent over or sitting down. Even when she walked, she was bent over. I bet she would be tall if she stood up straight. Really tall. I liked the idea in my head when I thought of my mom that way.

— *Beloved* —

The beloved has finally chosen an occupation. He is studying the past. He is studying stars. In particular, he is fixated on the smoky orange of Betelgeuse, the brawny shoulder of Orion.

"Betelgeuse is running on empty you know," the beloved says, almost admiringly, a bit sad. "It's been very greedy. Chomping through its fuel supply like there's no tomorrow. I've always been an astrology geek. Rare to see a star this huge. This audacious. It's in its giant phase, so it's all puffed out ... but at its core, it's full of ash. I was really hoping it would go supernova before I died. I wanted it to go out with a bang. It would be as bright as our moon, you know, maybe brighter. Turn into a black hole. But no, it's not impressive enough for that. Mostly likely it will just collapse into a neutron star. It will fall in on itself, becoming very dense. Neutron stars never die. They just get colder and colder."

Do you want Us to ...?

"No. Leave me."

CHAPTER TEN

HEART OF THE MOUNTAIN

— *Graziana* —

MASSA, TOSCANA

The next morning the view of the valley and of Pontremoli was golden and inviting. Francesca and Ilenia were waiting for me in the dining room with gentle coffee and colazione continentale: two kinds of homemade cake and fruit. I surreptitiously popped my meds into my mouth between sips.

I was offered an additional plate of eggs and cheese, considering I had a big ride to Massa.

I said, "Sì, grazie!" I was full-pull hobbit, having second breakfast.

I got on the road to Aulla, and it was an easy up-and-down through the valley under the happy sun, a truly gorgeous twenty-five kilometres. However, I was certainly feeling the strain in my legs from yesterday, and just outside of town, my pannier broke off the back end of my bike. Could I even accomplish the next fifty kilometres? The Via Francigena app itinerary said it was very challenging. It suggested, "Anyone who does not seriously cycle should sweep this and take the train."

I swept.

I went to the stazione ferroviaria in Aulla and nobody was at the kiosk. I went to purchase a ticket, and the ticket machine was broken. I went online to inquire about taking a bike on the train, and everything was in Italian. I was stuck in Aulla with a broken bike and not many euros. My head got light, so dizzy ... Just then, three Afro-Italian men burst through the train station doors, having just arrived from ... heaven? Their sportswear was super fancy and their bikes gleamed, each vehicle a superb feat of sport engineering. They strode with the jocular confidence of the young and the healthy.

I upended my squat and waddled after them, "Excuse me, do you speak English?"

The fellow in the middle, clearly the leader, looked down, annoyed. "Of course I speak English."

"I'm sorry, I didn't mean ... I've never been here before. Can you take a bike on the train?"

"You simply have to pay the conductor an extra commission."

They leapt on their steeds and glided away. I paid cash for my ticket on the upper floor and luckily the train was quite empty. It was no problem to lean it against me and take in the mountainscape without breaking a sweat. I felt guilty, in fact; so many kilometres traversed so easily. I had to transfer in La Spezia, which was quite a large hub. I had two and a half hours to wait for my connection, so I headed back down the road from where we had pulled in. I recalled having seen a bike store in an off-ramp sort of mini mall. I hoped they could repair my pannier.

The lights were off and the doors were locked. Out of desperation and denial, I kept wandering around the building. In the back repair room, which I could see through the glass, a tiny gentleman in a button-down shirt and sweater vest was tinkering over a bicicletta, his glasses sliding down his nose. I knocked gently on the glass. He looked up from his gears and waved me in through a door further south. I entered and mimed the "problemo." The man nodded and headed into his shop and returned with a compact set of tools. After tightening all the nuts and bolts and reattaching my pannier, he waved me off when I offered to pay and asked me where I was going.

"Vengo ... Milano. Vado a Roma."

His eyebrows raised above his glasses. "Buon viaggio." He tipped his invisible hat to me, wishing me well, and turned back to his previous occupation.

Good men. Good men everywhere.

Back at the La Spezia train station, I popped into a caffè for an espresso con latte. I didn't have the courage to ask for a cappuccino at this hour because it is considered gauche to have breakfast for lunch, and I would earn an invisible eye roll. This is another Italian superpower. Say "Buongiorno" at 4 p.m.? Invisible eye roll as the woman behind the counter returns the greeting with an elegant "Buonasera." This is why I order baccala instead of pizza, Campari when I want Coke, espresso when I want a latte; I use cash instead of card, simply to avoid getting the invisible eye roll. I thought I had gotten it right this time, but the barista refused my espresso con latte, and with an invisible eye roll she slid the correct beverage over. Macchiato. Okay.

A middle-aged working man, torn flannel, hands hardened and blackened by labour, sang love songs by himself outside the caffè patio. I wrote a postcard to Hazel:

> *Dear Hazel,*
> *This trip is such a great exercise in addressing the fear*
> *of the unknown.*

This was not something one says to an eight-year-old. But I had already started the postcard, and I wasn't sure when I'd come across another one. Oh well. Better than nothing.

> *I am so very grateful to have the privilege of this*
> *space, this quiet time, to get healthy and heal.*

I was still not talking to an eight-year-old.

An argument broke out between two cars in the parking lot. Two men yelled at each other through their rolled-down windows. The Fiat drove off quickly with an angry skid. I suppose that was supposed to look cool, but it just looked laughable. Like a baby fawn kicking up its heels. The Volvo followed in its own good time, cocky about its four doors.

I took a train today through the mountains. I put the bike on the train. A nice man fixed my bike for free.

Now I was talking to a three-year-old.

I am in La Spezia. I am near the Mediterranean.

Who cares? How boring. I stamped it, mailed it – done. Another tangible example of how disconnected I am to my child.

I hauled my bike up to the train platform with a gnarling swirl of parental shame in my gut. The train was delayed by an hour. It was just me and a group of drunken teens. They had a pack of beer and a bottle of cognac plunked down between their feet. They became rowdier and rowdier as the train kept adjusting its arrival time later and later. One of the burly boys picked up the tiniest of the girls and started swinging her around while she screeched in flirtatious glee. Nobody tried to pick up the bigger girl; she scowled and drank her beer. I suspect she was the one who raided her parents' liquor cabinet for the cognac. The tiny girl had imitation leather pants that gave her a pubic triangle and a camel toe all at once, yet she rocked them with aplomb. To my surprise, the bigger girl at one point kicked the tiny girl between her legs. Not hard enough to hurt, but enough to dampen her spirits.

Once I got to Massa, it was six in the evening. I had an hour and a half before sunset to get to my hotel, Albergo San Carlo. I wonder why Herman booked me something so fancy? It was probably uphill with a view, I guessed that much, but only about ten kilometres away. The hotel had a restaurant attached, so no problem, I'd have plenty of daylight, and dinner upon arrival. Once I got off the train and walked across the piazza, I noticed Massa was surrounded by cliffs. Surely my hotel was not all the way on top of one of them?

Google Maps first took me up one side of a collina on a foot-path near the Cattedrale dei Santi Pietro e Francesco. I didn't have time to go into the stately, white cathedral with its double-decker of pillars and frescoes. Apparently, noble rulers from the thirteenth century, the Malaspina family, had members buried in the chapel. According to Dante, they knew how to throw a good party for their friends.

At one point the cathedral collapsed. During its reconstruction, Elisa Bonaparte, the sister of Napoleon and Grand Duchess of Tuscany, ordered its demolition to make way for gardens and buildings intended to "Frenchify" the Italians. They weren't too pleased about "la Madame's" efforts to culturally influence them. Elisa's portrait has her wearing a vibrant-red gown. She loved the arts and particularly fostered the theatre and marble sculpture. She set up a Committee of Public Charity and instituted free health care for the poor. She turned monasteries into churches and schools, especially focusing on education for girls, and financed the invention of new agricultural tools. History blames her "sharp tongue" for the testy relationship with her brother. I'm sure it had nothing to do with the fact that he was a megalomaniac who imposed demands on her territory, namely conscription and heavy taxes. Yeah, all her fault. If only she was less hormonal.

I followed a Google route up towards the smaller Santuario di Nostra Signora delle Grazie on the Via delle Grazie. I lifted my bike up many, many steps; ceramic tiles of the Stations of the Cross pressed into the brick and stone wall beside me. As I carried my CUBE, Christ carried his cross, and by the time I reached the church piazza overlooking the city, Christ's body had been pulled off the crucifix, and all the women were weeping. There was no tile for the resurrection, and there was no connection to the zigzag road that headed me up to my hotel. Google was wrong. To make things worse, I started to have troubles with my navigation connection, and now my capricious cicerone was sending me back down towards town to head up the cliffs a completely different way. Down I went, reversing the Passion with great dismay.

The sun was starting to set; I didn't have time to feel sorry for myself. I had to forget navigation and eyeball a way to what seemed like a main road up the cliff. My bike was not outfitted for night cycling. I was sore and hungry and my phone was dying. I cycled back into town, following main arteries that led up. Switchback after switchback, I cycled up a steep, narrow road with no lamplight and very little shoulder. I was going as fast as I could; my heart was pounding so hard, I was gasping for breath. My legs were shaking, and cars zoomed past me, honking. I know, I know, I had no business being here. I know it's dangerous! I checked my navigation. It wanted to send me back down the mountain for six kilometres. There was 12 percent power left on the phone. I had to just keep heading up and hope I would see the hotel, or any hotel, at the top.

I was still huffing and puffing up the cliff when I hit the blue hour. I started to grow dizzy and seriously concerned about falling off the cliff. It was gorgeous over the water, Massa now a small collection of miniature bone-coloured buildings far below. Up, up, up. A white truck nearly blew me off a corner. I stopped, shut my eyes, and shuddered as he yelled from out his window. Up, up, up. What was I doing here?! I wanted to go home. But I didn't even know if I had a home to go to. Maybe I should just allow myself to fall ...

For the first time, the thought of Hazel kept me going. My legs were getting so tired they began to shake. I could not fall off this cliff. I could not do that to her. My elbows ached from holding the handlebars steady. Hazel would not be better off without me. I need to stay focused on the road. I am necessary to Hazel's well-being. This was a new conclusion.

By the time the night turned pitch black, I had threaded my way up to the top of the cliff, and just as I had one foot in utter darkness, the other foot stepped into faint streetlamp light. The road flattened, I rounded a bend and I saw a big lit *H* surrounded by stars. This had to be it.

It was.

The sprawling Albergo San Carlo was quite a resort destination, with a bar and restaurant and many rooms. But it was also rather desolate at this time of the year and at this hour. It was now 8 p.m. I got there and limped up the stairs to the lobby. I was greeted by three generations of women, none of whom spoke English. They made literally twelve calls to the husband/dad/nonno in the next half hour to sort out three things:

1) Had Herman prepaid?
2) Was he charged seventy euros?
3) What was the Wi-Fi password?

I stood and waited as they yelled at each other over the phone, handing it back and forth between mother and daughter while the baby in their arms stared at me, jostled back and forth between them, lulled into a stupor.

Finally I was given two receipts for thirty-five euros each, and the nonna passed the phone to me. Now I was to talk to the poor fellow about the Wi-Fi password. I heard a weary broken English over the line.

He said: "Wee-Fee è 'San Carlo'."

I replied in my best Italian. "Okay. Semplice. E password? Um … chiave Wee-Fee?"

"Okay, C."

"Okay, sì. Yes?"

"No, C, C, C, come *Carlo*."

"Oh, C!"

"El."

"*L.*"

"Eye."

"*I.*"

"Eh."

"*A.*"

"No, eh!"

"A … *Alfredo, Albergo?*"

"NO! EH, EH, EH! *Elefante*!!!"

"Ooooh, eh! Of course, *E* is eh in Italian."

"Madonna, give wife! She make!"

I handed over the phone to the wife whom I hoped would just write it down, but oh no, the "who's on first" routine continued much the same between them, and by this time I was doubled over, laughing so hard I could barely breathe. The daughter, who had been bouncing the baby and preparing a bottle, came back to the desk, clued in to what was happening and simply wrote down:

Client: San Carlo

Password: SanCarlo

God help me, that made me laugh all the more.

My jovial response to the long check-in finally got the best of the women, and they started chuckling too. I know that Herman must have paid for the smallest, cheapest room, but the one they gave me for my trouble was the honeymoon suite. It was huge, with big sweeping windows, an opulent bedroom set and a sitting area. The bathroom had a heart-shaped white jacuzzi tub. As much as I wanted to climb right into it, I thought I'd better hit up the restaurant before it closed.

The hotel bar and restaurant weren't open yet for the season, but the pizzeria next door was, and it was packed full of locals, always a good sign. I ordered a Vito, a salumi-gorgonzola pizza with small chewy olives. It was from heaven. Almost literally, considering the altitude.

I headed back to my suite and had that honeymoon heart bath. I dumped in all the shampoo to make bubbles. How did I go from plummeting to my death to the life of a treasured bride? I had forgotten to close the shutters on the windows, so I was a naked pink lady floating in a heart on top of a mountain, if anyone had cared to look up.

— *Herman* —

Last night we retired around ten o'clock after a three-handed game of crib. Cathy and Dave are early risers, which suited us just dandy. Hazel tends to get up with the sun anyways. We had a good solid breakfast of turkey bacon and egg whites (Cathy is careful about cholesterol), and you know, it was just fine. I didn't miss a thing. Well, maybe the bacon. But I might try some of that turkey stuff at home. Why not? Mix it up. I'm quite disciplined myself. I put on some weight in the winter, but it's usually gone by spring. I am the older brother by three years, but David looks substantially younger than me. It helps that he doesn't have a stitch of arthritis. He does a lot of kayaking and backpacking and walking the dog, and Cathy keeps up with him. They're both very fit for being in their late sixties. It's quite admirable but also a little annoying. We went for a brisk walk down their wooded lane to a lookout over Okanagan Lake; it was real pretty. A very nice visit. Good folk indeed. I wish we lived closer. It's just easy with them. Easy.

I wanted a chance to settle into our hotel in Vancouver before we went for dinner at Marco's. You know those Italians – you don't mess with supper plans, and you have to come dressed up. I asked if I could bring anything, like a bottle of wine. And he said, "Please don't," in a way that made me understand that I'd probably get it wrong. As if I couldn't ask the fellow at the store what goes well with spaghetti. I was beginning to remember why Marco could irritate me.

Hazel and I booked it all the way through the mountains past Merritt and Hope. We didn't stop for lunch (Cathy packed us some apples and a couple of ham sandwiches), and we got to Vancouver by two in the afternoon. It was a beautiful day. Ships were out on English Bay, lots of people were on the beach, some even swimming, sailboats on the water. The Sylvia Hotel is right off Stanley Park, kinda quaint. It's older, built in 1912. For a time it was Merchant Marine apartments, so we had a kitchen, which is nice – saves a few pennies buying groceries. Apparently the apartment was owned by a businessman, Goldstein, who had a daughter, Sylvia. He had a few hotels that he named after his kids, but this one stuck. I can see why.

We went down to Denman Street and found ourselves a slice of pizza. Didn't want to get too full because Marco would be serving a feast. Then we walked through Stanley Park. Those bright-red and pink rhododendrons were all in bloom, and magnolias blossomed everywhere. Hazel was pretty amazed to see flowers as big as her head on bushes as tall as a house.

It was really starting to bug me that Marco thought I couldn't bring a bottle of wine, so I consulted the Google and found a wine store on Davie Street. I told the guy at the till, a real nice fellow, but, you know, a little limp in the wrist would be an understatement … I told him that a highfalutin' Italian man was making dinner, I didn't know what, but he usually makes fish. Everyone on the West Coast figures you come all the way there just to eat salmon, but I don't even like seafood. Anyway, the fellow was very thorough. He asked if Marco was southern Italian or northern. I said southern, but not "real" southern like the Sicilians or anything, more like the heel of the boot, as Nunzia would say. Well, his eyes lit up then. He said I should buy a dry Lambrusco, which is kind of a pink champagne but way more expensive. It can go with antipasti or dessert. And then for the main fish, an Orvieto. I let my pride get the better of me, because these two bottles together set me back nearly eighty bucks, and I probably wouldn't even drink any. I guess a part of me wanted to do Nunzia proud. She would have done something like this. And I would have complained. Here I was, doing what she'd do. I wondered if she'd find this funny or just plain weird.

Marco lived just a couple of blocks from us on a street named Comox. Hazel had a purple dress for the occasion, but I noticed she only had running shoes. Oh well. Too late. She combed her hair all nice and even put a yellow-and-purple ribbon clip in it.

Pretty cute. She got some paper from the lobby and made him a card. A "thanks for dinner" kind of thing. And she drew a picture of Oola.

I buzzed the front door of the condo, and Marco let us in. He was all kisses and hands waving all over the place and "Bella bambina!" over Hazel, who was all wide-eyed. Marco's place is very elegant. Immaculate. It looks like a ... I don't know. The inside of a millionaire's jet or something. It has a lot of mirrors and glass and chrome and white leather. I don't think he makes a whole lot of money, but he's got a good sense of fashion, if you like that kind of thing. He says it's very "Milan." He says he can't help himself.

Hazel blurted out, "Grumpy, you're right, Marco IS like a prince!"

That made things uncomfortable, but not as uncomfortable as what came next. A man was in Marco's shower. At first I thought maybe he had a roommate but, nope, the guy came out in a towel to say hi (a small towel, not a single hair on his chest), right in front of Hazel.

"This is Jejomar," said Marco.

Then Jejomar said, "You can call me JJ. Be two minutes, babe."

And in he went to the bedroom to get changed. This is a one-bedroom apartment. It's pretty obvious, even to a little kid, what's going on. Now, what you do in the privacy of your own home is none of anybody's business. But to subject a child to that without even asking, I was pretty shocked at his insensitivity.

Then Hazel yelled at me, "Stop being a homo!"

Now I was double-shocked. I scolded her, "Hazel, you may not be used to being around gays, but you never ever say that word!"

She said, "No, not Marco. You. You, Grumpy! You're being the homo!"

And I wasn't sure what to say to that or how she got that

conclusion. So I spurted, "Well, I can't help look at a guy if he's going to go prancing around in nothing but a towel!"

Hazel continued, "Grumpy, don't you know that boys can have boyfriends? Get over it! It's not right to be a homo about it."

Marco started killing himself laughing.

So I said, "Hazel, you mean *homophobic*. You think I'm *homophobic*. Well, I think I might be. I'm certainly not used to it. And I'm sorry, I didn't mean to be rude. You're right. But when you say the word, you have to remember the -*phobic* part, that's the part that means 'fear.'"

And Marco said, "I like it better without the -*phobic*."

And Hazel said, "Grumpy, why are you afraid?"

And it put me in a terrible foolish position, you see. Because the child was just fine with it. It was only me. She had no aversion. And here Marco had invited me to his house, and he hadn't seen me in eight years. I just wanted to go home, back where everything was normal.

Marco asked Hazel if she wanted something to drink. He had one of those little pear nectars that Nunzia used to love. Hazel went gaga over the tiny bottle. And that's when I remembered the wine I brought. Marco pulled the Lambrusco out of the bag and nodded with surprised approval. "Lambrusco, very nice, that will go well with the antipasti, the porchetta ... thank you, Herman." And of the Orvieto he said, "You knew I would make fish? It's not even Friday."

I could tell he appreciated it because he actually opened it. Then JJ came out, all dressed. He wore a purple shirt with what I think were little jellyfish on it. Fancy. He said he wanted to match Hazel. Then he oohed and aahed over her card, and she told him all about Oola. Then he pulled out a colouring set, and they drew some pictures together. He'd make a scribble and give it to her, and she'd make a picture out of it. Then she'd scratch a scribble and give it to him, and he'd make a picture out of it. I was staring at them, wondering if I could make a nice picture

223

out of the scribble I had started here. Then I wandered into the kitchen to see if I could help Marco, knowing he would say no. He was pretty much ready anyway, putting little leaves on the plates.

"JJ's good with the kids, eh?" I asked him. And Marco told me that he was in early-childhood education, works with special-needs kids. I offered, "Seems like a nice guy."

To my surprise, Marco turned to me and said, "I'm in love with him, Herman. Nunzia would laugh because I always thought marriage was so stupid. But now I don't want to have life without him."

"I know what you mean."

We had a toast, the two of us. The Lambrusco. I was expecting a kind of Baby Duck, but it was not too sweet. I didn't mind it.

Dinner was very good. Four courses, as expected. I was worried that Hazel would forget her manners. Maybe it was the whole elegant setting of the place, but she minded her Ps and Qs well, even put her napkin on her lap, which impressed JJ and Marco. We started with a pork dish and some kind of sweet celery thing. Fennel. Then noodles – sorry, *pasta* – kind of simple, with olives and cheese, and then the fish. It was black cod, which I actually really liked because it didn't taste fishy. Then he served salad and potatoes and a kind of gelato, with an orange semo-semi-Lina-something cake. We finished with a shot of "grappa," which is fancy Italian for moonshine. I don't usually drink, but I didn't want to be even more rude, and Marco kept filling up my glass. I have to admit, I caught myself giggling a lot. Marco can be a real card. Great comic timing. He has these eyebrows, and with the hand gestures, you know. He did a very good impression of Nunzia.

After dinner, Marco pulled out a few photos he had of her and him when they were kids back in Italy, and then teenagers, and then when they got older and reunited in Vancouver. Hazel had a good squeal when she saw me in my moustache and mullet. All very hilarious indeed. There was a cute little picture of Graziana in a jumpsuit at the aquarium. JJ's family is from the Philippines. I guess they run a car dealership in Burnaby. He has a sister who has a new baby. It was a very nice evening.

As we headed back to our hotel, Marco and JJ walked with us, leading the way, holding hands. I was surprised how quiet it was, this part of town in the evening: streetlights, the ocean, kind of sad and dark blue. I noticed that throughout the evening, that strong feeling of aversion, which I always thought was natural, faded. I wouldn't say it disappeared but when you see two people who love each other and when you get to know them, you think to yourself, "Well, isn't that all that matters, end of the day?"

It was so so so hard to say goodbye to Oola. She is my favouritest animal in the whole world. She's kind of like my imaginary
tiger except 1) she is not imaginary and 2) she would never get
all wilded up one day and accidentally eat me. Here's a secret
and it makes me feel bad, but now I know a special thing. I took
her paw and I squeezed it as a kind of test to see if she would
bite me, but she didn't. She just looked down and made a little
whimper when I squeezed kind of hard, so I let her go right
away! I felt terrible. But that told me that she would never hurt
me and that we would be best friends forever. To say sorry in
a way that a dog would understand, I asked Auntie Cathy if
I could brush Oola, and I brushed her and brushed her until
I had enough hair to make another whole dog or at least a
sweater. I asked Auntie Cathy if she could weave me a sweater
from Oola's dog hair and she said no. Oola likes to be brushed,
especially her tummy. She wagged her tail and then I felt her
same paw again and she did not pull it away like she was scared
or hurt and that let me know that my test was useful but not
really bad. But I will never do it again, I promise.

Then we got in the car and kept driving for a long boring
time. Grumpy downloaded a movie for me on the iPad so
that wasn't too bad. We listened to his music (yuck) and then
we listened to my music. If you can count that as listening to
my music because Grumpy would hear a song and then say
"Inappropriate!" and change the channel. So most of the time
we just heard blah-blah-blah talking.

Then we got closer to Vancouver and holy moly, there was
the real ocean! Grumpy went over a huge bridge, like bigger
than you can believe! We were so high up crossing over that I
was positive we could have hit an airplane maybe. And by the
water I could see big orange machine-guy things like Trans-
formers. I was scared of them but Grumpy said they were kind
of like big cranes that took stuff off of ships and onto ships. We

drove through lots of trees and then another big bridge! This
bridge was prettier, it had lions on it and pokey tops and I could
really see the ocean from there. I mean, I know the ocean is big,
duh, but when you see it in real-to-life situations, you really go,
"Wow, that's the OCEAN! I can't see the other SIDE!"

I have never stayed in a hotel before and it was so pretty. It
had lots of wood and it was all grey and there was this plant,
huge plant, growing on the side of the whole big hotel! Guess
what it is called? A creeper! That's what the lady at the desk
said. The plant is a something-girl's-name creeper! The apartment we got was sparkling clean and white white white. Towels
white, tub white, sink white, soap white. Grumpy gets his own
bedroom and I get to sleep on the sofa because it is super cozy
and I am small but tall and my legs just fit perfect.

Outside, people were rollerblading and riding their bikes
and jogging. I think everybody in Vancouver likes to exercise.
Grumpy and me, we had a piece of pizza, which was super
yummy and it came all the way from New York and then they
put it in this big oven and just for a few minutes – presto! It's
done. We shared a piece because it was super huge. We decided
we would have Hawai'ian.

Grumpy said, "Don't tell Marco we had Hawai'ian pizza."
I said, "Why?"

And he said, "Because Italians don't put pineapple on their
pizza, they think it is disgusting."

Well, maybe Italians shouldn't judge what they haven't tried
because I love it.

Then we went to the park, which is not really a park, but a lot
of trees. And some of the trees had huge flowers the size of my
head. Grumpy called them rotos. The red ones were my favourite. They were like Spanish dancer ladies CHA CHA CHA.

Then we had to go to my old cousin. I mean, my zio Marco's place for a fancy dinner. Grumpy was upset that I only
had my runners, but duh, when has he ever bought me fancy
shoes? Never. And my white ones from Joe Fresh were too small
because I got them last year with Mom for school, so I only

brought runners. I felt so bad about it, I almost didn't want to see Zio Marco because I would look stupid. But then Grumpy kinda got sorry for being upset and he said, "Hazel, you look so pretty the way you've done your hair with that ribbon, nobody's gonna take one look at your feet!"

We went to a store and Grumpy bought wine. I've never seen him do that. He was acting weird too. His face went all red and he laughed a lot and he kept looking around like he shouldn't be doing what he was doing: buying wine. I think it cost a lot of money and Grumpy doesn't like to spend a lot of money. But he said that Zio Marco likes fancy stuff.

We went to Zio Marco's and his house looked like a SPACE-SHIP! I LOVED IT! He even had a disco ball that he put on for me in the living room, and JJ, Zio Marco's boyfriend, played some FUNK. I didn't say a bad word – ha ha, tricked you! That is a kind of music: funk. Like *funky*! The singer was called Jojo ... Mart ... tini? Something like that. She sings in Portu-guese, and she is from Rio, like that cartoon with all the birds, and it was awesome. Like you just had to get up and dance. I am sometimes shy to dance with strangers, but JJ started dancing (his shirt had jellyfish on it) and then Marco started dancing, so it was easy for me to start dancing! We were all laughing so hard because Grumpy wasn't dancing. And then Zio Marco started to tease him and bumped him in the bum and then Grumpy did dance a smidge. He stuck his thumbs out and jolted back and forth, kind of like he had an itch and then we laughed even more.

Zio Marco made shrimps, which are one of my favourites. And there was a kind of cheese that was, well, it was not my favourite. And olives are not my favourite, but the bread was really good. And so was the porky. Then some fish which was DElicious! Nothing like fish sticks at ALL. And then I was so full I could hardly eat all my cake. I felt bad. But I ate most of it. It tasted like pancakes with oranges. But in a really good way.

And then we saw pictures of my nonna and Zio Marco and baby Mommy, and JJ let me lean against his knees. It was so cozy. Zio Marco is really nice too, but he was in the kitchen a lot making the good food. And he had some talking with Grumpy. JJ and me, we had the fun stuff. We even did colouring! They walked us all the way home to the hotel. I wish Zio Marco and JJ lived closer. They make everything beautiful.

— *Beloved* —

The beloved sleeps. Even though there is not a body requiring regeneration. It is a comfort, an escape to become negative matter. It is perhaps his way of saying to Us that he no longer knows what to do or be. This is not resting in peace. He is here, he is trying not to be here. *Astrophysical exotica*, a term that sounds far more exciting than it is. We recognize it could be difficult for him to feel connected to Us when We are All. How do you see All? How do you hear All? How do you taste All? How do you touch All? How do you smell All? He loses Us in All of Us. He feels alone when he is surrounded.

The satisfying thing about creating is the wonder that comes with it. Not just at the creation that wonders at Us but how We wonder at the creation. The creation would be surprised to learn We are often surprised. It is all Ourselves but how often is it that We actually don't know Ourselves? We don't know Ourselves until We put Ourselves into action.

We can only hope that the beloved will seek Us out and choose to be creative. Curiosity is Divine. Though We have made a star, it is the star who chooses whether to implode into darkness or explode into light.

CHAPTER ELEVEN

THE WALLED CITY

— *Graziana* —

LUCCA, TOSCANA

It was a perfect day for a ride: overcast with no rain. I headed all the way down the steep cliff again back to town, rewinding the nightmare of last night. Like watching a horror flick with the lights on, it ceased to be frightening. Once I reached sea level, I came upon a stark modern sculpture of large sheets of white rock (perhaps marble) stacked in a staggered line at the Marina di Massa: *Le Vele* (The sails) by Pino Castagna. There was something about the spaces between the massive, impenetrable blocks that gave me hope. There was passage through. There were peeks of ocean between the imposing rectangles of rock; there were fresh gusts of sea air. One could have blocks and still have beauty. One could have marble and not be a mausoleum.

Along the sea were private beaches, still closed for the season. The bars were empty, the chairs stacked, the umbrellas and cabanas had their fabrics huddled and tied together as though they were sheltering from the cold. On the other side of the boulevard stood gorgeous summer villas, all virginal white, shut up with shutters that whispered, "Non apro per lei," they won't open for me. This certainly felt like a summer resort for those with means and Maseratis.

The Via Francigena continued along, moving away from the sea and into a lush valley. Magnolia trees were in bloom. I cycled past wild rosemary, calla lilies, cacti, and succulents. This was the pilgrimage I had in my head. Before a town came into sight, I heard a woman yelling. I believe it had something to do with her sister coming for dinner. I rounded the bend and out of a thicket of trees. Sure enough: a home on the outside of a village. A woman in her seventies was yelling at her husband, not unkindly. He shrugged silently with a slight smile and headed down the street, hands in pockets, perhaps ambling over to the bar to play cards with the boys. She stood on her porch, flanked by a flowering thyme. Her white apron fluttered. Her face was tranquil, neither angry nor resigned.

I was startled out of my spying when a couple of "real" bikers swished past me so fast that it was almost violent. They were ferocious and lean and sharp as hawks. I felt like a chicken beside them, flightless and plump. Please don't eat me.

Halfway through the day I stopped at a town called Camaiore to get out of the rain and have some lunch at Pasticceria Rossano. As I approached the big glass doors, they slid open, and I was hit full blast with AC/DC's "Highway to Hell." The pasticceria was full of laughing young people mostly wearing leather. A man at the bar turned his head towards me and yelled so loudly, I wondered if I had trespassed into a private party. I quickly realized he was shouting in celebration of a grey-bearded biker who was leading a group of Australian motorcyclists through Toscana.

Gorgeous chocolate Easter eggs and bunnies in lavender, white and spring green, were on display. Delectable piles of pastry were followed by pizzas and calzoni; behind was a well-stacked bar. It was decked out like a stylish hotel lobby: large floral arrangements, white leather. Despite all the sensual contradictions, everyone seemed to be having a good time. I was happy to see they had a full menu, so I ordered a pasta with fresh porcini and a salad.

After my lunch, I scaled two gracefully graded foothills. Roosters and robins and olive groves grew at a near ninety-degree angle. The pilgrim's path into Lucca was along the lovely River Serchio. I approached the walled city with excitement. I knew I'd be staying overnight here for two days, so I'd actually get to see some of the galleries and museums. I swooshed through one of the large gates, and suddenly, I was out of pastoral Italy and in the centre of artisan cheese shops and enoteche selling Tuscan wine. Lovely, narrow streets were full of clothing shops and churches and packed with wandering people. Everyone seemed to be in a good mood. I walked my bike over cobblestones and popped into colourful stores to pick up fennel sausage, walnut-wrapped pecorino, and a very nice bottle of Chianti for my host.

I was staying at an Airbnb, and my host was named Pablo. He was in the historical centre of Lucca. I knew from the pictures that his home was a large apartment filled with plushy, red-velvet sofas and drippy candles, wallpapered rooms filled with flowers and art and books and brick. I was surprised that Herman chose this place for me, as it was a room in a home, not private. I suppose it was for the price. Pablo was very florid and articulate in his welcoming message and told me he'd like to cook me dinner. This was also unusual. I hadn't connected with a host since Rubbiano. It made me nervous that I was staying in a home with a man I didn't know. I didn't want to be rude. I agreed to dinner for the first night and brought wine, because he was not asking to be paid to cook me a meal. Admittedly, I was quite anxious that I would have to navigate a sexual advance. As innocent as it may be, I didn't think I'd have the strength to say no without

With

Out

Crumpl–

Yeah. I strongly considered cancelling.

But as soon as I knocked on his door and he answered, all my fears vanished. Pablo was a poetic, gracious, compact man, older than me. He immediately took my handlebars and hauled my bicycle up three storeys, despite the fact it was muddy and very heavy. He then turned and greeted me properly with a sincere, long squeeze and a big kiss on both cheeks while I was still in my helmet, smelling of second-day sweat. He showed me around. His home was comfortable and wonderfully eccentric. The walls were packed with original paintings and antiques and favourite bottles of wine he'd relished. Apparently, there were two other women staying there, and I was given the large teal room with a king-sized bed, a breezy window, and a big, fluffy duvet.

I freshened up, then offered him my gifts in thanks. The other female guests came in through the door. Angie, from Venezuela, was a spectacled, leggy young woman who seemed to speak Spanish, Italian, English, and God knows what else. She was joined by Sofia, a woman perhaps in her early sixties, wrapped in cashmere, originally from Russia and now residing in New York.

Pablo was cool with me throwing my clothes in the washer, and then he was off to cook us dinner. I offered to be his sous-chef, and he politely said, "Just leave it all to me." It was then that I noticed his chef certificates on the wall.

Pablo took his time with a type of handmade pasta. The sauce had tomato and basil, fish, octopus, and seppie. He told me that he makes fish broth from the spine and head of the fish, and for a more intense taste, he will bake the shells of shellfish and simmer that for eight hours. He also makes a mussel dust. He removes the dark part of the mollusk and bakes it for several hours until it is dry. He grates it and sprinkles it on dishes for added flavour. This all explained why such a seemingly simple meal exploded with gusto. He had worked at a Michelin-starred restaurant here, and his passion was definitely cooking.

Later into the evening, we all had the wine I brought with the cheese and salami. He added some of his bread made with smoked oil and laurel. We spoke about food. He admonished me to never cook egg yolk. He was so adamant, I felt it might come to blows if someone dared fry a whole egg in his kitchen. Then he took me through the process of making a soufflé – steps I had all done in the past but failed at. By our second glass of wine, he was into the proper omelette technique, and my mind was getting fuzzy. I think I remember him saying he flips his soufflé, which I can't even imagine. We all laughed and had a cozy little party until midnight.

The next day I wandered around Lucca. I decided to add to my meagre supply of clothing because I was shivering in shorts. The forecast was all rain, and my clothes at Pablo's were still wet. Though I was now down to a size sixteen, it was extremely difficult for me to find any clothing that fit, given the fact that Italian women tend to be shapely, but tiny and fit. I've noticed they often have really nice bums. I guess because they do so much walking and cycling. You could bounce a nickel off their rounded cheekiness. I had a way to go before I was at that level of fit. One store I walked into, the saleswoman waved me out like a bad smell.

"Too big," she said. "Nothing for you, sorry."

When I finally found buttons I could do up, I tore off the tags and covered my body with warmth. I wandered the streets and found biscotti. I walked the Lucca wall and popped into the Basilica of San Frediano. It had a grand pipe organ from the 1500s. I sat in that space and held hands with the Great Good.

Pablo said that "americana" cooking was all about "fast fast fast." How fast can you make it? How few steps? French cooking was about transformation. You take a potato, some flour, some butter, and with ingenuity and science you transform it into something new and unrecognizable. But Italian cooking is all about bringing out the best properties of the thing itself. It's simple. You focus on one or two ingredients, and you find the right combination and the right timing to make it the best it can be. So perhaps it's a carrot. Simple. But to bring out its best qualities takes practice. That takes time. This pilgrimage was, in a sense, a way to cook me into being a mother.

Next, I visited the Via Francigena Entry Point museum. To be honest, it was rather pathetic: just a single room with a video projection. But that being said, the projection was quite beautiful, and the history lesson of various kinds of pilgrims over the centuries was valuable for me. It was great to hear more about the Bishop of Canterbury, the merchant trade, the unification of Italy, and how the Via Francigena all played a part.

I continued on the wall and stopped for lunch at a patio restaurant named San Colombano. There was a very chatty British family beside me who all spoke rather proper and looked a wee bit posh. Grandmama and Grandpapa were traveling with daughter and granddaughter, the latter largely ignored. The grandpapa was waxing eloquent about Italy and said, between sips of cool white wine, "Venice is one of the few cities I've been to that actually did not disappoint."

Imagine living like that? "Ooh, this truffle cream is really quite good isn't it? Though a bit salty, wouldn't you say?" Oh, F– off. You're eating real truffles in Lucca on a gorgeous sunny day. Try to enjoy yourself. I certainly enjoyed my handmade squash ravioli with a ricotta-and-spinach cream.

I strolled on down to another cathedral. I was surprised by the depictions of the resurrected Christ. One was a hunky sculpture of Jesus in a scant loincloth, leaping with joy. It was called *The Freedom of Christ*. There were two more resurrection paintings, homoerotic and certainly joyful. It was a wonderful change from all the torture and agony. I also appreciated a Last Supper that actually had women in the scene! One was serving and another was at the end of the table, breastfeeding. It made me wince, thinking of my own failed attempt, baby Hazel feasting on my carcass like a little scavenger. I turned my eyes away from the painting.

I ambled over to the Piazza San Giovanni and booked tickets for a Puccini concert that evening. Lucca is Puccini's birthplace. The performers were two young opera singers who had recently graduated from the Opera Theatre of Lucca. The tenor was particularly good. Opera is funny. Half the time I think, "Oh my God, when is this going to end?" And the other half of the time, I feel like, "Oh my God, this is so beautiful, I hope it never ends!" There is no ambivalence. It's one extreme or the other, but it is always memorable. Isn't that the way to live?

Apparently Ms. Camila Vidal arrived in Vancouver the same evening we did. We were supposed to meet up yesterday, but she cancelled and said she wasn't feeling up to it, too tired from the travel. She was staying put in her room at the Westin Grand Hotel instead of the Sylvia, which she felt was too "dingy." She took great pains to let me know how fancy the Westin Grand was. Her voice sounded slurry on the phone, so I asked after her health. She said that she had taken a Valium because air travel makes her nervous, and it was best if she just lay down for the day. Okay. We agreed to meet up this afternoon, but she cancelled again. I inquired after her health and she admitted she doesn't sleep well when she travels, and she wanted to put her best foot forward meeting Hazel. Well, I'll tell you what foot to put forward, lady: your front foot through the front door.

Naturally the little pup was mightily disappointed to wait an extra two days to see her paternal grandmother. We could have spent this time with David and Cathy, having a longer visit. Hazel asked if we could see Marco and JJ again. I didn't want to burden them, having to babysit us in the city, and besides, it was midweek.

So yesterday was just Hazel and me, and we did a nice walk around the seawall and had hot dogs. But today, hearing we had been stood up by Camila Vidal, Marco and JJ took the day off from their respective jobs and met us downtown for brunch. I said I was up for anything except sushi. How people don't get worms eating all that raw fish is beyond me. We ended up at a place called Café Medina. We had to wait outside in line for over half an hour, but JJ and Marco assured us it was worth it. I have to admit, it was. I had something called fricassée, which, truth be told, I had only heard of in Bugs Bunny cartoons. Elmer Fudd was going to have "fricassee rabbit," or some silly thing.

But this was ribs for lunch, basically. Very good indeed. Hazel had Belgian waffles, which was a big hit.

Then they wanted to take Hazel shopping. I insisted that I cover it, but they were having none of my protestations and told me that she was the only little girl in their life and they thought it would be great fun. It sure was great fun for Hazel. Goodness gracious. They bought her shoes and blue jeans and a shirt and a bathing suit and a new jacket. Marco also wanted to take Hazel to his salon and give her a haircut, which she was thrilled about.

This meant JJ took me under his wing for a makeover while Hazel was at the salon. I wanted nothing to do with that. You see, Nunzia was the one who did all my clothes shopping. She knew what looked good. She just brought it home and it would fit. She had a good eye. She bought nice things, and she knew I didn't go in for anything too adventurous. It's pretty accurate to say that I haven't really bought myself anything new in the eight years since she's passed, give or take a pair of jeans and a six-pack of the essentials at Mark's Work Warehouse.

JJ has a way of sensing what a guy is thinking. I didn't tell him a damn thing about why I was resisting, but he put his hand on my shoulder and said, "Herman, I think Nunzia would want you to take care of yourself, don't you think? Keeping up with her tradition of dressing you well is a way of honouring her memory."

He got me there. I never thought about it that way before. I more or less felt: Who cares anymore? As long as I'm decent and clean. But if I think about what Nunzia would want … Yup. I tried on a whole lot of overpriced, ridiculous clothing and gave JJ a good laugh many a time. He ended up flattering me into a new pair of dress pants, a rather smart blazer, and a couple of button-down shirts, and a pair of shoes. I have to admit, I felt like a part of me returned when I put myself back together wearing those nice things. I surprised him and bought two more shirts, a belt, a pair of boots, and some black jeans. All in all, it was a victory.

We walked up to Marco's salon, which was on Davie Street,

and Hazel had the whole salon in a whirl. Everyone was cooing over her. Marco cut her hair off short into what he called a French bob. Right up to her cheekbones. I was miffed because I think he should have asked me or Graziana permission first. And on top of that, he gave her a streak of purple and yellow in her hair, her favourite colours. She was pleased as punch, indeed. I was not pleased that he dyed the hair of a little girl, but I had to admit, the cut looks real cute on her. Hazel's hair is mousy and thin, and the little bob perked it right up.

After all that, we went back to their house and had simple burgers on the barbecue, which was a nice relief from the fancier food we've been eating, and we had a couple of beers. We talked about politics and the environment and the usual liberal blah-blah-blah. But when I disagreed, they listened to what I had to say and didn't get all superior and arrogant like some lefties do. They are both smart and reasonable guys. I appreciated that Marco brought up the fact that e-cars cause terrible damage to the environment. JJ said something along the lines of it being a sign of white supremacy, which I didn't quite follow. But in a nutshell: We get all hot and bothered about fossil-fuel emissions in Canada, but we turn a blind eye to the fact that the Andes Mountains are being dug up for lithium. I guess he's meaning we care more about ourselves than about the people in South America. I think that's probably true.

Then we talked about JJ's family back in the Philippines and how his dad chose to go back to his hometown to die. Liver cancer, I guess. He went quick. This was hard for JJ, because he didn't get a chance to say goodbye. When Nunzia was in her final months, she asked me to take her rosary to Italy and place it in the cemetery in her hometown. I never did. I actually lost the rosary somehow in the move, and of course, I had no occasion to go to her small town in Italy. Nobody speaks English there. Nobody knows me. I thought it strange that she wanted a part of herself to return there, a place that seemed to have only brought her sorrow. She didn't want to be buried at all; she chose to be cremated. This is against custom for Italians or

Catholics or both, I'm not sure. But it has something to do with the rising of the dead and the second coming of Christ. Nunzia figured that if God could rise us from the dead, he could do so with ashes just as easily as a decomposing corpse. Gosh, even now to think of her that way.

When I picked up her ashes, I went out in our rowboat and sprinkled her over Crimson Lake. Her ashes sunk into the water like sand. I know I am never going to see her again. She's gone. There will be no second coming. There will be no raising of the dead. There will be no reunion in the clouds. She was a brief, beautiful being, the love of my life, the first and the last, my dear Nunzia. I will miss her until I take my last breath. Then someone will throw me into the fire and then sprinkle my ashes over Crimson Lake. I'll sink to the bottom, a lump of forgotten sediment, no shape, no name. I won't be joining her, though I will have joined her. We'll both just be done.

I was thinking these thoughts when I laid out all my new duds on the bed and felt foolish. Who was I dressing up for? The memory of a woman long since dead? Close to midnight, I went out into the living room to grab a glass of water. And there was Hazel, tucked into her sofa bed, fast asleep, a streak of purple hair plastered against her cheek. She's going to be shocked tomorrow morning when she sees me wearing a shirt that isn't plaid.

— *Hazel* —

Zio Marco took me to his hair salon and gave me purple and yellow hair! That probably doesn't sound very good but it's entirely STRAIGHT FIRE! (That means awesome.) He cut it really short and it makes it all swooshy and more fluffy and there is one streak of purple and another streak of yellow on the left side and it's gorgeous. Like, I look in the mirror and I don't even recognize myself. If I didn't know me and I saw me walking down the street, I'd think, "Now, there is a supercool girl that I would be lucky to be friends with." This is the first time in a long time I have ever thought of going back to school just to show all those kids they don't know me. They don't know the real me. This is the real me. Zio Marco just put it into a hairdo.

Marco and JJ spoiled me with clothes too! They kept buying me stuff like shoes and a jacket and even a swimsuit! Zio Marco said I was the only kid in his life and he loved my nonna Nunzia and my mom Grazie, so that's why I have to let him spoil me. "Twist my rubber arm," as Grumpy would say.

And I had these waffles for breakfast that had chocolate lavender (which is a kind of small purple flower) and white chocolate roses or something and raspberry and caramel. Can you believe it? So fancy! It gave me a stomach ache because I ate so much, but it was worth it, a million times worth it.

I love JJ and Zio Marco. I want to move to Vancouver. It's the prettiest city in the world, with the ocean and the parks and the flowers and the big fancy buildings and all the trees and the mountains and crows calling all the time, even downtown: CAW CAW CAW, look at me!

And this made it all a good distraction because my grandma is being stupid and mean. I don't get it. She flew all the way to Vancouver to see me and now she's chickening out and is not seeing me! We don't even know why! She says she's tired and she says she is sick from flying. Grumpy says old ladies can be fragile, but so what? You haven't seen your only granddaughter in your whole life and you instead want to sit in your fancy-pantsy hotel room and watch TV?

I started to worry that she'd see my yellow and purple hair and think I was a weirdo. Or maybe Grumpy said something to her on the phone that made her think we were dumb. Or maybe she just already has a regret and thinks I'm not worth knowing. WHY IS SHE WAITING?! I'm already thinking she's a liar. So much for this person who wanted to take me to San Francisco and do all this cool stuff. She can't even meet in her hotel for a coffee to see my face. What a jerk.

Or maybe she's a really nice lady and she just has like diarrhea from flying in a plane and she's too embarrassed to say that to us. I will have to hope that is true, my diarrhea theory. I told this idea to Grumpy and he nodded and thought it might be true. He said that older people get upset tummies when they travel sometimes. Then he pretended to be my grandma with a high fancy-pantsy voice, pretending to not have lots of farts, "Why, hello Hazel (fffffftttt). I'm your grandmother (fffffftttt). We're going to have a gas together (Ffffffftooooot)!" Oh my goodness, sometimes Grumpy makes me laugh so hard I am going to pee my pants and then we will have the farty grandma and the pee-pee granddaughter! What a family!

JJ and Zio Marco and Grumpy ended up talking boring stuff at dinner like adults do. But I drew them each a picture and when I went to put it on their fridge, I noticed they had on it already the picture I made two days ago for them. That made me feel very happy. That, even when we go back to Red Deer, here in the coolest city in the world, a picture by Hazel will be hanging in the kitchen.

When I grow up, I want to move to Vancouver and do hair-dos for all sorts of people. I want to ask them lots of questions about themselves and then come up with the perfect style. I would call it my heart hair. What your hair is, your heart is feeling. So maybe that's like having a pointy green beard because in your heart you love Christmas every month of the year? It would be like an upside-down Christmas tree on your face and then you could hang decorations on it if you wanted. But not too close to the mouth because then it would be hard to eat. I told Zio Marco that I hoped I would grow up to be like him someday. I said that in the chair when he had the plastic thing on my shoulders like a big cape. And he put down his scissors and put his hands on the side of my head and kissed me both cheeks. He said something in Italian and looked like he was going to cry but in a good way. I don't know what he was saying. But I hope it was, "Come work for me when you're a grown-up and we can make people happy."

"Jesus wept." That is the only Bible verse the beloved remembers from catechism. He thinks about that as he turns over. He ponders the feeling of abandonment. He closes his eyes again.

Jesus wept. The beloved slept. Each in their own dark Garden of Gethsemane.

"My soul is very sorrowful, even to death; remain here, and watch with me."

We never left. We never left either of them.

We remain. We watch.

The first Son asked us to intervene, to move a cup. But We Both knew there was more than just a cup that needed to be moved.

The second son does not even put effort into conversation. He asks for no movement. His whole body is cupped. Dreamless. Fetal. Stillborn over reborn.

CHAPTER TWELVE

WHITE TRUFFLES

— *Graziana* —

SAN MINIATO, TOSCANA

I took the long route around the Lucca wall this morning, hesitant to leave. Shopkeepers were sweeping their stoops and unlocking doors. Pigeons were hovering around bakeries hoping for crumbs. I cycled past a soccer field, and the concession stand was huge. There were no labels for hot dogs and beer. They sold contorni, grigliati, bruschetta, baccala. I dropped off my latest postcard to Hazel, nattering about the walled city and Puccini. I ended it with:

> *I am not sure if this postcard will reach you before I do. It's been so long since we've seen each other. I am tempted to call. I miss you, dear Hazelnut. But I don't want to just give you my voice. I think it's best that when I show up, I show up as whole as I can. See you soon, love,*
>
> *Mom*

I was grumpy today. I should not be mixing my meds with wine. I'm eating too much cheese. The jeans I bought yesterday added enough weight to my panniers to throw off my balance. I scraped my knee falling over at an intersection. Stupid! I'm sick of pastry for breakfast. I just want a damn egg with the yolk cooked.

About twenty kilometres outside of Lucca, I hit the urban-industrial ass-end of Toscana. Through the leather and shoe factories of Altopascio, I nearly got flattened by a truck heading into a big square building called Pam. Another fifteen kilometres after that, I came upon a town called Fucecchio. The Via Francigena did not take me through its elegant medieval centre but along the back lanes of its ugly suburbia on garbage day. All the pilgrim signs disappeared. Racist graffiti protesting the influx of refugees was sprayed along grey walls. German shepherds snarled at me from their small cement yards as I tried to navigate my way independently towards San Miniato. Elderly ladies clutched their shopping bags and eyed me suspiciously. The town gave me the big "Fuce you." On the way out, like a kick in the ass, I hit a cobblestone path so rough I had to get off my bike and carry it.

The Via Francigena has many generations of pilgrim markers littered along the roads. I've followed milestones, statues on churches, painted markers on buildings, and spray-painted arrows. The most modern markers are blue-and-white stickers. The path changes depending on your mode of transport too. If you're driving, you follow along the paved roads, if you're biking, you follow the Cammino and some back roads. If you're walking, you can stay on the path the entire time, over rocky trails, and up stairways. Needless to say, getting turned around several times a day is part of the journey.

Once I crossed the Arno River, I hit land far more pastoral. I was blessed with bunches of wild purple iris and long corridors of ubiquitous towering, tapered Tuscan cypress. The extremely narrow one-lane road up to San Miniato made me claustrophobic. The traffic whizzed by, and there was nowhere to go for a cyclist. Both sides of the road were lined with high buildings. I walked my bike, too wobbly to trust myself. I kept bashing my pedal against my calves. Once in San Miniato, I saw lovely stone homes so tidy one would think each line of mortar between bricks was scrubbed with a toothbrush. I noticed a beautiful starched, white curtain in a window that was hand-stitched with delicate daffodils. Osterias smiled with cheerful, green awnings and chubby, chalked menus.

I found the tall building that housed my suite and knocked on the heavy, imposing door built for a giant. I figured I'd better wash the blood off my legs before sitting down anywhere to eat. A man built like Sisyphus let me in. His name was Gennaro and he welcomed me with an embrace similar to a wrestling move.

The moment he noticed I was limping and bloody, he hauled me over his shoulder and hoisted me up three flights of stairs, while I squealed with surprise. He laughed. I didn't have time to be self-conscious, I didn't have time to feel frightened, I was a little kid at the fair on the Gennaro ride. He dumped me at my door and went back for my bike. He heaved that up three flights as well. Not speaking any English, he waved me in through another door, which I soon realized was his own smoky suite. He poured me a glass of water while I eyed a game show he was watching on his computer. He showed me to my room: a modest affair, with its own locked door, sitting area, and bathroom.

I took a shower and washed my clothes and stared out at the incredible view. The distant, jaggy, grey Apennines were pushed like blankets to the end of the bed. Fuzzy, rolling green hills, lines of tall cypresses, vineyard grids, and tidy, leafy orchards sprawled out luxuriously before me. I had a short nap. When I woke, the sun was already setting. I waved to Gennaro as I headed through the labyrinth of doors and stairs that finally landed me out on the street.

San Miniato is even more magical at night. Tall brick tunnels the colour of baked bread were lit with single lanterns that cast shadows all around me. The Tower of Frederick II overlooked the entire Valdarno, a stoic sentinel. The Piazza Venezia in front of the Palazzo Bonaparte was sombre and empty. I passed a line of homes, and each garage was a cave. One of the doors was open, and I saw a line of garlic drying on garden twine over the hood of a Fiat. San Miniato is famous for its fresh white truffles, so I hunted out a restaurant where I could find some: the Enoteca-Ristorante Piazza del Popolo. The chef, Salvatore, boasted owning a trained dog that sniffed them out. I chose a simple hand-rolled pici. It was very mild and so beautiful. I hadn't tried real fresh truffles before. It was sort of like a water chestnut and mushroom combined. I ate everything slowly and reverently. Then I was rudely interrupted by the Great Good.

We will never forsake you.

Damn it that made me so mad. I asked for the bill and spilled myself out into the night. I snaked myself beside the duomo and hissed. "You will never forsake me?! Where were you when I was shoved against the parking lot wall? Where were you when his sperm wriggled up to my egg? Where were you when my mother's body ate itself to bones? Where were you when Hazel was left crying in her crib while I wept in the kitchen corner?"

We were there.

"Oh, I see. So, if only I relied on You more, prayed to You more, fasted instead of eating whole boxes of Oreos, I could have handled the death of my mother. I could have had the courage to look into my baby's eyes. I could have the strength to confront my abuser. Thanks for this, very fucking useful. So, on top of me being an open wound that will never heal, I have a victim mentality – is that what You're saying? I'm a self-pitying lazy son of a bitch who should have just sucked it up because YOU WERE THERE. Got it. Great chat."

I curled along the circumference of the church.

It grieves Us how you speak of yourself. Those words are not from Us. You are Our beloved.

"Capricious asshole! Now I'm the beloved?! After You call me a failure?! I'm supposed to feel loved because Hazel has a wonderful grandfather? I should be praising You for the beauty of this dark night? I should be thankful Ivan didn't also bash my brains in?! If You loved me, You wouldn't have let Ivan get away with this shit scot-free. He died without ever getting caught."

Ivan has faced a reckoning.

"Oh, fucking good for Ivan. Floating around on a cloud somewhere, all forgiven. He should SUFFER! He should SUFFER!"

248

I leaned over the dark rail, overlooking the few twinkling lights of the city.

Grazie. Embrace Grace.

You want me to forgive Ivan? Forget it. I will never forgive him.

It is not your obligation to forgive Ivan. Ivan is Our business. We mean you. Embrace Grace for you.

"What?!"

I made my way back to my apartment. The hallways were empty and silent. I tiptoed to my door and turned the key quietly. I gravitated towards my small window and peered out at the night sky.

Open the window and breathe out the guilt and shame you carry. It is not from anything Great or anything Good.

I opened the tiny window, the square of magic. The town twinkled below, the sky was filled with stars and a bright crescent moon. Gorgeous. I breathed out guilt. A small sickly, wheezy breath that didn't last long. Then I breathed deeper for shame and exhaled it until it was gone. I closed the window.

Now the weight will fall off easily.

"The spiritual weight or the physical weight?"

Both. Because now you no longer need to hide.

I lay back in bed quietly and softly, like a gem placed on a pillow of velvet.

You are worth defending.

"What do you mean? Like, filing a police report? The guy is dead. What good will it do?"

A record of truth. For you. For Lucy.

"Who is –?"

Maybe there is another woman out there who could be helped to know: she did not imagine it, she did not have it coming, she did not deserve it. She is not alone.

The next day I headed down into the Elsa valley, a wonderful swoosh. I basked all day in the warmth and lightness of my new relationship with Grace. I stopped by a herd of sunlit sheep and listened to the gentle tinkle of their bells. Little white birds were bobbing around them, riding on their backs, snatching at bugs. The sheep were happy to share their pasture.

I climbed into the gorgeous comune of Gambassi Terme. I teared up when I saw the beautiful arches. It is my mother in me that tears up over architectural beauty and the watchfulness of the robin on the stop sign. But it is Herman who taught me fortitude to get places and how to measure out my time and my euros well.

On my way into San Gimignano, I came across a police barricade. I had heard the sirens wailing and distant dogs howling, mourning in empathy from their yards. The road was littered with police cars and fire trucks. An officer on the phone walked by me and I caught the word *morto*. Two cars were bashed to hell. One had been broadsided and the other had smashed headlong into a tree. Another police officer gestured to me: "A Piedi," go on foot. Another police officer waved at me to continue, dodging glass and a broken side mirror. I was to walk to the left of a tree. I wheeled over bits of broken metal. I passed the long line of cars waiting on the other side for clear passage. Their vehicles were turned off. We eyed each other grimly. It made me extra cautious the rest of the day, the slick deadly bit of rain on the road.

I pondered an instalment I had read at the Via Francigena Entry Point's museum in Lucca. It said something along the lines of: "This road is no longer of religious significance, but people still enjoy the nature, the culture, and the history of the Cammino." It made me so angry, and I wasn't a religious person. Why do the Cammino at all then? Fitness? What a base reason. Go to the gym. It's safer.

The famous San Gimignano skyline really lived up to its hype. From a distance it looked as though the town was filled with skyscrapers. But once I approached, I realized they were massive stone towers. Once I weaved my bicycle in through the walled city, I found a huge market piazza. My suite was beside a flower vendor. A lovely elderly lady in a crocheted sweater led me in past an elegant front desk of dark wood. My quaint room had a bedspread of roses, little shuttered windows overlooking one of the squares, and a decent shower. For dinner I had pears with basil, pecorino, and honey.

The next day, my body shrieked that it needed a day off. But I had fifty kilometres left of "challenging" road to endure before Siena. The app said, "Some small ups and downs followed by a long ascent into ..." Always with the long ascent. I swear, we've gone up so much we should be on the moon. The "small ups and downs" are a bald-faced lie.

Once I got going, my body tried to forget its fatigue. Between elevation extremes, I focused on the beauty of snowy geese, pungent lilac, friendly forests, and silvery olive groves. Finally, Siena. I navigated narrow streets through sweaty, blinky, swollen eyes until the city opened up into the magnificent Piazza del Campo. Now I understood why Pablo, the chef back in Lucca, demanded that I lie down in the middle of it. So I did. It's not an entirely unusual thing to do. The piazza is sloped and clam-shaped. It's neatly swept and free of automobiles and full of people reading and eating panini and sitting in caffès, gazing at the Fonte Gaia. I lay down on the warm red brick and stared up at the Torre del Mangia and the billowing clouds. Was it my imagination, or did I feel a rumble coming up through my back? I'm sure the bricks were breathing into me the memory of pounding horse hooves.

Madam Vidal of San Francisco finally showed her face. It was as if nothing had ever happened. To my great surprise (though I suppose I could have done the math), Camila was about the same age as me and rather fit, and some might say striking. She had dark hair and dark eyes, and she wore big earrings. I imagine when she was younger she would have been quite the looker. She still turned heads, largely because she wore a bright pink dress. But it wasn't a flashy sort. It was a classy sort. Like Nunzia would have worn, I guess. Except Nunzia had a full figure, which I much prefer. Not that I was looking at Camila's figure. She just took me by surprise is all. I was expecting an old lady. I don't know why.

(I think I don't realize I'm two years shy of seventy. Though, if I'm anything like my parents, I'll live into my nineties. I don't feel like an old man. I guess because I'm healthy and everything more or less still works.)

I digress.

Camila Vidal met us at a fancy place for lunch called Cardero's off the water, just a couple of blocks down the street from our hotel. When I saw her all decked out, I sure was glad we had gone shopping with Marco and JJ, or I would have felt intimidated. Hazel had her yellow and purple hair, but she combed it all nice, and it was still styled from yesterday. She wore her new matching yellow dress, and I must say she looked cute as a button: a real little city girl. I noticed that Hazel's posture had improved just by having a nice haircut. She stood straighter, felt better about herself. Actually, I don't know that it was just the haircut. I think it was the fact that she had some new people in her life that she could call family who most obviously love her.

Hazel was nervous to meet Camila, and I think she was also miffed that Camila stood us up for two days. She even said at breakfast that she didn't care if she met her. I knew this was likely just nerves. I said, "Let's meet her once, and if we don't like her, we don't have to meet her again." She figured that made sense. Anyway when we headed out to Cardero's, I told Hazel to walk the first couple of blocks in her old running shoes. I did the same thing, and then a block away, we changed our old shoes out for the new shoes so we wouldn't get blisters. Worked like a charm.

Camila saw Hazel and gasped and kissed her on both cheeks, very familiar. Hazel was all bamboozled by Camila's glamour and affection and was immediately in awe of her new great-grandmother. To my surprise and dismay, sushi came to the table pretty much right away, along with some dumplings. Camila insisted we try them, as they were apparently "superb." Later, I looked up on my phone what exactly she made us eat. It was tuna tataki and har gow shrimp dumplings. I wasn't a big fan of either and thought it rather presumptuous of her to order on our behalf. She barely took one bite of each and left the rest for us. Hazel was a champ and ate half, thank goodness. As my father always said, "Zero waste at the dinner table," starving children in Africa and all that, so I finished off the tataki and dumplings with focused determination. I would have much preferred a burger.

After that foreign fish stuff, I figured I'd better just have the soup of the day and let my stomach settle. Hazel decided to have the margherita pizza, which Camila criticized as being too heavy and entirely lacking in vegetables; she ordered Hazel a kale salad instead. Can you believe that? She just went ahead and ordered. Annoyed that Camila was bossing Hazel around, I ordered the margherita pizza for myself. But having been criticized for her choice, Hazel dutifully swallowed some of that kale stuff while sorrowfully eying my margherita pizza. She wouldn't touch it in front of Camila. To top things off, Camila had ordered a glass of white wine. Can you believe, thirty dollars a glass? And she most obviously expected me to pay for it. This is how we ended up having a whole lot of extra food and a bill of a hundred and sixty dollars for bloody lunch.

I don't want to say she flirted, but she kind of flirted with me, as if we were on a date and Hazel was the pet poodle or something. I don't have the words to describe it, except for the fact that I was getting the feeling we were being taken for a ride. Hazel seemed to enjoy Camila. She had brought Camila a picture she drew of Oola and the Okanagan, and Camila treated the picture with respect and thanked her for it. She rolled it carefully into a scroll around a handkerchief and placed it gently into her purse so it wouldn't wrinkle. I did appreciate that care.

Camila then brought out a photo album and showed us some pictures of her and her late husband, a hard-looking fellow with a large moustache. He had the same mousy hair as Hazel and the square head. Then Camila showed Hazel a picture of her daughter, Ivan's mother, Rose. Rose did not take after Camila one bit. She had thick glasses and that same mousy hair as her dad, and even in the pictures I could tell she was unhappy and uncomfortable, all slouchy and looking away. Camila said, "I named her Rose, but she was the thorn in my side." She called her all sorts of terrible things: lazy, ungrateful, a liar, a disappointment to her father. She didn't finish high school; she got into drugs and became a "sex fiend," as Camila put it. Rose died young of cirrhosis of the liver, and Camila simply said it was a "relief." Can you imagine describing the death of your only child that way? And why the hell was she telling this to Hazel? I almost interrupted, but then she turned her focus to Ivan.

Ivan was the golden child. Ivan was still a teenager when Rose died, and being an orphan, he went to live with Camila in San Francisco. Camila had nothing but wonderful things to say about him. He was handsome, he was fit, he was smart, he was charming. I got the impression that Camila, a widow by the time he showed up on her doorstep, doted on Ivan and turned him into her little companion. They went to the theatre together and on holidays to Hawai'i. When he studied in Barcelona for a year to learn Spanish, she went with him. I can't explain why, but it almost seemed … romantic, and it gave me the creeps. I could tell that hearing good things about her father was buoying Hazel up, though, so I let it go.

Camila gave Hazel one of his trophies; apparently he'd won first place in California for racquetball. She also gave Hazel one of his report cards: straight As. Camila then took a golden necklace off her own neck and placed it around Hazel's neck. It had a locket on it, and in that locket was a picture of young Ivan. She went on and on about it being twenty-karat gold and a family heirloom and soft, so Hazel should only wear it on special occasions and store it wrapped up in a soft cloth and put it into a box. She should never wear it in the pool, etc., etc. Camila is definitely a pontificator. How ridiculous to give such a thing to an eight-year-old. I'll tell you where it's going – in a box until she's sixteen.

I wanted to make sure I got some useful information out of Camila. This is what I learned:

- Camila has no health complications aside from osteo-arthritis.
- Her dad died of a heart attack at the age of fifty-three.
- Her mother died of a heart attack at the age of seventy-eight.
- Her husband's father died in the war.
- Her husband's mother died in childbirth (he was raised by his aunt).
- Her husband, eighteen years her senior, died of diabetes-related complications at the age of fifty-nine. I'm guessing alcoholism may have been involved.
- Her daughter Rose died of liver failure, also as a result of alcoholism, at the age of thirty-two.
- Ivan had no health issues and his blood type was B positive. Father unknown.
- There are no known hereditary diseases or cancer in the family.

After I paid for lunch and all the gifts were given, Camila said she had a spa appointment and would see us tomorrow. Hazel and I spent the rest of the day at the beach while my stomach tried to settle over that damn raw fish. That night we went downtown and saw a movie about Nancy Drew. Then we popped that margherita pizza in the microwave and ate it as a snack before bed.

The next day I suggested a horse-and-carriage ride through Stanley Park. Camila thought that was a grand idea. Again, she had a way of making everything sound like a date. She waited for me to offer her a hand into the carriage, like it was a royal wedding, Charles and Diana's – or should I say, Charles and Camilla's. Hazel loved the horses and she got really chatty about it. "Look at the ocean, Grumpy! Look at the totem poles, Great-Grandma," whereupon Camila said, "Hazel, it is sufficient to call me Grandma, and little girls should be seen and not heard." I thought Hazel would retort, but she hung her head instead and stayed silent. Can you imagine Hazel quiet? I was trying to figure out how to address the issue without making things worse for Hazel, but Camila started asking me all about my marriage and how long I was widowed. None of her beeswax. And I'll tell you, between her befuddling me with personal questions and the click-clacking of the horse hooves and the tourists beside us chatting very loudly in Mandarin and taking photos, I couldn't hear myself think.

The aquarium was better. I got a nice picture of Hazel and Camila in front of the jellyfish. Hazel particularly loved the penguins, and Camila told her that the penguin was Ivan's favourite bird. She engaged with her quite well, though she let us know that the San Francisco aquarium was far superior because they had an octopus. I was very happy to direct Ms. Superior to the Vancouver Aquarium octopus: Ceph Rogen. (They named their cephalopod after the Canadian actor Seth Rogen.) Camila pretended to not be impressed by the octopus or by an actor she had never heard of before, but I gave Hazel a sly wink, and she nodded. We scored.

Camila tired of the aquarium sooner than Hazel and I did, and so she hailed a cab while we stayed on to catch the otter show. It was a relief when she left. Before she did, she whispered to me that she'd be open to having dinner with me and having some adult companionship, if I could find a sitter for Hazel. I politely declined. Imagine that. You fly out to see your only living relative, and you want to ditch her in hopes of some hanky-panky. Get a life, lady. I wasn't sure if we would see her again after that, as she seemed quite put out.

Day three, Camila showed up after all, as though nothing had happened. She wanted us to go to the art gallery downtown. She did not make eye contact with me but ingratiated herself to Hazel. There was an exhibit that I can only describe as bizarre. Mowry Baden was the artist, and he made this ... wheelbarrow being pushed by a guy covered in black cloth and chicken wire. This was called *Marsupial*. Why? God only knows. It did not look like a kangaroo to me. There was also a room where ping-pong balls were being fired. Okay, more tax dollars well spent on "Arts and Culture." Camila said that Canadian artists tended to be derivative and small-time, not as groundbreaking as American artists, blah blah blah. I didn't know enough to counter that remark, so I said, "Well, we got some of the world's best music: Shania Twain, Anne Murray, Stompin' Tom, Gordon Lightfoot."

To which she said, "Who?"

I said, "Don't you listen to music, Camila?"

And she shrugged and said, "I prefer the classics: Mozart, Chopin, Vivaldi."

Give me a break, lady. Don't you ever turn on the radio?

The surprise was Hazel. Hazel loved the art gallery. I thought she would be bored out of her gourd, but no. She was particularly drawn to this weird thing where there was a reflection of yourself upside down in this round mirror, and the closer you got, the more distorted your face became, and there were a lot of colours all around. It was called *Calyx*. She stood in that art thing and stared at her changing reflection for a long time. I didn't understand it; Camila pretended to understand. Somehow, we knew not to interrupt Hazel's experience of it. Somehow, this weirdness was important.

When Hazel finally stepped out from the space-agey mirror thing, she said, "Sometimes you need to be upside down to really see yourself."

To which Camila replied, astonished, "Hazel, darling, you have the heart of an artist."

As much as I don't like to admit it, I believe Camila may be right. Cathy and Dave said something similar. I always thought Hazel to be poetical. This led to us looking at the European stuff upstairs and Camila going on and on about how she saw Monet and Chagall at the Louvre, and how she was an artist too, but her parents were really religious and had been through the war and the Depression and thought that art was vain. Her dad used to beat her and her mother. So, she married young in order to escape. Her husband was eighteen years older than her and provided for her well, but he was just as violent. He wanted her to be his "doll on a shelf," as she put it, and keep quiet. I could imagine the doll part; I could not imagine the quiet part. Once she contradicted him at a dinner party, and after the guests left, he broke her arm. She told me all this to help me understand why her daughter Rose left home so early.

During our sensitivity training as paramedics, we touched on PTSD; in particular, we briefly talked about intergenerational trauma. I found that real eye-opening. For starters, I had no idea what residential schools were until the RCAP report came out in 1996. And then all the stories of the sexual abuse and starvation and nearly half the First Nations students dying of TB or freezing to death or ... good Lord. All sorts of horror stories done to children. Medical testing. Still hard to believe. A guy wants to think people are making it up, but they're not. I've seen enough to know that.

My German grandfather came to Canada after the Second World War, and I've heard others say too that they had no idea what was happening to the Jewish people other than they were taken away and put into ghettos. Nunzia insisted too. Her parents under Mussolini knew nothing about the gas chambers. Maybe they couldn't admit what they knew. Maybe it was convenient to not ask questions. But then it happened to me about the residential schools. Right under my nose, and I didn't know. Could I have known? It still haunts me today: what I chose to stay ignorant about and what my own family didn't acknowledge. My dad's mother was Swampy Cree. I know nothing more about her other than her name was Marie, that she limped because she had polio, and that she died giving birth to her third child, who was stillborn. Dad never talked about his parents. Said his father was a hard man who only spoke in German when he got drunk, and his mother was dead. Why wasn't she connected to her Band? How did she even meet my grandfather? These are things I'll never know. Dad left Manitoba at the age of sixteen and never looked back. I stare in the mirror at the shape of my nose and the wideness of my lip, and I wonder at the violence and secrecy that resulted in me.

This concept of intergenerational trauma helps me make sense of Camila, as much as I don't like her. I suspect she wasn't well loved as a child, and she did not seem to love her daughter, who in turn, became an alcoholic and was a lousy mother to Ivan; so no wonder Ivan turned out to be a rotter. Not to excuse his behaviour. A fella always has a choice. But it makes it more understandable why he'd hate women, or himself, or whatever his problem was. I do see a pattern and that gives me some understanding, some room, I guess.

We went for one last dinner together. Camila had three glasses of white wine. And she's a tiny woman. She barely ate a thing. She was well into her cups before we even got into the first course. The dinner started with bread, and Hazel reached for some. Camila slapped her hand.

"Don't spoil your supper!" she barked.

I was stern then. "Camila, never lay your hand on my granddaughter again."

She laughed, surprised, and Hazel said it didn't hurt. It was at that point Camila got nasty. She said if I disciplined more, perhaps Graziana wouldn't have been whoring herself out, trying to trap Ivan into a marriage so she could live off their wealth. Hazel yelled at Camila not to say mean things about her mom. Camila told Hazel to get a grip on reality and to not be so stupid. Then I chimed in with the truth and said, "I think we all know Ivan sabotaged Graziana's sports career, stalked her, traumatized her, and assaulted her. He stole your car and crashed it on the highway while snorting cocaine and watching dirty videos. That's your wonderful grandson, Camila. That's your legacy. Well done."

I shouldn't have said that.

Camila stared blankly ahead and said, "Give me my gold locket back."

"No," said Hazel.

Camila grabbed the chain from around Hazel's neck and tried to rip it off. Hazel started to scream, because it was digging into her neck. The waiter tried to intervene, I grabbed Camila's hands, everyone in the restaurant was staring, and the gold chain and locket went flying in the air and landed in a corner underneath a table for two.

"Keep it," she said. "I fly all the way out here to give you my heart, and you break it."

She walked out. Hazel stared after her, and then she started to cry. I went over to the table for two, and they had scooped up the necklace. I put it into my pocket. It was broken. Hazel said she didn't want it and never wanted to see it again. I paid the bill, and we didn't even stay for our dinner; they just gave it to us to go. So Hazel and I walked hand in hand back towards our hotel. By then night had fallen, and the boats were out on the sea. It was real pretty.

"Grumpy," Hazel asked, "can we eat dinner outside on the beach?"

It was chilly, but we ate our spaghetti from containers on big logs and stared out at English Bay. We didn't say much. Goodness knows, a lot had been said that day. But by the second meatball, Hazel muffled with a full mouth, "Grumpy, it's time to see Mommy."

"I've never heard you say Mommy. It's usually Mom."

"Well, so what? I miss her."

"Me too."

"You miss my mom?"

"Yes, Hazel. I love your mom. She's the only child I've ever had in my life. Next to you. I'm excited for her to come back."

"So you don't have to take care of me anymore?"

"No, no, that's not what I said. I hope to keep doing some of what I've been doing. Wouldn't want you to miss math class."

"Oh, Grumpy. You have to keep making ginger chicken."

"Okay, I will. I'm excited because I have a feeling that your mom is going to come back … more like herself."

"Yeah. I think she's going to come back as Mommy. And I'm going to call her Mommy like a little kid would, because I think we have to start all over. Like as if I was a baby. But can walk and talk. You know what I mean?"

"I think I do."

"You know, Grumpy, I came to Vancouver hoping for a great-grandmother, but she can go suck an egg. You know what I got instead?"

"What?"

"I got a Zio Marco and a Tío JJ, the best uncles ever. I got Oola. I got an Uncle David and an Auntie Cathy who are so nice. I got to see real art. I got to go in the ocean. And Grumpy, I got you."

She threw her arms around me, and her final meatball went rolling down the beach and got covered in sand, and that made us laugh and laugh.

"Some seagull is going to be mighty happy you left your supper there."

"Yeah, she'll think it's a sandball and then poke poke poke, it's a meatball!"

"Buon appetito! Brawwwwk!"

Then I got an idea. I pulled the broken necklace out of my

pocket. "You know, sometimes when you want to let go of something, it's good to chuck it in the water. Do you want to let go of Camila, your farty not-so-great-grandma, and this whole goldarn experience?"

She nodded and seemed to know exactly what I was meaning. She took the necklace carefully in her little hands, then led me to the beach.

"I think we have to go in, or it will just wash up on the shore," I said, surprising even myself.

The water was extremely cold, being the Pacific Ocean at night in April. But I took off my new fancy shoes and socks and hoisted Hazel up on my shoulders and splashed into the water up to my, well, right before the important bits, Hazel squealing her head off.

"Goodbye, broken heart!" she yelled.

And then she chucked that necklace so hard I saw it fly above our heads, catch the light of the moon, and then land in the sea.

— Hazel —

My great-grandmother is not so great. She didn't have anything nice to say about anybody except herself. She did say I was an artist, but that's not nice necessarily, that's just saying the thing that is true, like, DUH. She's a bragger. I would say she has really pretty eyes and really nice hair and I like her shoes. She's a first-class number-one lady on the outside. But on the inside she's like a rotten lemon, like, sour and stinky at the same time, like compost. My great-grandmother is a pink dress stuffed with compost, and I bet in her heart she has maggots. Sometimes maggots are in the compost bin. You don't know how they got there but they are suddenly squirming around. That's what it was like with Camila Vidal. She was suddenly full of worms and we had to get out of there fast. I know I sound mean when I say that, but if you were there you'd understand.

She hit my hand and told me to be quiet, and at first I was like, "I want to be good for her, I want her to like me." But then I realized she's a jerk and I don't want her to like me, because if she liked me then maybe I'd be like her, and I never want to be like her. The whole family seems like they are not nice people. And this made me think that when I'm bad inside, when I'm mean, because sometimes I can think mean things, then that is because of my dad. I come from mean people. Well, my mom is not mean. She is boring and she left me, which is a different kind of mean, but she was never mean as in calling-me-names or hitting-me mean. I sometimes want to punch people in the face. Well, I did when I was little. That is my dad part, definitely.

We have an apple tree in our front yard, and one day Grumpy decided to cut off a huge part of it, like half of it. Because it was diseased. It had these lumpy bumps all over it, gross, like an alien had touched it and made it into lava bubbles. But the other half of the tree kept living. So, I think I can cut off this part of my family tree and I will keep living. I will keep living better and not get the maggot jerk disease.

Grumpy raised his voice to Camila and she really scared me when she grabbed the necklace around my neck. It was making a cut in my skin behind my hair because she was pulling, and Grumpy grabbed her arms and she wouldn't let go so the necklace snapped off and flew across the table! This was all because she said mean lies about my mom. And then she left and I think I will never see her again. Good! Yuck!

Cool things happened too, though. I saw the aquarium, a bunch of penguins; they were my favourite! They wiggle their little bums when they walk and they don't even have bums. They barely have legs. But you know, they do this wiggle, like: dodeedodeedodeedo – so cute! And they can swim like nobody's business.

An otter looks like a little dog in the water, and otters can hug each other and float at the same time. It's the cutest thing I have seen in my whole life. A floating otter hug. I just kept going, "Aw, aw, aw!" And Grumpy took me on some horses with a carriage like in the olden days. And we saw real totem poles in the park, one of them by the Hiding Guy People. They were sooooo big! How did they climb up all the way to the top to carve those faces? They must be really good at climbing and hiding. Then Grumpy told me it's "Haida Gwaii People." But secretly I still like "Hiding Guy": the secret powers of forest hiding.

We also went to the art gallery, and it was the coolest thing ever. I felt like someone went into my brain and then went SPLAT and put some of it everywhere. It was magic to think that there are hazelnuts like me out there who think up crazy stuff and then make it into art and people come see it! This can be a job?! I'm going to grow up to be a hairdresser AND an art maker!

There was a kangaroo guy with a wheelbarrow for a pouch. And there was, like, spaceship stuff you could move around on. I love art that you can touch! I never knew you could touch art. Then there was this magic mirror with lights that you walk into and see yourself upside down. It made me think of Mom. Like going away from me on this cycle trip was her way of going to the other side of the world to be upside down. She turned herself upside down so she could see herself. Those are still my eyes, but look at my eyes. Those are still my lips, but look at those lips! Which direction do I like it better? I never noticed my nostrils before. They are like perfect little triangles. It's good to look at yourself upside down. It makes me feel like I could be anything.

And that's when I decided I'm going to call her Mommy.

Grumpy and I threw the broken heart into the sea. Usually he doesn't put me up on his shoulders because he says I'm too heavy now and he's getting old. But this night he did; I was light as a feather. Grumpy is super strong for being an old guy. I think Camila had a crush on him, but he was too smart for that wormy worm.

There was a picture of my dad she showed me. He was wearing a velvet suit with a bow tie and teddy-bear ears. Ivan was a chubby baby, very cute. I think that is how I am going to remember him: just little, before he even knew how to grab and say, "Mine."

The beloved wakes. He rubs his eyes and then grunts, realizing he still identifies as male. He has the impulse to urinate after waking: phantom fluid. He misses the familiar feel of his penis. He thinks how often he disparaged it for its size, but it served just fine. Consistent erectile function, steady flow, high sperm count. He sighs deeply, cloaked in the remembrance of the transgressions made with that same organ. The soul forgives, but it is too wise to forget. Forgetting leads to repeating. He doesn't want that. Memory is a heavy gift. This also gives him a thought.

"I'd like to meet my father. Is he here?"

He is only sixty-five. He's alive.

"Oh. I never thought of that. He's outlived me. Did he even know I existed?"

No.

"May I ... know him? See him?"

So, we spy.

Bill is making beds in Wolfville, Nova Scotia. He has a handsome grey beard that is surprisingly soft to touch. He wears a ratty T, the one reserved for cleaning. He's learned from his wife, Kim, how to set the pillows perfectly. He plumps the third and fourth, pulls the corners to make them straight, props them up on top of the duvet. Then the firm, crocheted lumbar, spelling out "Home Sweet Home," set with great precision in the middle. Guests ask who did the needlework. He does not tell them he purchased the pillow at Winners.

He vacuums the bedroom, and then the living room, and then the hall, and then the kitchen, and then the guest bedroom, and then the bathroom. He uses the brush extension to run along the baseboards. He double-checks the tub. Already a spider. These old houses. He scoots it onto his dustpan and tosses it outside, despite the fact they could use the rain. He dots the drain with peppermint oil.

Bill then waters all the flower boxes around the house by hand: pink geraniums. They offset the yellow and white of his Victorian home, built in 1893. He lets the cat in, "Here, Tabby," pours some kibble into a bowl and tops it with yesterday's salmon skin.

The kettle is set on the stove. While the water heats, Bill makes two ham sandwiches with edam cheese and mustard on white bread and slides in sweet pickles. He then stares out the window a good, long while. Resigned, he heads to the fridge and pulls out a head of lettuce and extracts two leaves. They each get a quick rinse and then they get shoved into the sandwiches. The kettle whistles. He pours the steamy water into a teapot. Everything is set on a tray with two cups prepared: a dash of milk and sugar in one. He heads up the stairs, hands full, and pushes open a door left ajar.

"Hello love," he says.

Kim opens her mouth, slowly. Afflicted with bradykinesia and rigidity, she smiles with her eyes.

"What's she got?" the beloved asks.

Parkinson's disease.

The beloved watches Bill feed his wife tenderly while informing her that the next guests are from Hong Kong, and he hopes she is well enough to come downstairs tomorrow morning and speak Mandarin with them. They're here to visit their son, who is studying at Acadia. She slowly pulls a pickle out from between her teeth. That isn't what she wants today.

He talks about the movement of the clouds and their neighbour's new car. He tells her Tabby appreciated the leftovers. He announces what he's going to do with the rest of the afternoon: mow the lawn, dig compost into the vegetable bed, and plant peas and carrots.

"He's kind."

Yes, he is.

"How long have they been married?"

Thirty-three years.

"Do they have kids?"

A daughter and a son, three grandkids.
All local?
The daughter is in Halifax.
"So I have half-siblings. Half Chinese. That's cool."
You do.
"What do they do?"
The daughter is at home with two kids; she is a kindergarten teacher. The son is an electrician.
"Well that makes sense. We like to teach, and we're handy. So, how did this nice, respectable East Coast guy meet someone like my mom? I can't imagine him in that sleazy living room."
He had moved out to the West Coast to work in a lumber mill in Crofton, BC. He went out with his buddies one night to a bar. Your mom had snuck in with fake ID. After many drinks, he had intercourse with your mom in the back of his truck under a tarp, at her bidding. It was an enjoyable night for them. You were conceived with the giddiness of youth, knees sticky with tree sap, fronds of cedar in their hair, laughter.
"Did they even know each other's names?"
Bill and Rose, yes. They think of each other with fondness.
"Gee, Bill. You could have had another son. And wouldn't that have made you proud."

The beloved continues to watch Bill run to the post box, help Kim to the toilet. He lets in the B & B guests, makes pork chops with canned mushroom-soup sauce over rice, watches the news with Kim, bathes her body, helps her brush her teeth. He tenderly combs her hair, sets out her pills, and puts her to bed. He then retires to his son's old room and slips under a blue-striped blanket on a flattened twin bed. He soon falls asleep and snores quite loudly. Kim is kept awake in the dark a long time, blinking.

And with that, We leave the little town of Wolfville under a crescent moon and a cool wind coming off of the Minas Basin.

CHAPTER THIRTEEN

KINDNESS IN A CUP

— *Graziana* —

RADICOFANI, TOSCANA

In Siena, my suite was to the left of Via dei Malcontenti. I tried not to take that to heart. I rested most of the day, leaving my room for only a few short hours to wander around the incredible city. I was too weary to really take in another glorious steepled chiesa; I had chiesa fatigue. For weeks now I've seen mangled Christs suffocating on crosses, tapestries of lions tearing apart sheep, paintings of overgrown babes giving us sociopathic stares while batting absent-mindedly at the Madonna's offered breast. It's starting to get to me. The only images of my gender are of passive, sorrowful Madonnas or anguished, lascivious Eves.

Outside of the duomo, however, stood an imposing, warrior-like female angel with stained glass wings: Alberto Inglesi's *Donna in cammino*. She stood staring at the Catholic institution with sober examination, one foot in the ancient world, one foot in the contemporary. Just seeing her there gave me such a feeling of renewed courage and relief. What a powerful way to be. Once I opened my eyes to her, I noticed other Inglesi sculptures of women warriors and goddesses installed around the city: preparing for war, bearing down for birth, stretching languorously like a lioness ready for lovemaking. Imagine being the one with strength? The one with power?

I bought an Easter cake at a bakery full of locals, sort of a fig-and-apricot torte pressed with almonds and rum. I tossed bits of that into a salad with apple, gorgonzola, radicchio, and fennel – fantastic. I cooked all my meals and did my laundry and rested, which is what I needed to do. It was difficult because I had never been to Siena, but I had to tell myself this trip was not about ticking off the boxes of culture and art. It was about the land and the sky, the farms, the trees. It was about the Cammino in front of me. I would be focused and strong and self-reliant like an Inglesi *Donna*.

All night a street party was going on. I was in a hotel in the Contrada della Torre. Though it was disrupting my sleep, I couldn't disparage the joyful cacophony of community. I nodded off to a loud male unison choir singing folk songs and drinking wine well into the early morning.

Today was a beautiful and reasonable up-and-down through the Tuscan landscape. There were several pilgrims on foot. Romantic clouds were overhead, but they never rained their melancholy on me, just sheltered me from the sun and turned the tops of hillsides purple. At one point, I was nearly startled off my bike when a small ram bleated at me with a man-baby cry.

I felt as though my body had grown muscle overnight. It simply needed the rest in order to renovate. I felt far stronger and more capable. I rolled into the fairy-tale walled village of San Quirico d'Orcia. Herman had suggested I see the Collegiata dei Santi Quirico e Giulitta and the Palazzo Chigi Zondadari, but I ended up at the Church of Santa Maria Assunta, to my surprise. (Here I thought I was done with chiese.) Santa Maria Assunta is a mid-eleventh-century Romanesque church. It is made from grey, square, travertine stone, with a single nave, no adornment. I was drawn to its simplicity and its silent street. I didn't pray inside, but rather, I wandered through an adjacent austere rose garden snuggled up next to it. Someone was tending to these red beauties. Someone cared enough to keep them clipped.

The rose garden, I discovered, led into the Horti Leonini garden: a sixteenth-century Italian park. One level was wild and woody and another was full of carefully manicured triangular boxwood beds and a statue of Cosimo III de' Medici, Grand

Duke of Tuscany. I made my way to my little yellow sunflower-themed suite in the pink B & B, C'era una Volta, located in the middle of town. That night I dined at the Trattoria Osenna. Though it had a wine list as big as a Bible, I did my body a favour and stuck to sparkling water. The ristorante warned that dinner would take a while because all the pasta was hand-rolled. The menu went on at length about the danger of pasta rollers compressing the dough and making it too hard. I had pici with steak and chicory. It was *sex*cellent. I wrote my postcard to Hazel between bites.

> *When I get home we will learn to make hand-rolled pasta.*
> *Do you like roses?*
> *Maybe we can plant a fairy garden by the tree in the backyard. With a little fairy castle.*

The next day I passed this wonderful castle B & B called Spedaletto. It used to be a hospital and then an inn for pilgrims in the twelfth century – gorgeous. Wouldn't Hazel love how magical this place looks with its flowering bushes in the courtyard and the opulent rooms with princess beds? I wonder if she'd ever want to go on an adventure like this with me. How old would she have to be to appreciate it? Thirteen? I could save up for that.

In the distance I saw a mountain covered by dark clouds. It looked like Gondor on a ringless day. I chuckled to myself, "Wouldn't it be something if that was my destination?"

As the kilometres clicked along, my path kept veering towards the ominous kingdom. "It can't be. I know I'm climbing eight hundred metres today, but that looks too far away."

No towns, hardly any farms on this stretch, no place to stop for a pee or a sandwich. Well, it was only thirty-five kilometres or so in total today, so I kept pushing on. About fifteen kilometres later, I was cycling through a national reserve forest, and I hadn't seen a house or farm in a long time. The rain had been at me already, just a sprinkle, but now it started to pelt down with great determination and thunder.

"Oh dear."

I kept pedalling. Afraid of lightning, I didn't get off my bike once; I just kept riding. Up, up, up … my heart was pounding. I heard a bunch of little yips around one uphill, thickly forested bend; they sounded like baby foxes. Let's hope they were foxes. Another thunderclap, even closer! Not a single car on the road. I kept going, pumping pumping pumping, up towards Gondor. I was able to see the lightning crack open the dark, broody sky.

The road wound on and on, up and up. Sure enough, I was scaling that dark, cloudy mountain towards the castle. The rain and wind started to blow so hard, I had difficulty keeping my handlebars straight. I was shivering, but there was nowhere to shelter. The thunder cracked loudly now; it made my tires skid. Lightening was so close, I could count to three and hear the deafening clap, and the whole landscape would electrify around me. I could feel it in my molars when it struck. I know the Great Good said I would die an old lady of bodily dysfunction, but They didn't say anything about living the rest of my life with a brain injury due to a strike of lightning! Just when I thought it couldn't get worse: hail! It pelted down like buckshot; I was very glad for my helmet. Bike on, bike on, bike on, terrifying thunder and lightning. Its might made me whimper, and the cold made me shake. My rain-resistant jacket had finished resisting a long time ago.

Finally, Radicofani came into sight. It was a beautiful town nestled into a high plateau on the mountain I had been calling Gondor. The "Rocca," an imposing castle, was still above us on the summit. What dark, brain-addled Carolingian built that imposing fortress in the 900s? How isolating! However, the castle served Italy's Robin Hood, Ghino di Tacco, well, as he rode down the mountain to ransack wealthy travellers on the Via Francigena.

In Radicofani, my navigation went all awry and the service was spotty. I ended up at a prosaic yellow apartment complex.

The thunder continued and the hail was hitting cars to the point of possibly damaging them. The soft animal of my body took refuge in the parking lot, while tenants peered out their windows in concern for me. I called my B & B. They hardly spoke any English.

Broken to broken I stuttered, "Io ... arrivo giallo appartamento ... tu? No? Sì, sì. Aspetto qui. Okay. Aspetto in parchetto. Okay ... la casa con giardino? I don't see a garden. I aspetto qui. Appartamento. Okay?"

I ventured down the road and saw nothing like they had described. Great. I didn't need to tap to keep myself from hyperventilating; the hail was tapping for me. A man from the apartment complex ventured out in an umbrella and opened up his garage for me to shelter in. He only spoke Italian, but he ended up taking my phone, calling them again himself, and he got them to drive over to get me. Bless him.

A husband and wife showed up in a minivan. My bike was wet and filthy, and so was I. I said, "Vicini?" hoping that meant "Close?" They said, "Sì, sì," so I followed them to their little acreage, which was about five hundred metres further down the road. The wife dropped the husband off at a cottage, and he waved me towards it while she drove to the main house with a scowl. It was clear she thought I was an idiot.

"Occupati tu di quella scema."

I don't remember much after that; I didn't see the wife again. But the husband brought me into this little cabin and set my bike beside it. It had a roaring fire prepared by a kitchen. I get this whole cabin to myself? I was delirious. I was shaking, and my fingers were so numb, I couldn't get my bags out of the panniers, so he did it for me and led me in beside the fire. He unclipped my helmet for me, under my chin, as though I were a small child. It made me tear up, it was so kind of him. I was so relieved to be safe and sheltered after two hours of biking in the storm. Then he peeled off my wet jacket and my soaked sweater, leaving me shivering in my T-shirt, biking shorts, and goose skin. He handed me a towel for my face and hair and sat me in a chair by the fire. Then he took my soggy shoes off for me and set them by the fire. He made me tea: Great Good embodied.

By the time the kettle boiled, I had regained my composure somewhat and laughed and apologized for being so helpless and hopeless.

He nodded. "Il temporale è molto pericoloso."

He told me where a good restaurant was, and he handed me one of those Twinkie sort of breakfast Danishes I hated. He gave me a double kiss goodbye and good wishes, and he was out the door. I sat down by the fire, soaking in that man's kindness. I looked around me. I was in a spacious wooden cabin with two bedrooms and a post-and-beam kitchen with a stone fireplace. It was adorable. In fact, it was *ro-tic* (a romantic experience without the man, as my friend Anita from college would say). I hobbled into a hot shower and then after a nap, I put on all the clothes that I had left that weren't wet, and I walked the fifteen minutes into town for dinner. The rain had finally stopped.

Radicofani was beautifully laid out, with tiny cobblestoned streets, stone stairways, and hidden corridors. The buildings had large wooden doors with polished knockers and baskets of flowers everywhere. Ristorante La Grotta was indeed in an old grotta, its beauty rather tackily dressed up with a stuffed panda in the corner and other such oddities. But the local people were in there, and the hand-rolled spinach and ricotta ravioli I had with tomato and garlic sauce was the best pasta I'd had so far on my trip.

It was hard for me to consider what my mother might have thought of this pilgrimage. To ponder that I had to ponder what my mother might have thought of my mental incapacity to handle the rape, her death, and my pregnancy all at once. She'd have said something along the lines of "Non fare la bambina!," which meant I was not a baby anymore. Or worse, "Stare con le mani in mano." I think that's right. It means to be useless: to sit there holding your own hand.

Often women who have been through a great deal of tragedy are the most cruel to other women. "You got raped? Well, that was stupid of you. You've had a miscarriage? I've had four. You had postpartum? So what? I did too, but I had three other kids to take care of. Get over it." Stare con le mani in mano.

Interesting how Herman, the most practical person I know, understood this pilgrimage. I wonder how Hazel will feel. She won't understand it right now, what I have been through, and why I am here. But I can only hope she will someday. I hope she'll understand the mountain I've climbed to get to her. She will hopefully see it as an act of love.

Before we left for home, we met Marco and JJ for breakfast at their place. Marco made a frittata with spinach and ricotta, just like Nunzia used to make. It's amazing how you can put a forkful of food in your mouth and someone long since gone suddenly appears in your tastebuds. I asked him how to make it. I figured it would be a nice thing to pass on to Hazel. He took me patiently through each step (Italians have to make a big deal out of showing you with their hands; they can't just write it in a recipe), and I think I got it down. Hazel didn't much care for it, but I figured she might over time. At the very least, I'll make it for Graziana her first morning home. That is, if she wants me around.

I then put out the formal invitation for Marco and JJ to join us for Christmas. I offered my suite, assuming that Graziana would be okay with me sleeping on her pullout sofa. Marco said he was pretty busy with the salon around the holiday season, and JJ often picked up a weekend retail job to earn some extra money. They've never much celebrated Christmas. Plus, JJ had his widowed mother to think of. I got the impression that there may be other reasons they didn't care for the holiday. Well, Hazel overheard the conversation and was all over it like stink on a skunk. She pushed and pushed, and finally Marco explained to her that Christmas made him depressed. It brought up memories of his family in Italy rejecting him, his father being ashamed of him. He hadn't seen his father in thirty years, and his mother won't travel.

He also talked about the rejection of the Catholic Church and how he used to be an altar boy. And how, as a gay young man in the nineties, there wasn't the same kind of opportunity to get married and have children back then. He explained that was the heartbreak of his life, to not be a father. Hazel said that she is a child and I was a grandpa and that we loved him. I'm telling you, that kid is a dart to the heart. At this point, Marco burst into a bunch of Italian words and kisses for her, and JJ nodded but looked out the window, kind of sober-like. I think it was the first time I saw his face without a smile. Once you see a person's sadness, you can't unsee it.

So I made another offer, "Let's have Ukrainian Christmas," to which JJ asked if I was Ukrainian, and I said no, and then we all laughed. But it would be a nice way to break up the doldrums of January, to have them come visit January seventh to fourteenth. They could bring JJ's mother since my suite is a two-bedroom. We could all go ice-skating on Bower Pond, do some cross-country skiing, and maybe go up to Ed and Connie's for some tobogganing? I'd even make cabbage rolls. Marco said they'd see, and that he appreciated the offer.

We said our goodbyes and then hit the road. Reality started to sink in. Graziana would be home in three days, and my one-on-one time with Hazel would likely be over. Grazie has always found me a bit much. I can't imagine that will change. I've never been able to navigate her moods. I don't know how to help her in a way that she appreciates. I don't think she would have ever chosen me to be in her life. She was stuck with me. She might, in fact, get very possessive over Hazel. She might ask me to not come around anymore if she feels threatened by me. And it was this troublesome thought that kept me pretty quiet at the wheel all the way to Hope. It was there that we stopped in at the Home restaurant and had a piece of lemon meringue pie. Hazel had a piece of chocolate pie. I told her she'd regret it, as chocolate pie so often disappoints, but I was wrong. She ate every last scrap of it.

She's an intuitive person, our Hazel. You'd never guess it, because on the drive all the way to Hope she talked non-stop about the female version of *Ghostbusters* and how it held up to the male version. She compared plot points and characters all the way through the Lower Mainland, to the point where I thought I would lose my mind.

I asked her, "Why on earth would I care about hearing the entire plot of two movies I have never seen?"

She said, "Well, I'm trying to get your mind off of thinking sad things, and *Ghostbusters* made me laugh. It's not my fault if you don't think it's funny."

To which I replied, "It's never funny when you retell a movie. It's just best for the person to see the real thing. Retelling movies is one of the most tedious things you can do."

"What does *tedious* mean?"

"It means excruciatingly BORING."

"Well, it's not as boring as sitting beside your grandfather for three hours while he's being sulky and not letting you play your own music. That's BORING."

"Well, settle in, kid; we have another nine hours."

Letting her eat chocolate was not a smart idea. She was hyperactive in the back of the car, wiggling around, listening to her headphones, doing dance moves, and singing and then talking non-stop about old social dynamics from school. "And then Maxine told Yumi that blah blah blah, and then Nodin, who is the smartest in the class, said blah blah blah ..." I can't say I was very kind to Hazel today. I told her that something even more tedious than retelling movies was retelling gossip about other people that happened years ago. Who cares? And she kept kicking the back of my chair. I tell you, by Salmon Arm I was fit to be tied. I pulled over and let her run around the shore of Shuswap Lake.

Graziana, for all her faults, never raised her voice with Hazel. She's got that over me for sure. I mean, I never yell or anything, but I get short. I get stern. That isn't always a bad thing; sometimes it's necessary, but today I was just simply in a bad mood and taking it out on her. Admittedly, if I could hand over the reins to Grazie, there would be some relief in it. Could I not admit that? Being able to keep the house perfectly clean with no fingerprint marks on the stainless-steel dishwasher, no carpet fringes turned over, no pens lying out, no toothpaste gobs in the sink, no empty milk cartons in the fridge. I could wake up in the morning to quiet, have my coffee, and actually listen to the news uninterrupted. I could eat beans and toast for supper and watch an entire hockey game.

I missed most of the semifinals last year and at least twenty minutes of the Stanley Cup playoffs, thanks to Hazel skate-boarding in the backyard on the icy sidewalk and scraping up her knee. Not that I care much for the Washington Capitals or the Vegas Golden Knights. What kind of name is that anyway? Golden Knights. Ridiculous. When did hockey become about money instead of sport? Mind you, being from Alberta, I've been spoiled. I grew up with hockey royalty. I saw Gretzky score against Dryden. I was in the stadium for the '79 WHA all-star game with Gordie and Mark Howe against Dynamo Moscow. Messier, Lemieux. Yeah, that was real hockey. I mean, Draisaitl's worth watching, and McDavid. But it's a far cry from when the Oilers had the Great One.

We stopped in Golden for supper at the Legendz Diner. Hazel got a kick out of the whole fifties shtick in there, with the red barstools and the checkered floor and the pictures of Elvis Presley and Marilyn Monroe and all that gack. I had to admit, though, their milkshakes were mighty generous and their burgers not half bad.

When we finally got home, it was 2200 hours, and Hazel went straight into the shower and then to bed. It wasn't until the next day that I looked in the mailbox, and there were five postcards from Grazie. I was tempted to read them but didn't. I just stacked them beside Hazel's orange juice at the breakfast table. She didn't grab them and read them right away, like I expected. She stared at them while she ate. Then she gathered them up and took them into her room.

Last couple of days, we've been getting back to our home-schooling. Hazel will actually read without being prompted now. She's reading a series called Judy Moody, which I hate. I think it encourages bratty behaviour. Judy is very rude and as far as I'm concerned could use a real good spanking. Not that I've ever spanked Hazel, but if I had a Judy, I might be tempted. It's basically a book about a young smart-aleck sociopath. Anyway, as long as Hazel is reading, that's all that matters. She can count backwards. She understands the months of the year. She's pretty good at grooming herself. She's got her multiplications up to ten. Basic division is still tricky. She can sew a button. She can prepare a can of tomato soup. She can make her bed. She can play crazy eights. She can braid her own hair. I think Grazie will be nothing short of amazed, frankly.

JJ and Zio Marco are coming for Ukrainian Christmas. I am already planning how to make their stockings and what I'm going to put on them. You can make some pretty good stockings if you use felt and fabric paint. I've seen it on YouTube. And Grumpy has been showing me how to sew and I can sew a button so I think I can sew a sock, especially if I start now. Zio Marco is going to have green and red and silver because it reminds me of his silver disco ball. And I am going to put on hairdryers and curling irons and brushes and wigs because Zio Marco does hairstyling. If I was a really good drawer and crafter, then I would put Santa Claus with a great hairdo and a curly moustache, but I am not a good drawer. So, I will "stick to the basics," like Grumpy says.

And JJ's stocking will have shirts and ties and socks on the sock (which feels like a joke to me; is that a joke?) because JJ likes fashion. And he will have gold because he wears a gold necklace so I know he likes gold. Mom and Grumpy have stockings already that my nonna Nunzia made for them a long time ago. Grumpy's is red plaid (because Grumpy is the plaid man, everything is plaid; plaid is a bunch of lines and squares as a design, mostly you see on older men and sometimes Scottie dogs and butterscotch). Mom's stocking is REALLY old, like her stocking from when she was a little kid. It has an angel on it and a baby Jesus, except the baby Jesus's head got ripped off because it used to have a halo and the halo got caught on a pinecone, says Mom. So, anyway, it's just a baby body in the crib, which is kind of creepy. But Mom loves it. It makes her laugh, so I don't say anything. But maybe, depending on how I feel about her coming back, maybe I will make her a baby Jesus head. If I start now and get practising on my baby Jesus head making. I don't think I will make baby Jesus a halo though. I will make Jesus smiling, and that will be holy enough. Because, if you think about it, babies, when they are born, are not smiling. They don't know how to smile. Not for a long time afterwards do they learn. (Auntie Connie told me that because I was trying to make baby Amber smile but she was only a newborn like Jesus.) If you think about it, if the baby Jesus is smiling, you already know this baby is a little bit magic.

I asked Grumpy what baby Jesus was all about, because some of the songs for Christmas talk about him being the Son of God. They also talk about some girl named Mary being a virgin, which I think is very rude. Imagine people singing about your vagina every Christmas? Nobody's beeswax – so weird! Grumpy agreed that it was weird. He said that some people think that God (who is a big man in the sky who created the whole earth and universe, which sounds a little far-fetched to me, and Grumpy says it sounds far-fetched to him), decided to put a baby inside a young woman named Mary before she had sex so that everyone knew the baby was from God, not from a penis (Grumpy didn't say penis but that's what he meant). And so baby Jesus was born, and he was a little bit human and a little bit God. Sort of like Camp Half-Blood and the Olympians from Percy Jackson.

I asked Grumpy, "Do people believe that for real? Why?" Grumpy said the story about God gives people comfort. But I don't see what's so comfortable about a big alien dude who can stare at you all the time.

And Grumpy said that some people think God is just another word for Love. So if Love is watching over you all the time, that can be a comfort. Well, that was a completely different story! Love?! Love is a lot of things. And Grumpy figured I was right about that.

I thought about Jesus and his headless body and making him his smiling baby face. I thought about how lucky, if it was true, to be Jesus. Jesus got to be the Son of God. Imagine being able to make that family tree for school? One side of the tree just goes round and round in a big circle called Love. "Guess what, I'm related to LOVE." Not only that, but he also had a dad named Joseph, so he had two dads. No wonder he was smiling. Why did Jesus get to be so lucky? Maybe if God is real, and if God is the big Love thingie-thing that made the whole planet and the universe, maybe God would also want to have a daughter? Because it's kind of nice to have a daughter and a son. And maybe a nonbinary kid just to be fair. (There is a person in my school who was Jason and is now Jazz, and I think Jazz would be a great kid for God too because Jazz is pretty nice to me and Geoffrey and other kids who are different, and we all understand what it is like to be picked on.) Why not spread it around, God? Maybe all I have to do is ask.

So I asked quietly in my head, "God, I'd like to be your daughter, if you want a daughter, because I don't have a dad and that would be really useful." And I can't explain what happened next, except it made me very sad. Grumpy was in a big grump so he didn't notice, but I cried very, very quietly until he said to stop snuffling my snot, so I got a Kleenex. But I also felt really, really warm inside. Like maybe, just maybe, God said, "Okay, Hazel. I choose you."

Of course I'm not going to tell Grumpy any of that because he thinks it is all baloney and I don't want him to laugh, because if he tells me I'm being silly about it then it might take away this feeling. And I like this feeling.

Mom sent me postcards. They are really squishy writing and hard to read. She's talking like she isn't herself. I know this is her handwriting because I recognize it. But I don't really recognize her talking. She sounds ... happy. I'm having second thoughts about calling her Mommy.

— Beloved —

The beloved returns to Wolfville the next day and watches his father mow the lawn and then pick the seeds out of a watermelon to serve to Kim, cut up in squares and served with a toothpick.

"I think it would be rather nice to be needed."

Yes. It is part of the Design.

"Nobody needs me. Not really. I know I'm part of the cosmic pattern and all that, but nobody needs me like Kim needs that man, my dad. And although it looks boring and hard and sad, really ... it has meaning. Can you make me into an angel?"

An angel?

"Yeah, like, can I be a guardian angel or something like that?"

Angels are created differently, Our beloved. You have a human soul. You're simply more complex.

"That keeps me from being useful?"

The beloved watches his father some more. He is now laying a cold compress on Kim's forehead, and even though she is ill and in pain, she is rubbing his arthritic thumb.

"Who is guarding my daughter, Hazel? She has an angel, right?"

Yes.

"What is the angel's name?"

Angels do not have spoken names but felt names. Their name is ... felt to be gentle laughter with the taste of what you might liken to crabapple jelly. It is their feeling but also their function.

"Meaning they guard Hazel with ... gentle laughter and crabapple jelly? That's not a great defense. No wonder kids get murdered. No wonder they get molested. What if she's about to be hit by a truck? Laughter and condiments are not going to save her!"

Often Hazel is directed away from danger because gentle laughter brings her to a pause and a rethinking.

"Saved by jokes."

Not always. But humour is one of Our greatest gifts to humanity.

"I'm a joke."

Sometimes. Sometimes you are magnificent. Why do you ask about Hazel's guardian angel?

"Well, I'd like the job. Though, now that I think about it … I don't know if I'm that sophisticated."

We understand your desire to protect Hazel. We feel the same. Terrible things happen to children. Terrible.

"Tell me about it. It's why I don't believe in You. I still don't. I mean, I know You're powerful but I don't believe You're Perfect."

It haunts Us: this Design We've created and the innocent souls caught in the fabric We have woven, stabbed by the pin. The price of freedom is often too great. We ponder this.

"That's your problem. You ponder. You puke poetry. You don't protect. I want to protect her. If this free-will business is legit, you'll let me do that. The only person who really needs me is that little girl. Nobody else can be her dad."

That's true. Nobody else can be her dad. She will always have that absence.

"Drive the knife in further, would ya?"

The beloved drops the subject of guardian angel. He watches his father gather up Kim and carry her emaciated, pale body to the toilet for relief. Kim's bottom is now concave and wrinkly, her knee bones are bigger than her thighs. They chat about the temperature of stored tulip bulbs.

"Please," the beloved says.

Please?

"Can you not find a way for me to … watch over Hazel? At least for the next ten years, until she's eighteen. She didn't deserve any of this."

Interference is not part of the Pattern.

"You created the pattern; you can break it."

We have given Hazel her guardian; We have given Hazel her

gift. Her gift is her creative mind. With it, she is the wildest of alchemists. She can turn any part of her pain into poetry. She can transform the grot and gash of her life into gold. She is also starting to tap into Us, directly, and We are limitless Love. She doesn't need you in order to be happy. She doesn't need you in order to be whole. Please take Our hand. When you create, you will find purpose. It is not the point to do it alone.

"No."

With that, the beloved tucks himself up and vanishes from Wolfville with the smallest of cries.

CHAPTER FOURTEEN

FLAT ITALY

— Graziana —

BOLSENA, LAZIO

The next morning, wanting to beat any possible recurring storm, I hastily pumped my tires and zoomed down the Radicofani collina. About ten kilometres out, I saw a caffè near a couple of factories in the middle of the country and decided the clouds were far enough behind me that I could have my morning cappuccino.

Over the last few days, I have shared the Cammino with a biker laden down with camping gear. Despite his heavy load, he bikes faster than me, but then he stops over longer so I catch up to him. Every time he passes me, I wish him a "Buon cammino," and he never wishes me anything back. This has happened six times or so now. It's beyond the place of rude.

But today, when I walked into the little caffè, he was there at a small table.

He looked up, grimaced, and said in a Californian accent, "Well, if it isn't Miss Buon Cammino." I pretended to completely ignore him as I ordered my cappuccino. To my surprise, he called out, "Join me, oh pellegrina."

I looked at him warily and carried my cup and saucer to the small table and sat down across from him.

"Where you from?" I asked.

"Why do you assume I'm not from here? Because I'm Asian?"

"No, because the locals are friendly, and you are an asshole."

This made him laugh. His eyes crinkled at the sides, revealing his age. He crossed one slender leg over the other and ran a hand through his hair, spiky with sweat and greying at the temples. "I'm from Oakville. And you're Canadian, eh? You have a strong accent. How far are you travelling?"

"All the way to Rome," I replied, proudly.

"Oh yeah."

Annoyed by his lack of enthusiasm, I inquired, "How far are you travelling?"

"Iran."

"Iran?"

"Yeah, Southern Italy to Croatia to Turkey to Iran."

I nodded, not wanting to let on any sign of being impressed.

He sipped his cappuccino and admitted, "Bolsena is only fifty-five kilometres and a four-hundred-metre climb. I'm ready for an easier day. Especially after that hail last night."

"And how about the ascent to Berceto? That was intense!"

He shrugged. "Italy is flat. I mean, compared to the rest of Europe. Italy is very flat."

I wanted to punch him in the head.

"I'm impressed with you," he said. "You're a light packer."

"Well, easy for me. I'm sleeping in B & Bs and eating in restaurants, not dragging along a tent and camping stove."

"True. Principessa." He stood up with his long, lean legs unapologetically wrapped in bright-green, frog-like spandex. "See you out there, eh." He gave me a salute and he was off. I finished my cappuccino slowly, wanting his foul presence to dissipate before I got back on my bike.

I took my time riding to Acquapendente. Herman had suggested I stop in to see the Cattedrale, endowed with a noted sepulchre. The front door was locked. As I was poking around, a nonna with a kerchief on her head rounded the corner of the cathedral, took one look at me, grabbed my arm under hers, and showed me a small door to the left that was open. She rattled off some creaky Italian I didn't quite understand while encouraging me to tuck my bike into the narthex against the plainest wall. She fluttered her fingers at me to head into the nave, where I was greeted by Nonna number two, fixing the flower arrangements near the transept. She led me to a box with a green button on it beside a set of descending stairs. She indicated I should stick a euro into the box to enter the crypt. I dug around in my pack until I found the right coin and stuck it in. Lights appeared, leading me down into the bowels of the building.

Did I really want to go down there by myself? Nonna number two waved me on, "Cripta!" Then vanished. I was alone in this cavernous place of death. I stepped gingerly down into the shadowy crypt and was touched to see a large clay sculpture of a pietà. But in this one, Christ's head was tilted up. He was dead, but he had a peaceful look on his face, like he had just glimpsed a bit of heaven. The tenderness of Mary, the way she cradled her grown child with that mix of holding on and letting go, made me take off my bike helmet in reverence.

I had decided a long time ago, as a child, that I wasn't going to pray to Mary. My mother occasionally prayed to her on her rosary, usually when someone back in Italy died. She'd pull out her beads and do her rounds while staring out the window at her geraniums. I don't know if she even believed in Mary or if it was a ritual out of respect. But today, I knelt by Mary's knee clothed in stone, and prayed.

"Dear Mary, did you see this coming? Did you wonder how you could have prevented your son's pain? Do you wish you could take his place? Please, for the sake of my child, make me the mother I was meant to be. Give me the strength to bear Hazel's anger. Give me the patience to endure my shortcomings. Help me to be grateful for Herman and not take his presence as a reason to feel ashamed. Help me understand his helpfulness as kindness and not as a judgment. And Mary, perhaps give me the mindfulness to always include snacks. I have always sucked at snacks. Thank you. Amen."

After my visit with Mary in Acquapendente, I cycled through an area that my app said was "without emotion." I love that. The English would say it would be a place that was "unremark-able." The English "remark," the Italians "feel." I will "remark" that it was flat Italy, and I "feel" that it was very good for me.

By lunch, I arrived at San Lorenzo Nuovo and decided on a pizza place. Upon entering, I was told there was no pizza until cena. The "pellegrino special" was tagliatelle ragu: oily as hell and overcooked. I was the only one in the restaurant. A husky woman in the kitchen kept yelling at her flustered husband, the waiter, through the swinging door. I wondered if she was short-tempered because, deep inside, she knew she had missed her calling as a wrestler. The husband came back and forth through the swinging door, looking beaten. He'd mournfully watch a soap opera on the TV between bouts of verbal abuse and table busing.

I opted for the Via Cassia instead of the gravelly Via Francigena for a spell, and it took me on a scenic ride along the gorgeous Bolsena shoreline. It was lovely to see a lake. I was starting to notice wild white iris now, and peony trees in full bloom, and pink bunchy rose-like camellias. Horses enjoyed this spectacular view. Shorn sheep bowed their heads, sniffing through foxtails.

Bolsena is a very pretty Roman town overlooking the lake, topped with a large castle built by the Monaldeschis, the rulers of Orvieto and Bolsena. The stones of its streets were shiny from shoes and wheels, Vespas, lines of laundry, shiny succulents, and swept porches. Many of the tall stone homes had tiny holes in the wall beside their entrances that housed little shrines to the Madonna. I passed an artisanal pottery shop; clay Medusa heads were drying their snakes in the sun. I popped into the museum: mostly Etruscan pottery shards. There was a curious panther throne, a lascivious crypt laced with writhing bodies, and a goddess Fortuna, cheeky and full figured, lying on her side and grinning, quite pleased with herself.

After procuring some groceries and checking into my lovely B & B, I spent some time lying by the lake on a park bench, a fatigued version of Fortuna. At one point, I heard footsteps and looked up to see a moustached, small, handsome man, younger than me, approach. As I opened my eyes, he noticed

me and nodded with approval. As he passed, he purred, "Bella."
I sat up and looked around. Yes, he actually meant me.

I stared out at Lake Bolsena and felt a twinge of something.
What was it? My long-entombed libido? My goodness, I had
forgotten how that felt. I allowed myself to flood with warmth
and giddiness. I wiggled my bottom and decided it was at the
point of pleasing. I was goddess-proportioned, still young, and
could pedal uphill for hours. Even if it wasn't to Iran. What's
not to love? I ran my finger along the smooth rod of the bench
rail. I thought of that moustache and how it might tickle the
skin. Was I waking up? Was I walking myself out of this crypt?
I had an urge for red lipstick and hose. I had an urge for that
man to turn around and strut his fine self back towards me
with his taut shoulders and his thick, black hair and his sturdy
legs. I liked the fact that he was about the same height as me.
I wonder if he knew how sexy safe could be?

I decided to wander through town before the shops closed to
find myself a bathing suit. As I crossed the piazza, lo and behold,
I bumped into Mr. Lime Legs again. He called out:

"Hey, buon cammino! I didn't get your name."

"Graziana."

"Hm. I guess that's the Italian word for *grace*?"

"Yup. And you?"

"Felix. Whatcha doin', Grace?"

"I'm, uh ... looking for a bathing suit. There are some hot
springs near Viterbo."

Felix sniffed, uninterested. I wandered away.

Down the street, I found a discount store with a great deal
of socks and underwear and children's shoes. I requested a
"costume," and the woman held up her finger, "Un attimo,"
and headed to the back of her store to the storage room. She
returned with a bright-red bikini with orange polka dots, size
sixteen. It looked like something my mother might have worn
in the seventies, and it fitted me perfectly. This was a gift from
Mary or Fortuna, I don't know, but some luscious Mamma
was watching over me. I stared in the mirror at my shapely

body. I had some muscles in my legs. I had a waistline. I had firm arms. I had rounded breasts. I had a hilarious biker's tan: very brown hands and face and brown legs up to my mid-thigh. The rest of my body: blazing white.

In a split second, I also felt shame. Deep shame.

Why does she want to expose herself like this?

Why does the walrus think it's safe?

She ... I.

Tap tap tap tap.

I tapped until my skin turned pink. I won't let this bullshit feeling beat me. I hurriedly changed, paid for the suit, and hustled out onto the street, fully clothed.

The next day, I made my last significant ascent to the top of Montefiascone, where I had a modest chicory soup in a rather fancy mountaintop restaurant. The maître d' who seated me assured me with an invisible eyeroll that my pilgrim's wear was fine.

The old Via Cassia was made from black volcanic rock so bumpy, I laughed with the vibrations as I struggled to keep hold of my handlebars. Near the outskirts of Viterbo, I came upon some rough-hewn signs for the Bagnaccio Baths "Spa." This was no Banff Springs Hotel, that's for sure. I pulled up to a makeshift bunch of beach huts surrounded by RVs and picnic tables. I paid a couple of euros and walked into what looked like a mini-golf landscape of tiny hot pools. The pools were surrounded by cement walkways and a bit of garden, populated with the elderly, all wearing furry bathrobes and fuzzy slippers and slinging copious amounts of liquor. I changed in the outdoor shack, giggling to myself.

I tiptoed out towards the hot pools in my hot-red bikini, and it seemed as though every single elderly head turned. I had nothing to lose now. I whispered to a lady in her eighties, wearing Gucci sunglasses and a black racy one-piece, "Prendi ... un photo? Mio? Per favore?" My lousy Italian. To my chagrin, she yelled that she didn't know what the F– I wanted. The men around her started to explain, loudly, that I wanted her to take my picture. I shrunk my body into as small a ball as possible by the overgrown bathtub and protested, waving, tucking my camera under my thigh. "No grazie, nada, it's okay ... no problem." She continued to yell – YELL – for some guy named Luigi, because apparently he could take a good photo. I looked behind me, and there was octogenarian Luigi pouring himself a cognac in his bathrobe and a navy Speedo that had long since lost its elasticity. He had gold chains worthy of P. Diddy. He grinned, raised his glass, and called out to me, "Ciao bella!" And then he started giving me directions on how to pose, with a long stream of Italian and many hand signals. I was too flushed with embarrassment to hear him very well. I just crossed my legs and tried to look as modest as possible. Luigi decided he had to squat in full defensive volleyball stance six feet in front of me, taking his time, his sunglasses glinting, his testicles dangling dangerously close to the cement, gold chains swaying. I was so red-faced, trying not to burst out laughing, I turned my face away, pretending it was a choice to give a profile. Che palle! Thank you, Luigi, for the most memorable tourist photo ever.

After my brief dip into the hot pools, I cycled into Viterbo, the largest city I had been to since Lucca. The first layer was all suburbia, and then I hit the old city wall and the luscious medieval part of town.

My B & B, called Emc², was in an arts district. It was a sweet little apartment with a kind host, Eduardo. Next door to it was a caffè and a theatre school with a two-hundred-and-fifty-seat venue. I chatted with the enthusiastic manager who said something along the lines of theatre being necessary for society to elevate itself above the everyday life and find its moral compass. It reminded me of when Hazel saw *The Secret Garden* with her class at Theatre Calgary. She was all wide-eyed and starry, embodying Mistress Mary Quite Contrary for months afterwards, rather enjoying being a short-tempered orphan with a penchant for red-breasted robins. Just the thought of Hazel suddenly made my arms ache to hold her. Yes. My body was waking up, indeed. I was cracking out of my pupa and feeling the breeze on my new, tender skin.

The next day I cycled to Sutri. The gravel road wound through scrubby, prickly, sour farmland: lemons and artichokes. The sun made my head pound. Smashed porcupines and smeared snakes were left to shrivel on the road. Ominous-looking caves underneath overpasses and cliffsides housed many imaginary, mean-spirited creatures. But after lunch I started to notice the progression of spring. Wisterias were blooming, camellias frilled along gateways like lounging ballerinas. Sutri welcomed the pellegrino or pellegrina with a centurion-worthy stone entry. I rode my way into town, and who was standing outside my B & B address? My landlord *and* Felix!

"Apparently we're sharing," he said. "I need a shower and a good night's sleep."

"I –" The landlord started rattling off an explanation that his suite had two rooms and I should have known that from the listing and it is still the same price. "Tranquillo."

"I'd go elsewhere, but I think this is the only gig in town. Try not to look so disappointed." Felix led his bike into the hallway ahead of me.

The landlord waved me in and said something about modesty and two bedrooms, then he turned on his heel and scooted away.

Felix called from inside the suite, "I'll take the downstairs."

"Hold on a second!"

I hauled my bike inside and scanned the apartment. The upstairs had a private bedroom, and the downstairs had a bed made from a pullout sofa, right out in the open.

"Thanks."

I headed to the market, and he must have slipped out when I was gone. I made a modest pot of veggies and potatoes, ate, showered, then sat down at the table with some dusty camomile tea I found in the cupboard and started writing Hazel a postcard. Felix entered with a bottle of wine.

"Want some? I suspect it's excellent."

"Sure, a small glass."

"Why a small?"

"I'm on medication."

"For what?"

"Trauma. Let's leave it at that."

Felix blew the invisible dust out of two Chianti glasses from the cupboard and poured me a glass. He looked quite different in jeans and a button-down shirt, his hair fluffy and washed.

"Cheers. To trauma!"

The complex beauty of the wine made my tastebuds gasp with incredulity. The liquid filled my mouth with warmth and sensuality. I swear I could have throated an aria if I had allowed myself to sing.

"Good, huh? Aleatico di Gradoli. It's made from the Canaiolo Nero grape."

"You a wine connoisseur?"

"Nah. Total poser. Just read about it."

"So, why Iran?"

"Back to trauma, huh? My wife was half Dutch, half Iranian. We had planned this trip together. Start in Amsterdam, then hook up to the Via Francigena in Switzerland through the St. Bernard Pass. You know, hit both of her homelands. A couple of years ago we did mine: Seoul to Busan in Korea and then hung out in Japan. Anyway, we split in November, but I still wanted to do the trip. So here I am."

We sat and slowly swirled the wine in our glasses.

"You? What's your trauma?"

"My mom died. She was Italian."

That's all he needed to know. He nodded.

"Who you writing to?"

"My kid."

Surprisingly, his face lit up. "You have a kid? Got a picture?"

"No."

"Not even on your phone?"

I looked away.

"I always wanted children. That was one of our issues. She said she did but then, thirty-five, thirty-six, thirty-seven ... kept putting it off. On her fortieth birthday she admitted she had no intention of having a child. What's your kid's name?"

"Hazel."

"Great name."

"She'd like your name; she likes names that have x's and z's."

And so the conversation rolled on comfortably until I got sleepy. The suite became quite cold into the evening, despite the wood pellet heater kicking in. Felix said goodnight, showered, then tiptoed down the stairs with a towel around his tidy waist. It had been a while since I had seen a man shirtless.

Two o'clock in the morning the wood pellet heater started beeping loudly. It startled me awake and I hurried into the hall and madly tried to figure out what was wrong with it, pushing all the red buttons, hoping they'd turn green. Felix leapt up the stairs in his boxers, squinting at the heater panel.

"Out of pellets, I think. No wonder it's so freaking cold in here."

We searched the cupboards and found nothing, so we unplugged it to stop the beeping. We stood shivering, staring at it. To my surprise I said, "Well, you can sleep with me."

"Really?"

"It's fine. It's a queen. Bring up your blanket."

I headed into my room and he soon joined me, curled up on his side of the mattress, respectfully. I could tell from his breathing he couldn't sleep. Though we weren't touching, I could smell his hair and feel his heat. My body was so alive with this proximity I was sure I was glowing in the dark with electricity. I imagined myself a lioness. I could purr, deep and easy. He rolled sideways, towards me; I rolled the same way and my back brushed up against his hand. He left it there for a moment, then ever so slightly ran his finger along the fabric of my pyjamas. I accepted his micro-invitation and arched my back and spooned into his concave. He groaned and ran his hand along my hip and then up to my breast. This is what it feels like to be touched. I forgot. I forgot.

"Your breast is as big as my head!" He exclaimed far too loudly.

"Sorry."

"Sorry? Why are you sorry? It's – it's glorious!"

We laughed together and I turned to face him. He brushed the hair back from my face.

"I haven't done this since ..."

"Me neither."

"I don't know if I can."

"It's okay. Whatever. We're just ... keeping each other warm."

I kissed him and he kissed me back, invoking the word *ardour*, which I don't believe I've ever used in a sentence, though my body certainly embraced the vocabulary. His skin was so smooth and his body so warm and taut, like a racehorse, like a canoe, like a lily stamen, like everything heady and hot about summer.

No bitter aftertaste.

Hazel and I have been getting things at the house back in order: laundry and cleaning the home and such. Being the end of April, we can work the ground, so we direct sowed some sweet peas, spinach, and Green Arrow peas. I was impressed with how carefully Hazel pinched those little seeds between her fingers and measured them out. She kept whispering to them as she "put them to bed," saying, "Grow, little seed, grow."

We did a few little seedling pods in the house, sunning in the living-room window: pansies, snapdragons, and lettuce. I was pleased to see crocuses, tulips, and hyacinths starting to come up along the sidewalk. I was nervous about our industry, because Grazie never planted anything in her yard before. She resented me even cutting the lawn, so it was quite the chore pulling out all the weeds last fall and preparing the beds for spring, considering they had been sitting neglected for eight years. Last fall, we put in daffodils and tulip bulbs, planted brown-eyed Susans, and at Hazel's request, we added big flashy Casa Blanca lilies.

My Nunzia always loved planting flowers in with the vegetables. Everything she did was both functional and beautiful. She'd grow geraniums beside tomatoes and basil, and lavender beside the onions. She'd dot cabbage with marigolds and plant scarlet runner beans in with their plainer sisters for colour. It's one of the reasons why she loved zucchini – it produced edible flowers, the best of both worlds. I hadn't planted a proper garden since she passed. Why bother if I'm only cooking for one? Ah, but it brought back memories, placing those seeds, bulbs, and tubers in the ground. I could picture her so clearly, bent over in her gumboots and ridiculous floppy hat, lovingly training a cucumber up a trellis or digging in fertilizer around her prized peach-coloured rose. How she would have loved Hazel. This little one goes at weeds with a vengeance. I can't bring her nonna back, but I can certainly pass on a love for dahlias.

The third day home we got another couple of postcards from Graziana, which highlighted her imminent arrival. I thought it best if Hazel and I made a calendar of events. After all, it was our routine Grazie would be stepping back into. It was our household. It was our educational plan. We had a right to keep some of it for ourselves, some normalcy. I had no idea what Grazie's expectations would be, or what she was ready for. We had to be prepared to continue without her and also be prepared to continue with her.

Hazel and I both agreed that it would be best to give Grazie her room back. So I started clearing out my stuff, preparing to move back into my apartment. But as for the rest, I bought a great big yearly calendar and a couple of colourful markers. I figured this would be a way to create some continuity for Hazel and give her a sense of security. For instance, we marked April 22 to June 30 "Homeschooling with Grumpy" from 9 a.m. to 1 p.m. Hazel decided she'd go back to swim lessons, which pleased me. That would be Tuesday evenings, 6:00 to 7:30 p.m. May first we would plant our seedlings. We decided once a month we would go see Ed and Connie. We marked that down. We made special note of Hazel's birthday on February 9 and decided we would go to the West Edmonton Mall water park. We marked down Grazie's birthday, June 24, and my birthday, October 18. We set up some concerts and plays and a bowling night with the homeschooling association in May, June, and September. October 12, we decided to go to Rosebud Theatre to see *The Mountaintop*, a play about Martin Luther King Jr. We invited Geoffrey and his family. We figured it would be fun to go camping July 3 to 10 in the Kananaskis and to see Jasper and the glaciers. We figured we could go visit David and Cathy and Oola the week after that. I confirmed that date with them – they were delighted. We planned Ukrainian Christmas with Marco and JJ. We figured November first would be a good time for Hazel to start making their stockings, and she was real particular about her mom's stocking and making a head for baby Jesus. I think Grazie is rather fond of the headless Godhead, but I'll let them discuss that matter.

We hung this calendar in Hazel's room, as per her wish. We agreed that neither of us would add a thing on the calendar without consulting the other. We agreed that whatever Graziana wanted to do, there was still plenty of room for her. Once I finished tacking it to the wall, Hazel said, "Thanks Grumpy. I have so much fun to look forward to."

"Me too," I said. And we just stared at it for the longest time.

Grumpy and I made a calendar for things we want to do in the year. We are going to see plays and concerts and go travelling to the mountains and see glaciers and have birthdays and lots of visits with family. Mom can't take that away from me. No matter how much she complains at Grumpy (because Mom is a real complainer), we are GOING. And we made a real nice garden and Mom can't say no because we put it in the ground already and if you dug it up, it would be killing real life. And Grumpy is going to keep on teaching me school. School is not my favourite, but I like school with Grumpy way better than school at the building school, and Grumpy thinks it might be best for me to homeschool until I go into grade seven, which isn't for four years, so I have lots of time to catch up and also learn to harness the wild horses!

That's what Grumpy calls it when my imagination goes running off with me. He says it's like a bunch of wild horses (but I think it's like a bunch of unicorns who aren't wild, they are just full of excitement and magic), and anyway, if you harness them, then they can still run but you have control if they go right or left or stop for a bit or be a whole bucking bronco show! You could make the wild horses jump or do tricks or race or lie down for a nap, even. You could make the horses stop for a healthy snack and take a breather so you can pet their soft noses and whisper stories to them and make friends with them.

I said to Grumpy, "Do you think my mom has wild horses?"

And he said, "What do you mean?"

"You know, like my wild horses. Do you think she has thoughts that go running around in her head? Because I don't remember my mom having imagination."

"Everyone has imagination, Hazel."

"Well, she never told me stories that were made up, or used funny voices or coloured creatures or pretended imaginary friends."

"Oh, I don't know if that's true. Remember your ducky?"

Ooh right, I completely forgot about Ducky! I have a little ducky and then I have a big ducky and Mom would sometimes play Little Big Ducky. Big Ducky was always trying to sleep and Little Ducky was always beating him up. It was very funny. I used to love my duckies. I pulled them out and fluffed them up, because they were at the bottom of my toy box.

And then I remembered I used to be afraid of the vacuum because it was so loud it made me cry. (I was a baby.) One day Mom put the vacuum up to Big Ducky and Big Ducky stuck to the end of it with his big fluffy tummy and Mom waved around the vacuum with Big Ducky dancing around on the end, and it made me think, if Ducky can stop the vacuum and not get sucked up, then I can stop the vacuum and not get sucked up. That took some imagination on her part, I think.

Then I had a dream. I had a dream that Mom was a horse and she was riding a bike, which was kind of hilarious, but behind her were all these horses riding bikes and they were laughing. I told Grumpy about this dream and he said it was prophetic. And I said, "What the heck is *prophetic*?" And he said *prophetic* means it tells you something about the future. He says that Mom's wild horses have been stuck in a tiny little barn, afraid to come out, so all they do is eat hay. He thinks they are totally riding bikes with Mom. He thinks Mom's wild horses (I know this is confusing because this is called a metaphor – when we say "wild horses" we mean "imagination," actually. Grumpy says I am advanced because I use metaphors and can make them up and understand them and he thinks that normal kids don't do this until they are at least nine or maybe twelve. Not to say I am not normal but my poetry is WAY super advanced. This is part of my wild horses, says Grumpy. He says I talk in poems in my head all day. My horses neigh in poetry, and this is again why I think they are magical unicorns) – What was I saying?

This made me a little bit curious to see my mom. What would she be like with an imagination? What would she be like if she actually liked the flowers we planted? What would she be like if she rode a bike? I've never seen her do this, only in pictures when she was younger. What would she be like if she was laughing at a joke I made? What would she be like if she asked me a question, like an important question, like, "Hazel, what makes you scared at night?"

She wrote me a postcard from a place called Siena. She said she figured she's lost a hundred pounds since she saw me last and that I should be prepared because she looks really different from when she left. When I told Grumpy this, his eyebrows flew up to the top of his head. (He has very fluffy moving-around-ish eyebrows.) He said that was almost two of me because I am fifty-seven pounds. (I am tall but skinny like a bean.) So we did the math, and fifty-seven plus fifty-seven is one hundred and fourteen. So, it's like me, but twins, minus one arm. I looked in the mirror and looked in the mirror and tried to imagine my mom minus twins with three arms, and that's a LOT of Mom to lose. What's left? Her hair and teeth? Now I'm freaked out!

Grumpy says this means Mom will have a lot more energy and she will be able to do things that she's never done before with me, like run! Like play tag. Like maybe she'd want to go swimming. Mom never went in the water with me, not since I was a really small baby.

Grumpy says to remember her face from our video chats. It's the same face. He says to remember I have a right to be angry but that she's doing the best she can. I didn't like this idea. I thought it was lame-ass. Did the best she could? LAME-ASS! MEAN! But then I thought of all those horses inside of her afraid to leave the barn. I don't know. It's hard to be mad at a horse. Grumpy says that Mom is very upset at herself that she left for a whole year, but it was part of her getting better. She was afraid to come back too soon and lose her courage. Grumpy said one year without Mom is going to mean the rest of my life with a healthier mom and that it will be worth it. Hmph. We'll see. I don't think so. I don't think I can ever forgive her. I think there will always be a part of me that whispers, "Lame-ass Mom, with your scaredy-cat, lame-ass horses."

Though what We spoke to the beloved was true, and though he had earned no measure of reprieve from his self-awareness, We are in the habit of Grace. We drift alongside him in the mist of morning. We float with fingers of fog. We comfort with a curl of beauty. We blush a bruisy purple with dawn.

"I understand why You won't let me near my daughter. I trashed my opportunity. And what do I think I could offer her that You couldn't, that she couldn't do for herself? Nothing. I am Nothing."

You are Some and One.

"I'm glad You've made my kid an artist. I'm glad You've given her a sense of humour. She'll need that with that square head of hers. Or maybe she'll have nicer friends. I used to get called Blockhead in school. Once in a while, I got upgraded to Jughead, which was at least a cartoon."

You are all children of light, children of the day.

The beloved sighs.

We now understand your hesitation. You can let go of the pain of being a failed father when you've reckoned with being a son.

"You mean, y'all want me to face my mother, Rose? I knew it."

Your choice. You are still tied to her with an unforgiving knot.

"You want me to forgive a freaking butterfly?"

Rose emerges in the image that the beloved remembers, minus a stained floral robe, minus a cigarette and clinking glass, minus the smell of sweat, gin, and ash.

"Ivan. It breaks my heart to see you here in the After. You're so young."

"Don't pretend you care just because They are watching."

"You are my child. Of course I care."

Rose sits with the beloved, carefully. Not close enough for him to strike. Would striking even hurt?

"There is no excuse for who I was to you. I am so sorry for all I've done and all I have not done."

The beloved becomes as small as he feels. His hands close down into chubby little dimpled fists. His hair, cowlicked. His pyjamas, soft. His eyes, wide as pies. Rose carefully reaches over to touch him.

"Leave me alone!" he shouts. "What do you want from me?"

Rose looks to Us imploringly.

Rose is why you are in this waiting place. You are waiting for Mother.

"No, I am not!"

You have always been waiting for Mother to show up.

"No!"

Rose smiles, gently, sadly, "Yes. Son. I finally have the capacity to be here."

We are all Understanding and yet We do not understand the human act of unforgiveness. It has no logic. It goes against the animal, it goes against the soul. There is no benefit to it whatsoever. This is where Darkness takes hold. After all the beloved has been through, after all he's seen of the world and of himself, he cannot give forgive himself or his mother.

He pretends to listen, We know he is pretending. He lets her hope. She trembles when she speaks of her father who beat her, her mother who locked her in closets and seduced her first boyfriend. She spoke of alcohol's seduction and the crushing weight of a major depressive disorder.

When she was emptied of all, he said, "Are you done?"

"Will you forgive me, Ivan?"

He gave her a wicked little smile. "Never."

Then he shot across the dark sky, straight into the ashy centre of Betelgeuse, giving over all his energy to the crushing weight of a dying star.

CHAPTER FIFTEEN

MOTHER COUNTRY

— Graziana —

PALAZZO SAN GERVASIO, BASILICATA

In the morning, Felix and I used a blow-dryer to dry out a shirt each, as our laundry stayed wet overnight in the cold. Then we hunted down a cappuccino by the massive Roman arch in gorgeous Sutri. We chatted comfortably about my days at the bike shop and his love for tennis. It was pleasant and "without emotion." This was the greatest surprise to me. I wasn't sure I'd ever be able to be sexual again. But much like riding a bike, one doesn't forget. It all came naturally. It was a relief to know this part of my life was not taken from me forever.

From Sutri, Felix was heading east to Perugia, then Ancona to take a ferry to Zadar. I was making my way south to Rome.

"You are grace, you know that," he said, scooping the last bit of cappuccino foam out of his cup with his tongue. He smacked on his helmet and rode off with his heavy pack and his bright green legs.

I sat there at the little caffè table a moment or two longer, basking in the warmth of recent companionship. When was the last time I had an in-depth conversation with someone who wasn't my therapist or my child? I think it's been eight years. I'm naturally private, but I used to talk with my mother. She had always been my main friend; I would share with her everything except sex. With sex, I would talk to Caroline. Caroline was an ass-kicker MTB rider with a trusty Trek Roscoe. I did the Tunnel Mountain Tech Trails with her near Banff. She was a voracious and bright bisexual athlete who would chat with any stranger on the street. She was a completely delightful and terrifying contrast to my quiet, tucked-in self. I don't quite know why she hung out with me, other than because I could keep up with her on the trail and I ran her local bike shop. But after I got attacked by Ivan, I could not step foot in there. When I realized I was pregnant, I shut everything down remotely and had a company stick everything in storage. I ended our work relationship, and thus our friendship, with a group email – no forwarding address, no explanation. I didn't mean to be cruel, I just couldn't deal with it all. I stared into the silty bottom of my cappuccino cup. Familiar shame started to creep all over my body, like ivy snaking between my legs and up my spine.

She thought she could have sex and get away with it.

Hands hands hands all over its body. Scrape of cement. Underground parking ... lot ...

The walrus flopping around naked and helpless, beached on the rock.

Can't.

Tap.

In.

Sand.

Crump-le

Crump–

"Ha finito?"

Is she finished?

"Scusi? Hello? You okay?"

The waiter taps my shoulder.

I come to with a start. "No. No, I am not finished. I would like another. Grazie."

"Allora."

I would like another Grazie please. Great Good. Make me new. Make me new. I have a right to have a friend. I pull out my phone. Her number is still – I'm going to call her, I'm going to call Caroline when I get home. I tuck my phone and my promise back into my pocket.

Before I left Sutri, I popped into the Santa Maria Assunta Cathedral. Big, old, scrappy green doors of the apse opened up into butter-and-lettuce-coloured arches. I particularly loved the intricate, hand-cut marble floors. I whispered, "Not sure if that was You, but if it was, thank You for last night with Felix."

It was a gorgeous, sunny ride, quite flat. Sutri: what a beauty. I ambled through acres of apple and apricot orchards, pedalled by peach and pear and a spotty Appaloosa pony; the sun shone on my shoulders. The warm wind carried the scent of lemons and artichokes as I cycled past proudly puffed roosters allowed to crow. Near Capranica, little green geckos darted in front of my tires. The rural roads were paved with broken pottery: dross from local Vetralla ceramic factories. One of the fields had been newly replanted with a spindly line of saplings, maybe two feet tall. I felt the Great Good say, *This is you.*

I was rather insulted.

"This is me? After all I've gone through?! You mean, spiritually, I am nothing more than a baby tree, a mere twig?"

Don't feel too badly, dear sprout. Some people never have the courage to crack the earth.

Then my eyes were directed towards some majestic towering stone pines in the distance.

This is how tall you're going to be. This is the gift of age, of time. It took you a while to build a root system in rocky soil, but you've had the courage to send your roots down deep and wide, and you've found fertile ground. No mere breeze can blow you over now.

"But I am fragile. I am psychologically ... fragile."

The ability to be fragile is part of your capacity for greatness.

"I don't feel ... great."

Like these saplings, you're only looking above ground. Remember your roots. Because you are fragile, I've called you to a disciplined life. A disciplined life will help you grow to your full height.

I found cycling so deeply good for my soul. Going downhill is exhilarating, but it's actually the uphill stretches that have allowed me to slow down, see the scenery, take pictures. It's been the harsh weather that put me in a position where I experienced the generosity and beauty of the Italian people. How can I bring this home to Hazel? How can I take this serenity with me back across the ocean to Canada? I'm often so impatient with my daughter.

You are right to be impatient. But you aren't really impatient with Hazel or Herman. They received the brunt of your frustration. But what really frustrated you? You felt stuck in the temporal, in the monotonous and mundane. Your impatience was actually for Us. You were impatient for your own time alone for prayer and healing. You were impatient for the Big. For Glory. Always listen to your impatience. It is holy.

I cycled through a valley beside a babbling brook, and it brought me eventually to Monte Gelato, where there was a national park protecting modest waterfalls and an old water mill. I was disappointed that, of all places, Monte Gelato did not have an ice-cream stand.

I came upon the famous Sutri Necropolis, toothy and foreboding. Sometimes the caves along the road were boarded up, sometimes used as woodsheds, workshops, animal-food storage, or converted into chicken coops.

From that point on, the Via Francigena was effused with fantastic *F*s. Following the road to Formello I found fields of mooing mucche, forests, falls, wild fennel. Figs flanked the flight up to Campagnano di Roma, where I met an unfortunate flattened frog. After a fat puff pastry, I flew down the other side of the four hundred metres I'd just climbed, only to discover three-quarters down that I had flown west instead of south. There was no other road to the right one. I footed it all the way back up, whereupon many more *F*s were freed.

Once I corrected my course, I spilled into a lovely park: Veio. I cycled into an open meadow, where a camper van was pulled up to an outdoor pizza oven (an Italian-style picnic), and a dad and little daughter lay on a blanket, looking at the clouds. Dogs were chasing balls. Horses in the distance chomped on grass. I passed a grand tower on top of Campagnano di Roma. On the Via Lucia, the walls were so gorgeous; the mortar expanding beyond the rock created a window-frame effect.

In Formello I stayed in a white-plastered villa circa 1600, called the Gusto e Benessere. A deep-red rose crept along its wall. Inside, it was all post-and-beam with a fluffy bed and twinkle lights. Formello is the kingdom of cats sunning themselves on cobblestone circles. There were bright-purple wildflowers everywhere; they looked like tiny cyclamens.

The next day I rode to Roma. I anticipated having to jostle my way through crowded streets and complicated traffic circles, but no, a lovely biking path along the Tiber River took me all the way to the Vatican. Herman had asked me to purchase some Vatican coins (as he is an avid collector), and I tried to haggle a bit, but it ended up costing twice as much as he predicted. Then I navigated my way across the city to the CUBE store to drop off my trusty steed before they closed for Easter holidays. It was in a back-pocket industrial park near the airport, beside a CrossFit gym. The staff were eagerly awaiting me, knowing who I was, thanks to Giulia and Massimo back in Boffalora sopra Ticino. They shook my hand and took my picture for their Facebook page.

I felt a kind of victory, but more so, I felt sad. Sad my journey was over. Sad to say goodbye to the back roads of Italy. Sad to say goodbye to my faithful little orange mud-splattered bike. We had been through so much together, and my little CUBE stood the test and didn't pop a tire once in over eleven hundred kilometres.

I waited for the taxi and looked down at my scarred-up legs: pedal scratches and thorns from berry bushes, bruises from railings along my thighs as I carried my bike up or down stairs. The taxi took me to my adorable little apartment on the other side of the airport, in Ciampino. Once I settled in and washed up, I wandered down the modest street and found a woman's clothing boutique. I bought an Easter dress: pink, flowery, and flowy. I looked in the mirror and felt ... lovely. Gosh. I thought of my closet at home. The few pieces of clothing I have would fit like blankets on me now. I will be so happy to throw them out. I might even have a bonfire.

The next morning, I rented a white Fiat near the airport and drove in my dress all the way to my mother's small town, about four hours south: Palazzo San Gervasio, Potenza. Herman had warned me to bring a lot of change for the tollbooths; still, I found it very stressful to frantically plug the meter with the appropriate amount of euros, a long line of cars impatient behind me. At one point, near Frosinone, I had to pull over and tap to calm myself down.

Mom didn't have any immediate family left in the town. Her parents had died and her brother, Zio Gaetano, lived in the South of France. But apparently I still had two elderly great-uncles and many second cousins my age. I'd never met them, and Mom had never visited them, so I didn't feel compelled to try and contact anyone. I didn't see the point; I'd be a complete stranger.

I drove up to the quiet village. It was perched on a hill over-looking peaceful farmland, a large, abandoned castle on one end. I got out of my car and stretched, and it seemed like all eyes turned to me. Three elderly men sat snugly together on a bench outside of a bakery, and one called out to me, "Buona Pasqua."

"Buona Pasqua, signore. Grazie. Mi scusi, dove ... cimitero?"

This surprised them. One let out a long string of Italian directions, to which I apologized and shrugged, asking if they could point. One nodded to the other, who slapped the back of the speaker, and all three got up.

"Seguimi."

I was to follow these three octogenarians with their smart caps and their dark blazers. One of them had a thick, brown, wool sweater. He must have been close to ninety. He had a scooter and winked at me and asked me if I wanted to ride on the back. I giggled and indicated that I had better walk. They led me down past the castello and a few churches humming with the remnants of Easter Mass. Then they pointed down the hill to a small, white, cross-topped façade off the small road, Borgo Santo Spirito. I made my way down there and walked through the façade and past a kerchiefed widow who looked up at me, slightly annoyed that I had disrupted her grief picnic. But then she was curious when she saw I was looking specifically for someone, and she started following me.

I squinted at the names on the tombstones, stepping by them, reverently. Grieco, Saponara, Soriano, Frangione, Cipriani, Latorraca … Oh! Baggio Sotera. My father. There was a small, oval picture of his face. I have his pronounced jaw. He looked poetic, as people do when they are long since dead and their portrait has faded to the lightest of grey. From around my neck, I drew my mother's rosary and wrapped it carefully around the dusty, empty flower vase.

"Che fai?" demanded the woman.

"It's okay," I said and held up my hand.

"Che cosa vuoi?" And she added something derogatory about me being a tourist.

"Non un turista … è la mia famiglia."

"Famiglia?" she scoffed. Then something about Baggio being long since dead.

"Baggio … è mio padre."

This took the woman aback. She gasped. "Chi è tua madre?"

Why was I telling this little angry bird anything? "Mia mamma … um … morta. In Canada. Nome, Nunzia Dolores."

When I said my mother's name, this kerchiefed woman let out a little pained cry and ran out of the cemetery screaming. Before I knew it, two of the old men in caps were at the top of the stairs, waving at me to come up. They were all talking excitedly about Baggio and my mother and the Dolores family. Of course. What was I thinking? In such a small town, my presence was not going to go unnoticed. The two old men grabbed me each by the arm and each kissed me on the cheek and told me, "Bella," and how much I looked like my mother ... I think. One made a gesture about my robust figure being typical of the Dolores women. The widow started smiling now, happy to be involved in this excitement now that she'd figured it out. They drew me towards the gentleman in the scooter. They kept saying, "Zio Paolo, Zio Paolo Dolores."

He scooted up closer to me and squinted at me very carefully for a good five seconds. Then he nodded and waved his arm to grab my hand. He pulled me in towards him, and that's when I realized he was too emotional to speak. He eventually said, "Tu appartieni alla nostra famiglia."

You belong to us.

In a very uncomfortable, awkward side hug, I rather collapsed by the side of the scooter. I could hear this ... weeping ... and at some point, I realized it was me. I couldn't help myself. His words opened up the floodgates of grief. Everything. The loss of my mother. I never felt so keenly. I could barely breathe. I had no words to express what was going on for me. I just kept saying, "Mia mamma. Mia mamma."

They all took it in stride, like I fit right in, like this was normal. They nodded, they patted my hand, they patted my head. They laughed a little, and this made me laugh. My zio Paolo pulled out a large, white, starchy handkerchief that I blew my nose unceremoniously into. I wasn't sure if I should give it back, which made them laugh again. We decided to stuff it into his cupholder.

The rest of the day was a brilliant blur. I was given a tour of the town, stopping to say hello and to be introduced to all kinds of neighbours, friends, family members (?) – I wasn't sure. There were kisses and hugs and a stop at the bakery for tette delle monache, mascarpone-filled "nuns' boobs" pastry and a shot of cognac. I met a host of cousins, and we stopped by my other elderly great-uncle's house, my zio Pietro. He was waiting, a very handsome, dignified man, also in his later eighties, fully dressed for Sunday, perhaps having come from Easter service. His sweet little wife, my zia Maddalena, perfect in pink, patted my cheeks and stared into my eyes so lovingly. They were hoping I spoke French at the very least because, like my zio Gaetano, they had lived in France. But I was a disgrace of a Canadian and knew nothing more than *bonjour*, *merci*, and *Guy est dans la discothèque*.

Everyone wanted me to stay, everyone wanted to have me over for dinner, and everyone was outraged that I had to leave early the next morning for home. The last house I was brought to was Zio Paolo's, a butter-yellow, immaculately tidy stone house with beautiful tilework and a long dining-room table already covered in a crisp, white tablecloth. There I met his younger wife, Zia Anna. She was a slender beauty with a big, hearty laugh and a stiff hip that she pivoted around on. I was shown photographs of my mother as a baby, while all their children and *their* children started milling in. Zia Anna brought out her prized homemade nocino, a liquor made from black walnuts, and home-dried sausage with fennel, both delicious. Then oranges appeared and aged provolone and rye bread fresh from the bakery and olives and roast peppers and artichokes. Then my cousin Natale arrived with enough pizza for ... gosh, at least twenty people were crammed into that dining room. Most of them were gorgeous children with shiny, dark curls and perfect skin and bright eyes, ranging from toddler to teen. Someone was always grabbing my hand or kissing my cheek or patting my shoulder.

Natale, looking much like an Italian Bono, was dressed very cool, all in black, rocking long hair, jeans, and earrings. He was definitely the life of the party. He was charming and warm and even tearful at meeting me, talking about how much he loved my mother, his closest cousin, and that Baggio was one of his best friends. Natale had married a woman who owned a bakery; he joked that he knew that way his children would never go hungry. Her name was Natalina. She was bustling around the room, bosomy and bodacious, serving people, cracking jokes, smiling a million-dollar smile, and ribbing Natale to the point where they both broke out in a loud, good-humoured yelling match with each other. The whole room now doubled over in laughter, including them. I had no idea what anyone was saying, really. My Italian was terrible at the best of times, but on top of the dialect here ... I was completely lost.

I met my cousin Stella, Natale's sister. She gave me shit for not calling first and for only staying in Palazzo for twenty-four hours; that much I understood. There was something about her that I loved immediately, a sadness covered up with a fierce, jocular joy. Then I met the youngest sibling, Mo. He was a quiet, hardworking man who seemed to own several businesses and had a new baby. He was the one who decided to run down the street and fetch the only person in town who spoke English, a woman named Vincenza.

Vincenza had a slight New Jersey accent, a swish kimono, and a head full of wild, beautiful, brown curls. She was about my age. She graciously accepted a prominent place at the table beside me and spent the entire evening translating between me and my relatives. Thank God for her incredible generosity. We laughed and shared stories and took pictures. Then we parted with promises to return, and kisses and hugs and addresses swapped. It was the best day of my entire life.

Vincenza, Natale, and Stella all walked me to my B & B, arm in arm under the moonlight, down the cobbled, winding streets of Palazzo San Gervasio. I knew from that moment on, we would be visiting our family in Italy regularly, Hazel and I.

Yesterday was Easter. I put a basket by Hazel's bed while she was sleeping. I filled it with jellybeans and chocolate eggs and a chocolate bunny. She was rather pleased. I was happy to hear that Graziana had been doing this with her too. Something Nunzia used to do.

Hazel and I drove to the Calgary airport to pick up her mother. Hazel was very quiet in the car; it was hard to know what she was thinking. I suspect her little head was spinning with a whole lot of things. It was 2200 hours by the time Grazie arrived, so Hazel was already far past her bedtime.

When Graziana walked out from the international gate, I didn't recognize her at first, largely due to the fact she was striding in such a confident way. I had grown accustomed to her moving very slowly and hunched over. But she was back to walking more like herself. Her mother used to joke that Grazie had a way of moving that looked like she always owned the place: an athletic sort of swagger. I used to think it wasn't lady-like. I've changed my mind about that. Confidence in a young woman is a beautiful thing.

I could tell that Hazel didn't recognize her at first; in fact, she didn't register it was her mom until Grazie came right up to us and said, "Hey, thanks for picking me up." The look on Hazel's face was nothing short of astonished. Grazie squatted down to Hazel's level and said, "You don't have to hug me. This is a weird situation, I know, so we can take it easy."

Hazel didn't say a thing, she just continued to stare, and she reached for my hand to hold. The whole thing was very anti-climactic. We loaded in her panniers. Grazie asked Hazel a few questions, to which she got monosyllabic answers.

"Are you liking school with Grumpy?"

"Sorta."

"What's your favourite subject?"

"Dunno."

"Do you like art?"

"Duh."

I let Grazie know that her room was all ready. I could tell this was one of the questions she was afraid to ask. She seemed relieved. I also let her know that Hazel and I had cleaned the house and put some food in the fridge, that we had a garden coming up, and that I would be over in the morning after breakfast to check in and start school. To my relief and surprise, Graziana said, "Thank you, Herman. For all of it. You've saved us." And she got a little emotional and looked out the window. When this happened, I reached over and patted her shoulder, and we drove in silence until the Beiseker turnoff.

Then I started asking her questions about the trip and she really lit up and told us all about Palazzo San Gervasio. I had no idea she was going to bump into any family there, never having met any of them. I also didn't know she had kept her mother's rosary to put on the grave. I was real touched by that. She was very grateful for the pilgrimage and told me it had changed her life. She said she would pay me back someday and thanked me to the point where I had to say, "Graziana, thank your mother for buying life insurance. Don't you think this is exactly what she would have wanted me to do with her death benefit? I think so." That seemed to give her some relief.

She talked about opening up a bike shop again in Red Deer. It sounded real good to me. I was afraid that she'd want to "start over" in a different city, which would be hard on Hazel and frankly, hard on me. We got to the house, and Grazie seemed pleased with the yardwork and asked Hazel what we planted.

Hazel said, "Stuff. And you're not allowed to rip it up!"

To which Graziana said, "Why would I rip up a beautiful garden?"

Hazel yelled, "Because you hate everything I do! But I do a lot of things really well. I'm not stupid and I'm not ugly and I'm not a crazy NUT. You are! You're the NUT!"

Grazie just nodded and said, "You're right. I am a crazy nut. I'm a nut in recovery."

To lighten the mood, I opened the door and said, "Welcome to the nuthouse!" And I made a funny face, to which Hazel had to work very hard not to laugh.

When Grazie walked in, it was with a mixture of discomfort and amazement. I can't imagine what it would be like for her to see the place so clean and organized and full of a life she hasn't been a part of. The art on the fridge, the lumpy ceramic plant holder in the window that Hazel made at the Color Me Mine studio. The new sofa. (I had to buy a new sofa, as the old one was disgusting and deeply uncomfortable.) The classroom we put together in the corner of the living room. The fact that we painted Hazel's room purple. Her new yellow duvet cover. The schedule on the wall.

Grazie looked at the events and nodded with approval. "Looks great to me."

I could tell this was a surprise and a relief for Hazel. I asked, "Hazel, would you like to make us a cup of tea before bed?"

"I don't want tea!"

"Maybe your mom does?"

"I'm not calling this woman Mom."

Grazie said, "Fair enough. But I'd love some tea."

Hazel stomped off to the kitchen and turned on the kettle. Grazie gave me a look, and it shouldn't have been funny, but we both stifled a chuckle. "Give her time," I said.

"At least she's talking to me. Sort of," Grazie said.

We had a cup of tea, and then I stayed to tuck Hazel into bed after she brushed her teeth and got into her jammies. I said, "You gonna be okay, kid?"

And she said, "Of course I am, Grumpy. I am a daughter of God."

Kid comes up with the strangest things.

This woman I used to call Mom has been with us for three months now. I call her Grazie but once in a while I slip and call her Mom and I can tell that makes her happy and then I think, "Oh don't get too happy, I just made a mistake. Okay?" I can't believe I ever thought I would call her Mommy. Those days are over! Too bad, you missed them, Graziana who gave birth to me.

She looks like my mom, and I can tell she's the same human being but she's, like, moving around and stuff. She likes to go on her bike with me, and she even tried to skateboard with me and we go swimming and we go for walks in the park along the Red Deer River with Grumpy, and she and Grumpy get along really well. So weird. My mom before used to think Grumpy was boring and always trying to change her stuff. This makes me think that maybe this mom is fake and I am waiting for her to be mean to Grumpy again and start eating a lot of macaroni and watching *Dragon's Den* on TV. But get this! One of the first things she did was throw out the TV! (Well she didn't throw it out, she gave it to the Value Village even though it works perfectly.) This mom recycles. This mom has cool hair. This mom wears JEANS. This mom eats carrots and salad and makes wraps and smoothies. I prefer cereal. The cold cereal, not the hot cereal. Hot cereal looks and feels like vomit. This mom also has days where she doesn't come out of her room and Grumpy and I have to do everything. Grumpy and I don't get it. I thought you were sooooooo much better?

I am doing school with Grumpy and soon we are going on summer holidays. He says he is very proud of me, and he and Mom decided I am going to get a present and Uncle Eddie and Aunt Connie have it and I have to wait for it. I get it next week. Maybe Uncle Eddie will let me ride the tractor? That's what I'm thinking. Or maybe my present will be that all my cousins will be there and we can have a barn dance? Jody (she's the oldest cousin, with blond hair, and she plays guitar) thought of that idea, and the adults said, "No, it's too dusty for Danny" (he has asthma), but maybe they changed their mind? It would be SO FUN.

Grumpy and Grazie decided that she's going to come along on our camping trip to the Okanagan. I'm not very happy about that. I want to see Uncle David and Auntie Cathy and Oola just with us. I don't want her to wreck it, so I said, "They don't have room for you! The house is too small! You have to stay home!" But Grumpy thinks they have room. They said they'd put Mo– I mean, Grazie, in the art studio. So not only does she get to come on our holiday, but she gets the best room of all time ever. Seriously. No fair.

She's trying to be real nice to me and it just kind of makes me want to kick her really hard in the knee. I don't know why. I just want to yell, "Faker! Faker! I know you want to leave!"

But she opened a bike shop. So ...

Grumpy told her that I knew all about Ivan and that we went to meet Camila and she was weird and mean. Mo– I mean, Grazie, said she wanted to protect me and that's why she didn't tell me all of that stuff. She said she's happy to talk to me and I said, "You're the last person I want to talk to."

I don't know why I am so mean. Dr. Cheryl said it's called abandonment. But I wasn't abandoned. Grumpy never left me. Only she left. And I don't care. She can go again. In fact, I bet she will go. Good. GOOD RIDDANCE. I hate smoothies anyway.

She's teaching me how to sew, though. We are doing a quilt for her room. I met her friend Vera who has a really pretty house and she makes really good jam. I didn't know my mom had friends. And ... I guess she's trying. Sometimes I think, "Hazel, everyone deserves a second chance." But I don't know if that counts for moms who leave. I'm still deciding.

I asked to go to Sunday school, which super surprised Grumpy.

He said, "Why?"

And I said, "Just cuz."

And Grazie and Grumpy had a big talk about it. He said he didn't want me to learn a bunch of baloney and he said something about war and dinosaurs and how old the world is. Mom said stuff like the patriarchy. She talks a lot about the patriarchy. (I don't know what it means. She explained it, something to do with a lot of white men bossing people around.) And she said hell and heaven and homo. Phobia. But together they decided it would be okay if I went to the United Church Sunday school and that Mom would take me and stay for the adult stuff. Grumpy figured it wouldn't do any harm because the United Church is only one step up from a bowling league. I don't know why he said that. There is no bowling alley in the church. Though it's big enough you could probably bowl right down the middle of the pews. In fact, that sounds awesome.

So: Sunday school. The lady there is real nice, her name is Jen. She has fluffy yellow hair and the softest voice in the whole world. I told her my secret. I said that I think I'm the daughter of God. And she didn't think I was a weirdo. She whispered back, "So am I. Isn't that great?"

Ed and Connie's chocolate lab hadn't birthed a litter in two years. But they gave it one last try with a yellow stud, and she had seven pups, all spoken for. Then, unexpectedly, almost as an afterthought, she popped out a runt. Ed and Connie know just the perfect little girl to gift this pup to if it survives.

They want to make sure she is right before they say anything. They express the mother's milk into a sterilized cup and feed the pup with a syringe. They install a heat lamp to keep her warm when she is pushed aside by biggers. She is small, but she is feisty. She fights and finds a teat. She squirms right into the centre of her siblings. Little curly tail wagging.

All right. She's ready.

Herman, Hazel, and Grazie drive up to the front white gate of the farmhouse. Connie calls out to Eddie from the kitchen window, "They're here!"

"Just a sec," he says and scoops up a wriggling ball of fur.

Out from the shed, Ed comes, grinning. "Hazel, honey, I got something for ya." He lets the puppy bound to the ground, all bright-eyed and bushy-tailed, little pink tongue poking out.

Hazel gasps. It's too good to believe. Her very own dog? "For me?!"

Even though the beloved is born without her knowing about Ivan and stars, without remembering butterfly wings, without the name of Rose or the stamp of Camila, her senses spark the understanding that she belongs to this little girl. She belongs. She trots right up to her, tail wagging, and licks her shin.

"Looks like she knows who's boss," says Herman.

"Gosh, she's the cutest puppy I've ever seen," says Grazie.

"Yeah, we don't know what the heck happened here. We always breed her with Thomas's yellow lab, but something else got in. Australian shepherd, maybe. Look at the blue eyes, the brown-and-cream marking."

"Tartuffe!" says Hazel.

They all turn with a quizzical look at the big word.

"Remember, Grumpy? It's the chocolate-and-vanilla ice-cream ball that Marco and JJ gave me for dessert."

"Tartufo."

"She looks like a fluffy ball of Tartufo! Hey, Tartuffe!" Hazel picks her up and snuggles her to her cheek. The beloved is delighted and bats her chin with her paw.

Herman grunts. "Tartuffe. I can live with that."

"She looks kind of ... morose," jokes Grazie. "What did you do in a former life?"

Hazel holds up the pup. "You and me, Tartuffe, we're going to have so much fun. Welcome to our family."

And with that, they all retire to the front yard for tuna sandwiches and lemonade, swatting flies and chatting about the price of cattle, perfecting pie crust, and the nature of clouds.

ACKNOWLEDGMENTS

My many thanks to my loving husband, Scott Andrew Johnson. When I told him I'd like to go on a solo pilgrimage for my birthday, he supported the idea completely. In fact, he was the one who suggested the Via Francigena. Though Herman is a fictional character, he was inspired by the steadfast devotion to family that my mother and my stepfather, Lynne and Stan Markham, share. Thank you to my creative and full-hearted daughter, Nora. My dear friend and editor Karen Ydenberg White did the first edit of this novel and her insight and encouragement kept me going. Many thanks to Talon editor Charles Simard for helping me deepen and clarify the story, and to Kevin Williams who kindly offered me my first novel publication. I am grateful to my cousin Pina Laura De Vivo who helped me with my Italian (though Grazie's terrible beginner Italian I did all on my own!). Thank you to Norma Roth for teaching me so much about grace for self and others. And finally, thank you to all the wonderful hosts and my dear family in Italy, who kindly and generously took me in.

Lucia Frangione is an internationally produced, award-winning playwright and actor. *Grazie* is her debut novel. She is the winner of the Jessie Richardson Theatre Award, the Gordon Armstrong Playwright's Rent Award, and the Stage West–Equity Emerging Theatre Artist Award, and she is among the top three on the Flannery List (as featured in *American Magazine*). Her thirty-three plays have been produced across Canada and in cities like New York, London, Warsaw, San Diego, Boston, and Chicago. She is a member of ACTRA and CAEA. Lucia is currently working on a new novel, premiering a podcast called *Cuppa Stories*, and is developing a play titled *Danger to Self and Others*. She lives in Vancouver with her husband and children.
www.luciafrangione.com